BLAZING SUMMER

BLAZING SUMMER

DARLING INVESTIGATIONS

DENISE GROVER SWANK

Montlake
Romance

Published by Montlake Romance, Seattle

www.apub.com

Amazon, the Amazon logo, and Montlake Romance are trademarks of Amazon.com, Inc., or its affiliates.

ISBN-13: 9781503901803
ISBN-10: 1503901807

Cover illustration and design by Edward Bettison

Printed in the United States of America

BLAZING SUMMER

CHAPTER ONE

I was full of regrets as I walked into the office bright and early on Monday morning.

For one, I regretted not making more demands before signing the contract for three more seasons of my new reality TV show, *Darling Investigations*.

The first six-episode season had started out as a joke—twenty-nine-year-old Summer Butler, the washed-up former teen actress who played Isabella Holmes on the once mega-popular show *Gotcha!*, becomes a real-life private investigator on a reality TV show. A funny enough joke if you weren't me. Isabella had been a nosy amateur sleuth who solved small mysteries involving her classmates and family. Now I was a PI with a business license to prove it—and no training whatsoever other than that I'd solved a murder on camera two months ago, much to the irritation of my on-site producer. While she was happy we'd garnered so much success, she couldn't stand the fact that I was responsible for it. I'd gone behind her back to get the footage that had made us so wildly popular, and to say she harbored a grudge was like saying the *Titanic* hit a piece of ice.

Another regret: I should have pushed harder to remove Lauren from the show.

So now I was back, starting production of Season Two less than two weeks after the airing of the finale. The masses were demanding more *Darling Investigations*, and the network execs were eager to feed them.

Last week I'd sold the contents of my recently foreclosed Malibu beach house. Thankfully, my best friend, Marina, had just started her new job as an assistant to Renee Rouchard, world-renowned self-improvement guru, and had left for an around-the-world book tour, which spared me a dramatic goodbye. Yesterday, after a cross-country trip, I moved in with my grandmother and two adult cousins. That was another regret, although to be honest, it was more of a semi-regret. I was accustomed to living alone, so it was going to take some getting used to . . . especially since the house was small and crowded, and there was only one functioning bathroom. (Okay, so I'd forgotten you couldn't flush tampons in a septic system . . .) But the more important issue was that eternity wasn't long enough to make me unsee my cousin Teddy's surprisingly tan ass.

My least serious, though most annoying, regret was my decision to curl my long blonde hair for today's production meeting instead of putting it up in a ponytail. While it was only 9:00 a.m., we were in southern Alabama in the middle of June, which meant it was eighty-three degrees and 80 percent humidity. My hair currently looked like my wigs back from my childhood pageant days. Thank God we weren't on camera today and no paparazzi were in sight.

When I opened the front door, a bell hanging from the doorknob let out a little chime. The production studio had set up a PI office for me prior to shooting the first season. While they'd rented it since April, I was taking over the lease on July 1, one thing I'd insisted on including in my new contract. If I was staying in Sweet Briar, Alabama, full-time, I needed to have a job, and it looked like sleuthing was it. That, and getting filmed doing it.

"Hey, Summer," Tony, one of the cameramen, said when I walked in, "I saw you on *Live with Kelly*. Good save."

My face flushed. I didn't need a reminder that I'd nearly fallen flat on my face during the segment. "I should get some credit for getting out of the way in time. No one ever told me that kangaroos throw punches."

"That's right," said my cousin Dixie, walking in behind me. "That's something they don't teach in Sweet Briar schools."

Lauren had hired Dixie as my assistant just before we started filming, and she'd been invaluable in helping me investigate our big case from the first season.

"Hey, Dixie," Bill, the second cameraman, said as he walked down the hall toward us.

"Bill!" Dixie threw herself at him, wrapping her arms around his neck.

He looked embarrassed but quickly hugged her back before stepping away. He and Dixie had started something while we were filming the first season, although she was reluctant to define what it was exactly. Based on Bill's reaction, he felt the same way.

I knew he had a crush on her—it had been pretty obvious since April, when we first started filming. But everything was upended when I stumbled upon Otto Olson's body just days into production. Lauren refused to get to the truth of his death. Every single case *she* wanted me to work was faked or greatly embellished. Thankfully, Bill and Dixie agreed to help me solve Otto's murder with our own off-the-books investigation. Bill had been instrumental in getting footage of our real investigation, including the confession of Cale Malone, a Sweet Briar police officer turned drug dealer and murderer. Hence the massive ratings for the season finale. Thanks to Dixie and Bill, the executive producer had promised the second season would be filled with real cases, not the fake ones Lauren had cooked up for Season One.

Bill had gotten shot in our final showdown with Cale, something I'd never forget. Dixie had been at his bedside at every opportunity, but he'd returned to Atlanta after his discharge. While they'd kept in touch, he'd just returned to Sweet Briar last night.

"Glad to have you back, Bill," I said with a warm smile.

"Thank for insisting they bring me back," he said. "I was worried they would keep the temporary cameraman who replaced me."

"It wouldn't be the same without you," I said, meaning every word.

Looking around, I realized there were twice as many crew members today as normal. Our office was on the small side, making me wonder how we were all going to fit.

"What's with the extra people?" I asked.

The guilty look in Bill's eyes set me on edge, but before he could tell me what Lauren had planned, she walked out of the editing room and into the hall, holding up her finger. "Uh-uh-uh! Don't you dare tell her the surprise." She looked me up and down, her eyes finally coming to rest on my hair. "Fully embracing the stereotypical big hair, Summer?"

I reached up to my hair and tried to smooth it down, wishing I'd brought an elastic band. "I'm here and ready to get started."

"Good idea." She put her hands on her hips and looked around the room. "Let's all take a seat." She turned to some of the new crew members in the middle of the room. "You new people can grab chairs out of the editing room."

It was then I realized that Dixie's desk was much closer to the door than usual. It was hard to make out any details because the crew was packed in like sardines. From inside, the door to Main Street opened on the far-right wall, and the front section of the space faced large picture windows. The walls were painted sage green on the bottom and pale yellow on top. There was a large map of the county on the wall—which was mostly obscured by the people in front of it—along with our framed business license, the only credentials I needed to work as a PI. I caught a glimpse of my desk and realized it

4

had been shoved into the middle of the room. The two client chairs that used to sit there were now crammed against the front windows.

That was weird.

But I quickly figured out why when the crew headed toward the video edit room. My desk had been shoved forward to make room for a third desk, but *make room* was relative. The desk had been shoe-horned into a too-small space.

"Why is there another desk?" I asked guardedly.

"That's the surprise," Lauren said with a huge grin.

My stomach dropped. "What surprise?" I asked, silently registering that she'd used that word in the hall. Any surprise from Lauren was likely to be torture wrapped in a bow. Especially if she looked this happy about it.

She gestured toward the desks. "Why don't you girls have a seat?"

I cast a questioning glance to Dixie, who shrugged, her long blonde hair falling over her shoulder. Cousin or not, I hated her a little for still having nearly perfect hair in this heat. Our hair was almost the same shade of honey gold, but that was where the similarities ended.

My imagination ran wild with what Lauren's surprise could be, or rather, who. It was obvious we were getting a new cast member. Was she getting a real PI to help us with cases? That might not be a bad thing.

I pulled out my chair to sit down and immediately knocked it into the desk behind me. I swiveled the chair and sat down, banging my knee as I slid forward. Gritting my teeth, I pulled a folder out of my large purse and set it on the desk. I'd printed out all the potential cases for this season, and Dixie and I had gone through them the night before.

After everyone got settled, I folded my hands on the desk and smiled at everyone. "Hi, and welcome to the new people. I'm sure a lot of you know who I am, but if not, I'm Summer. I'm excited to start a new season of *Darling Investigations*! This is my cousin Dixie." I gestured to her.

"Hey, new people," she said, wearing a huge grin.

I pulled out a stack of papers. "After our big case in April, we decided to use real cases for this season. With that in mind, we created a website so people could apply for us to investigate their real cases on the show. We got seventy-six cases, but last night Dixie and I whittled it down. We came up with twenty-six cases that have real potential, ranging from minor ones to a couple of more major investigations."

Lauren began to laugh.

That was a bad sign . . .

"That's so cute," she said, giving me a saccharine grin. "But don't you worry your pretty little head"—she paused, her grin spreading as she shot a pointed look at my hair—"well, your *large* head about it. We've already picked out the cases."

"*What?*" I shook my head. "Scott Schapiro said I would have a say in the cases this season."

"Well," Lauren said slyly, "if you want to run and tattle to Scott again, then be my guest." She held out her cell phone. "Here. I'll even make the call for you."

I'd been adamant about replacing Lauren, who'd made filming miserable, but Scott had insisted that I "be a grown-up and learn to deal with it." Of course, Lauren had been there listening. She knew good and well I wouldn't call him and *tattle*. And now she'd just successfully made me look like an idiot in front of the new crew.

I was having déjà vu.

Lauren glanced down the hall and motioned to someone. "Bring in the board."

I heard wheels rolling down the hall, and Lauren's assistant, Karen, appeared, dragging a whiteboard on wheels. She gave me an apologetic look as she turned it to block the entrance to the hallway.

"As you see here," Lauren said, looking a little too pleased with herself, "I have twenty cases split up into two lists. I bet you all are wondering why there are two lists . . ."

"I presume it has something to do with the empty desk behind me," I said in a dry tone.

Lauren looked downright giddy as she glanced at Karen and said, "Tell him to come in."

Karen shot me another guilty grimace, then tapped out something on her phone.

Dixie looked just as confused as I felt, but a knot had already formed in the pit of my stomach. Whatever Lauren had planned was going to be bad.

The bell on the front door dinged, and I looked up and gasped when I saw who was walking through it.

This was worse than I could have ever suspected. "This is a joke, right?"

Lauren was practically glowing. "No joke. Summer, welcome your new partner, Connor Blake, but then again, you two know each other, don't you? Connor was your costar—and nemesis—on that cute little show *Gotcha!*"

Regret suddenly took on a whole new meaning.

Chapter Two

Connor hadn't changed much since our *Gotcha!* years. He was tall, and his blond hair was still styled in that longish boy-band style that had been popular when we filmed the show. Connor was good-looking in an average kind of way—think catalog model. Nevertheless, girls had gone crazy for him back in the day. Last I'd heard, some of them still did. He had a very active fan club that had been known to stalk him at public events. All ten of them. But that was pretty much all he had going for him. His career had taken the same downward spiral mine had, and rumor had it that he blamed me for his failures.

He walked through the door and opened his arms at his sides. "Surprise!" Then he did a double take. "Wow, Summer. You've really let yourself go."

So it wasn't just his looks that had stayed the same. Connor Blake was still an utter asshole. He'd convinced me to stage a huge (and very fake) scandal with him ten years ago so we could get out of our *Gotcha!* contracts, and fool that I was, I'd played along. The photos had made it look like we'd slept together, and it had worked all too well. Too bad I hadn't anticipated that my boyfriend, Luke, would break up with me for supposedly cheating on him.

"What did he just say?" Dixie demanded.

I tried to smooth down my hair again without being obvious about it. "It's humid in the South, and it's not kind to people with coarse hair."

He pointed to his heavily hair-sprayed hair. "My hair stylist sent me a hair gel to deal with it." He gave me a leer. "As a peace offering, I'll have him send you some too."

And now I was getting hair-styling advice from a man whose hair was stuck in the past decade.

"And . . . ," he added with a flourish as he pulled a book out of the back of his pants, "another peace offering. Something to help you get your life out of the shitter."

He handed me a hardback book with a photo of him on the cover. The photo showed him holding a copy of the book in his hand while pointing to it and winking.

I read the title out loud. *"Living the Connor Life: Connor Blake's Guide to Spiritual, Physical, and Emotional Wholeness in Less Than Thirty Days."*

Connor mouthed the words while I said them, bouncing his head and tapping his index finger in the air with each word.

Dixie's eyes bugged out of her head. "I'm sorry. *What?*"

Connor gave her a sly grin. "Sorry, Dixie, I know you're a mess too, and I would have brought you one, but that was my last prepublication copy."

Dixie turned to me. "Is this guy serious?"

I grimaced. "As a heart attack."

Connor reached over and opened the cover. "It's personalized and signed."

Sure enough, I read, *"To Summer: I know getting your life in order seems impossible, and it probably is, but hopefully I can help you gain a tiny bit of balance. I'm here to guide you every step of the way to living the Connor Life."* I glanced up at Dixie as I finished. *"XOXO, Connor."*

He looked pretty pleased with himself. "We'll have plenty of time to get you squared away with the Connor Life before I leave."

Dixie tilted her head. "It's a wonder you have time to do the show and all with your busy schedule."

He graced her with an attempt at a humble smile. "I'm a giver."

"Of herpes," she mumbled under her breath.

I tried to suppress a laugh.

"Now that you're all reacquainted," Lauren said, "let's get to work."

I pushed the chair back and crashed into the desk behind me. *Connor Blake's* desk. I shoved it even harder, pushing his desk against the wall and banging my knee in the process. After I got my legs untangled, I stood and gave him a death stare, choosing to ignore the fact that the whole effect had been ruined by my clumsiness.

How had this happened? But the beaming woman in front of the whiteboard was answer enough. Lauren knew working with Connor would make my life a living hell.

I shifted my attention to Lauren, who looked like it was Christmas, her birthday, and the release of a new *Sex and the City* movie all rolled up into one. "He goes, or I go."

If possible, she looked even more excited as she held out her hand to Karen.

Karen cringed and handed her a thick stack of papers, which Lauren brought directly over to me. She cast a quick glance up to Connor and said, "You just hang tight for a moment while we talk about things you won't understand."

Connor blinked but didn't say a word, and I took malicious satisfaction from Lauren's insult even though I knew she had something worse planned for me.

Lauren flipped several pages until she reached one with a yellow sticky tab on the side. After clearing her throat, she said, "All hiring decisions will be made by the on-site producer." Lauren looked up and touched her fingertips to her chest. "That's me."

"Fine," I said with plenty of attitude. Time to call her bluff. "Hire him. But I refuse to work with him."

A smug look filled her eyes. "That's why you both have separate cases."

"Noooo . . . ," I said slowly, dragging out the word, "I refuse to be on the same show with this asshole. One show with him was too many."

A tight smile thinned Lauren's lips as she flipped through the pages again, this time stopping on a page with a blue tab. "If Summer Butler voluntarily leaves the show within the time frame agreed upon by all parties in the contract, she forfeits all royalties as creative director, which acts retroactively."

What the hell? My manager, Justin, had sworn an attorney had gone over the contract with a fine-tooth comb.

Lauren tilted her head. "What that means is that you'll have to return that $23,000 check Scott Schapiro just signed for you last week, and while *we're* raking in the dough, you won't get a cent—either in salary or in royalties." She winked. "And don't forget those residuals you'll lose. Rumor has it that your greedy mother screwed you out of those too."

I caught the *too* and gritted my teeth. My mother had been my self-proclaimed manager for nineteen years, from when I was nine months old until I turned nineteen. I'd caved to her every demand right up until she convinced me to do something so horrible it imploded my life. At her behest, I stayed in Thailand to finish filming a movie instead of going to the funeral of my grandfather and aunt and uncle. My grandmother disowned me, and I lost the one place that had felt like home. I'd stood up to my mother soon afterward, and the moment she realized she'd lost control of me, she emptied my bank account and scuttled back to Sweet Briar, the one thing she'd always pledged she'd never do.

I could have sued her—everyone who knew the truth encouraged me to—but Dixie had just been arrested for setting the barn fire that had killed her parents and our pawpaw. When the police added manslaughter charges, the case made national news—all because they were related to me. If I'd brought a civil lawsuit against my mother, Dixie's case would have received even more attention, so I let it go, thinking I'd make more money from future projects to replace it.

Only my mother's underhanded way of dealing with agents, producers, and contracts had painted me out to be a diva that no one in their right mind would want to hire. Aside from a few commercials and one Lifetime movie, my career had suffered an almost decade-long dry spell.

Now that I was back in Sweet Briar and feeling stronger, I planned on confronting my mother. But I had to deal with this issue first. One user at a time.

"So much negative energy, darling," he said with a fake smile. He knew how much I had hated being called America's Darling—the name the press had given me when I was a fresh-faced teen. "You're filling the space with negative chi." He moved over, rested his hands on my shoulders, and began to rub. "Summer, Summer, Summer. You're so tense. Just let all that negativity go."

My back stiffened. "That's *exactly* what I'm trying to do." I shook off his hands and jerked my gaze back to Lauren. "I do *not* want to work with this man."

"And you don't have to," Lauren said in a sweet voice. "You only have to share an office and very limited screen time. Otherwise you'll be doing your thing, and he'll be doing his."

"Why are you doing this, Lauren? Our ratings were through the roof."

"Our ratings were amazing because you stumbled onto a once-in-a-lifetime situation, and you managed to take down a rogue policeman on camera. People wanted to see that, Summer. That's great reality TV." She picked up the list of cases off my desk and scanned the sheet. "Nobody, and I mean nobody, wants to see you chasing a pet alligator who eats the neighbor's chickens." Then she paused and glanced up at the ceiling, an evil gleam filling her eyes. "On second thought, that could be good. Add it to Summer's list, Karen."

My mouth dropped open.

Lauren lowered her gaze to mine. "When I came to your house months ago with the contract, I told you I could make this stinkbug of a show a success."

"You had absolutely nothing to do with the success of last season," I protested. "Bill, Dixie, and I were the ones who pulled this show out of the gutter. *I* should be running things."

Her eyes widened with surprise and then narrowed as if she was reevaluating me. I'd just unintentionally made myself a threat, and it was obvious Lauren Chapman made a point of eliminating threats. Great. "But you're *not* running things, so you better suck it up, buttercup. You're stuck with me producing this show whether you like it or not."

Dixie flashed me a thumbs-up sign. I had no idea what it meant, but I knew I had no choice but to let it go. Our first season had garnered me a lot of professional offers, all of which I'd turned down to come back to Sweet Briar and spend more time with my family and, truth be told, to become reacquainted with my first and only love, Luke Montgomery, Sweet Briar's police chief. I wasn't sure if I wanted to go back to Hollywood after this series ran its course, but I didn't want to be painted as a diva again. "I'm *not* working any cases with him."

Triumph flashed in her eyes. "And I've already stated that you won't." She turned to Connor and winked. "Why don't you take a seat at your new desk, hot stuff."

He preened as he walked past me to his desk, then stopped and tried to figure out how he was going to sit behind it since it was smashed against the wall. "Uh . . . this doesn't work with the Connor Life philosophy."

"I agree," Dixie said. "The office is too small for three desks. The Connor Life program needs to go back to whatever loony bin he pulled it out of."

Lauren's mouth twisted, and she tapped her chin. It was a good thing she worked behind the camera because she was a terrible actress. "You know what, Dixie," she said, dropping her hand, "you're right. So we have two choices. One, we get rid of your desk, or two, we move the office to the empty train station down the street."

"What?" I asked.

"In fact"—she threw her hands up in the air, then put one hand on her hip and pointed her finger at me—"gotcha!"

My signature move from that stupid show. People were forever asking me to do it, and I took great satisfaction in turning the situation around and getting them to do it instead. But I wasn't feeling any satisfaction right now.

"As of tomorrow," she continued, "the train station will be our new office." Then she leaned closer to me and lowered her voice. "Don't ever try to outmaneuver me again, Summer, because I will win every time."

I knew she'd caved too easily on letting me have this office.

Lauren stood and graced Connor with a smile. "Don't try to shove yourself behind that desk." And then she said to one of the new people, "Give Connor your chair."

Dee, a meek-looking woman who appeared to be in her midt-wenties, hopped up and pushed her folding chair toward Connor, who sat down with no hesitation.

"Quite the gentleman," Dixie muttered, but if Connor heard, he didn't let on.

"Okay, then," Lauren said, "as you all have figured out, Connor Blake has joined our show this season, which is why we have all these new people. They'll be Connor's film crew; and Bill, Tony, and Chuck will be working with Summer. As Summer previously stated, since Scott Schapiro insisted we use real cases this season, we had a website where people could nominate their issues to be investigated. Karen's done a lot of legwork and has come up with a list of nine to ten cases for each team to work on. We have a thirteen-episode run this time, so with two investigators, we'll be busy. We'll add more cases as they come, and edit them into the season." She scanned the room. "Any questions?"

Everyone remained silent. Even if they had questions, I doubt they would have asked for fear Lauren would jump down their throats. At least I'd be working with my old team. Tony was the other cameraman who'd worked with me last season, and Chuck was the sound guy. Although they'd been leery about working with me in the beginning because of my previous diva reputation, they'd grown to respect me by the end of production.

"Okay, Karen's going to e-mail you the list of cases with all the facts that we know. She's scheduled times for you to meet with the clients and suggested places for you to look."

"Shouldn't that be my job?" Dixie asked. "I'm the assistant."

Lauren laughed. "That's so cute. You think you have a job besides being a pretty face and throwin' in some cute Southernisms while wearin' your short denim shorts." Her fake southern accent grated on my last nerve.

Dixie shot her a scowl and looked like she was about to tell her off, but I beat her to it.

"As I stated before," I said in a shaky voice, "Dixie had more to do with making this show a success than you did, Lauren. It's obvious that you feel the need to put her in her place so you can feel better about yourself."

Lauren's face reddened. "I can make your life a living hell, Summer. Don't push me."

I walked in front of her, pissed that my five-foot-three stature ensured I would always need to look up to Lauren, who was nearly six feet tall with heels. "I'm a creative producer on this show, Lauren. Don't forget that."

She crossed her arms over her chest, probably so she didn't reach out and strangle me. "You know what, Summer? You want creative control? Fine. You can have it. You be the producer of your own segments. Run them any way you please while I run Connor's, and we'll see who can produce the better show."

I gaped at her, certain I'd heard her wrong. "You're giving me total control of my own cases?"

"Yep," she said in a clipped tone.

"What's the catch?"

"No catch. You work out of the train-station office, and you agree to be in the combined segments I insist upon, and the rest you're free to do on your own."

I was smart enough to realize that filming was only one part of it. "I want to oversee the editing of my clips too."

"Fine."

She was up to something, I just didn't know what. This was exactly what I wanted, and she'd just given in way too easily.

"You have to agree that you won't try to take any of Connor's cases, and he won't try to take yours," she said.

"Not a problem," I replied.

"Then we're good," Lauren said. "Now if you'll excuse us, Connor, his crew, and I will head down to the train station to work out our schedule. We'll leave you and your crew to work out your own."

Karen opened the door and stood to the side as the four new crew people filed out the door with Connor and Lauren following behind. Before she stepped out after them, Karen shot me a mournful look and said, "I'm sorry, Summer. I really am."

Why was she apologizing? It didn't take long to figure out.

Lauren had given me all the crap cases.

CHAPTER THREE

An hour later, we'd reached the conclusion that Lauren had been planning this all along. She didn't want to work with me any more than I wanted to work with her, so she'd devised a strategy that would allow her to keep her job and make me look like a fool in the process. Score one for Lauren.

After I marked down which cases had been given to Connor, we erased the board and listed the cases that were salvageable, coming up with only three from her original list and three more from the twenty-six Dixie and I had worked on.

"Six cases isn't enough," Tony said with a frown.

"True," Dixie said, "but we'll get more as the season goes on."

"We hope," I said, staring at the board. There was the alligator case (kept for the novelty), a child-support case, a husband who suspected his wife was cheating, and a few other minor cases. "There's nothing big enough to carry us through a few episodes, let alone half a season."

"That was her plan," Bill said, sounding disgusted. "You're sharing airtime with boy-band-wannabe dude, and he'll get more attention. She's trying to squeeze you out of your own show in your own hometown."

Oh, my word. He was right.

"We need a big case," Dixie said.

I heaved out a sigh. "We have to face the reality that this is a small town in a pretty boring county. There aren't many big cases."

"Certainly not enough for *two* detectives," Tony said.

"Well, we still need a big case," Dixie said with a mischievous look.

"We've established that, Dixie," Chuck said.

She didn't look deterred. "Except I know who can get one for you."

"Who?" I asked suspiciously.

"Luke."

"Whoa." I held up my hands. "Oh, no. I am *not* going there."

"Why not?" Bill asked. "He helped us with our other investigation."

"That's because his hands were tied. Otto's murder fell into the sheriff's jurisdiction, not Sweet Briar's, and we could find out information that Luke couldn't. *And . . .*," I added when I saw him open his mouth to protest, "I'm sure he only agreed to it because I was under suspicion of moving Otto's body."

"Well, it wouldn't hurt to ask him," Dixie said in a smug tone.

Thankfully, I had a two-day reprieve. "He's at that conference in Atlanta. He won't be home until Wednesday night."

Her smile spread wider. "I think maybe he got back early."

"What makes you say that?"

Her eyebrows rose, and I glanced at the front door just as the bell dinged.

Luke filled the doorway, stealing my breath away. He was wearing khakis and a blue short-sleeve, button-down shirt with the top two buttons undone. I was used to seeing him in his uniform or in jeans and a T-shirt, so his business-casual appearance caught me off guard.

His gaze went straight to me, then he smiled, and funny things happened to my insides.

I felt about as sure-footed as Bill and Dixie had seemed earlier. I hadn't seen Luke for seven weeks. While we were technically together, and had been since the last week of shooting, we hadn't texted or talked on the phone much in the months we'd spent apart. I wasn't sure if we were still on the same page.

But the look in his eyes assured me that we were not only on the same page but likely in the same paragraph.

"Hey," he said with his hand still on the doorknob.

"I thought you were in Atlanta at that police-chief conference." My heart was pounding in my chest, and I sounded breathless.

"I was sitting in an air-conditioned conference room, waiting for a guy to talk about training reserve police officers, and all I could think about was the fact that you were here. So I left."

I swallowed, suddenly unsure of what to say or do. We stared at each other for a few seconds before Dixie said, "I think it's a good time for a lunch break."

"It's only ten thirty," Chuck said.

"Then brunch," Dixie replied with a hint of irritation. Turning toward the front door, she said, "Luke, are you free to take Summer to brunch?"

He grinned. "I would love to take Summer to brunch." He paused, his smile fading a bit. "If *you* want to go."

I felt my face flush, and I told myself I was twenty-nine years old, not the seventeen-year-old girl who'd fallen hard and fast for him. "Now's a good time to take a break."

"I need to talk to the manager at my motel about changing rooms," Bill said. "That'll give me plenty of time."

I knew where he was staying. It was a dump, and I was afraid to ask why he was changing.

Bill continued, "How about we meet back here at noon? Then we can go over our cases again."

It was obvious he hoped I'd bring back a new case, which I had no intention of doing.

Probably . . .

I grabbed my purse and flashed Dixie a tight smile. "We'll reconvene at noon, Dixie."

"Of course we will."

Luke waited for me to walk out the door. I smiled to myself when I saw his truck parked at the curb about ten feet from the entrance—obviously Dixie had noticed him parking. He opened the passenger door and waited for me to get in.

"You don't want to go to Maybelline's Café?" I asked.

He gave me a devilish grin. "And be plastered on *Sweet Happenings in the Briar* before we even leave the restaurant? I'd rather have you to myself."

Maybelline's runaway success with her gossip blog had encouraged her to choose a more "marketable" name (her words). The way Luke was watching me now, I suspected it was a good idea for us to steer clear. I had enough issues with the national gossip sites. I didn't need to be on the local page. "Then where do you want to go?"

I'd stopped in front of him, and he rested his hand on the upper door frame and leaned down so his face was inches from mine.

"I was thinking my place."

"Oh." I hadn't been to Luke's house before, although I was certainly curious. He'd invited me over the night before my showdown with Cale, but I'd turned him down, saying I needed to get back to Dixie. Truth be told, I wasn't sure I was ready to sleep with him yet.

"I make a pretty good hash-brown scrambler," he said in a sly tone.

"While you can put that away without a worry," I said, "I put on five pounds when I was here last, and it took me all seven weeks to work it off."

"I can make you an egg-white omelet. I have some spinach and feta cheese."

My eyebrows shot up. "You have spinach and feta cheese? The meat-and-potato guy I spent a summer with?"

"Hey, I grew up," he said with a chuckle. "What do you say?"

Butterflies took flight in my stomach. "I have to be back by noon."

"That's plenty of time."

"Luke . . ." God, this was embarrassing, but I needed to tell him how I felt so there wouldn't be any misunderstanding. "I'm not ready to sleep with you yet."

Surprise filled his eyes, and he stood up taller. "Okay."

"I like you." I probably still loved him, but I wasn't willing to admit it out loud yet. One embarrassing confession at a time. "It's just that it's been a while since we were together. I think we should take it slow. I know you suggested a fling last time—"

"Summer," he said in a husky tone, a hint of a smile at the corners of his lips, "I already told you that I was an idiot when I suggested that, and I also told you I was willing to accept whatever rules you set. If you want to take it slow, I'm good with that. In fact"—he placed a soft kiss on my lips—"I think it's a good idea."

"Thanks for understanding, Luke."

"But we can still go to my place for brunch. I have no devious plans to take your clothes off."

Part of me was disappointed, but I'd made up my mind. "Okay."

I got inside his truck, shoving his duffel bag to the middle of the seat. When he got in the driver's side, I said, "Are you sure you won't get in trouble for skipping your conference?"

"I paid for it out of my own pocket and took vacation time to go. We had to borrow a sheriff's deputy to cover for me, so the city council will be happy to see that I'm back, especially since the officer we hired to replace Cale just started last week."

"Oh, you already found someone?"

"He's Mayor Sterling's son, but at least he has an associate degree in criminal justice."

"How's he working out?"

Luke frowned. "Too soon to tell."

He drove past the police station and turned left two blocks later. My mouth parted in surprise when he pulled into the driveway of an old bungalow.

"Your house is adorable."

He laughed. "Just what every man wants to hear."

I grinned. "I didn't mean to call your masculinity into question."

"I can handle it."

I got out and walked up his front steps. "You have a porch swing."

Luke dropped his duffel bag on the porch as he turned his attention to unlocking the front door.

"I've always wanted a porch swing." I'd told him that multiple times when we were teenagers, sitting on the swing on his parents' front porch.

He pushed the door open and picked up his bag, as though purposely ignoring my statement. "Go on in."

Curious, I walked past him and went into his living room, surprised again when I realized it had been updated. The wood floor was refinished in a dark stain, and freshly painted built-in bookcases surrounded a redbrick fireplace. A TV hung over the fireplace, and a gaming system sat on one of the bookshelves, wires attached to the TV.

"It's clean," I said with a grin. I recognized his furniture—it had belonged to his parents, but his cluttered high school room hadn't prepared me for this degree of organization.

"I'm not that seventeen-year-old boy anymore. I know how to clean my room."

One more reminder that we really were starting over. "It's nice."

"It's small, but it's just me." He walked through a door off the living room, and I saw a bed with a brown comforter. After dropping his bag on the bed, he walked out and motioned to the back of the house. "The kitchen's this way."

I headed through a dining room with a table that was too small for the space, and into a small kitchen that hadn't been redone. "Are you hungry?" I asked.

"I'm starving. I left the conference before the breakfast was served."

"I feel bad that you left early for me."

He shook his head. "You shouldn't. I left without one ounce of regret."

Luke got out a carton of eggs and the fixings. I insisted on helping and found a whisk. When I handed him the bowl of scrambled eggs, our fingers brushed, making my stomach cartwheel, and the look on his face said he felt it too.

We made two omelets and brewed some coffee, and despite the sexual tension between us, it felt homey too. I was amazed at how natural it felt to do this with him. It gave me hope that we could actually work, but I tried not to let myself picture us playing house. Not yet.

He studied me, and a smile spread across his face.

"What?" I asked, then reached for my hair. "I know, it looks like I walked off a pageant stage, but I never thought it would get this big."

Laughing, he shook his head as he reached out and caressed my upper arm. "That's not why I'm smiling."

"Then why?"

"I can't believe you're in my kitchen."

"I can't believe it either."

After we plated the omelets, we carried them into the dining room along with the fresh-brewed coffee. "So how's your first day back to work goin'?" he asked as he set his plate on the table.

I groaned. "Don't ask." I set my plate down and grabbed his hand, realizing I needed to warn him about one part of it. He'd been jealous of Connor before, so this would be a good test of how we were going to work out. "I don't want you to be alarmed—"

"It's always a bad sign when someone leads with that," he said with a frown.

I took a breath. "I want you to know I had absolutely nothin' to do with this, okay? In fact, I threw a fit when I found out, but it turns out I have no say in it, even if it's my own TV show."

"Summer, darlin', just tell me."

My breath caught. "You called me darlin'."

His eyes widened slightly, and he looked uncomfortable. "I used to call you that before . . . Do you not want me to now?"

"No," I said, warmth flooding through me. "You're the *only* one who can call me that." He'd started calling me that as a joke. When we'd first started dating, he'd called me *darling* just to tease me, but something about the way he said it, long and husky, had sent a thrill through my blood. It still did. "I like it."

He graced me with a sexy smile.

I couldn't let him distract me. I needed to get this over with. "Okay, here it goes: Connor's workin' on the show."

"*Your* show? *Darling Investigations*?"

I nodded. "This is Lauren's payback for standin' up to her. But . . ." My fingers dug into his hand. "We're each workin' our own cases, so hopefully I'll hardly ever see him. I didn't want this, Luke, but there's nothin' I can do to stop it."

He gave me a long look. "I'm sorry."

Ice ran through my blood. "What does that mean? Are you breakin' up with me already?"

His eyes shot wide-open. "*What?* No. It's exactly as it sounds. I'm sorry you have to work with the asshole, but thank God you don't have to deal with him much."

I stared at him in disbelief.

"What?" he asked, pulling out the chair in front of my plate. "You didn't think you were gettin' rid of me that easily, did you?"

I sat in the chair, slightly confused by his lack of reaction. "But Connor's the reason we broke up."

Luke shook his head and sat down. "No. *I'm* the reason we broke up, but I'd rather focus on the future than on my past idiocy." He picked up his fork and cut into his eggs. "How's Dixie doing?"

That was a weird question, given that he'd just seen her. "She's fine."

"So she's handling Trent Dunbar's return okay?"

I lowered my fork. "Wait. *What?*"

His eyes widened. "She didn't tell you?"

"No."

His eyes clouded. "If she hasn't mentioned it to you, then maybe it isn't bothering her as much as I thought it would."

"I've been gone for weeks, and I barely had time to talk to you, let alone Dixie. It's not the kind of thing she would probably mention on the phone, and I didn't pull into the farm until late afternoon yesterday, so we didn't get much of a chance to talk," I said, although we'd spent more than an hour going through cases in her room, so that wasn't exactly true. "It's Trent Dunbar. Of course it's a big deal." Trent Dunbar was her first boyfriend, and he was with her when she accidentally started the barn fire that killed her parents and our grandfather.

"I meant maybe she's distanced herself from him. She never seemed to hold a grudge against him, and when I tried to charge him as an accomplice, she insisted it had only been her."

I stared at him in shock. "Luke, Dixie said she doesn't remember how the fire started."

"That's what she told me at first, but later she insisted she'd remembered something—that he had nothing to do with it."

"Why would she change her story?" I asked, but it was a stupid question. "Of course. To protect him."

"Trent Dunbar was never worth protecting," Luke said with a scowl. "Typical rich boy who had Daddy bail him out whenever he got into trouble. Just like his older brother, Troy. Both boys were into drinking, drugs, and stirring up shit. And based on Trent's recent record, he's still a mess. He's the one who supplied Dixie with the drugs and alcohol the night of the fire, but she would never accuse him of it. She refused to say where she got them."

And now he was back. I wondered if Teddy knew. He was liable to freak out when he found out about Trent. "Where's he been that he just got back from?"

"College, believe it or not. But rumor has it he never got his degree. Maybelline said he got into trouble with the law in Mississippi. I can't find any recent arrests or convictions, but plenty of arrest charges were dismissed in Birmingham."

"So why did he come back?"

"I hear he ran out of money, and his daddy insisted he come back home to learn the family business."

"Huh." If I remembered correctly, Trent was the Dunbars' only surviving child, and Dunbar Lumber was privately owned. Troy had died in a car accident a few years ago. Screwup or not, Trent would be his father's successor.

"My biggest concern is that Trent and Elijah were big buddies in high school."

"Your new officer?"

"He and Trent went to school together, and they were on the middle school and high school football teams together."

"Well, crap. When did Trent come back to town?"

"Last week."

"And Elijah started on the police force last week too?" I asked. "That looks mighty suspicious. It's the perfect way to continue to cover up Trent's bad behavior."

"I'm glad I'm not the only one who thinks so. Especially since the mayor and the board didn't consult me about hiring him. They ramrodded it through. In fact"—he pulled his cell phone out of his pocket—"this reminds me that I need to make a quick call to the office. If you don't mind, of course."

"Not at all."

He unlocked the screen and placed the call. "Amber," he said after a few seconds, "I'm just letting you know that I'm back in town, so let me know if anything big comes up. Also, if you get any calls regarding Trent Dunbar, hand them over to me and not Elijah, okay?" He paused and made a face. "Well, that didn't take long, did it? Text me the location."

"He's in trouble *already*?" I asked after he hung up.

"Yep," he said with a frown. He shoveled a big bite of eggs into his mouth. When he swallowed, he said, "I really hate to do this, Summer, but I have to take you back to your office."

"Oh."

He must have picked up on the disappointment in my voice, because he looked down at his phone and shook his head. "No. I'm at least taking today off. I'll get back to it tomorrow."

All I could think about was the asshole who'd given Dixie the drugs and booze that had ruined her life. He was back in town, and he was already causing trouble. I had to make sure he didn't hurt her. "No. I want you to go. This is important."

"Are you sure?"

"Yeah, I'm positive." I stood and picked up my plate, then reached for his nearly empty one. "Do you need to change?"

"Ordinarily I would, but I don't want to take the time. Besides, the person who called it in knows me. She won't care whether I'm in uniform or not."

I carried the dishes into the kitchen and set them in the sink. Luke walked up behind me and wrapped his arms around my stomach.

"I've missed you," he whispered into my ear.

I sank into him and covered his arms with my own. "I've missed you too."

He slowly spun me around to face him, then his lips captured mine. The kiss started slow and tentative, but I slid my arms around his neck and pressed my chest to his.

His arm tightened around my back, holding me close as his kiss became bolder. He lifted his head and gave me an apologetic look. "Sorry. You want to take this slow."

"Yeah." But I could already see how impossible that was likely to be. "We should go."

"You really don't have to be back until noon?" he asked.

"If you're suggesting I stay here and wait for you," I said, "I don't think that's a good idea."

"No. I was thinking you could come with me. It's not an emergency call. Amber said April Jean Thornberry reported some kind of incident involving Trent, but she wouldn't explain it over the phone. I'll see if she minds you being there while I take the report."

"Really?" I asked in surprise. "I wouldn't think you'd want me around anything official."

A solemn look filled his eyes. "You were instrumental in Cale's apprehension. I think that means you can watch me take a statement . . . unless you'd rather go back."

"No," I said. "I want to go with you." Especially since it involved Trent Dunbar.

"Good." He gave me another kiss, and an ornery look lit up his face. "Then you can run interference with April Jean."

I was suddenly questioning my decision.

CHAPTER FOUR

April Jean Thornberry lived in a mobile home on the east end of town on a plot of land off the highway. The mobile home looked like it had been there a few decades, and the junk around it looked just as decrepit. I couldn't decide if it was a wannabe junkyard or a thrift sale gone awry. There was a mannequin under a tree wearing a boa around its neck; a few rusted musical instruments hanging from a scrawny artificial Christmas tree that was missing a few branches; and a riding lawn mower that had been painted black, red, and silver to look like a race car, with the number three and the words *Dale Earnhardt Forever* painted on the side.

I didn't have time to examine much else because a young woman walked out of the trailer as Luke pulled into her partially graveled driveway. She wore short denim shorts and a red halter top that showed off quite a bit of her ample breasts. Her blonde hair was bigger than mine, but her face was free of makeup. Not that she needed it. April Jean was pretty without it.

Luke opened his door and called out to her as he got out, "Hey, April Jean. Amber told me you had an incident this morning."

"An incident?" she said from the top of the rickety steps. "Is that what you're callin' it?"

I got out and stayed next to the truck as Luke walked toward her. "I'm not sure what to call it, April Jean. Amber didn't tell me much about what happened, so why don't you fill me in?"

"That no-good Dunbar boy is up to his old tricks again."

"And which ones are those?" Luke asked.

Her gaze drifted past him and landed on me. "Is that Summer Butler wearing a bad wig? Is she trying to be undercover?"

I rolled my eyes. "It's the humidity!"

She narrowed her eyes. "Am I gonna be on that reality show?"

"No," Luke said in a stern tone. "You definitely are not."

April Jean's full lips formed a pout. "That's too bad. I wanted to be on it."

An idea was percolating in my head, so I made a mental note to be sure to leave her a business card. Thankfully, I had a few in my purse.

"So what's she doin' here?" she asked Luke.

"It's my day off, but I wanted to take your statement myself. Summer was with me, so I brought her along. If you're uncomfortable with her being here, I can take her back to her office before I take your statement."

"Nah, she can stay." She motioned her thumb toward the front door. "Y'all come on in."

Luke's body tensed. "That's okay. We can do this out here."

She shook her head. "No way. I feel like a piece of bacon fryin' on a black iron skillet."

April Jean went inside, but Luke stayed put until I reached him. Lowering his voice, he said, "Just remember I'm not responsible for what goes on in there."

"What's she gonna do?" I asked in a whisper.

"Probably nothing since you're here, but just know that I didn't approve of anything you might see inside."

"Okay . . . ," I said a little too eagerly based on the hesitation on his face. If he was trying to scare me, it had backfired. I was dying to go inside and check it out.

Cringing, he motioned for me to follow April Jean across the threshold.

The flimsy metal door creaked when I went inside, and I was relieved to feel a blast of cold air. I'd been in plenty of poorly air-conditioned trailers before I'd moved to Hollywood. Heck, my aunt and uncle had lived in a mobile home behind my grandparents' farmhouse.

But as soon as relief over the a/c washed over me, horror quickly replaced it. Now I could see why Luke had given me his warning, but it had been completely inadequate.

"You like my artwork?" April Jean asked as she opened her refrigerator and pulled out what looked like a pitcher of water.

"Uh . . . yeah . . ."

She grinned.

Luke walked in behind me, and I felt his body grow rigid. Not that I was surprised. There were multiple drawings of him completely naked and in all his sexual glory. Or maybe he was pissed that he had competition. There were drawings of multiple men plastered on the walls, their male appendages all at very full staff—Cale, Willy, several other men I didn't recognize, and finally my cousin Teddy. And here I had thought seeing his bare butt was bad. I held up my hand to block my view of him.

"Hey, Luke. I added to your collection," April Jean said. "What do you think?"

"Uhhh . . . ," he stammered.

"This is amazing," I said, still holding my hand to the side of my face. I couldn't escape Teddy's image. I was going to need therapy after this. "How'd you get all these men to pose for you?" I cast a sideways glance at Luke. I was definitely reading Teddy the riot act tonight.

He held up his hands. "I swear to God I never posed for her."

April Jean rolled her eyes. "Please. I'm an artist who is in touch with the universe. I don't need them to pose. I can sense their proportions." She grabbed a glass out of the cabinet and filled it with water. When she offered it to me, I noticed she'd etched her drawings on the glasses too. I shook my head. I had no desire to be wrapping my hand around—from the looks of it—Mayor Sterling's . . . parts.

Luke crossed his arms over his chest. "So you had an issue with Trent Dunbar?"

"I sure as hell did," she said in a huff. "He stole my car."

Luke dropped his arms, seeming to take her more seriously. "When?"

"This morning. Or maybe in the middle of the night? I noticed it missing when I woke up about an hour ago."

"So Trent stayed here last night?" Luke asked.

"Yeah."

"Maybe he borrowed it," I said. "You know, maybe he went to get coffee and croissants."

April Jean burst out laughing. "Somebody's been livin' in fancy-pants land. Is that what they served on the set of that TV show you did? What was it called? *You Done It*?"

I scowled, and when I didn't answer, Luke said, "*Gotcha!*"

I shot him a dirty look.

She snapped her fingers. "Oh, yeah! You used to say that corny line." Then she thrust out her hip and pointed her finger at me. "Gotcha!"

My jaw tensed. Twice in one day was more than enough.

Luke shifted his weight. "*Anyway* . . . Summer has a point. Maybe Trent went to pick up breakfast . . . or lunch, and he borrowed your car."

"While I love a man who brings me a bear claw and coffee, we all know that Trent Dunbar's too damn selfish for that."

"I'm sure I can track down your car, but the question is, do you want to press charges?" Luke asked.

She hesitated. "I don't want anything official. Just the threat of it is good enough."

Luke was silent for a moment. "So you want me to try to reason with him first?"

"Would you? Maybe put the fear of God into him?" she asked, holding her glass up and pressing it to her cleavage.

"I think it would take God igniting a bush to make *that* happen," Luke said.

"Well, then, just get it back. I really need my car. Today's when the trash service dumps all the big items at the landfill. I need to be there to sift through it."

What? I shot Luke a sideways glance, but his mouth was pursed as though he was considering something he found distasteful.

"It's my day off, so how about we handle it this way: I won't take an official report, but I'll have a chat with Trent and see if he'll willingly return it."

"Would you do that for me, Luke?" she cooed, setting the glass down on the counter. "He's ignoring my calls and texts."

He leaned sideways and peered out the window at the yard. "I didn't see another car out there. How'd he get here?"

"I brought him home with me from the Jackhammer last night."

The Jackhammer was a bar outside of Sweet Briar city limits. I'd been there once, and while the crowd looked tame enough, I'd had an encounter with a guy that would have been a disaster if Luke hadn't stepped in to defend me, much to my irritation. It didn't surprise me that wild-child April Jean would pick up someone like Trent Dunbar there.

"And where was *his* car?" Luke asked.

"We left it in the Jackhammer parking lot. He was too drunk to drive."

He gave her a hard stare. "And you?"

"In better shape than he was."

"I've talked to you about drinking and driving, April Jean," Luke said in a stern voice. "You're gonna get someone killed."

"I wasn't drunk, Luke. I swear it."

"Hmm . . ." He obviously had his doubts. "Are you sure you didn't give him permission—either expressly or implied—to use your car this morning?"

"No, because we came home and started having sex, but he couldn't get it up. Then he fell asleep with me right on top of him." She turned to me with an incredulous expression. "Who *does* that?"

I shook my head. "Really drunk guys. You deserve better than that." Even if she'd mocked my show, because, really, even potbellied pigs deserved better than Trent Dunbar.

With her lips pursed together, she nodded. "Yeah, you might be right." She flicked her gaze to Luke and then back to me. "I bet Luke's never fallen asleep with you sitting on top of his d—"

Luke's eyes flew wide. "*And I think* that's all the information I need for now, April Jean. Thanks."

She looked startled. "Oh. Okay."

He made a move for the front door. "Like I said, I'm gonna keep this unofficial, but I can fill out the paperwork and file a report if you change your mind."

"Thanks, Luke," she said with a genuine smile. "You're the best."

He flashed a tight smile. "Just doin' my job." Then he wasted no time beating it out of her trailer.

I started to follow him, but April Jean grabbed my arm and pulled me to a halt. She tilted her head sideways toward the drawings of Luke. "How'd I do? Am I close?"

I allowed myself another quick glance at the four pencil drawings of him. He was completely naked in all of them, but the backgrounds were different. In one he was in the woods. He was holding an ax with one hand, the handle resting on his bare shoulder and his very well-endowed manhood in his other hand. He was grinning with that devilish grin he sometimes wore. She'd definitely gotten that part right. The next one was of Luke sitting on his desk at the police station, wearing his badge on his bare chest. He was holding a pair of handcuffs in one hand, and in the other . . . It was obvious there was a common theme linking all the drawings.

"That looks painful," I said, gesturing toward the image with the badge.

Her mouth twisted into a look of concentration. "I guess when something becomes engorged like that, it could be. But I think it only happens when a guy uses Viagra. At least the guys I know."

My mouth dropped open, and I quickly tried to recover. "Uh . . . I was talking about the badge."

"Oh . . ." She studied it for a moment with a perplexed look. "You know, I hadn't thought about that."

"Summer!" Luke called from outside.

I leaned closer to April Jean as I dug a card out of my purse. "Say, I take it you're interested in bein' on my show."

"Your PI show?" she asked in surprise. "Yeah, but what for?"

"Trent."

"Oh . . ." Her eyes lit up, but then a guarded look slid into place. "I dunno. I want to, but what do you want to put on there?"

"I take it this wasn't the first time you've had a sleepover with him."

"Not by a long shot. We go *way* back."

Which meant she had a wealth of information. "Do you know if he's still using drugs?"

She laughed. "Using? He's deal—" She clamped her mouth shut. "I don't know nothin'."

That was an outright lie that I hoped to unravel. "Here's my card." I handed it to her. "Text me your number, and either me or one of my crew will be in touch with you to set up an interview here in your trailer."

"On camera?" she asked hopefully.

"Yes, you *will* be on camera. But," I said, lowering my voice, "let's keep this between us for now, okay? I'm still working things out, and I don't want to let the cat out of the bag."

"Yeah, sure."

"Summer!" Luke shouted, starting to sound grumpy.

"Thanks, April Jean." I paused to look at her drawings again, holding up my hand to shield the view of Teddy. "You know? I think you've got real talent." And she did. Other than the exaggerated proportions of the parts in every man's left hand.

Luke was standing in front of his truck, looking like he was about to leave without me.

April Jean followed me out onto the porch and hollered out at Luke, "Don't be a fool and let her get away this time, Luke Montgomery."

He grimaced and climbed into his truck.

When I got inside, he wasted no time before pulling back onto the highway.

"That was . . . interesting," I said with a grin.

He didn't say anything for a second, his hands gripping the steering wheel at ten and two. "She's added more drawings."

"She's an artist?" I asked.

"She fancies herself to be one, but she doesn't make any money from it. She's livin' off disability."

"Disability for what?"

He rolled his eyes. "A bad back, but it doesn't stop her from sleeping with Trent and a list of other guys."

"Well, in her defense, she *was* on top . . ."

He shot me a dirty look.

"Are you gonna let me come with you to look for Trent?"

"I don't know. Don't you need to get back to the office?"

"I'll just send Dixie a text saying we got held up. Besides, she has to do the legwork of setting up some interviews. They've got plenty to do without me." I could see he was about to protest, so I quickly added, "*And* it's an unofficial visit. So it might look better if I'm with you. *Plus*," I said with a sweet smile, "we can spend more time together."

The hard set of his jaw softened. "Why do you *really* want to go?"

I couldn't tell him the real reason, but I could tell him a partial truth. "I'm curious. I want to see the guy who ruined Dixie's life."

"All the more reason to take you back."

"I'm not gonna do or say anything, if that's what you're worried about."

"That's what you said before we dropped in on April Jean."

"In my defense, it was impossible to remain silent after seeing all that." I shot him a grin. "She asked if she'd gotten the proportions right."

He coughed as though he were choking.

"Don't worry. I redirected her attention to the fact she had your police badge attached to your bare chest. So are you goin' to let me come with you? I might come in handy."

He groaned. "I may regret it later, but yeah, you can come. But if you butt in, I'll never bring you with me on something like this again."

At the moment, this trip was all I needed.

Talk about being shortsighted.

Chapter Five

"Where are you going to look for him first?" I asked as I pulled out my phone and started composing a text.

"Maybelline's Facebook page says he's been working at the lumberyard every day, so we'll start there."

Dunbar Lumber was located a couple of miles northeast of town, but still within city limits. I knew from when I'd lived here before that there was a massive lumberyard and sawmill in the back of the property, and an office building in the front.

"Well, I'll be damned," Luke said. "He's really here."

"How do you know?" I asked.

"Because there's April Jean's car." He pointed to an ancient-looking white Ford Explorer with two stickers on the back window. The first was a yellow road sign with a swerving car that read *Blow Job in Progress*, and the other was an interstate highway symbol with an *I* in the top part and a *69* in the bottom.

"So she's a fan of oral sex," I said.

"I wouldn't know anything about that," Luke said, his face turning red.

"Gotta love a woman who knows what she wants," I said with a hint of approval.

He turned to me, his eyes darkening with lust. "And do you know what you want, Summer?"

That was a loaded question. "Let's just say I don't want to make any mistakes this time."

His eyes searched my face. "Fair enough."

We headed toward the office, and as Luke reached for the handle on the front door, he said, "You stay in the background and let me do the talking."

"Of course." I gave him a sweet smile.

"You reminded me of Dixie just then," he said with worry-filled eyes.

He meant I was acting like a loose cannon, but I took it as a compliment. I had learned a thing or two from my cousin. My smile widened, and I walked inside the front office.

"Hey, Luke," a young woman said from a receptionist desk. "Can I help you?"

"I'm here to see Trent."

She froze for a moment but quickly recovered. "Is he in trouble?"

"I just need to speak to him. Unofficially."

"Oh. Okay." She stood, then walked through the doorway to the back.

About a half minute later, a cocky but undeniably good-looking guy walked out, literally strutting. He was shorter than Luke, probably about five-ten, and had short, styled brown hair. He wore jeans and a dress shirt. When he saw Luke, a shit-eating grin spread across his face that said *I know why you're here, and you can't touch me.*

I disliked him on sight.

"What can I do for you, *Chief*?" Trent asked in a patronizing tone.

"The *chief's* not necessary at the moment," Luke said in a deceptively calm voice. "I'm here as a private citizen."

"Then what can I do for you, *Luke*?"

"April Jean would like her car back."

He made a look of disgust. "It's not like I want it."

"And yet you left it in the Dunbar Lumber parking lot."

"It's better than leaving it on the street to get hit by a semi, although I'd be doin' her a favor."

"April Jean can't afford a new car, and you know it," Luke said with a hint of an edge in his voice. "What made you think you could just take it?"

"Obviously, I was desperate. I woke up and had to get to work, so I did what I had to do."

"By stealing her car?" I asked.

His gaze raked me up and down before a smile lit up his eyes. "Well, well, if it isn't Summer Butler. Or should I say, Summer Baumgartner? And *stealing*'s a harsh word. I only borrowed it."

I gave him a pointed look. "Without her permission."

Luke shot me a glare, reminding me I'd already broken our ground rules, but the warning came too late. Trent had shifted his attention to me.

"So you're back in town too," Trent said, thrusting his foot to the side. He gave me an appreciative look. "Looking for some fun?"

"You were just sleepin' with April Jean last night."

"I only went home with her because I was drunk off my ass."

"And I'd have to be drunk off mine to go home with you," I said.

His face lit up. "Woo-hoo. Summer's got some *fire* in her. I bet you're a hellion in bed."

"Summer," Luke said in a low tone, "go wait in the truck."

I gave Luke an irritated look. I'd handled worse than this, and after a childhood spent in pageants, I didn't like being treated like a little princess. But I had another reason for wanting to stick around. I'd come up with a plan for our big case—one Luke was sure to disapprove of. We could investigate Trent, prove him to be a lawless lowlife, and clear Dixie's name in the process. Whether Luke invited the interference or not, we'd be helping him out if we took Trent down.

Alienating Trent right now might be a bad idea, but I sure wouldn't kiss up to him either. Even Meryl Streep wasn't up to *that* performance.

Trent laughed. "Are you screwin' America's Darling, Luke?"

Luke's hands fisted at his sides.

Great. The man who was slow to anger, unless it involved me, apparently, was now riled up.

Since this was an unofficial visit, I decided to take over before Luke did something he regretted. I walked around him and held out my hand to Trent. "I'm gonna need those car keys."

"When did you become friends with April Jean?"

"Never you mind about that. Just give me the keys."

He dug into his jeans pocket and pulled out a set of keys with a pink, fuzzy pom-pom on the end. Dangling them over my hands, he said, "How long are you in town for?"

"Never you mind about that either."

He laughed. "We should entertain the idea of getting together for drinks."

I wiggled my fingers. "All we're entertaining at the moment is you handing over April Jean's keys."

He dropped the keys into my palm. "I'll win you over, just wait and see."

"Don't hold your breath waiting or you'll die from oxygen deprivation. You should head back to work," I said, motioning to the doorway to the back. "It's not easy trying to transform yourself into a productive member of society. You need to give it your full attention."

He laughed again. "You tell Dixie I'll see her later. And if you want to join us, the more the merrier. I love me a good threesome." Then he turned around and started to head back through the doorway, only to stop and swivel back toward me with an expression that screamed *arrogant asshole.* "Aren't you supposed to say *Gotcha!*?"

I clenched my fists at my sides, and my words came out in a low growl. "How about I say—"

Luke spun me around and pointed me toward the door. "And that's our cue to leave."

I was steaming, but not so much from the *Gotcha!* dig as what he'd said before it. Dixie was planning on seeing him? Over my dead body.

I turned around to leave, and Luke followed on my heels. I could feel his irritation before we even stopped next to his truck.

"I thought I told you to let me handle it," he said.

"It was an unofficial visit, Luke, and the way he was talking about April Jean was pissing me off."

"And the way he was talking about you was pissing *me* off."

"No kidding. I was scared you were gonna hit him."

His brow furrowed, and he glanced toward the office. "He was insulting you."

"I'm a big girl, Luke, and I've dealt with a hell of a lot worse than that."

He turned back to me. "You should have stayed out of it, Summer."

"I'm sorry." That I had upset him. Not that I'd jumped in. "But did you hear him say he was meeting Dixie later?"

"He was probably just saying that to rile you up, and he added the threesome part to get me on edge. I have to believe Dixie's smarter than that."

I lost some of my bluster. "I sure hope so."

Luke's phone rang, and he pulled it out of his pocket. "What's up, Amber?" He paused and pushed out a sigh. "I'll be right over. Tell Willy to hang tight."

Willy was Officer Willy Hawkins, which meant there was trouble. "What's goin' on?" I asked, realizing my southern accent was back in full force. *That* had taken less than twenty-four hours this time.

"There's a house fire on the south edge of town."

43

"Do you usually show up to those? Can't Willy handle it?"

"He could if it were an ordinary house fire, but the fire department's calling it arson."

"Oh." That hit a little too close to home. A shiver ran down my spine.

"I need to head over there. Do you think you could get Dixie to pick you up there?"

"We need to get April Jean's car back to her. Maybe I should have Dixie pick me up at her trailer."

Luke snatched the keys out of my hand. "No way. That car's a piece of crap and liable to break down ten feet after you pull out of the parking lot."

"Fine," I said, heading toward the passenger door. The truth was that I *wanted* to go with him. While I planned to investigate Trent Dunbar, I wasn't sure we'd actually be able to use it for the show. It was a dangerous proposition, since it involved Dixie. I wouldn't air anything that might hurt my cousin in any way, which meant I needed a backup plan. The house fire was probably nothing, but I was desperate.

During the drive, I could tell that Luke was still irritated with me, but he finally broke the silence after five minutes. "You are not allowed anywhere near this crime scene, Summer."

"I know, Luke."

"*No.* I want your word that you won't go near the crime scene."

"I promise I won't go near the crime scene." Releasing a sigh, I reached for his hand. "Like I said, I only jumped in with Trent because it wasn't an official visit. But the fire is different. I would never do anything to compromise an investigation. I swear."

His hand squeezed mine, and he nodded. "Okay. Maybe you should call Dixie now about coming to get you."

"Actually, I'm thinking Dixie doesn't need the reminder. She was a mess when we visited Otto's old house." Otto's family had died in a fire too, just like Dixie's parents and our pawpaw had. "I was thinking about asking Teddy."

"You're right. That's probably a good idea."

After he gave me the address, I sent Teddy a text asking him if he had time to pick me up. He responded right away and said he was leaving the feed store and could be at the house in fifteen to twenty minutes.

"That means you'll be hanging around for about ten minutes before he gets there," Luke said.

"I already gave you my word that I wouldn't bother the crime scene."

"Yeah, I know."

I didn't blame him for his skepticism.

The house was smoldering when we pulled up. Although the fire had been put out, it had done quite a bit of damage first. Two fire trucks were parked out front as well as an ambulance and a Sweet Briar police car. There was also a bunch of people gawking at the scene from the other side of the street.

Luke reached for his door handle, then stopped and turned to face me. "Are you free for dinner tonight?"

I made a face. "Meemaw has called a family dinner . . . but you could come."

"To a Baumgartner family dinner?" He sounded leery.

"Too soon?" I said with a hint of a challenge.

He cast a glance at the smoldering house, then leaned over and gave me a kiss. He sat back and smiled. "I want this to work, Summer, and I know your family is important to you now that you got them back. So yes. I'll come to a Baumgartner family dinner. And I'll even try my best to get along with Teddy."

"Thanks for making an effort," I said. And I knew what a supreme effort this was. Teddy held Luke responsible for putting Dixie in juvie all those years ago, something I doubted he'd ever get over. He also held a grudge against Luke for breaking up with me over the Connor photos. Luke had an uphill battle as far as my oldest cousin was concerned.

He rested his hand on my neck, and his thumb lightly brushed my jaw. "You're worth it. What time should I be there?"

A pleasant shiver ran down my back and all the way to my toes. "Meemaw knows my days tend to run late, so she's made the concession of a seven o'clock dinner time, but be forewarned—bodily harm is a distinct possibility for anyone who's late. If you come, make sure you're a few minutes early."

"I'll be there. Be safe, Summer."

"You too."

Luke got out of the truck, and I realized that a few people had been watching us, which meant what just transpired would be all over Maybelline's Facebook page in a matter of minutes. I could only hope that the novelty would wear off sooner rather than later.

I got out of the truck and decided to ask the neighbors what they knew about the fire—there was more than one way to get information.

I headed toward the crowd, trying to figure out who to talk to first, but I stopped in my tracks when I saw Connor Blake already talking to someone in the crowd. Worse, he had his film crew with him.

"What are you doing here, Connor?" I asked.

He turned to me and grinned. "Looks like I had the same idea you did—I just got here first. Which means I get dibs."

I put a hand on my hip. "First, there is no client, Connor. Second, this is an actual fire, and someone's house was destroyed. I think the police and the fire marshal have it covered, and three, this isn't a game."

"Says you," he said with a grin. "But this is still mine."

"I'm only here because I was with Luke. My cousin's on his way to pick me up."

"Yeah, sure."

I shrugged. What did I care if he believed me or not?

"Summer," Lauren said as she made her way to me through the crowd, "why am I not surprised to see you here?"

"I was with Luke when he got the call about the fire."

"Using everything at your disposal," Lauren said. "Just like me." The gleam in her eye told me she knew it was the worst possible insult she could have leveled at me. Worse, it kind of struck home.

"I don't need Luke's help to come up with cases," I lied. "We've got some exciting things lined up all on our own."

"I can't wait to see," she said. "Can you give me any hints?" She knew we didn't have squat.

"You'll have to wait to find out like everyone else."

She was about to respond, but her gaze shifted away from me, and a smug smile broke out on her face. "Looks like you were telling the truth."

I turned to see Teddy walking up behind me, and he didn't look happy. No wonder Lauren was excited. The *Darling Investigations* fans *loved* Teddy. I was sure she planned to take full advantage of that.

"Summer, you didn't waste any time finding trouble, did you?" he asked with a frown. His gaze shifted to Luke, who was talking to Willy and a man in a firefighter's suit.

Little did he know . . . "I'm only here because I was with Luke when he got the call, and he didn't have time to drop me off at the office."

"Didn't waste any time with him either, huh?" Teddy asked.

Lauren's eyes lit up at the smell of conflict in my life.

I grabbed Teddy's arm and tried to drag him away, but my producer caught his attention.

"What are all y'all doing at Bruce Jepper's house?" he asked.

"Is that who lives here?" I asked.

"Back off, Summer," Lauren said. "We were here first. The case is ours."

I rolled my eyes. "Like I said, I have my own cases."

Pissed, I started to walk toward Teddy's truck. He caught up with me in two strides. "What's goin' on, Summer? I thought you were workin' with Lauren."

"It's a long story," I said. "I'll explain in the truck."

A man who looked to be close to my age was standing next to the crime scene tape, and he nodded as we passed. He was wearing jeans and a T-shirt, and even though Luke was wearing civilian clothes too, this guy looked so nervous I suspected he wasn't a first responder.

Teddy came to a halt when he saw the guy, and I stopped with him. As anxious as this bystander looked, he had to know what was going on, not to mention he was standing right next to the crime scene tape, and no one was shooing him away. Sure, maybe I couldn't do anything with *this* particular case now that Connor had claimed it, but it would drive Lauren crazy that I was talking to him. Whoever he was.

"Bruce, what happened?" Teddy asked.

He ran a shaky hand over his shaggy, brown hair. "I have no idea. I left for work around eight, and then my next-door neighbor called me about an hour ago and told me she saw smoke pouring out the back window of my house. The fire chief says it's probably a total loss."

"That sucks," Teddy said. "Do they know what caused it?"

"No, but he asked if I had any chemicals stored in the kitchen. All I had was some cleaning supplies. Nothin' crazy."

"Do you live alone?" I asked.

Bruce eyed me up and down. "I ain't got a wife or a girlfriend, if that's what you're askin'."

"Don't waste your time," Teddy said with a groan. "She's goin' out with Luke."

He shrugged. "Can't blame a guy for tryin'."

"I'm sorry about your house," I said. "Do you know anyone who might have started the fire on purpose?"

He shook his head. "No. I ain't got any enemies that I know about."

A fireman headed toward us, and I was sure he was going to tell us to back up, but he turned his attention to Bruce. The new guy was tall and good-looking and had a mass of dark, thick hair and an air of confidence that didn't look forced. "I thought I'd give you an update, man." His gaze lingered on me before moving to my cousin. "Hey, Teddy. What are *you* doin' here?"

"Pickin' up my cousin. It's a long story as to why she's here, so don't ask."

The firefighter grinned. "I know why she's here. She showed up with Luke. I saw 'em makin' out in his pickup."

"We didn't make out," I protested. "It was one kiss."

Teddy scowled. "I said don't ask. I don't want to know any of the details."

The guy laughed. "I didn't ask. I made a statement of fact." He turned to me. "Hi, I'm Garrett Newcomer. You're obviously Summer."

"You have me at a disadvantage," I said. "You know about me, but I don't know anything about you."

"Garrett, Bruce, and I have been friends since kindergarten," Teddy said. "Garrett escaped Sweet Briar for a couple of years. Then, fool that he is, he came back and got a job at Dunbar Lumber."

"I got a degree in forestry, jackass. White-collar job. It's not like I'm loading the trucks."

"Wearing a dress shirt all day." Teddy said it like it was an insult.

"Sure as hell beats gambling with the weather every year," Garrett said good-naturedly. "And I still get time out in the field with a guar-anteed salary."

"But you're working for Trent Dunbar," Teddy sneered.

"Hey, now. I'm working for his daddy," Garrett said.

I held up my hand, then gestured to the clothes Garrett was wearing. "Wait. If you're working for Dunbar Lumber, why are you dressed up like a firefighter?"

"I'm a volunteer firefighter," Garrett said. "Most of us are. Sweet Briar's not busy or rich enough to pay for a full-time fire crew, and Roger Dunbar's good about letting the guys off for fire calls." He turned to Bruce with a solemn look. "Which brings me back to the reason I walked over in the first place. You can't stay here tonight. In fact, you can't go inside at all. The fire marshal is still investigating, and the house isn't fit to live in."

Bruce's face turned ashen. "What am I gonna do?"

"I was about to tell you to call your insurance agent, but Thelma Kuntz just pulled up." Garrett gestured to an older woman who was climbing out of her car. "The benefit of living in a small town. She should get you all sorted out." Then he lowered his voice. "Don't worry, Bruce, you've got a dozen friends to help you."

"Since Trent's back, he might help too," Bruce said in a hopeful tone.

Teddy's brow lowered so much it was a wonder he could see. "I wouldn't count on that asshole to put you out if *you* were on fire. Besides, I thought he was pissed at you over that poker game last night."

"He was drinkin'. He probably doesn't even remember," Bruce said, but he didn't sound like he totally believed it.

Trent Dunbar had been one busy guy last night. "Who else was at the poker game?" I asked before I could stop myself. I'd always been a little too curious for my own good—a trait I shared with the character I'd played on *Gotcha!*

Teddy gave me a look that said he didn't appreciate my nosiness, but Bruce wrinkled his nose. "Just a few guys. Me, Trent, Wizard, Mark, and Garrett."

Garrett, wearing a grave expression, clapped Bruce on the back. "I need to get back to it, but if there's anything you need, let me know, okay?"

Bruce nodded.

Garrett turned to me. "And if you need a forester who also happens to be an experienced firefighter as an expert on your show, I'm your man."

I laughed. "If the situation arises, you'll be the first one I call."

"Good." Garrett ducked under the tape and walked over to a group composed of a couple of firefighters and Luke and Willy.

"I better go meet with Thelma," Bruce said with a sigh.

"Say, Bruce," I said, lowering my voice, "I have no right to ask you this, but if that guy with the camera tries to ask you questions, shoot him down, okay?"

He scanned the crowd, and then his eyes widened in surprise. "Isn't that the guy from *Gotcha!*?"

"Yeah," I grumbled.

Teddy strained his neck, trying to get a better look. "What's he doin' here? I thought you hated that guy."

"*Hate*'s a strong word, but it's safe to say I'm not happy about him being here. At. All." I rested a hand on Bruce's arm. "Which is why I'm asking you something I shouldn't be askin', but I'm askin' anyway."

"Does he want to put me on TV?" Bruce asked, keeping his gaze on my former costar. Connor was trying to conduct an interview while holding up another prepublication copy of his book—he'd given me the last one, my eye. A few middle-aged women had flocked around him and were grabbing his shirt in a bid to get his attention.

"Yeah," I said. "But he's more concerned with selling *The Connor Life* and makin' himself look good."

"*The Connor Life*?" Teddy asked.

I rolled my eyes. "Don't ask. But, Bruce, if you'll let me interview you, not only will you get on TV, but I'll make sure you look amazing."

"Can you take away my beer belly?" He grabbed a handful of it through his shirt.

That wasn't exactly what I'd meant. "Um . . . yeah." It was nothing a table or tight frame on his face wouldn't hide.

"Then you've got yourself a deal."

A smile spread across my face, and I felt happier about this than I had any right to. "Great! We'll be in touch about your interview. Probably in the next day or two, if that's all right," I said. I had no idea what we would interview him about since I'd agreed to stay away from the fire investigation, but he'd mentioned something about Trent being pissed over a poker game. I could ask him for more details. "We might want to interview you in front of your house." It would definitely be a better backdrop than an office wall.

"There's not much left of it," he said.

All the better, but I wasn't crass enough to say it. Still, I felt like a vulture circling a wounded animal and waiting for his dying breath. Maybe Lauren's comment about our supposed similarities had pissed me off so much because I worried she was right. "That's okay," I said, trying to hide my guilt. "We'll figure out the location later."

"Okay." He headed over to the insurance agent.

"What did you think of Garrett?" Teddy asked, shuffling his feet.

I half shrugged. "He seems nice."

He tried to play nonchalant. "He's a good-looking guy, don't you think?"

"Yeah. I think you two would make a lovely couple."

His eyes flew wide. "Not for me."

"Then why bring up his looks?" But I knew exactly what he was doing; we both did.

Teddy leaned down and whispered into my ear. "Garrett's a stand-up guy. Let me set you up with him."

I glared up at him. "I cannot *believe* you."

"I'm looking out for you, Summy. Luke's gonna hurt you, just like he did ten years ago."

"Things are different this time."

A sad look filled his eyes. "Not all that different. You're still workin' on a show that takes up a lot of your time, and Luke Montgomery is a man who's used to getting what he wants when he wants it. Sure, he's tolerating your travel and your crazy schedule for now, but the novelty's gonna wear off, and where's that gonna leave you? Heartbroken all over again."

"Teddy," I said in warning. He wasn't saying anything I hadn't already considered. My career had broken up Luke and me before. We were all grown up now, but part of the reason we'd agreed to try again was that we still felt like the two people who had fallen in love the summer before my senior year. What if we were too much like those people? What if we were doomed to repeat the same pattern again and again?

"I worry about you, Summy. Just like I worry about Dixie."

While I loved the idea that he cared about me so much, I'd seen how obsessive he could be about protecting the people he loved. He'd gone undercover for the sheriff to take down Dixie's no-good drug-dealer ex and "catch" Luke, whom he'd suspected of selling drugs.

"I'm a big girl and used to taking care of myself." I shot a glance at Connor and his crew, who were shooting footage of him talking to bystanders.

I only hoped I could save myself on my own show.

CHAPTER SIX

"That no-good, slimy toad," Dixie said. I'd only been an hour late returning to the office, and I hadn't wasted any time before telling my team about Connor getting the jump on us at the house fire.

"Look," I said, "it's not necessarily a bad thing. I mean, Luke and Willy are on it, so they'll probably find the arsonist, and Connor will be left with a whole lot of nothing." I gave them a sly look. "Especially since I coerced the homeowner into not talking to them. Which reminds me, I promised Bruce we'd interview him."

"Does this mean you're breaking the rules?" Tony asked. "We're going to cover the house fire anyway?"

I wasn't ready to tell them about my plan to ask Bruce about Trent. "No. I want to win this fair and square. We can beat Lauren without being conniving."

"Then why are we interviewing him?" Dixie asked.

I especially didn't want to tell her my idea about investigating Trent in front of everyone else if she was really planning to meet him tonight. "We'll come up with something."

I could see by the look in her eyes that she suspected I had a plan.

"So aside from interviewing a guy for a case we can't use, where do to we stand?" Tony asked. "What did you get from Luke?"

"A whole lot of nothing."

They all groaned.

"We'll figure it out, okay? I have an idea, but I'm not ready to share it yet."

Dixie didn't look surprised, but the three guys protested. "We should be brainstorming ideas together," Bill said. "I thought we were a team."

"We are," I said. "But it's a sensitive matter, and I need to talk to the people it directly involves before I share it with the group."

"Then, what are we going to do?" Tony asked.

"We still have our smaller cases. We should focus on those and get them out of the way first."

"We have three weeks, Summer," Chuck said. "Three weeks, and we're already at a disadvantage because Lauren controls the final edits. Sure, there's going to be a Season Three, but that doesn't mean we'll be on it."

"We'll get a big case. I promise," I said. If the Trent idea fell through, I'd figure out something else.

"What are we going to do about interviewing clients on camera?" Tony asked. "We're supposed to be operating out of the train station."

I groaned. I'd forgotten about that part. "Maybe we can call this a satellite office."

By five o'clock, we'd set up several appointments and put together a tentative game plan for the next couple of days. I sent the guys on their way, and as soon as they walked out the door, I dragged one of the client chairs over to Dixie's desk.

"Dix, I need to talk to you about something."

"Okay . . . ," she said, her voice rising an octave.

"When I was with Luke, I found out a few things that were . . . concerning."

Her back tensed. I suspected she knew where this was going.

"First, Luke told me that Trent Dunbar is in town and that he's supposedly back for good."

"He's said that before," she said, looking down at her lap and tugging on a loose thread at the hem of her shirt.

My mouth dropped open, and I blinked. "You've been in contact with him?"

She squirmed in her seat. "It's a small town, Summer."

"Does Teddy know?" I doubted that he did, or he'd probably lock Dixie in her room.

"Teddy doesn't know every aspect of my life," she said in a sharp tone.

That was a no. "I saw Trent this morning."

Her gaze snapped up to mine. "When? How?"

I studied her closely, not liking the hopeful tone in her voice.

Crap. Whatever she might feel for Bill, it was clear Dixie was still interested in that slimeball Trent Dunbar.

"Well, that brings me to issue number two. Did you know that Mayor Sterling's son was just hired by the Sweet Briar Police Department?"

Surprise filled her eyes.

"Luke said he had no choice in the decision. That Mayor Sterling and the board ramrodded it through. He said Elijah Sterling and Trent are friends. I think Roger Dunbar convinced Mayor Sterling to hire his son to help cover for Trent's bad behavior."

"Trent's turning over a new leaf," she said at once. "He's trying to make things right."

"What does that mean? Make *what* right?"

She remained silent.

I hated to hurt Dixie, but she deserved to know the truth. I needed to protect her from this jerk who obviously didn't give two figs about her. It wasn't lost on me that Teddy had the same goal. "April Jean brought Trent home with her last night from the Jackhammer; then he stole her car."

Shock filled her eyes. "Who told you that?"

"April Jean herself. But she didn't want to press charges, so Luke and I went to Dunbar Lumber to see if Trent was there."

She kept her gaze on her desk.

"He was, and her car was in the parking lot. I have to say he didn't act like a guy who was trying to make things right." When she remained silent, I said, "He implied you two were meeting up tonight."

I was met with silence. So she *was* planning to meet him. My disappointment in her was surprising.

"He also said I should come along because he loves threesomes."

Her face lifted. "He was joking, Summer."

"He didn't seem like he was joking to me."

A defiant look crossed her face. "So what is this? An intervention? Are you planning on telling Teddy?"

"No, but I'm worried about you, Dixie."

Tears filled her eyes. "And where were you when I was sitting in juvie for two years?"

A lump burned in my throat, and I resisted the urge to defend myself. She was right. "I was a terrible cousin. I was too busy feeling sorry for myself after Momma stole all my money. It's not a good excuse . . . in fact, it's no excuse at all. But I can't change the past. The only thing I know to do is try to be a good cousin now." I leaned forward and said emphatically, "Trent Dunbar isn't good for you, Dixie. He's only going to hurt you."

"And you know this after talking to him for a minute or two?" she asked in an accusatory tone.

"You didn't see him, Dix. He was an arrogant asshole."

"Only because Luke was there. He hates Luke." A shadow crossed over her face, and I could see that it bothered her. Even though Luke had been the one to arrest her, he'd stuck with her through the whole ordeal, getting her an attorney and convincing the judge to try her as a juvenile and not an adult. He'd even been there for her after her release. She felt a loyalty to him that Teddy didn't understand, and I was sure she got tired of constantly having to defend it to him. And now she had to defend this thing she had with Trent—whatever it was—to all of us. It had to be exhausting.

"Three people came to see me, Summer: Teddy, Luke, and Trent. And not only that, Trent wrote me letters. I was lonely, and he made it more bearable."

I wanted to say that he owed her that and so much more, but I bit my tongue. "I'm so sorry I let you down, and I'll spend the rest of my life trying to make it up to you. But I need you to see the person I saw today, Dixie."

"No," she said, choking on her tears. "I need you to see the man I see."

She'd made up her mind, so I had two choices: continue to push her away or love her no matter what. Loving her was easy—staying quiet was the harder part of the equation, especially since I could see she was destined for heartbreak.

But then again, didn't Teddy think the same about me?

"I love you, Dix, and I only want you to be happy. I'll stand behind whatever you do."

She gave me a wary look.

"It's not a trick," I said. "I swear. And if he hurts you, I'll be here to help you pick up the pieces without a single 'I told you so.'" I tried to swallow the lump in my throat, but my voice cracked. "Just like I hope you're there if Luke hurts me."

So where did that leave my idea to investigate the fire? Dixie came first, so was I hurting or helping by digging into the past? And if we didn't investigate Trent, where did that leave my show? I couldn't worry about any of that right now. Dixie needed her cousin, not her boss.

She got up and walked around her desk as I stood. She threw her arms around me, and I pulled her close, her tears wetting my cheek. "I love you, Summer."

"I love you too." And I realized this was what unconditional love looked like, something I'd never gotten from my mother or even my grandmother. Our pawpaw had showed it to both of us, and I'd give it to Dixie now. She needed me, and I'd never let her down again.

"Let's go home and get ready for our family dinner."

"Oh . . . ," I said, realizing I'd forgotten to tell her about our dinner guest. "I invited Luke to dinner."

She pulled free and wiped her tears. "Meemaw will be thrilled. She loves Luke."

"And Teddy not so much."

She grinned. "So dinner should be entertaining."

Understatement of the year.

An hour later, Dixie and I were setting the table even though it was only six thirty. I was nervous about Luke coming, especially since I hadn't warned Teddy. We'd spent the whole drive back to the office talking about Connor Blake and Lauren's efforts to push me out of my own show.

I had started setting out five plates when the front door opened. It was too early for Luke, and Teddy usually came in through the kitchen. I looked up in shock as Lauren walked through the door, followed by the new crew members and Karen. "Hello!" Lauren called out in a cheery voice. "Is everyone ready for a family dinner?"

I nearly dropped the plate in my hand. "How did you know we were having a family dinner?"

"Who do you think planned this little shindig?"

I turned to Dixie, about to ask if she'd known Lauren and the crew would be showing up, but she looked as shell-shocked as I felt.

"However, unlike last time," Lauren said, "the cameras will be rolling before and after dinner, so we're just going to get set up and start rolling. Summer and Dixie? Brad needs to hook up your mikes."

"Where's my crew?" I asked. "Why are you using Connor's crew?" I leaned to the side to see if he'd come with them. Thankfully, he was nowhere in sight.

Lauren gave a lazy shrug.

The crew began unpacking their equipment, and I pulled my phone out of my pocket and texted Bill.

Did you know Lauren was filming our family dinner tonight?

His response was immediate: Lauren just told us about five minutes ago. Tony, Chuck, and I are packing up our truck right now. We'll be there soon.

Lauren must have hidden it from my crew to keep me on my toes, but at least they were coming. I trusted them more than the new people. What troubled me most was that Meemaw had insisted on this dinner, which meant she'd arranged it with Lauren without warning us. That was totally unlike her.

I set the fifth plate on the table and nearly gasped. Luke had made it clear back in April that he wanted nothing to do with being on camera. I had to warn him, so I typed out a quick text, turning away from the crew as I did so.

Our family dinner is being filmed by Lauren and the crew. We can just plan something for tomorrow night . . . if you're free.

The disappointment was stronger than it should have been over a measly dinner, but I hadn't seen him in weeks. What little time we'd spent alone together this morning had been eclipsed by Trent Dunbar and the fire. I reminded myself that we'd only be filming the show for three weeks, and then the crew would be gone. We could try to find a normal life . . . well, as normal as I was capable of.

After I sent the text, I brought Luke's plate back into the kitchen and found my grandmother mashing potatoes with her ancient hand masher.

"Why didn't you tell me they'd be filming dinner?" I asked after I put it away.

"Why would I tell you how you're running your own TV show?" she asked, putting even more force into her smashing.

"I can't figure out what convinced you to let the camera crew back into your house in the first place. After the last family dinner, you said never again."

She poured milk into the potatoes before continuing her task. "Turns out cleaning out septic tanks is expensive business."

I put a hand on my hip. "I'm not falling for that. You announced the family dinner before I clogged the toilet."

Meemaw shrugged, still not looking at me. "Money's tight, and that fool boy is still talkin' about raisin' organic chickens."

This had been an ongoing argument for a while. At least since April. The farm had been losing money, and some of the other farms in the county had set aside tracts of land to raise organic chickens. But Meemaw had thrown a fit when Teddy suggested it at the last family dinner. "Raising chickens makes sense, Meemaw. Teddy's done his research. He knows what he's doin.'"

She looked up with a glare, pointing her masher at me. A thick glob of potatoes fell on the floor. "This is a cotton farm, Summer Lynn Baumgartner, and a cotton farm it will stay."

"And it will still *be* a cotton farm. Just one that also raises organic chickens."

"Over my dead body."

I hoped it wouldn't come to that, because I was pretty sure that Teddy had already purchased the lumber to start building chicken coops. The county had paid him a $10,000 reward for his part in the sting operation that had taken down Cale Malone, and he'd earned a small stipend from appearing in the first season of *Darling Investigations*. He'd pooled the money together to fund the project.

But now didn't seem like the best time to bring it up. I had a more immediate concern. "Are Momma and Burt comin' tonight?" I asked.

"I didn't invite them."

"That didn't answer my question."

She shrugged again. "I can't stop that woman from doin' what she wants. The only way I get the money she promised is if I let her go hog wild. So that's what I'm doin'."

Great.

I pulled out my phone. Luke hadn't texted back, so I sent him a second message.

In case my last text was too subtle—stay away from dinner. Not only is Lauren filming, but I'm pretty sure Momma's coming with Burt.

My mother's appearance would bring plenty of conflict to the table. I didn't need to add Luke to the mix. She hated Luke, the only thing she and Teddy agreed upon.

"Meemaw."

She stopped mashing and started scooping the potatoes into a bowl.

62

"Meemaw," I said, softer this time, "I'm sorry I brought this mess to your door. I'll try to make sure it doesn't happen again."

Her face lifted, and I was surprised to see tears swimming in her eyes. "This show was what brought you back to us and made me swallow my stubborn pride . . . well, some of it anyway. I can't begrudge it that much."

I would have rushed over to hug her, but my grandmother was the prickly type who would likely shiv me with the potato masher if I tried. So instead, I nodded and hurried out of the kitchen before she shivved me anyway to keep me from telling anyone about her rare display of emotion.

The crew had unpacked, and one of them was attaching a mike to Dixie, but Lauren was nowhere to be seen. Another crew member wordlessly approached me with a mike.

Dixie did a sound check, and when I finished mine, I checked my phone. Still nothing from Luke.

I heard my mother's voice before I saw her, but at least I was somewhat prepared this time.

"I would love to host the next dinner at Tantara," she said from outside the front door. "Tantara is our home out on Highway 10. It's much larger and grander than the farmhouse."

She'd named her house Tantara? She was obsessed with *Gone with the Wind* and had once confessed that she'd almost named me Bonnie Blue after Scarlett O'Hara's daughter. Thank God for small favors. But where had the *Tan* part come from?

"That sounds like a wonderful idea," Lauren said. "We'll talk dates after we finish tonight."

I noticed the two crew people had picked up their cameras and were ready to capture my reunion with my mother. How did I want to play this? Try to minimize the conflict like last time, or let it all out?

I was leaning toward the shit show.

My mother smiled when she saw me and stopped several feet to my left, posing to ensure her left side—her best side—was angled toward the camera. And it was obvious that she'd come dressed for the spotlight. She was wearing a pale-pink pencil skirt and a white blouse that clung to her artificial boobs. Her bleached-blonde hair had obviously been styled by her hairdresser, and her makeup was flawless. My mother had always been a pretty woman, but it was obvious a plastic surgeon had helped her achieve this new level of beauty.

"Summer, dear," she said with a fake smile, "are you getting enough sleep? You have monstrous bags under your eyes. I have a cream that will do wonders for you."

"It must be bad lighting," Dixie said, moving up behind me. "Because I'm sure your plastic surgeon guaranteed your bags wouldn't come back for ten years, and yet it looks like your eyes have been on a three-day shopping binge."

My mother lifted her fingers to her cheek, but as soon as she saw the grin on Dixie's face, she dropped her hand, and her face contorted into something ugly. "You think you're so cute, Dixie Belle, but everyone knows you're only hangin' out with Summer for your fifteen minutes of fame."

Dixie put her hand on her hip. "And you're here trying to hang on to yours."

"I'm a respected business owner. I train girls in southern Alabama and Georgia to win pageants. What do you have to show for yourself other than killing your parents and my father?"

I gasped and resisted the urge to punch my mother in the throat. "Momma," I said, my voice tight, "maybe you should get back to those girls, the ones you find so much more important than any of us."

My mother turned her glare on me. "I knew you were jealous of my success. I can't help it if you're a washed-up failure at twenty-nine."

I heard hard foot thuds behind me, followed by Teddy's harsh voice. "It's better than being a bitter old hag like you, Aunt Bea."

My mother drew in a breath so sharp she nearly sucked in a fly that happened to be buzzing past her head. When she realized her close call, she started screaming and waving her hands in front of her face.

Dixie and Teddy burst into laughter, but the gleeful look on Lauren's face told me we were playing right into her hands. I had to get this runaway circus under control.

"Momma, I'm gonna go grab another plate for you. Is Burt comin'?"

She lifted her chin. "He's staying home with his bursitis. I'm thinkin' I should be gettin' back to him." Her full accent was back in full force.

"You'll do no such thing," Meemaw said as she burst through the door with a bowl of mashed potatoes. "I called this family dinner for a reason, and like it or not, you're family, Beatrice Mae."

My mother looked like she was going to bolt anyway, but instead, she excused herself to the restroom to wash up, probably so she could see if Dixie had been lying about the bags under her eyes.

My grandmother pointed her finger at the three of us cousins, holding our gazes with a look that made my toes curl. "All y'all, behave. I need Beatrice here tonight, and I don't want the three of you runnin' her off."

By the time Dixie and I helped Meemaw bring out the rest of the food, my mother was already sitting at the table with a look of righteous indignation. Teddy sat one chair down and across from her with a mischievous grin on his face.

I just wanted this dinner to end.

Meemaw said grace, and we all started to fill our plates with meat loaf and potatoes. After a minute of silent eating, I heard loud voices outside. I jerked up my gaze, shocked to see we had another dinner guest.

Luke pushed his way through the crew and stood at the foot of the table.

"Am I too late to join y'all for dinner?"

"Oh, hell no," Teddy said as he got to his feet. "What's *he* doin' here?"

Dixie grinned from ear to ear. "This family dinner just got good."

Chapter Seven

"Miss Viola," Luke said to my grandmother, "would you mind if I go into the kitchen and grab myself a plate?"

He'd done it more times than I could count the summer we were together, and my grandmother hadn't changed a thing in the kitchen since then, but I hopped up from my chair, my heart pounding with anxiety. "I'll help him."

"The boy did nothing but eat the summer he was always here," my mother said in a snotty tone. "He knows where the plates are."

Meemaw broke into a huge smile—one I hadn't seen since that long-ago summer. "Your face is always welcome here." She good-naturedly waved her hand toward the kitchen. "Summer, you go with him."

Teddy looked like he was about to bolt, but Meemaw shot him her death stare. He tucked his chin to his chest and shoveled in a mouthful of meat loaf, probably to force himself to keep quiet.

Luke didn't seem to notice the tension. He ambled toward the kitchen door as if he were walking up to the Dairy Queen window after a fun day on the lake, while I walked along the other side of the table, feeling like I was on a Spanish Inquisition rack about to be pulled in half. He pushed the swinging door open and waited for me to go in before following behind me. I reached around to the box attached to my skirt waistband and turned off the mike. I didn't need Lauren hearing this conversation and using it against me.

Once the door closed, he snagged my hand and pulled me closer. His smile faded into a serious expression as he studied my face.

"I know you told me to stay away, but I felt like I'd be failing you if I didn't come."

This was a huge gesture, no mistaking it. "But you told me you wanted no part of being on camera."

He grimaced. "That was when you first came back to town. But you're on this show for at least three more seasons, and I know your life will be this show while you're filming. I'll be honest, I'm not interested in being in the spotlight. I'm hoping to fade in the shadows, but I know if I want to be part of your life—all of it—I have to suck it up and deal with it. I can't compartmentalize us."

A lump filled my throat, but I whispered past it. "I think that's the sweetest thing anyone has ever done for me."

Relief filled his eyes, and he grinned. "Better than when I took you to the county fair and spent forty dollars on that milk-bottle game to win you a giant teddy bear?"

I grinned too, feeling better about the two of us than I had since we'd agreed to try again. "Okay, it's a close second."

"That game was rigged, you know."

I laughed and wrapped my arms around his neck, suddenly regretting my insistence on taking things slow. "Of course it was." But I didn't sound convincing.

He slid his arm around my back and pulled me closer. I felt his deep inhale as our bodies connected. "Are you really okay with me being here?"

"Momma's already stirred up crap, Teddy's raring to take your head off, and Meemaw has some cryptic reason for wanting all of us gathered here. Why not add you to the mix?"

His eyebrows shot up. "That doesn't make it sound like you're happy to see me."

"Sorry. I'm just worried is all, but I really am happy you care enough to do this despite your reservations. And I apologize in advance for anything my mother or Teddy says to you. That's what has me worried the most. I don't want them to run you off."

His shoulders tightened. "I can take it, Summer. I know I hurt you back then. I know neither of them have forgiven me for it. I'm willing to do my penance to make amends."

If only that was why my mother hated him. If anything, she'd seen my broken heart as a cause for celebration, hoping I'd abandon the idea of quitting acting and running back to Sweet Briar. She hated him because he was the first person who'd made me question her intentions. My relationship with Luke had been the beginning of the end of her hold on my life.

"Besides," he said, "after I watched your show, I realized it wasn't that bad."

I slid my hands down his chest with the intention of pushing him away, but my palm touched a small lump under his collar. My eyes flew open wider when I realized what it was. "Are you miked?"

He looked confused by my reaction. "It was the only way they'd let me in. I told you, Summer. I want this to work."

"Oh, my God. They heard everything we just said." I turned him sideways and found the box hooked to his jeans.

"But we're not on camera."

After I turned it off, I took two steps back, running over our conversation and trying to determine how bad this was. "Luke, they can just use the sound and fill the screen with the swinging door." I did a quick glance up at the ceiling to see if I could find a camera. I wouldn't be surprised if she'd installed one here.

"I didn't say anything I'm ashamed of. This is us—the real us—so what's the big deal?"

"I don't show the cameras *everything*."

He grinned. "I sure hope not. I don't care to see my bare ass on my TV screen while I'm watching your show. My own personal video, maybe, but not your show."

I put one hand on my hip and pointed the other at his face. "First of all, who says your bare ass is gonna be anywhere near a camera, let alone me? You must have a whole lot of ego to think that's gonna happen."

His grin spread. "Oh, it's gonna happen, Summer, it's just a matter of when and where."

A needy ache filled my core, and I sucked in a breath to help the rest of me cool down. I could try to deny it, but we both knew he was right.

"And what was the second?" he asked, loving every bit of this.

That brought the irritation right back. "I will never make a sex tape with you, so if that's on your future agenda, you might as well move along." I wagged my finger at him, then pointed at the back door.

He didn't seem the least bit phased by my statement. "I've never made a sex tape before. I understand the risk it would pose to you if it got in the wrong hands, so I'm good with that stipulation. Was there a third objection?"

It wasn't lost on me that Luke was making a supreme effort to communicate. That had been a huge problem before—for both of us—so this was nearly as much of a grand gesture as showing up here tonight. "I can't believe you watched my show."

He closed the distance between us, leaving a few inches between us. "I recorded and watched every episode of *Darling Investigations*."

I smirked up at him. "You wanted to see how Lauren portrayed the Sweet Briar police."

"I'll give you that, but I also wanted to see you. Especially since you were gone. And in the interest of full disclosure, I own all five seasons of *Gotcha!* on DVD."

That one caught me by surprise. "You didn't burn them after you broke up with me?"

He sobered. "No."

"Summer!" my mother shouted from the other room. "How long does it take to get a plate?"

I grinned up at Luke, and the next thing I knew, he leaned over and gave me a sweet and tender kiss.

When he lifted his face, he smiled at me. "Time to face the firing squad."

He looked far too happy to be walking into a room full of conflict.

He spun around and opened the cabinet to grab a plate while I took advantage of his position to turn his mike back on. While I reached around to do the same with mine, he got a set of silverware and then pushed open the door to the dining room.

Three faces turned to face us—Dixie's beaming smile, my mother's irritated frown, and Teddy's murderous glare—and nearly a dozen more if you added the crew, including Bill, Tony, and Chuck, who had arrived while I was in the kitchen. (Meemaw considered her hot, buttered roll more attention grabbing than the commotion.) I ignored them as I wrapped my hand around Luke's wrist and pulled him around to my side of the table. Part of my motivation was that I wanted to sit next to him, but I also hoped that some separation between him and Teddy, who was sitting on my other side, would eliminate the glaring contests.

"What were y'all doin' in there, Summer?" Momma asked in a snide tone. "Havin' sex like you did that one time we went to the—"

71

"It's lovely to see you again, Miss Beatrice," Luke said without a hint of malice as he sat down. "I hear your pageant business is doin' well."

My mother looked caught off guard. "Why, yes, it is." Then she realized Luke had given her the perfect opportunity to promote her business and spent the next couple of minutes monologuing about her pageant the previous weekend and how her girls were sweeping the awards. "Everyone says my girls are the best, and it's all because of me," she said with a smug smile. "Summer's the perfect example. When she fired me, her career was flushed down the toilet, which only proved it was my management that created her success, not her talent."

I stared at her in disbelief. I'd written her off almost a decade ago, so why did her barbs still hurt?

Dixie, my tiny mountain lion of a cousin, wasn't about to let that one go. She dropped her fork on her plate with a loud clank and turned halfway in her seat. "Are you *kiddin'* me?"

My mother turned slightly to face her, and one of the new camerawomen moved in next to Luke to capture the upcoming fight.

Dixie's cheeks turned pink. "Everyone knows that you sabotaged her because she told you she wasn't doin' it your way anymore. And you'd burned so many bridges that no one wanted to work with her again."

Oh, my Lord. Were we really doing this now?

My mother put her fingertips to her chest as though she'd never been so offended in her life. "I love Summer. Why would I sabotage her career? Is she spreading vicious lies about me?"

"Lies?" Dixie demanded. "You told Summer you were comin' back home to take care of your family, yet you've never spent any time with us. It was obvious the moment you got back to town that the only thing that interested you was building your own version of Tara with all the money you stole from Summer."

"And how would you know?" Momma asked in a snooty tone. "You were too busy in juvie jail to notice, Dixie Belle."

I had to stop this disaster.

"Say, Teddy," I said in a loud voice, "how are the crops doing? We've had a dry spell. Have you had to irrigate?"

He shot me a look that suggested I'd lost my mind, then launched into my mother. "Dixie's right. You don't give a shit about this family. You never did. Dixie may not remember much about you and Summer before you dragged her off to Hollywood, but I remember plenty. Summer was nothin' but a Barbie doll for you to play with and put in those idiotic pageants she hated, not that you gave a shit. She was your ticket to Hollywood and all the money and attention you craved. Unless you needed her to advance your master plan, she lived with us. I can't imagine how awful it was for her to go from everything and everyone she loved to that godforsaken hellhole."

"She had me!" my mother shouted.

"Like I said"—Teddy's voice hardened—"she was all alone."

My mother's mouth hung open, and for once she looked at a loss for words.

Luke sat quietly next to me, his plate still empty.

"Where are our manners?" I gushed loudly, trying to interrupt this debacle. "Luke doesn't have any food yet." I grabbed the meat-loaf platter and handed it to him.

The hard set of his jaw suggested he was about to jump in to defend my honor. I gave him a slight head shake. I didn't need him fighting my battles. Especially this one.

But my mother's eyes lit up as she watched us, and I realized I'd given her a way to divert the negative attention from her.

"What are you even doin' here, Luke Montgomery?" she asked with forced attitude. "This is a family dinner."

"Yeah," Teddy said as he leaned over the table and around me to get a good look at him. "What *are* you doin' here?"

Luke picked up a slice of meat loaf and dropped it on his plate. "I was invited." He set the platter on the table and glanced over at Dixie. "Would you hand me the potatoes?" Then he shifted his gaze to Meemaw. "No one makes meat loaf and mashed potatoes like Miss Viola."

Meemaw smiled. "And no one can put 'em away like you do."

"What the hell?" Teddy said. "I can put 'em away too!"

"This isn't a competition," I said with a tight smile. I had to find a way to salvage this, all the way around. "Meemaw, did you hear about the house fire today? The house belonged to Teddy's friend Bruce. He's pretty much homeless right now."

"Bruce Jepper? The boy you went to school with?" she asked.

"Yes, ma'am. That's him," Teddy said, clearly unhappy at the change in conversation. "It was arson." He glanced over at Luke. "Why are you here eating our food when you should be out lookin' for the guy who did it?"

"It's my day off," Luke said, reaching for the rolls next to me.

"Well, it's not the first fire," Teddy said. "There was one on Saturday at the Civil War marker on Highway 10. The sheriff's deputy said that was arson too."

"Oh, my goodness," my mother said in a breathless voice. "How far was that from Tantara?"

"I doubt the two are related," Dixie said with a tight voice. "The roadside fire was probably a cigarette." Her eyes went round, like she hadn't meant to blurt it out.

Teddy's eyes narrowed. "How did you know that?"

She lifted a shoulder into a half shrug. "Lucky guess."

"Dixie's right," Luke said gruffly. Now he was the one who was leaning around me to look at Teddy. "It was a cigarette, although you knew that too, didn't you, Teddy? Are you still working for the sheriff?"

"Whether I am or not isn't any of your damn business."

"True, but that last case you helped them with nearly got Dixie and Summer killed," Luke said, the first hint of anger creeping into his voice.

Teddy scooted his chair back and got to his feet. "That had nothin' to do with me! I told Summer to drop Otto's case, but I also told her to stay the hell away from you, and look what good *that* did."

Luke turned his chair slightly, but thankfully he remained seated. "Summer is a grown woman with a mind of her own. Perhaps you should respect that, Teddy."

"Respect?" Teddy shouted. "You mean the way you respected her a decade ago and broke her heart over that bastard Connor Blake?"

I heard some whispers and shuffling behind the crew. I turned my attention toward them, gasping when I saw the cause.

"Did someone say my name?" Connor asked, pushing his way past the cameraperson and standing to the side of the dining room entrance so the camerawoman next to Luke could capture Connor without the crew in the shot behind him.

Lauren was grinning from ear to ear.

I was steaming. That woman would do *anything* to piss me off. And if it brought good ratings, even better.

Luke was instantly on his feet, his chair scooting out behind him. "What the hell are *you* doin' here?"

"This isn't your house!" Teddy said to Luke. "You have no right to ask him that." Then he turned his attention to Connor. "What the hell are *you* doin' here?"

Connor gave him a patient smile. "It's my first night alone in town, and I knew how gracious Summer always was when we were on *Gotcha!* together, so I decided to drop by and catch up on old times. It looks like I'm in time for dinner."

Meemaw looked up to the ceiling as though asking the good Lord to grant her strength. Then she motioned to the kitchen. "Grab a plate."

"You can't be serious about letting him stay!" Teddy said to our grandmother.

"You know it's impolite to send a guest away."

"It's also impolite to coerce your innocent costar to pose for nude photos with you so can advance your own career and destroy hers," Luke said.

"Stay out of this, Luke!" Teddy said, then his eyes widened, and he turned his attention to me. "Is that true?"

"It didn't happen exactly like that . . ."

My mother reached for the pitcher of lemonade. "I always liked that boy."

We all stared at her like she had just announced she was having George Clooney's baby.

Meemaw waved her fork in the air. "Everybody sit your keisters down."

Luke took his seat, looking none too happy about it, but Teddy remained standing while he glared at the kitchen door.

"Why don't we talk more about the two fires," I said, trying not to panic. It wasn't lost on me that Lauren hadn't stopped us yet to replay anything, probably because she knew she had one shot and she was going for it.

Connor returned from the kitchen carrying a plate and silverware. He took a seat next to my mother, who gave him a gracious smile.

Luke was now sitting directly across from him, which was even worse than if I'd placed him across from Teddy. And Teddy, realizing this was really happening, sat down and scooted back to the table, now giving Connor his full attention.

"It's so good to see you, Connor," Momma said. "How's your mother?"

"She's well, Ms. Butler. How are you? I hear you're filling the world with charming little princesses." He graced her with his posed smile, the one he always used for photo shoots.

My mother preened. "I'm doin' my part to make the world a better place."

Dixie made a gagging sound.

Momma ignored her and continued her conversation with Connor. "I'm surprised to see you here." She grimaced. "What with how everything ended."

"Life's too short to hold grudges, don't you think? Besides, I'm doing my part to make the world a better place too. I'm spreading the news about the Connor Life, and the Connor Life only embraces positivity."

"The Connor Life?" Teddy asked drily.

Connor's grin spread. He'd been looking for an in. "It's my new philosophy on life. Clean living, which means no animal by-products cross our lips. No chemicals of any kind. We fill our lives with the joy of giving—just like I'm doing now by giving you the gift of my presence."

Teddy stared at him like he'd lost his mind. "Uh-huh."

"Gift, my eye," Dixie mumbled.

"So no grudges, huh?" Luke asked with a wicked gleam in his eyes.

Oh, crap.

I patted his leg under the table. "Luke, tell us more about your new police officer."

"I want to hear more about this grudge thing." He shot a quick glance at Teddy before shifting his gaze back to Connor. "How's *that* work?"

Connor was practically jumping up and down in his seat. "It's important to know that resentment creates bad carma." He gave a pleased-as-punch grin to my mother. "I trademarked that."

"Karma?" Dixie asked. "I believe the Buddhists came up with it long before you were born." An ornery grin lit up her face. "But then again, judging by the wrinkles around your eyes, maybe not so long."

Connor gasped and touched his face. "It's carma with a *c*, not a *k*. It's different."

"Oh, brother," Dixie groaned.

"You really should embrace it, Dixie. Especially since you were responsible for killing your family with that fire," Connor said as he looked over the spread of food on the table. "I only eat vegan."

Teddy rested his forearms on the table and stared Connor down. "What did you just say?"

"Vegan. It's when people don't eat anything that came from an animal."

"Not that, even though that's crazy nonsense. I'm talkin' about the fire."

Connor blinked, obviously having the good sense to fear my cousin. "You know, the fire that killed your family. People were talkin' about it today at the scene."

"What exactly were they sayin'?" Luke asked in a hard tone.

Connor shifted his attention to my right, suddenly looking worried. "Just whisperings . . . speculations . . ."

"Which are?"

Something shifted in Connor's eyes from fear to gloating. I suspected he thought he'd just one-upped the police chief. "You know . . . she started the fire before, did she start this one now." He lifted the bowl in front of him off the table. "What's in the potatoes?"

"Milk and butter," I said in a flat voice. People were gossiping over Dixie and linking her to the fires?

"Huh." He grabbed the tip of the basket holding the rolls. "And these?"

"Butter and eggs."

"Why in the hell would you hold a grudge against Summer?" Luke asked.

I shot him a questioning look. We'd long moved past that topic, but one look at Dixie's flushed face was my answer. He was trying to take the heat off her.

"Is there anything without animal products?" Connor sounded exasperated.

"No," Teddy said.

Connor glanced around at us as though we were ogres. "Then what am I supposed to eat?"

"Nothing," I said. "Because you weren't invited."

"Summer Lynn," Meemaw said, "we don't talk to guests like that."

"But, Meemaw . . ."

"Enough," she said, pushing her chair back from the table. "The boy doesn't eat anything that came from an animal, so I'll get him something he can eat."

"Meemaw!" Teddy protested, but our grandmother disappeared into the kitchen.

"Thank you, Mrs. Butler," Connor called after her, wearing a grin that suggested he knew he'd put her to a lot of trouble and was loving every minute of it. "You know," Connor said, "it's funny how the people here love to talk about the past, but no one in the know wanted to talk to me about the fire today. I thought people in small towns loved to gossip."

"That's a stereotype," I said.

"Even if it's true," Dixie muttered under her breath.

"I still learned a few things," Connor said in a smug tone.

"So what have you learned?" Luke asked, then added sarcastically, "Maybe you can help out my investigation."

"Well . . . ," Connor said, leaning his elbow on the table, clearly missing the insult, "I've learned the fire was arson, and it started in the kitchen. I also overheard the homeowner talking to his insurance agent. She's expediting his case."

Luke gave him a hard stare. "Anything else?"

Connor shrugged. "I'm still working on it."

"You should go back to *Dancing with the Stars*," Dixie said. "You had better luck there, and you got voted out the first round."

Connor's jaw clenched. "I can't help it if I have a bad ankle, just like I can't help it if Summer sabotaged me, just like she did back on *Gotcha!*"

"What on earth are you talkin' about?" I asked.

"I know you told the homeowner not to talk to me."

I remained silent. I wasn't going to lie, but I wasn't going to confirm it either.

Dixie looked down and pulled her phone out of her lap. "I have to go soon."

"Where?" Teddy asked, his voice full of suspicion.

"I'm a grown woman, Theodore Stanley. I don't need you to babysit me."

"I do if this concerns Trent Dunbar."

Dixie gave me an incredulous look. "Did you tell him?"

"No! I swear!"

Teddy's eyes hardened. "So it *is* about Trent Dunbar."

"Who's Trent Dunbar?" Connor asked.

"Shut up, Connor," Teddy said. "This is none of your damn business." Then he turned his attention to Dixie. "What the hell, Dixie? That boy is responsible for our parents' deaths!"

"No, he's not," Dixie said with tears in her eyes. "*I* killed them. I was the one to start the fire."

"Well, it's about time she fessed up," my mother said.

"Stay out of this, Momma," I said with a shaky breath. I hated when Dixie and Teddy fought, and this was a doozy, not to mention Dixie's heart was clearly breaking. I grabbed Teddy's arm. "Maybe we should talk about this later . . . when we don't have *company*."

Teddy swallowed and sat back in his seat. Dixie looked down at her plate as a tear slid down her cheek. I squeezed my hands together in my lap and nearly jumped when I felt a large hand cover mine.

Luke.

I turned to look at him and soaked in his reassuring gaze.

He cleared his throat. "Dixie, you and I have discussed the circumstances of that fire until we're both blue in the face, and we both know that what happened was a terrible, unfortunate accident. You've paid your dues, Dix. Don't torture yourself any more than you already have."

She glanced down at her phone again, then pushed her chair back. "I have to go. I'm sorry, Teddy. I'm especially sorry you don't trust me enough to let me make my own decisions."

His mouth fell open. "That's not it, Dixie."

"Really?" she asked, swiping a tear from her cheek. "Because that's exactly how it looks from where I'm standing." With that, she turned and ran through the kitchen door.

Silence descended on the table—broken, of course, by Connor. "Where's your grandmother? I'm starving."

"Shut up, Connor," I said in unison with Teddy and Luke.

As if on cue, my grandmother came through the kitchen door with a big bowl in her hand. "You want vegan?" she asked. "Here's your vegan." She scooped a handful of daisy heads from the bowl onto his plate. "Here's your daisy appetizer. And then a dandelion-weed entrée." She dropped a handful of leaves and dandelion flowers next. "And for dessert, you have blackberry cobbler." She shoved the bowl on top of his head and smashed it for good measure, blackberries dripping down his face and into his lap.

"What the . . . ?" Connor shouted. "What'd you do that for?"

"That's for ruining my granddaughter's life, you good-for-nothing, backstabbing, yellow-belly, conniving Yankee!"

Luke leaned closer, whispering under his breath, "She pulled out *Yankee*. She's not playin'."

He was right. And while I was loving every minute of my grand-mother's performance, all I could think about was Dixie.

And how I was going to have to apologize to vegans the world over.

CHAPTER EIGHT

Connor didn't waste any time leaving, shouting that he was going to sue my grandmother for ruining his shirt. My mother ran away right after him, saying she was leaving before she was accosted too.

Without saying a word, Teddy grabbed his plate and headed into the kitchen. A half minute later, I heard his truck start up behind the house. From the sound, he was headed toward the county road.

Luke and I sat at the table, and I watched Meemaw for a clue as to how she wanted to handle this. She pushed out a sigh and sat back in her chair. "There's still some blackberry cobbler left. I didn't dump it *all* on his head."

I grinned. "It would have been worth the sacrifice."

"Speak for yourself," Luke said. "Miss Viola makes the best blackberry cobbler in the state. It would be a shame to waste it on that Yankee." Then he winked, and I knew he'd called Connor a Yankee to commiserate with Meemaw.

She offered him a smile, but her eyes looked sad. "Then you be sure to take home the rest of it with you." Lifting her plate, she stood and headed into the kitchen.

I rose from my chair and turned to the crew, who were still filming. "And that's a wrap. See you tomorrow."

"You're not the producer," Lauren said from behind one of the camerapeople. "You can't call it a wrap."

"No, but you're in my grandmother's house. You got your pound of flesh, which should fill up an entire episode, so pack up your cameras and go. *Now.*"

Bill and Tony weren't in the group, and a quick glance out the front window confirmed that they were stuck outside interviewing Connor and Momma about their evening. The rest of the crew cast nervous glances between Lauren and me.

Luke got to his feet and turned to me. "Summer, does your contract say the cameras have unlimited access to your private life?"

"No. It says I have the final say as long as I provide them with enough suitable footage."

He turned to face Lauren. "I'd say you've gotten more than enough 'suitable' footage. Now pack up your cameras and get out of Viola Baumgartner's house before I arrest you for trespassing."

The crew lowered their cameras and started to pack up, but Lauren gave me a death glare that rivaled my grandmother's. "You've got a bright-and-early call time, Summer. Don't be late." Then she turned around and left, leaving the crew to deal with Luke.

I grabbed my plate and Teddy's and headed into the kitchen. I found Meemaw at the sink, rinsing off her plate. "Meemaw, Luke and I have got this. You go rest."

"I can clean off the plates, Summer Lynn."

"Of course you can, but I feel bad that Lauren made you host this dinner."

"I already told you that I was the one who called the dinner. I had something to tell all y'all."

Something that included my mother. That was frightening. "What is it?"

She shook her head. "Nope. This is an all-or-nothing deal."

Which meant we would have to do this all over again, but hopefully minus Connor.

Meemaw dropped the dishrag in the sink. "I'm gonna take a walk. Clear my head."

"I'm sorry, Meemaw."

She turned to look at me. "I know I gave you a hard time, and if I had to do it over again, I'd do it different. I'd do a lot of things different."

I nodded, and my voice cracked. "Me too."

She reached out and patted my cheek, then headed out the back door. As I set the plates on the counter, I noticed Dixie's and Teddy's mikes on the small breakfast table. I also noticed Dixie's car next to my car from LA. If Dixie's car was still here, where was *she*?

I went back into the dining room to clear off the rest of the table, surprised to see Luke supervising the crew's exit while holding his plate with one hand and his fork in another.

He cast me a sideways glance before turning his attention back to the crew.

Five minutes later he walked into the kitchen, where I'd brought the haul of dirty dishes, with his empty plate. "Your grandmother still doesn't have a dishwasher?" he asked, grabbing a dish towel.

I chuckled. "After nearly fifty years of livin' in this house, why would she get one now?" My smile fell. "I could have handled that, Luke."

"I know. You handled all the chaos just fine."

"I'm not talking about the mess we call a family dinner. I'm talking about you threatening to arrest the crew if they didn't leave."

He did a double take. "Lauren was making a stand, and I had the means to put her in her place."

"And now it looks like I couldn't handle it on my own."

"You've handled her just fine on your own until tonight, so why not let me help?"

I turned to face him, putting a hand on my hip. "Because I'm not looking for a man to save me, Luke. I'm looking for a man who will support me."

He grabbed a plate from the rack and started to dry it. "So you wanted me to stand back and let that woman walk all over you?"

"I could have handled her."

"But why not let me help?"

"Because I didn't need to be saved."

He stared at me like I was a Martian with three heads. Then he grinned and leaned forward, giving me a kiss. "Was that our first fight? Because I think that means we get to make up."

I shook my head, but the corners of my lips lifted up despite my orneriness. "There won't be any makeup sex tonight."

"Get your mind out of the gutter, Summer Baumgartner. Who said I was interested in sex?"

I lifted my eyebrows. "So you're not?"

He wrapped his arm around my back and slowly pulled me to his chest. "I most definitely am, but I'm following your lead on this. You want to take it slow, so we're taking it slow."

"Thanks for understanding."

"I've waited ten years to get you back. This is enough for now."

◆ ◆ ◆

Luke stayed for a couple more hours, and we walked the farm. I showed him where Teddy was planning to put the chicken coops and explained Meemaw's resistance to it. Before he left, he walked me to the front door, pulled me into his arms, and gave me a long, lingering kiss.

"Next time we'll have a real date," he said, then got in his truck and left.

I got ready for bed, worried that there was still no sign of Dixie and Teddy. Teddy could handle himself, but I didn't trust Trent Dunbar farther than I could throw him.

Around ten thirty, I sent Dixie a text.

I'm sorry about dinner. I love you.

Five minutes later, she texted back.

Love you too.

At least she was still talking to me. I drifted off to a troubled sleep, waking to the sound of a text on my phone.

I checked the screen and saw Dixie's name. The time was 2:14.

Summer, I need you to get me. Now. I'm at the recreation area at Lake Edna. By the pier.

My breath caught in my chest for two reasons. One, it sounded like she was in trouble, and two, that was where I'd found Otto Olson's body. A cold sweat broke out on the back of my neck as I called her. She didn't answer.

Why didn't she answer?

I snagged my truck keys off the dresser. Still wearing my pajama pants and a tank top with no bra, I slipped my feet into a pair of flip-flops and bolted out of my bedroom, through the kitchen and then the back door.

I was practically hyperventilating by the time I reached the recreation area twenty minutes later. The thought of facing the place where I'd been attacked—and in the dark, to boot—freaked me out.

But the fact that Dixie hadn't answered any of my multiple phone calls terrified me even more. I parked the truck in a lot facing the pier and started to panic when I didn't see her.

I hopped out and headed toward the beach. "Dixie!" She didn't answer, and it felt like someone had slapped my panic button. *"Dixie!"*

I found her on the beach, lying on her side on the sand. I started to cry before I even reached her. *"Dixie."* I dropped to my knees next to her and brushed her long, blonde hair out of her face. She reeked of smoke, which scared me nearly as much as her unresponsiveness. "Dixie. Answer me."

"Mmm . . . ?" she said. Her voice was slurred, and her eyes were half-closed.

"Oh, thank God. What happened?"

She tried to get up but fell back onto the sand. I wrapped an arm around her back and helped her sit, her legs extended straight out in front of her. She started to weave in place and almost tumbled onto her back.

I brushed her hair back, searching her face in the moonlight for any sign of injuries. "Dixie, honey, you're scaring me. What happened?"

She leaned her head on my shoulder. "Party . . ."

"You went to a party?"

"Hmm . . ."

Maybe there was a bonfire. That would explain why she smelled like smoke. "Can you get up?"

"Uh-huh . . ." She tried and fell back down.

How was I going to get her to the truck? "Dixie, I'm goin' to call Teddy."

Her eyes flew open. "No Teddy!"

She was right. Teddy would lose it. We didn't need that right now. "What about Luke?"

"No . . ." She turned over on her hands and knees. Pushing up on her hands, she stood upright on her knees and then tried to stand. I wrapped her arm around my neck and helped her to her feet.

"Dixie, how did you get here?"

"I don't know." Her eyes were only half-open.

"How much did you have to drink?"

"I don't drink. I promised Luke."

Now that I thought of it, I'd never seen her drink. Now I understood why. "What about drugs? No judgment, Dix. I just need to know."

"No. I didn't take anything. Not anymore. Not since . . ."

Not since the fire.

With her arm around my neck and my arm around her back, we set a slow pace toward the parking lot. I was amazed we made it to the truck, but she almost fell when I released her to open the passenger door.

I was scared. If Dixie wasn't drunk or high, then what was going on? I wondered what she'd been doing for the last six hours. She'd met up with Trent, that much I knew, but who else? Why did she smell like smoke?

What if something terrible had happened to her? It would need to be reported. I wanted to call Luke, but I wasn't sure that was the right decision. Then again, what if she'd done something that could get her in trouble? I couldn't forget that Luke had been the one to arrest her after the barn fire. The fact that he was her friend wouldn't protect her.

I got her buckled in, but by the time I got to the driver's side, Dixie was leaning her head against the window.

"Dixie. I need to know what happened."

"Mmm . . ."

"Dixie."

She tried to sit upright and rested the back of her head on the head rest, her eyes closed.

"Did you hit your head somehow?"

"No . . ." Her answer was so quiet I could barely hear her.

I couldn't do this alone. I needed help, and in the end, there was only one person I trusted to make sure Dixie was safe, no matter what.

I pulled out my phone and called Teddy. He answered right away.

"Summer? Is everything okay?"

"No," I said, my voice breaking. "Where are you?"

"About to leave the Jackhammer. Why? What's going on?"

I'd passed the bar on the way to the lake, but I'd been too preoccupied to notice his truck in the parking lot. "It's Dixie."

"Dixie?" he sounded panicked.

She moaned, her head rolling on the seat. "Don't call Luke."

She wouldn't have to worry about that. I lowered my voice. "She's with me, and she's uninjured as far as I can tell, but she's not right. I'm headed home now. I'll stop at the Jackhammer."

"I'll be waitin'."

Dixie slept during the ten-minute drive. The bar's neon's lights were turned off, and the parking lot was nearly empty, but Teddy was pacing next to his truck.

I pulled in next to him, and he had Dixie's door open before I came to a full stop.

"What happened?" he asked, fear filling his eyes when he saw her.

"I don't know," I said, my voice cracking. "She texted and asked me to come get her at the lake. So I jumped in the truck, and when I got there, I found her lying on the beach." Tears filled my eyes. "I was scared she was . . ." Dead. But I couldn't bring myself to say it.

"She smells like smoke."

"I know. I don't know why. She mentioned a party . . . and she's clearly on something, but she said she didn't have anything to drink and that she didn't take any drugs."

He squatted next to her and patted her cheek. "Dixie. Wake up."

"Teddy?" she murmured, sounding surprised. Her eyes opened a crack.

"It's me, little sister. Tell me what happened," he said in a soft, soothing voice. "Did you see Trent?"

"He took me to his party, but I wanted to leave."

Teddy's jaw set, but he brushed her hair back from her cheek. "Was there a bonfire, Dix?"

"No."

Teddy looked up at me, and the fear in his eyes was nearly my undoing.

"We've got to get her home, Summer. She needs a shower, and we have to wash her clothes. Tonight."

I nodded, unable to speak.

"Are you okay to drive?" he asked when he saw my hand shaking.

"Yeah."

"Drive the speed limit home. I'll follow behind you." He paused. "Summer—we can't tell Luke. I mean it."

"But we don't even know what happened."

"Exactly. We don't know what happened, and until we do, this stays between us."

I took a deep breath and nodded. "Agreed."

I was a nervous wreck driving back to the farm, terrified I'd get pulled over, terrified Dixie had been involved in something awful.

As soon as we pulled in behind the house, Teddy parked beside me. He had Dixie's door open before I was out of the truck. Scooping her into his arms, he said, "Summer, hold the door open for me, then go upstairs and start the shower."

"What about Meemaw?"

"We just need to be quiet."

Several minutes later, we were settled in the upstairs bathroom. The water in the shower was warm, and Teddy had set Dixie down on the toilet lid. She seemed to be coming around.

"What are you doin'?" she asked. She was still bobbing around, but at least her eyes were halfway open.

"You need to take a shower, Dix, okay?" he said. "Can you stand?"

"I don't know."

Teddy glanced at me.

"I can help her," I said.

The gratitude in his eyes caught me by surprise. "I'll stand outside the door and wait for her clothes."

He stepped out of the small bathroom and shut the door.

Dixie was rousing enough that she helped me strip her down to her bra and panties. After I handed her shirt and shorts out to Teddy, I helped her into the shower and got in with her. She leaned against the shower wall while I washed and conditioned her hair, then I scrubbed the rest of her with a scrubby and some of my good-smelling shower gel. My pajama pants and tank top were soaked and clinging to my skin, but that was the least of my worries.

When I finished, she'd come around enough for me to turn my back while she stripped out of her underwear and wrapped a towel around herself. I did the same, leaving my sopping pajamas on the shower floor. We went into her room, and I helped her put on a nightgown, then grabbed a pair of her pajamas to put on since my clothes were downstairs. I turned around to ask her more questions, but she was already lying on her side in bed, her eyes closed.

I found Teddy in the hall, and now that Dixie was out of sight, he looked like a nervous wreck.

He gazed found mine. "Did she say anything else?"

I shook my head. "No."

"Do you have any idea what happened?"

My stomach twisted. "No.

He scrubbed his face with his hand. "I have to protect her, Summer. I can't lose her again."

I grabbed his forearm and squeezed. "*We* have to protect her, and we will. The both of us. I'm here to help this time."

I'd do whatever it took.

Chapter Nine

We had an 8:00 a.m. call time at the train station, but I was worried Dixie wouldn't be up to it.

I'd slept with her in her full-size bed, terrified to let her out of my sight, so when the alarm on my phone went off at six forty-five, she roused too.

I rolled over and studied her. She lay on her side, some of her long blonde hair covering her cheek. Partially asleep, she looked younger than twenty-five, and a surprising surge of protectiveness rushed through me. Dixie had lost her mother when she was fifteen. She'd spent the remainder of her teenage years locked up in juvie, motherless, and except for Teddy, alone. Though Meemaw had eventually come around, she still blamed Dixie for the fire.

Dixie was one of the sweetest people I knew, and she'd gone out of her way to welcome me back to the family. It only confirmed my vow to protect her at all costs.

She opened her eyes and looked confused when she saw me.

"How are you feelin'?"

"I have a splittin' headache, and my stomach feels like it's leading a rebellion . . ." She rubbed her forehead. "Hopefully a hot shower will take care of that." She paused and slid her hand to the hair at the nape of her neck. "Why is my hair damp?" As if coming more fully to her senses, she tried to sit up. "Why are you sleepin' with me?"

I sat up too. "Do you remember anything about last night?"

Her confused look quickly morphed into fear. "No."

"What's the last thing you remember?"

She closed her eyes as she tried to concentrate. "That gosh-awful dinner. Then Trent picked me up and took me to a party. I don't remember much after that." A troubled look crossed her face, telling me she had remembered *something*, but then her eyes opened wide, and I could tell she'd hit a brick wall—the place where her memories ended. "Why don't I remember what happened?"

I grabbed her hand and held on, searching her face. "I don't know, Dixie, but we'll figure it out."

"Why is my hair wet?"

How much should I tell her? Deep in my gut, I knew something bad had happened last night, and Teddy seemed to feel the same way. She had a right to know everything. "After we got you home, I helped you take a shower."

Terror filled her eyes. "I don't remember that."

"Do you remember texting me?"

"No."

"Last night you said you weren't drunk and hadn't done any drugs . . ."

She shook her head and winced. Nevertheless, she was adamant when she said, "No. I don't do either of those things. Not anymore."

"Do you think someone might have slipped something in your drink?"

Her eyes bugged out. "You mean roofied me?"

"Yeah. Why else wouldn't you remember anything? You were totally out of it when you called me and I picked you up. Teddy carried you upstairs. You don't remember any of that?"

"Teddy knows about this?"

"I had to tell him. I was scared, Dixie. I wasn't sure what to do."

"And you helped me take a shower? Why? Did I puke on myself?"

I was scared to tell her the truth, but she had a right to know. "No. You smelled like smoke."

Terror washed over her face, and she backed up to the headboard. "What?"

"Last night Teddy asked you if there was a bonfire at the party. You said no. Are you sure about that?"

Her hands began to shake. "I don't remember a bonfire. We were at Trent's ranch."

"The Dunbar ranch is on the north side of town. I picked you up from Lake Edna. You were alone. Do you remember how you got there?"

"*No.*"

My stomach churning, I said, "If you were drugged, we need to report it." Yes, Teddy and I had agreed to keep Luke out of it. But we'd also agreed to keep Dixie safe, and I was beginning to think that meant reporting it. The way she'd acted last night and her complete lack of memory pointed to the involvement of someone else, someone with questionable motives.

"You mean report Trent?" she asked suspiciously.

"I mean report whoever did this to you. What if you were raped?"

She paused for a moment, considering it, then shook her head. "I'm not sore, so I don't think I was."

"Dixie. That doesn't necessarily mean you weren't. We should be safe."

"Trent was the last person I remember being with, which means he'll be the one they blame. And with his record . . . No."

"But—"

"No." She slid out of bed and nearly fell. "Besides, everyone already thinks I'm a murdering druggie and a slut. No one would believe me." She headed for the bedroom door.

"Dixie."

She turned to face me with tears in her eyes. "This is my life, Summer. My choice. No."

Tears filled my eyes too. I hated that she felt this way, but I'd seen some evidence of it myself with the people in this town. Some of them *did* look down at her. And Connor said people were whispering her name next to Bruce Jepper's still-smoldering house. She didn't need any more gossip.

I scrambled to the end of the bed and grabbed her hand. "Okay. Fine. No police. No Luke. But I want you to pee in a cup."

"*What?*"

"I read somewhere you can test for date-rape drugs in urine. So pee in a cup and we'll send it off for testing ourselves."

"You're kiddin' me, right?"

"No. I'm serious as a heart attack. The only way I'll agree to keep quiet is if you pee for me."

She grinned. "You know that sounds perverted."

I wiped a tear from my cheek and grinned back. "Then, so be it."

"Well, I really have to pee, so get a cup quick."

I hopped out of bed and hurried down the stairs and into the kitchen. I expected to run into Meemaw, but she wasn't in there—although the coffeepot was full. I scoured the cabinets and selected a small mason jar and a lid, then headed back upstairs and found Dixie standing in the bathroom doorway.

"Here," I said, holding it out. "Use this."

She took it and then shut the door.

I leaned my back against the door frame. Now I needed to figure out where to send it. I'd read a post somewhere that you could send urine off to a private lab, but the results took one to three weeks. I needed to find a way to get them back sooner. At least I'd gotten her to agree.

Teddy's bedroom door opened, and he did a double take when he saw me.

"Dixie's in the bathroom," I whispered.

He wore a grave expression. "How is she?"

"She doesn't remember anything, even texting me. I've convinced her to pee in a mason jar to test for date-rape drugs."

His face paled. "You think she was raped?"

"Honestly, Teddy, I have no idea what happened to her, but she swears she didn't drink anything or take any drugs, so *something* happened. I'd feel better if we tested her pee to be safe. I just need to figure out a lab to send it to."

His shock had faded, and anger was taking its place. "I know somebody in the county crime lab. I'll see if she'll run it for me."

I lifted my eyebrows. "She?"

He groaned. "Don't you start matchmakin' too. I get enough of it from Dixie." He leaned closer. "Delores is fortysomething and happily married with three kids. And she was friends with Momma. She's one of the few people who continued to check on me after the ruckus died down."

Just one more reminder that I'd let my cousins down. While I was off sulking because my momma had finally revealed her true colors, Dixie was alone in juvenile detention suffocating from guilt, and Teddy was stuck here at the farm, dealing with the gossips, our surly grandmother, and the loss of his family in a matter of days.

I lifted my hands. "Sorry. It's just that most people don't know a crime lab tech well enough to get them to run a drug test off the record. Platonically, anyway."

He kept infuriatingly silent.

The bathroom door opened, and Dixie stood in the doorway, holding a mason jar half-full of pee. "Teddy . . ."

"How are you feelin', Dix?" he asked.

"I'm sorry I freaked you two out, but I'm fine."

"Don't worry about freakin' us out," he said. "We just want you to be safe. What do you remember?"

She pushed out a breath. "I already told Summer, and I don't have time to get into it again now. I need to get ready for work. We'll talk about it tonight."

Teddy looked like he wanted to say something, but instead he held out his hand. "Give me the pee, and you do what you need to do."

She handed it over, her cheeks slightly pink, then went into her room and shut the door.

"Keep an eye on her today, okay?" he asked.

"Of course."

◆ ◆ ◆

Dixie was quiet on the drive into town, staring out the window and lost in thought, but she jerked upright when her phone dinged. After a few taps on her screen, she went still.

My chest tightened. Had word gotten out about last night? "What's on Maybelline's Facebook page now?"

"It's not the Facebook page. I have a Google alert set up for your name."

I used to have one set up several years ago, but my signature *Gotcha!* pose had been turned into a meme, and I'd decided enough was enough. "I'm scared to ask what it is."

"Oh my . . ." She glanced up at me. "There's a video on TMZ."

My heart stopped. "Of what?"

"Yesterday morning. When Connor showed up in the office."

I resisted the urge to grab the phone from her, worried I'd run the car off the road. "Did someone passing by the office take a video?"

She looked up. "No. Someone in the office."

"Who?"

"Based on the angle of the video, one of the new people." She paused. "Do you want to see it?"

"No." I had no desire to watch my tirade. "What's the headline?"

"'A Not So Happy Reunion?'"

"I would complain about this to Lauren, but I suspect she instigated the whole thing, including the leak. People are going to want to see me and Connor butt heads. Which means I can't blow my top again."

She smirked. "Good luck with that."

"No kidding."

Dixie tapped on her phone. "I figure I better check the Facebook page."

I pulled into a parking space in front of the abandoned train depot with ten minutes to spare. Maybe I could even walk down to the coffee shop and get a latte.

"There's something on here."

"What now?" I said with a groan, but then I saw Dixie's hand begin to shake. "Dixie, what is it?"

Her face lifted. "There was a fire last night."

My heart skipped a beat. "Where?"

"April Jean's trailer." Her chin began to tremble. "Arson."

I tried to hold my anxiety at bay. "Poor April Jean."

"Yeah," Dixie said, but something seemed off.

"Dixie?"

She glanced up at me. "April Jean was at the party last night." She looked like she'd seen a ghost. "And you said I smelled like smoke."

There was no denying it was all suspicious and strange—Dixie had been upset to hear about April Jean and Trent yesterday, and now April Jean's trailer was gone—but I was convinced my cousin was innocent of any wrongdoing. She was the last person who'd start a fire after her parents' deaths. I had to put her at ease. "So? It's just a coincidence."

"Summer . . ." She reeked of fear. "What if I started that fire?"

"That's ridiculous. When I found you, you could barely get to your feet. How could you have started a fire? And April Jean's trailer is a good ten miles from the lake, where you were waiting for me. Without a car, I might add. How would you get to April Jean's and then out to the lake?"

"How did I get out to the lake, period?" she asked.

"I don't know, but I plan to find out." I was starting to think someone had intentionally set her up. I turned to face her. "You can't tell anyone about blacking out last night."

She hung her head. "Why would I tell anyone that?"

"Even Luke."

"Why?" Her breathing became shallow, and her gaze shot up to meet mine. "You think I did it."

I grabbed her hand and squeezed tight. "I think no such thing. I believe you are perfectly innocent, but I can't help but wonder if someone is setting you up. How many times have you blacked out since your parents died?"

"Never before last night."

"That's right. That seems like a huge coincidence, doesn't it?"

Some of her color started to return. "It also seems like a huge coincidence that I blacked out and set the fire in the barn . . . and then blacked out after having an argument with April Jean, and what do you know, her trailer caught on fire."

"You had *an argument* with her?"

She gave me a dry look. "Changing your mind about my innocence?"

"No. I'm thinking it encouraged the person to go through with this. That it maybe gave them an alibi."

"Summer, I appreciate what you're trying to do, but I need to talk to Luke."

"No, you don't. Promise me you won't call him."

Her mouth dropped open. "I don't believe you. You're datin' him! He's my friend."

"And he was your friend the first time, but that fact didn't stop him from arresting you."

"Either you trust him or you don't, Summer."

And there was the rub. I was less than twenty-four hours into my official second chance with Luke, and I was not only keeping secrets from him, but I was doing so because I didn't trust him to keep my cousin safe.

"Dixie. Let's just find out more information before you tell Luke anything about last night."

"But it's his job to investigate things like this."

"And it's our jobs too."

Her eyes widened. "You want this to be your big case."

"Maybe . . . ?" It was a risk, a huge one, but I'd never believed in anything more than I believed in Dixie's innocence. Was I willing to bet her life on it?

"What if you find out I'm guilty, Summer? What then?"

"But you're not guilty. That's why I want to do this."

"Because you don't trust Luke."

"I do trust him, but this is your life, Dixie. When it comes to you, I'm not willing to take chances. Not again."

"Why are you doin' this?" she asked. "Is it because you feel guilty for not bein' here before?"

"Honestly? I don't know. I just know I love you, and I want to keep you safe."

"Which makes you just like Teddy, treatin' me like a child." She opened the door and got out.

I hurried after her. "Dixie."

She ignored me, but I blocked the door. "I want to investigate this, but only with your blessing."

"Well, thanks for askin'," she said in a snotty tone.

I gasped. "You think I'm trying to control you?"

Tears filled her eyes, and she covered her face with her hands. "No. I'm sorry." She dropped her hands and gave me a pleading look. "I'm scared, Summer. I'm scared I did something bad."

"I know you are, so that's why I'm askin' you to wait to go to Luke until we have more information about what really happened. At least until the results of the test come back. *Please.*"

She glanced out into the street, and a single tear streaked down her cheek. "Okay."

I pulled her into a hug. "Trust me, Dix. I'll sort this out."

I only hoped I could keep my promise.

CHAPTER TEN

"You two have a spat, then kiss and make up?" Lauren asked as we walked through the door.

"What does it matter?" I asked. "You'll just spin it however you want."

She laughed. "That must mean you saw TMZ."

Dixie took several steps toward her. "There's a special place in hell for people like you."

Lauren smirked. "Since you're a murderer three times over, maybe I'll see you there."

Dixie froze, but I was pissed as all get-out. "You've crossed the line, Lauren."

"As far as I'm concerned, I've barely even touched it."

I couldn't let her get so much as a whiff of what had happened to Dixie last night. The best way to handle this was to change the topic.

I glanced around the much bigger space, surprised that Lauren hadn't decorated this place like she had the smaller office. While they'd cleaned it up, the walls sported peeling paint and a cracked-tile floor. There were three desks spread out on the left side. One of them was the desk they'd shoved into my office space, and I suspected the other two came from Walmart up in Eufaula, or more likely a yard sale. The right side had folding tables set up against the wall with several chairs and computers, presumably for the editors who would show up today to go through yesterday's footage. Stacked around the tables were the equipment cases for the cameras and sound gear.

Bill, Tony, and Chuck stood by the back wall, all three wearing scowls. Karen and the new people didn't look any happier. Maybe they'd already had a butt chewing or two from Lauren.

"Where's Connor?" I asked.

"He'll be along shortly. Why don't you girls get miked up then have a seat? Oh, and Summer? I'm glad to see you're wearing a dress again today." She winked. "It gives you a softer look."

I knew it wasn't a compliment.

She'd insisted that I wear dresses during the last season, so she probably thought I was following her orders. In reality, I'd worn a dress because I planned to have a chat with Trent and everyone else who'd attended the party, and I might have to use my womanly wiles to get the men to talk.

Chuck gritted his teeth as he hooked up our mikes. "The sooner we can get out of here, the better," he said under his breath as he attached the clip to my collar.

"I hear you."

"I have a question," Dixie called as she sat in a chair that was too low for her desk. "You don't expect me to work for Connor, do you? I'm Summer's assistant, not his."

"Well, funny you should mention that," Lauren said, then her face lit up. "Oh, hold that thought. Connor's here. Chuck, why don't you go outside and get him wired up out there, then we'll have him walk in on camera. Dixie, there's a sort of script on your desk. Look it over and try to stick to it as closely as possible without resorting to reading it."

A few minutes later, Chuck gave them a thumbs-up and walked back inside, while Connor remained on the sidewalk.

Bill held up a clapboard and called, "Action."

The two new camerawomen were both filming as Connor walked through the door with a shirt in his hand.

"Good morning, ladies. Which one of you wants to get these blackberry stains out of my shirt?"

Dixie let out a harsh laugh. "Not on your life."

"Summer?"

"I'll take care of your shirt, Connor," I said with a sweet smile.

His eyes widened, and he faltered, clearly caught off guard by my response. He quickly recovered, then sidled over with a huge grin. "Good to see you got your hair under control today." Then he tossed his shirt on my desk and headed for his own. "We've got a busy schedule, ladies. I hope you're ready to put in some serious hours. This isn't like last season. We're going to get into some nitty-gritty cases."

"Nitty-gritty?" I asked with a patronizing grin.

"You know Summer brought down a killer, right?" Dixie asked in an incredulous voice. "A drug-dealing, murdering, dirty cop. Single-handedly."

Connor sat down and shrugged with a bored expression. "Eh . . ."

I just smiled at him like he was an imbecile. It wasn't hard.

Dixie folded her hands on the desk and gave him a blank stare. "Connor, you have three appointments today, and Summer, you have an appointment with Sylvia Rush at ten. She thinks an alligator is eating her chickens."

My appointment couldn't be on Lauren's script because Dixie had set it up the day before. I needed to play along. I made sure my smile was as genuine as possible. "Thanks, Dixie. I can't wait."

Connor gave me a blank look. Obviously he'd expected a more antagonistic attitude from me, which was why I was bound and determined not to give him one. No Summer-Butler-flies-off-the-handle headlines for me, thank you very much. I didn't need to cut Connor down publicly in order to beat him.

Lauren called, "Cut," and Connor went back outside so we could film his entrance again—this scene nearly identical to the last one. I expected Lauren to run it a third time, but she was obviously bored. I wouldn't be surprised if this tame entrance scene ended up on the cutting-room floor.

"Can we go now?" I asked, drumming my fingers on my desk. "We have some actual work to do."

"So you're really taking the alligator case?" Lauren asked with a smirk.

"That's right," I said. "But from now on, I'll conduct my interviews in the *real* Darling Investigations office."

Lauren waved toward the door. "Have at it."

"We're done here?" I asked in surprise.

"That's what you want, isn't it?"

It was, but she'd agreed much too easily. She was clearly up to something.

I picked up the shirt Connor had tossed at me, and Lauren gave me a confused expression.

"I said I'd take care of it," I said, the shirt fisted in my left hand. "I'd hate to break my word." Then I headed for the door, taking deep, cleansing breaths and trying to figure out what horrors she was planning next.

I tossed the stupid shirt on the front seat of the truck, then rolled down the windows and waited inside while Bill, Tony, and Chuck packed up their equipment and loaded it into the back of my truck.

Dixie climbed in and curled her upper lip when she saw the stained shirt next to her. "Are you seriously going to clean Connor's shirt?"

"Not a chance in hell." I gave her an ornery grin. "I said I'd take care of it. I never said what I'd *do* with it."

Bill banged the back of the truck when the equipment was all loaded, and we drove the block and a half back to our real office. All the parking spots were full, so I stopped parallel to a car in front of our office, making sure there were no cars behind me.

Dixie looked pale and clutched her lower abdomen. "I need to use the restroom. Those eggs Meemaw made went straight through me. I may not be done in time to help."

"Okay," I said, worried as she hopped out and practically ran to the office. Dixie unlocked the front door while the guys unloaded the equipment from the back.

I heard a rap on the side of my truck the same moment I felt someone's hot breath on the side of my face. "I'm going to need your license and registration, ma'am."

I yelped and jumped in my seat, then turned to see a police officer glaring at me. He was young, with dark hair, and sunglasses covered his eyes. Smirking, he lifted his glasses to the top of his head. There were only three police officers in this whole town, so it wasn't hard to figure out this was Elijah Sterling, especially since he looked so much like his father. "Can I ask *why*?"

"You're double-parked, ma'am."

"Uh . . . no, I'm not. My engine is still running, and I'm behind the wheel. I'm only letting them off with the equipment so they don't have to lug it down the block."

"I'm still going to have to see your license and registration, ma'am."

"Would you please stop calling me ma'am?" I said, sounding defensive. "I'm about two minutes older than you."

A car pulled up behind me and honked.

Officer Sterling grinned, but it wasn't friendly. "I'm going to have to ask you to park around the corner. I saw several parking spaces over there only a few moments ago."

The car behind me honked again, and I lifted my hand in an apologetic wave before driving to the intersection and turning right. I pulled into a parking space and dug in the glove compartment for the paperwork, then retrieved my license from my wallet. Officer Sterling—who had been parked on Main Street in front of the office—pulled his police cruiser up next to my truck. When he approached my window, I handed him my paperwork.

Even if he seemed like an ass, I decided to make an effort to get along with him. If I wanted to make it as a real PI in this town, it would be smart to be in all the officers' good graces.

"So . . . ," I said, "I hear you joined the police force just last week, Officer Sterling."

He studied my license. "Yep." He glanced up. "Your license says you weigh one hundred and ten pounds. You look closer to one twenty-five. Do you typically lie on government paperwork?"

"What?" I asked in shock. I'd barely weighed one hundred and thirteen after eating Meemaw's and Maybelline's cooking, and I'd worked my ass off the last month to lose it all.

"I'm going to need you to step outside the vehicle."

"What on earth for?"

"I need to look through your truck."

"Why?"

"I know for a fact that you were in April Jean Thornberry's trailer yesterday. And the damn thing was set on fire in the middle of the night. I plan to see if I can find any evidence."

My mouth dropped open. "I'm a *suspect*? Have you lost your ever-lovin' mind?"

Officer Sterling shot me a glare that assured me he didn't appreciate my evaluation of his mental health. "If you don't have anything to hide, then why not let me look?"

"By that logic, I suppose you'll let me go through your things too?" I said, my voice shaking with anger.

"Of course not." Then he hooked his thumbs on his waistband and gave me a smart-ass grin. "Just doin' my job, *ma'am*."

"No," I said. "You're on a witch hunt."

He started to open the door with the outside handle, but I quickly locked it.

"You need to unlock the door, ma'am," he said through gritted teeth.

"For the last time, I'm not a ma'am!"

"Is there a problem here, Officer Sterling?" Luke said from across the street.

I pushed out a sigh of relief as he strode toward us.

"I need to search this perp's truck."

"Perp?" I said in disbelief.

Luke stopped next to the officer, wearing a nonchalant look, but I knew him well enough to realize that the squint of his left eye meant he was pissed. "Why?"

"She's refusing to cooperate with an officer."

"What did she do?"

"She was double-parked on Main Street, and when I saw her license, I realized she perjured herself."

Luke's eyebrows shot up. "And how did she do that?"

"She lied about her weight."

"And that's grounds to search her truck?" Luke asked in a dry tone.

Officer Sterling reached inside my window, blindly feeling for the "Unlock" button.

I tried to shove his hand away, but he grabbed my hand and jerked it behind my back, forcing my chest down toward the wheel. I released a cry of pain and shock, and the next instant I was free, and Luke had the asshole shoved up against my truck.

"You lookin' to bring a lawsuit on this town, Sterling?" Luke asked, his face shockingly calm as he pinned the officer over the hood. "Because if you think a woman fudging her weight on her driver's license is grounds to search her car, you better line up the entire female population in town. But the capstone on that lawsuit, which

Ms. Butler is sure to win, is your abuse of power, which, I might add, has been captured on film for the judge and jury to see."

Sure enough, Bill was in front of the truck with his camera, and Tony was at the back bumper. Added to the fact I was still wearing my mike—Chuck was sure to have captured the sound—we had plenty of evidence to file a lawsuit.

I unlocked the door and got out, shaking out my arm.

"Would you like to file a complaint, Ms. Butler?" Luke asked in a cool tone.

I tried to reason this through. Elijah Sterling had to know that I was dating Luke . . . and yet he'd approached me anyway. What was his end game? But then, I was sure he hadn't planned on Luke showing up so quickly. He'd asked me to pull over after the bogus double-parking claim—and then he'd immediately demanded to search the truck.

Oh, my God. He really *had* intended to plant evidence to incriminate Dixie or me.

I tried not to freak out, but Luke became more alert when he saw the change in my demeanor. "Summer?"

Calm down. "I want him to stay the hell away from me."

"Do you want to file a report?" Luke repeated.

"Can I think about it?" I needed to weigh the pros and cons.

"Yeah, but the sooner you do so, the better."

I nodded.

Luke released Officer Sterling, who shimmied and backed up as if Luke had the plague. Officer Sterling stepped back onto the sidewalk and glanced at Bill. Rage covered his face when he realized the camera was still pointed at him, and he lunged for it.

"Get that thing the hell out of my face!"

Luke jumped between the two men, shoving Elijah back. "He has every right to film this. It's his constitutional right, something you obviously need a refresher course on. Get your ass over to the station right now." Luke turned to me, his jaw clenched. "And I need you to come and file that complaint." It wasn't a request.

I glanced at the time on my phone. "Will this take long? I have an appointment with an alligator in forty-five minutes."

Luke's eyes widened slightly. "Do I want to know?"

"No."

He blinked. "Okay. Then I need you to come by *today*. Amber will have the form ready even if I'm not in."

"Okay." I suspected Luke needed my complaint to get Mayor Sterling's son off the force, and if that was true, then I'd be more than happy to oblige. The man was as crooked as a dog's hind leg. But now I was completely freaked out. If Elijah Sterling had been trying to plant false evidence, this whole mess definitely involved Trent.

Why did they have it out for Dixie and our family?

Elijah Sterling got in his police cruiser and headed toward the station while Luke watched him leave. As soon as he was sure Elijah was gone, his expression turned grave.

"Summer, I need to talk to you. Without cameras, please."

I nodded and made a shooing motion toward Bill. I turned my back to Luke and said, "Can you turn off my mike?"

He turned it off, then put his hands on my shoulders and turned me back to face him, his expression serious. He made sure Bill and Tony were both around the corner before he said, "What happened with Elijah?"

"It was pretty much like he said. I stopped the truck in front of the office to let the guys off with their equipment. There was a parked car next to me, but the truck's engine was on, and I was still in the driver's seat, ready to take off. I swear, I hadn't been there more than ten seconds. I wasn't even blocking traffic. At least not until Officer Eager Beaver demanded my license and registration."

"Then what happened?"

"I drove around the corner, parked just like he told me to, and handed him my paperwork. Then he accused me of lying about my weight on my license and demanded to search my truck, which I refused."

"Are you sure you didn't leave anything out? Lyin' about your weight isn't grounds to search a vehicle. Did you give him cause to suspect something else?"

I jerked out of his hold and took a step backward. "What on earth do you think I did?"

He pushed out a breath. "I don't know, Summer, I'm just trying to make sense of it is all." He gave me a dark look. "But the next time an officer of the law asks you to do something, you need to do it, no matter how outraged you might be."

"Are you serious? You think I should have just let him search my truck without cause?"

"If he's insistent, yes." When he saw the shock on my face, he said, "This could have gotten even more out of hand. You could have ended up shot." The fear in his eyes led me to believe he thought it an actual possibility. "Not to mention, you could have ended up with resisting-arrest charges. Just cooperate next time, and we'll sort out the facts later."

"Oh, my God!" I said in horror. "You're serious! You have a lunatic in your department, and your solution is to tell me to obey him if there's a next time." And, one way or the other, I suspected there would be. Elijah Sterling's brand of brazen wasn't quiet.

"You *know* I don't want him on my force!" he shouted. "You know I'm stuck with him, which is why I want you to file a report."

"I know," I said, losing some of my anger. "I'm sorry."

He hauled me to his chest and held me close. "When he manhandled you . . ." His arms tightened. "Please be more careful. I know you didn't do anything wrong, but defying him wouldn't have done you any good. If I hadn't shown up . . ." He shuddered.

"But thank God you did." I glanced up at him and grinned. "This is one time I'm grateful to have you save me."

He grinned too. "You're gonna be nothin' but trouble, aren't you?"

I gave him a saucy look. "I suspect I will, but you'll love every minute of it."

He gave me a lingering kiss, then lifted his head. "Dinner tonight? At my place. No guests. No cameras. Just you and me."

The smoldering look in his eyes set me on fire, but the mere thought of *fire* doused it. I was keeping a secret from him—a big whopper of one. "I might have to work late."

"You came up with a big case?" he asked in surprise. "Last night on our walk, you said you hadn't found one yet."

"Well, I had the eight a.m. call time at the train station this morning, and . . ." I let my voice trial off to insinuate that I'd found something. But I hated this. I didn't want to keep secrets from him. I wanted to share everything. Maybe I could test the waters without giving Dixie away. "Say, Luke, if you found out I had done something illegal in the course of an investigation, would you arrest me?"

His eyes shuttered his emotions. "Have you done anything illegal?"

I made a short scan of everything I'd done last season. "I don't think so." Although some were morally suspect.

"Are you *planning* on doing something illegal?"

"In the spirit of truthfulness, I don't know. This big case has potential, but it's going to be tricky getting the information I need."

He frowned. "Are you planning on doin' something dangerous?"

I batted my eyelashes. "Of course not."

His frown deepened. "That's a yes."

I realized I'd been too vague. I had to throw him a bone to test the waters. "Okay, let's say I broke in somewhere to get important information I needed. Would you arrest me?"

He squirmed. "Are you plannin' on breakin' in somewhere?" He shook his head. "Nope. Don't tell me. I don't want to know the answer to that."

"What if I got caught?"

"If the owner wanted to press charges, I would have no choice, Summer. You have to know that," he pleaded.

I gave him a soft smile. The takeaway was if I was doing something illegal, he didn't want to know, but if presented with the evidence, he would have to do his job. That was no less than what I'd expected, and it confirmed my decision to keep what I knew about Dixie from him. I reached up on my tiptoes and gave him a soft kiss, then smiled up at him. "You're a good and honorable man, Luke Montgomery, and I'm damn lucky to have you."

He gave me a wary look. "Why do I feel like there's a 'but' in there?"

"No buts, but . . ." I grinned. "I think to be safe, I need to keep some parts of my job from you." When he started to protest, I added, "Just like you keep some parts of your job from me. As you should. I have no business knowing everything." I didn't add that he had no business knowing everything about mine either.

"You're serious?"

"Yeah." I wrapped my arms around his neck and gave him another kiss, this time with more heat.

His hands dug into my waist. "Dinner. Tonight," he said in a tight voice.

"Yes."

When he kissed me again, I knew we were done going slow, and for the life of me, I couldn't remember why I'd wanted to.

Chapter Eleven

Luke dropped his hands and took a step back. "You make me forget myself." But the expression on his face made me think he wasn't entirely happy about that. "We can touch base about the time later."

I nodded. "Okay."

He started to cross the street, then turned around and took a few steps back toward me, stopping at the end of my bumper. "I had a purpose for coming to see you."

"What?"

"April Jean's trailer burned down last night, and it's lookin' like it was arson. With the fire yesterday and Dixie . . . I just thought you should hear it from me and maybe let Dixie know so she's not caught off guard."

"Thanks, Luke." Then I gave him a sly look. "You could have called or texted with that information."

He grinned. "But then I wouldn't have been able to see your sexy legs."

I flushed, and his grin spread before he headed back toward the police station. I took a few seconds to admire the way his pants clung to his nicely shaped butt.

"Earth to Summer," Bill said behind me, and I jumped.

"If you're done checking out the police chief, maybe you could come in and tell us what just happened."

I cringed. "Yeah. Sure."

When I walked into the office, I couldn't help but smile at how normal it looked. No sign of Connor anywhere.

Bill followed behind me and shut the door. "We talked to some of Connor's crew. Lauren never intended for us to run our office out of the train depot."

My jaw dropped. *"What?"*

"She's pissed that you didn't play her game. She was hoping you'd pitch a fit this morning so she could film you storming out of the office. They were going to have Connor give a couch interview implying you kicked him out for no reason. They're planning a competing agency."

"It would coincide with the video they leaked yesterday," Tony said.

"That doesn't make any sense," Dixie said. "Why didn't she set up the big fight in *this* office? Why would she move us there?"

"It's Lauren," Tony said. "Who can figure her out?"

"No," I said. "I bet it was because there isn't enough room to film it here, especially not with the two crews."

"She's right," Chuck said. "They never would have gotten clean shots."

"Back to more important issues," Bill said, turning to me. "What just happened with the new police officer? I mean, I saw what happened—I got it on film—but I still have no idea why."

I sat behind my desk and told them what I'd told Luke, then filled them in on my version of Officer Sterling pinning my arm behind me.

"Luke's right," Tony said. "That doesn't make any sense."

I turned to Dixie. "I want to tell them about what happened last night. I still want to use this for our big investigation. Especially after what just happened with Elijah Sterling."

Dixie's face lost color.

"They won't judge you, Dix," I said. "They'll want to help you, especially after I tell you Luke's theory about his new position."

"Summer's right. Whatever it is, we want to help you," Bill said.

She shot him a guilty look. Although she and Bill weren't really a couple, there was still something between them. Or there had been. "You might not say that after you find out what I did."

"We'll still help," Chuck said.

"Especially if we get an awesome case out of it," Tony said. He shrugged in response to the dirty looks the other two gave him. "What? You're both thinking it."

Dixie gave me a long look, then turned to face them. "I need to start with the fire that killed my parents."

She told them about the argument she'd had with her mother that afternoon—her mama wanted her to clean the barn, but Dixie only wanted to hang out with Trent Dunbar. So she snuck out the back and met him at the overseer's cabin, and they partied with the Xanax and vodka provided by Trent's older brother. She blacked out, but when she came to in a field, she reeked of gasoline, and the barn was on fire. Hence her arrest and incarceration in juvie.

"And what about Trent?" Bill asked. "What happened to him?"

"Nothing," she said.

"He supplied the drugs," Tony said. "That should have made him partially responsible."

"There's a couple of things you should know," I said. "Trent Dunbar is the only living child of Roger Dunbar, the owner of Dunbar Lumber, the biggest employer in the county. The Dunbar boys practically got away with murder."

Dixie shot me a glare.

"And Officer Elijah Sterling—Mayor Sterling's son—was hired just last week. The same week Trent came back to town. Rumor has it that Trent's back in Sweet Briar because he got in trouble with the law in Birmingham too many times, and his daddy ran out of favors. Luke said his arm was twisted to hire Mayor Sterling's son. Elijah Sterling was good friends with Trent *and* Troy Dunbar."

"Wait," Bill said. "Are you insinuating that Mayor Sterling hired his son to help smooth things over for Trent?"

I pinned my gaze on Dixie. "We need to keep this between the five of us, but that's Luke's theory."

Dixie looked down at her desk.

"Something happened to Dixie last night. She went to a party, and then she blacked out. She texted me around two this morning, and I found her on the beach at the lake." I glanced up at Bill. "Where I was attacked in April."

He nodded slightly, and his eyes hardened.

"Dixie was incoherent and could barely walk to my truck." I paused, giving her an opportunity to stop me, but she remained silent. "And she smelled like smoke. She still doesn't remember anything. I made her pee in a jar this morning, and Teddy knows someone who's going to test it for date-rape drugs."

All three men looked at me with stunned expressions.

"You think Dixie was raped?" Bill asked, his voice tight.

"I don't know. I think she may have been dosed for a different reason. April Jean's trailer burned down last night, and they think it was arson." I paused. "Dixie remembers getting into an argument with her at the party."

"You think Dixie started that fire?" Chuck asked.

Bill whacked him in the back of the head. "Idiot."

"Ow." Chuck rubbed his scalp. "What?"

"No," I said. "I think the opposite. Dixie is innocent. She could barely walk when I found her. How could she purposely start a fire at a trailer and then find her way to the beach? Trent picked her up from our farm. Someone must have driven her."

"You think someone is setting her up?" Bill asked.

"Yes. Especially after Elijah Sterling—in an official capacity—demanded access to my truck for a bogus reason. Not to mention he brought up me being at April Jean's trailer yesterday morning."

Tony's eyes widened, and he quickly picked up on my train of thought. "You think he was going to plant evidence framing Dixie *and* you?"

It was a serious accusation. I hated to outright say it, even if I believed it. "Honestly, I think he's more interested in Dixie. I was just an excuse. But you have to admit that his behavior seems pretty suspicious."

Bill nodded. "Damn suspicious."

Dixie remained silent.

"Our case," I said, keeping my eye on my cousin, "is to find out what happened to Dixie last night at the party and clear her name." I scanned the men's faces. "So who's with me?"

"What if we get an answer right away?" Chuck asked. "What will we do then?"

"We'll thank the gods, you fool," Bill said. "We're a team. We're doing this to save Dixie. Using it for the show is a bonus."

Chuck turned in his seat to face the cameraman. "The show is what funds our paychecks. Summer has a contract for three more seasons. I'd like to stick around for all three of them, and if Connor has better cases, Lauren is going to squeeze Summer out. Our job security depends on a case that entertains the viewers *and* beats out Connor."

Tony hung his head.

"I could force us to do this," I said, "but I don't want that. I want us to be a team. This only works if we all agree."

"I'm in," Bill said without hesitation.

"And I'm in, obviously," I said. "Tony? Your thoughts?"

He looked up at me. "Chuck's right. If we screw this up, we could all be jobless by the end of the season." Then he looked at Dixie. "But Summer's right too. We're a team, and that means we should support one another. If Dixie's in trouble, then we need to help her." He glanced at Chuck. "Summer has good instincts. That's why we had a kick-ass first season. Hell, she brought down a cop. I have no problem taking down another bad cop to help a friend." He grinned. "And, of course, to get even higher ratings."

"Chuck?" I asked. "If you'd rather work with Connor's crew, I understand."

He made a look of disgust. "And let you all get all the credit for another big case?" He grinned. "I'll take my chances with you all. Besides, we know that Dixie didn't do it. That was never my issue. My protest is that we're counting on this to be a huge case, when there's every likelihood that we'll prove her innocence this afternoon."

I hoped he was right, but my gut told me it wouldn't be that easy.

Bill shifted in his seat, discomfort making him grimace. "I don't think Dixie should work on the case with us."

"What?" Dixie asked, her eyes wide.

He sighed. "It's just that people won't talk to us if you're there. You have to know that."

Pain filled her eyes. "So I'm fired?"

"No," I said, realizing Bill was right. Dixie was too close to the situation to be objective. Besides, I could tell she barely believed in her own innocence. "You can do preliminary interviews with the clients in-house. We'll leave Tony here to film."

"You're leaving me out of this investigation too?" Tony asked.

"No," I said. "You and Bill can take turns, but you have to admit that if Dixie's here interviewing, it will throw Lauren off if she comes by to check on us."

No one looked happy with my suggestion, but they didn't argue.

"I'm happy you all came up with a plan," Dixie said in a dry tone, "but right now we have an alligator to catch."

Chapter Twelve

Sylvia Rush lived on a small parcel of land outside of Sweet Briar city limits. Dixie and I were quiet the entire drive, but when we pulled in front of Sylvia's shoddy-looking house, I asked, "What do you know about Sylvia?"

"She's got a bunch of kids, I think."

The rusted bikes in the yard suggested the same thing.

I climbed out of the truck and waited for the guys to unload, watching multiple little faces peer through the windows.

"I think we should try to capture my introduction to Sylvia as realistically as possible." I glanced back at Bill. "The sky's overcast, so the lighting should be good to film outside, don't you think? Especially since we're talking about chickens."

He glanced around as he lifted his camera out of its case. "Yeah. If the sun comes out and causes a glare, we can go under the shade of that oak tree."

"Dixie," I said, "why don't you go warn Sylvia that we'll introduce ourselves at the door and then invite her outside."

"Okay."

Dixie walked up across the gravel driveway and up to the front door as Tony slung his camera strap over his head. "We've got two cameras. Which one is A, and which one is B?"

"Tony, why don't you take A? I think we should get plenty of shots of the kids' bikes and toys for the B-roll, Bill."

He nodded as Tony headed toward me, Chuck tagging along with his laptop. We walked closer, and Tony pointed to the chicken coop. "Why don't you meet her at the door, then lead her toward the coop? If you keep your backs to it, I can keep it in the background as you interview her."

"Okay."

Dixie headed back toward me, trying not to laugh. "I know why Lauren picked this one out special for you."

Dread clenched my gut. "What does that mean?"

A grin lit up her face. "I'd hate to ruin the surprise."

Oh, mercy.

Tony had me walk back over to the truck and mimic getting out and walking up to the door with Dixie by my side. I'd barely rapped on the window of the storm door when the inside door opened and a woman appeared.

My mouth dropped open in shock. I tried to recover, but my reaction had been captured by Bill, who stood to the side. Obviously, Dixie had told him to be prepared.

Sylvia pushed the storm door open. "Oh, my God! I can't believe Isabella Holmes is standing at my front door!" She danced in place in her canvas tennis shoes and squealed.

I took a backward step down the front porch, nearly falling on my butt. The fortysomething woman I was facing was dressed in a plaid school-uniform skirt, a white blouse, and a plaid tie. Her blonde hair—a very cheap wig—hung halfway down her back, and two skinny braids at her temples were pulled back with barrettes. Fringe bangs brushed the top of her eyebrows.

My signature hairstyle in season four of *Gotcha!*

Facing my unfortunate choice of hairstyle was uncomfortable. Facing it on Sylvia Rush was a nightmare. This was undeniably a score for Lauren.

My best friend, Marina, would have *loved* this . . .

Thankfully, Sylvia seemed clueless to my horror. "I am your *biggest* fan."

I turned to Dixie, shooting her a glare for not warning me, then gave the woman a bright—albeit fake—smile. "That's so sweet of you, but I'm just Summer Butler. I left Isabella behind a long time ago."

She leaned to one side and then the other as she scanned the yard behind me. "Where's J.P.?"

"Who's that?" Dixie asked in confusion.

But I knew exactly who she was talking about. "Connor Blake, the actor who portrayed J.P. Stanley, has his own cases," I said in a patient voice, the one I used with crazy fans.

"I thought y'all were workin' together now. That's what the whole town is sayin'."

"Well . . . ," I drawled, "we're both private investigators in the same town, but we're workin' our own cases. Would you rather work with Connor?" *Please say yes.*

Her smile drooped, and for a moment I was sure she would agree, but she shook her head. "I can meet him next time."

Good Lord. I hoped there wouldn't be a next time. I smiled again. "Obviously, you know who I am. You must be Sylvia." I held out my hand to shake hers.

She bobbed her head in a nod, and her hair slid forward, the ends of her bangs hitting the tip of her nose. After reaching up to slide the wig back into place, she hastily shook my hand. Her palm was clammy.

"And I'm Dixie," my cousin said, offering her hand. "Her cousin."

Sylvia shook her head as she took her hand back from mine. "Nope. Isabella doesn't have any cousins. She said so in Season Two, Episode Twelve, 'The Case of the Missing Twins.'"

Holy crap. She knew more about the show than I did. "You're right, Sylvia," I said in a cheery voice. "Isabella didn't have any cousins, but I—Summer Butler—have two. Dixie here, and my cousin Teddy."

Confusion clouded her eyes.

"So, Sylvia," I said, hoping the repeat of her name would help get her back on track. This ship was sinking, and I needed to steer it toward a deserted island. I started walking toward the chicken coop, and she followed me. "Dixie and I are here because we heard that you have some missing chickens."

"Yeah."

"When did this first happen?" I asked.

"A few weeks ago. Them worthless boys of mine was supposed to put the chickens up in the coop, but it done turned dark, and I heard the chickens squawking and shriekin', so I ran out there with my shotgun. That's when I saw something with a long green tail slink into the cornstalks behind the coop. Sure enough, my hen Mae Whittaker got snatched by a gator."

I ignored the fact that Mae Whittaker was the name of Isabella Holmes's best friend on *Gotcha!* "There aren't alligators around these parts," I said.

"Actually," Dixie said, "they've made a comeback. They caught a monster alligator in Lake Edna a couple of years ago."

"Don't they need water?" I asked, glancing around. Miller Creek was a good mile to the west.

"My neighbor behind me has a big stock pond behind his house," Sylvia said. "I hear he's got a big gator back there."

My eyes bugged out. "And he's just on the loose?"

"Yep."

"How big is he?" Dixie asked.

"I'd say about ten feet long. I only saw his tail that time, but the second time he came at my chickens, I saw him in the whole. That was the day he took Derek Matthews."

J.P. Stanley's best friend on the show. This woman was obsessed.

The wind gusted and blew up Sylvia's short skirt, revealing her panties, but what was more shocking was the tattoo on her upper thigh—very bad likenesses of Conner and me in our *Gotcha!* roles. I was looking dead-on with a gaping mouth, and Connor was turned sideways, his tongue hanging out. I could only guess that this was from an episode when J.P. had tried to kiss Isabella and accidentally licked her face instead. Sylvia batted down her skirt with one hand and covered the top of her wig with the other while she looked at me expectantly.

I blinked, wishing we had bleach in the truck to wash out my eyes. Some things just couldn't be unseen.

Dixie covered her mouth with her hand as her shoulders shook with laughter.

"Are you okay?" Sylvia asked.

Dixie nodded, her face now turning red with suppressed giggles.

"Dixie," I said, "why don't you go out to the truck and look for a bottle of water?"

Nodding again, she bolted for the truck, stopping halfway to bend over and try to cover her laughter.

"Is she really okay?" Sylvia asked.

"My cousin's prone to fits sometimes. She'll be fine."

I finished the interview, finding out that other neighbors had complained about the alligator prowling on their property too.

"Have you tried calling the sheriff?" I asked. "Or animal control?"

"They won't help me."

I found it hard to believe that animal control didn't care about a ten-foot chicken-eating alligator on the loose. "I'm not really sure what Dixie and I can do for you. You know who owns the alligator, or at least who shelters it. I can't haul it off, and if your neighbor doesn't want to do anything to stop it, I'm not sure I can say anything to convince him."

"But you're Isabella Holmes. He'll listen to you."

"No," I said, striving for a patient tone. "I'm Summer Butler, and I suspect he'll tell me to mind my own business when I go over there."

"You'll go over?" she squealed. "I *knew* you would help."

Crap. I pushed out a long sigh. "What's your neighbor's name?"

"Rick Springfield."

I narrowed my eyes. This woman had an obsession with celebrities. "What other name does he go by?"

"Sometimes he calls himself Big D, but usually he just goes by Rick."

My mouth parted, but I reconsidered the wisdom of responding to that, and instead asked, "Do you have an address?"

"He lives on County Road 46. Turn on the gravel road with the mailbox shaped like an alligator."

Of course he had an alligator mailbox. "I'll see what I can do and let you know how it goes."

"Thank you, Isabella!" she said, throwing her arms around me.

I started to correct her, but a chicken squawked loudly, and I jumped back, thinking the alligator had returned for another snack. Sylvia started to laugh, pointing at me like I was a fool. I scanned the yard for the predator, but it was empty but for two chickens, one light brown and the other dark, both covered with extra-fluffy feathers, even on their legs. They sure didn't look like the farmhouse chickens I'd expected.

"You're scared of Isabella and J.P.," Sylvia said, her laughter dying down.

"*Excuse me?*"

"The light one is Isabella, and the darker one is J.P. because his hair's a little darker than yours."

"Uh-huh."

Bill said "Cut," and then Tony insisted that we needed to conduct the interview again, which earned him a death stare from me.

"Come on, Summer. There's a reason reality shows repeat things. Just to make sure we get what we need."

I refused to start back on her front porch—some things just couldn't be re-created—and insisted we just repeat our discussion about the chickens and alligator in front of the coops. We gathered a few more pieces of additional information that might work on screen, but I knew they wouldn't help at all when I confronted Big D.

Oh, mercy. I was not looking forward to talking to a guy who went by *Big D* and kept an alligator in his backyard.

I was ready to leave, but Bill suggested we get some shots of Dixie and me holding the chickens. I swore under my breath and vowed revenge, but Bill just grinned. He got some great clips of me screaming when the chicken I was holding—Isabella, of course—flapped its wings, and I tossed it into the air. I knew he was about to suggest I try again, but one look from me made him close his mouth.

Smart man.

I thanked Sylvia for talking to us on camera as the guys headed toward the truck. They decided to leave their gear unpacked for the short drive over to the neighbor's house, especially since we hadn't gotten Big D's permission beforehand.

Sure enough, we easily found the alligator mailbox and drove down the gravel road toward a small house that was in better shape than Sylvia's. I could see a large pond behind the house, but no alligator was in sight.

"Maybe he's not home," I said hopefully as I put the truck into park.

"Then why's that big, shiny truck parked in front of that detached garage?" Dixie asked.

Sure enough, a decked-out truck was parked in the gravel driveway partially behind the house. I scowled, glancing at the pond again. "Do you think that alligator's out there?"

"Dunno," she said, leaning into me as we both looked out the driver's side window. "Maybe it's sleepin'."

"How fast do alligators run?"

"How would I know?" she asked, sounding irritated. "Just because I knew there were gators in Lake Edna doesn't mean I'm a walking alligator encyclopedia."

"Look it up," I said, still watching for the gator.

"How fast do alligators run?" she said slowly as she typed it into her phone. "Um . . . this says people can sprint at twenty miles per hour—but usually around ten—and while alligators usually walk around seven to eight miles per hour, they *have* been known to get up to twenty-five."

I vigorously shook my head. "Nope. Not gonna do it."

She grinned. "Do what?"

"Get out of this truck."

She laughed. "Do you want to drive up to the front porch, honk the horn, and see if the guy will come out?"

"Can I?" I asked in a hopeful tone. I turned around and looked out the back window, knowing the guys could hear us with the mikes.

Tony and Chuck were laughing and shaking their heads no, but Bill was nodding and mouthing *yes*.

Dammit. "If I get eaten by an alligator, I swear on Maybelline's country-fried steak I'm coming back to haunt y'all, and it'll be an ugly haunting, not one of those cute ones that just moves keys and such."

My statement was greeted with more laughter, Dixie's included.

"I'm happy to see y'all take my safety so seriously," I grumbled.

My cell phone rang, and Bill's number showed up on the screen. I answered it on speakerphone.

"You know we'd never knowingly put you in harm's way, don't you?" Bill asked in a cajoling tone.

I started to protest, then stopped. Bill had proven beyond a shadow of a doubt he had my back when he'd faced Cale Malone with me.

"Look," Tony said, "we have a better view of the pond than you do, and we don't see a thing. You're safe. Besides, he's more afraid of you than you are of him."

"Are *you* getting out of your truck to shoot this?" I asked.

"No way," Tony said. "You said Bill was camera A next time."

"Thanks a lot," Bill groaned.

"I'm warnin' you right now," I said, "you're only gettin' one shot at this, so make it count." I turned to Dixie. "Are you comin' with me?"

Her mouth was pressed into a tight line. "I haven't decided yet."

"Traitor." I pushed open the truck door, glancing down to make sure an alligator wasn't underneath the truck, and gingerly put a foot on the ground, ready to get back inside, if need be.

"Just get out of the truck already," Dixie said good-naturedly. "You think it might be hiding under there?"

"Well, now that you mention it . . ."

"Then you would have run it over. We didn't drive over any lumps, and if you *had* run it over, it would be dead, and Sylvia would likely get another tattoo of you."

I shuddered at the thought.

"Oh, come on, you big baby," she said as she shoved her door open, but I noticed she glanced around before she actually got out.

I hopped out too and told myself that Tony was right—it was likely more scared of me than I was of it, which meant it was probably on Xanax and so lethargic it wasn't capable of running after me, let alone eating me.

If I could get so lucky.

We headed for the front porch, but Bill told us to slow down as he adjusted his camera and started recording. He followed us up the steps and onto the covered porch, then moved to the side to capture the front door.

I knocked and waited, then knocked again. Rick Springfield was liable to be cranky at my impatience, but I couldn't bring myself to care. I needed to talk to him now because I never wanted to come back.

Ever.

I heard a grumbling voice, and then the lock was unlatched. As the door swung open, a guy said, "This better be damn important since you woke me—" He took one look at us, and a hesitant smile spread across his stubbly face. I got the impression we'd caught him off guard. "Well, good morning, ladies."

We were face-to-face with a scruffy-looking guy wearing a stained white T-shirt and a navy bathrobe. He had a serious case of bedhead, but my eyes were drawn to his messy, dark hair and his pajama pants, which were covered in bloody zombies being chased by guys with hatchets.

"Hi." I forced my eyes to his face. "I'm Summer Butler, and this is my cousin Dixie."

He leaned his shoulder into the doorjamb while leisurely looking me up and down, but an undercurrent of something dark hummed beneath his casual demeanor. "I know who you are. You're big news around here, or at least you used to be. You were on that stupid show about the girl detective."

My brow lifted, and I bit back a retort. *Let it go, Summer.* I forced a smile. "That's neither here nor there. I'm here because your neighbor Sylvia Rush says you have a pet alligator that's eating her chickens."

For half a second he looked surprised, then he crossed his arms over his chest and grinned. "Chickens are meant to be eaten."

"But only if you pay for 'em," Dixie said. "So you owe Sylvia for her chickens."

I stared at her in astonishment for a half second before I recovered. I wouldn't have gone that direction, but it was a good idea.

Rick let out a barky laugh. "Like hell I'm payin' for her chickens."

"If your alligator ate them, then, yes, you will be," I said with more confidence than I felt.

"First of all, little lady, nobody tells Big D what to do." He winked. "Unless it's in bed, then I'm open to suggestions."

I didn't try to hide my disgust.

"And second, I ain't got no pet alligator."

"So you're saying you don't have an alligator in your pond in the backyard?" I asked.

"Oh, yeah, I have one all right, but he's not my pet. He comes and goes as he pleases, and I leave out raw meat to entice him back."

"Why would you entice him back?" I asked.

"To keep nosy girls away from my house." Then he slammed the door in our faces.

Dixie looked disappointed. Bill kept the camera running, and I realized that Big D never said anything about the camera. I wasn't sure what to make of that. Had he been expecting us? As prepared as Karen had been last season, she'd probably already scoped him out and hopefully gotten him to sign the waiver to appear on the show. If she hadn't, we wouldn't be able to use any of the footage from his house.

Either way, there was no reason for us to stick around. I spun around to leave when I heard clanging behind the house. Then Rick shouted, "Come on, Kitty, Kitty. Come and get the tasty meat."

Dixie's eyes widened. "Oh, crap! He's calling that thing!"

"And he named it Kitty," I said as I hurried down the steps. That lunatic was siccing his alligator on us.

Dixie hurried after me, then tripped and fell to her knees.

I could see Rick holding a pie tin and a steak with one hand, and banging the tin with a wooden spoon.

"Oh, my word!" I shouted. "He's crazy!" The alligator surfaced and wiggled out of the pond.

"I'll say," Dixie said as I pulled her to her feet. "He's giving that gator a ten-dollar steak!"

Bill was still filming, though he'd taken the precaution of running around to Dixie's side of the truck.

Dixie was already climbing inside the cab, but I remained in place. I had moved past scared and well on to pissed. Who the hell did this guy think he was?

Rick was already at the front corner of his house, and I could see the alligator lumbering after him. The front door opened, and another guy walked out of the house and onto the front porch.

"Rick! What the hell are you doin'?"

"Lettin' these fine ladies meet Kitty."

The guy—who was dressed in jeans and a light-gray T-shirt that clung to the muscles of his upper arms, shoulders, and chest—had short, dark, damp hair. He rushed down the steps in bare feet and raced toward me.

"Just get in your truck and get out of here."

"Not until Mr. Springfield pays for Ms. Rush's chickens."

The new guy's mouth dropped open. "*What?*"

"He's named this alligator and is feeding it, which proves it's his pet. Turns out he lets *Kitty* roam free and terrorize his neighbors."

The new guy's head jutted forward. "*What?*"

I put my hands on my hips. "Are you deaf? He's paying Sylvia Rush for the two chickens his alligator ate." While part of me was terrified of the advancing alligator, the fact that the two men were out here with it proved it couldn't be *that* dangerous. Maybe Tony was right that it was more scared of us.

The new guy glanced over at the alligator. Rick tossed the steak about six feet from where we stood, then scampered up onto the porch, all while wearing an amused grin.

The new guy's eyes widened, and he dug into his pocket and retrieved his wallet. "How much?"

"How much what?"

"How much for the damn chickens?"

"Are you the alligator's owner? Because you payin' for those chickens defeats the whole purpose of this exercise."

He started to pull some bills out of his wallet, and a condom package fell onto the ground.

"Classy . . . ," I said in disgust, starting to get nervous when the alligator continued advancing. But surely Rick wouldn't sic an alligator on his friend.

Right?

The gator snatched up the steak in a quick movement, then eyed the two of us speculatively.

The new guy bent down and threw me over his shoulder. Before I could even register what was happening, he'd scrambled up onto the hood of my truck. He tossed me on top of the cab while he sprawled across the windshield. His long legs stretched across the hood, and his feet dangled off the edge.

The alligator tried to climb the front wheel, and the guy jerked his feet up onto the hood. Rick burst out laughing on the front porch.

My new hero turned to me, fury in his eyes, and shouted, "Are you *crazy*?"

"*Me?*" I shouted, flinging an arm toward his friend on the porch. "He's the crazy one! He just tried to kill us with his alligator!"

"Kitty wouldn't have killed you," Rick said with a chuckle. "He might have eaten Nash's foot, though."

"This is gettin' out of hand, Rick!" his friend shouted. "Now call this damn thing off, pay the lady for the two chickens, and let me get to work."

"Oh, come on," Rick said, resting his palms on the front-porch railing. "I'm enjoyin' the show." Sure enough, he'd taken a seat on an Adirondack chair, as if he were watching a movie or a live performance.

Nash shook his head, looking like he was about to vault over the alligator and wring his friend's neck. "I swear to God, Rick, if you don't call off this alligator, I'll go get my .22 and shoot the thing right in the head."

Rick scowled and grumbled under his breath as he picked up the pie tin and wooden spoon, which he'd set on the table next to his chair. "You used to be fun, Nash Jackson. What the hell happened to you?"

"I grew up, you asshole," Nash said, his chest heaving.

Rick walked down the steps, beating the pie tin. "Here, Kitty, Kitty."

The sound caught the alligator's attention. It lowered to the ground, watching Rick walk backward to the other corner of the house, and started following him like he was the pied piper and not some fool with a pie tin.

Once the gator was almost to the corner, Nash slid off the hood and grabbed his wallet from where it had landed in the yard next to his condom package. He snatched out two bills and strode toward me with murder in his eyes.

I was still on top of the cab, watching him move toward me.

He lifted his hand and shoved two twenties at me. "And before you say it's not Rick's money," he said through gritted teeth, "I plan to get it from him—plus twenty more for my inconvenience—so I suggest you take it and get the hell out of here while you can."

I slid down the windshield to the hood and took the bills.

"Listen," he said, his anger fading, "I don't know who you are or what you want, but do me a favor and stay the hell away from my cousin."

"Rick's your cousin?"

He ignored my question and started to stomp off to the souped-up truck, but he stopped and did a double take when he saw Dixie through the windshield.

"You know Dixie?" I asked, thrown off by his reaction.

His gaze lifted to me. "Dixie?"

"My cousin, although I actually claim her, as opposed to you and *your* cousin."

He didn't answer. Instead, his face paled as he took another glance at Dixie and then took off for his truck.

Nash Jackson knew something about Dixie, and I planned to find out what.

CHAPTER THIRTEEN

We decided that it would be better for Dixie to deliver the forty dollars to Sylvia, so we dropped by, and I ducked down and hid in the truck while Tony filmed Dixie handing her the money and declaring the case closed. Afterward, we all headed to Maybelline's for lunch and grabbed a table in the front facing the street.

"What in the world got into you?" Tony asked me as he grabbed a menu. "You were afraid to step foot out of the truck when we first got there, and then you decided to stare that alligator down."

"I did not," I said, my brow furrowing. "But I reasoned if those two men were standin' there, I wasn't goin' to back down." I turned to Bill. "How much of that did you get?"

"All of it. When I realized the alligator was goin' after you and that guy, I moved to the side and got a great shot of him picking you up and vaulting you onto the hood of the truck. Who is he?"

"Nash Jackson," I said.

I'd quizzed Dixie about him on the ride into town, but she'd sworn up and down that she'd never met him before, which made me wonder if Nash had been at Trent's party. He'd definitely acted like he recognized her.

"Dixie, was *Rick* at the party?"

"I don't remember seeing him there."

"How many other people were there?"

"I don't know. At least twenty, maybe more."

"On a Monday night?" Tony asked.

She shrugged "It's Trent. He parties when he feels like it, and he's such a good host, people come."

"By good *host*, you mean supplying refreshments?" I asked.

She shrugged again. "I guess."

"How old is this kid?" Tony asked.

"Twenty-five," I said. "Old enough that calling him a kid doesn't let him off the hook anymore."

"Sorry," Tony said. "I just meant that he's old enough for free alcohol not to have the same draw as it would for underage minors."

"Tony's right," Dixie said. "Back in high school, Trent and his brother were known for the parties they threw. And now I guess he's known for the samples he provides."

"Drugs?" I said. "After what happened with Cale, you condone what he's doin'?"

I expected her to get angry—instead, she looked sad. "I had no idea what he was up to until last night, but as soon as I figured it out, I asked him to bring me home."

"And he refused."

"He told me to lighten up. Then he handed me a red plastic cup of Coke and told me to go enjoy myself."

Which probably explained how she was drugged. "What happened after that?" I asked.

"I sat with a group of people, and then April Jean showed up and found out that Trent had picked me up. She stomped over and threatened to snatch me bald for tryin' to steal him back. I told her she could have him, but she thought I was lyin' and lunged for me. I told her to back off, that I didn't want Trent anymore and she was welcome to him. I remember thinking about calling you to come get me, but my body felt weird. I couldn't feel my legs."

Which proved she'd been drugged. "What do you remember after that?" I asked. Why hadn't she told me all this before?

She smoothed a few strands of hair from her forehead with a shaky hand but didn't answer.

"We don't have to talk about this now," I said. "Especially here. You can tell me later, and I'll fill the guys in."

She shook her head and lifted her chin, determination filling her eyes. "No. I'll tell them. I've got nothin' to hide, whether I did it or not."

"What do you remember next?" Bill asked, his eyes guarded.

"Wakin' up to Summer's alarm and wonderin' why she'd slept in my bed. I have no idea what happened."

"What time did you ask Trent to take you home?" I asked.

"Around eleven." A half hour after she and I had first texted each other.

"Can you give me a list of who was at the party besides Trent, April Jean, and Rick Springfield?"

She hesitated. "I guess it depends on who's gonna see the list."

"Not Luke," I said. "I told you I want to prove your innocence before he gets anywhere near it."

"Because you don't trust him," she said, sounding disappointed.

"No, because I trust him to be a good and honorable man. He'll do everything by the letter of the law, including arrest *me* if someone turns me in for doin' something illegal." I gave the men a half smile when I saw their shocked faces. "I asked him what he'd do if confronted with the situation. I wasn't surprised at his answer, but it confirmed that we keep this to ourselves for now. Teddy's gettin' the drug screen, and we're workin' on the investigative part. When we have everything to prove your innocence, we'll present it to Luke."

She paused for several seconds, then nodded. "Okay."

"So you'll give me a list?" I asked.

"Yeah. As long as you don't give it to Teddy either."

Maybelline came over to take our orders, and we changed the subject, going over our encounters with Sylvia and Rick. Discussing what we could have done differently.

"We need to get that other guy to sign a release," Tony said. "And verify that Karen got one from Rick."

"Agreed. But we need to track him down," I said. I glanced at Dixie, about to ask her to do it, then quickly changed my mind. Rick seemed like the logical person to ask, and I didn't want her anywhere near either one of those guys. "I have an idea on how to get it." From someone who had recently been knee-deep in the county riffraff . . .

"How's that?" Dixie asked, narrowing her eyes.

"Never you mind. I have it covered. Your job is to call the woman who thinks her husband is working some side jobs and not reporting it to pay less child support. Oh, and that guy who thinks his wife is cheating is coming by this afternoon. After you get some preliminary information on camera, we'll schedule some surveillance on both cases." I paused. "Oh! I completely forgot about Bruce Jepper. You feelin' up to interviewin' him?"

Her eyes flew wide. "Me? What would I ask him?"

I started to give her some suggestions, then stopped and gave her a warm smile. "You've got great instincts, Dix. You can figure it out. You can ask me for help or suggestions, of course, but you take point on this one."

Her mouth pinched tight with anxiety. "But I can't investigate cases, I'm not a PI."

"You won't be investigatin' his case," I said with a smile. "You'll just be askin' questions." I turned to Bill. "I want you to stick with Dixie for the rest of the day until one of us is done."

"You think I need a babysitter," she said, sounding forlorn.

"No. I want you to have an alibi. If another fire pops up and you're with someone, it will automatically prove you weren't responsible for April Jean's fire." It didn't mean any such thing, but I hoped Dixie believed it. At least for a little while.

◆ ◆ ◆

After lunch, Dixie headed to the office with Bill, although in hindsight, I wasn't so sure I should have left the two of them alone together. Bill undoubtedly had questions about Trent's and Dixie's involvement, and my cousin was liable to tell him the truth, no matter how hard that might be to hear. I was sure she had feelings for Bill, but her loyalty to Trent had been stronger. Thankfully, his sample party may have cured her of that. But at what cost? Had she pissed off Trent enough for him to set her up?

We headed to my truck, but I stopped and took a long look. While the county was full of older trucks, most weren't as old as my pawpaw's farm vehicle. "I think we need something more subtle."

"What have you got in mind?" Tony asked.

"My car. It's out at the farm, but I'd like to talk to Teddy while we're there. I think he's out working the fields today, so he should be around."

"You want to get some clips of your personal life?" Tony asked as he turned onto the four-lane highway.

I started to say no, then realized this could be part of the show—not to mention it would give Teddy more screen time, something fans were begging for. "I hadn't considered that. This is for the case. Teddy knows a lot of people in this town, and with his work with the sheriff's department, I have a feeling he has a better feel for the baser elements in the county than Dixie does." Thank God for small favors. "I'd like to ask him about all the people we know were at the party. Hopefully, Dixie will have texted her list by the time we get there."

"Sounds good."

"We'll have to mike Teddy," Chuck said. "And I need to switch out your battery."

I nodded and sent Teddy a text.

I'm coming out to the farm to trade the truck for my car. Are you around? I need to ask you some questions.

His response came a few minutes later.

I'm out in the back field. Can you come out here? Bring your camera guys.

I relayed the message to Tony and Chuck, and they looked worried.

"What do you think it means?" Tony asked.

"Maybe he got the results of Dixie's drug test."

"Does he know you're investigating this for the show?" Chuck asked.

I frowned. "No." And I wasn't sure how he'd take it. I'd just push the proving-Dixie-was-innocent pitch and hope he'd go for it.

When we reached the farmhouse, Tony pulled over. Chuck switched out the battery pack for my mike, then climbed in the back of the truck so Tony could film me while I drove.

I steered down the dirt road, past the fields and the overseer's house, toward the back corner of the property. Teddy's truck was parked at the beginning of a curve in the road, and he was a good twenty feet behind it, watching for me.

I pulled to a stop about ten feet in front of him. My nerves were about to get the better of me. Why had he asked the cameramen to come?

"Stay in the truck," Chuck said as he hopped out of the truck bed. "Let me mike up Teddy."

"Okay. But hurry." I wasn't sure I could wait much longer to find out what he had to tell me.

Chuck hurried over to my cousin and clipped the box to the back of his jeans before quickly threading the cord up his shirt. Teddy helped get it clipped, keeping a serious face, then shooed Chuck away.

As soon as Chuck got behind the cab, I opened the door and ran to Teddy. "Is everything okay?"

A grin spread from ear to ear. "Better than okay." He put an arm around my lower back and started ushering me toward his truck.

I tried to guess what he was so happy about—specifically in regard to Dixie—but I couldn't think of anything related to Dixie that would make him smile like that right now. Whatever the outcome, there was no reason for either of us to be happy about the results of her drug test.

Before we reached the front of his truck, he said, "Close your eyes."

"Why?"

"Just do it."

Wanting to make him happy, I closed my eyes and felt him grasp my wrist and tug.

"I won't let you fall."

"Now I'm really scared," I teased. "You told me that once when we were kids. We climbed the oak tree out back, and I had to get a cast on my arm a few hours later."

He chuckled. "We're not climbing any trees this time."

We continued to walk for nearly half a minute, and I asked, "Are we walking to the Georgia state line? Because I would have changed out of these sandals."

"Stop your griping," he said good-naturedly and stopped moving. "Besides, we're here. Open your eyes."

My eyes fluttered open, and I gasped. We stood on the gravel road between two cotton fields, and on either side, the lower branches of the plants were covered with white flowers. Only white flowers. Acres of them.

"The cotton plants are blooming," I whispered, realizing how much I'd missed this.

"When I planted in April, I started in this back corner, so that's why they're blooming first, but the weather's been perfect—hot and dry, but not too dry—and while they're a little early, the plants seem to have set well. Not too many leaves, and the squares are good. Barring any issues with Mother Nature, this could be our best crop in years, Summer. The best crop I can ever remember."

I walked over to the side of the road and squatted to get closer to the delicate white petals that contained both male and female parts. They would only stay white while they pollinated themselves. Tomorrow they would turn pink, then one or two more flowers on each branch would open and greet the world a day or so later. But today was the only day the field would be entirely white, and it was magical.

To see the first flowers . . . I turned to Teddy with tears in my eyes. When we were little, Pawpaw used to tell us they'd been touched by fairies, and if we saw the very first flowers on the day they bloomed, we'd be touched by magic too. Every year after that, Pawpaw had brought me out to see them . . . until my mother took me away.

Teddy had remembered.

"Thank you," I said, forcing the words past the lump in my throat.

"I've been checking them and thought they were close. I meant to tell y'all at dinner last night, but things got out of hand, and then I stomped out. I'm sorry."

"That's okay. I liked finding out this way better."

He gave me a tender smile. "You saved this, Summer. You did what you had to do to save a farm you hadn't been to in over a decade. This would all be gone if not for you."

I shook my head, wiping a stray tear. "No, Teddy. You would have found a way. We Baumgartners are stubborn folk."

He leaned over and hugged me. I rested my chin against his shoulder, so thankful that I was back in Sweet Briar. That he and Dixie and Luke and even Meemaw were back in my life. But it wasn't just that—I was happy to be back at the farm too. I'd forgotten it was an entity of its own, one that had seeped deep into my bones before I was old enough to realize it. It was part of Teddy too. I tried not to think about what he would have done if he'd lost the farm. Other than Dixie, it was his everything.

I pulled away and looked up him. I had to tell him about my plan to help Dixie, and I was ready to fight him on it if necessary.

"Teddy, I've figured out my big investigation for the show." I paused to make sure I had his full attention. "I plan to find out what happened to Dixie. This morning she heard that April Jean's trailer had burned down, and now she's scared to death that she started it. I aim to prove that she didn't."

His body went rigid, and his smile fell. "You're gonna film it and put it on TV?"

"Only if it helps her. If it hurts her, no. I'll dump all the footage."

"How will you control that?" he asked, getting pissed. He turned toward Tony, as if only then realizing he was still filming. "Turn that off."

Tony looked to me for confirmation, and when I nodded, he lowered the camera and walked back toward the trucks.

When he was out of earshot, Teddy lowered his voice and asked, "How can you be sure it won't get used?"

"We'll treat it like we did the footage we got on our own back in April. Bill used his own cloud storage and dumped the recordings every night. We'll do the same thing this time. Lauren will never see this unless I show it to her."

"What about those two?" Teddy asked, gesturing toward them. "They weren't any part of helping you last time. How do you know you can trust them?"

"The only reason they didn't help last time was because I never asked them. Bill and Dixie cooked up the secret investigation while I was in the hospital. We kept it between the three of us to be safe. But Tony and Chuck are firmly on board. They want to do this too. They won't tell Lauren."

"And what if it falls through?" Teddy asked, looking like he was about to be sick. "What if you find evidence that incriminates her?"

I leaned closer and lowered my voice. "Then I'll bury it. I won't hurt her."

"And those guys?"

"They've agreed to do the same."

"What about Luke? He'd arrest her in a New York minute."

I shook my head. I couldn't deny it because I knew he was right. "He doesn't know what I'm investigating, and I won't tell him. Dixie comes before Luke, Teddy. I swear it on Pawpaw's grave."

He drew in a deep breath and ran a hand over his head, then dropped his arm to his side. "I'm scared, Summer."

I grabbed his forearm and held on tight. "I am too, but I believe she's innocent—on both counts. She's lived with far too much guilt for far too long. I want her free of it."

"You don't think she started the fire in the barn?" he asked in a guarded tone.

"No. I just can't see her doin' something like that." I paused. "Even if she was out of her mind on drugs."

He was silent for a moment. "Why does she think she burned down April Jean's trailer? Does she remember bein' there last night?"

"No. She remembers telling Trent she wanted to come home. Then he handed her a soft drink and told her to lighten up and enjoy herself."

His face went rigid. "Trent Dunbar drugged my sister."

"We don't know that yet." But I'd bet my entire season of earnings on it.

His jaw clenched so tight I was afraid he was going to grind his teeth to dust.

"She remembers an argument with April Jean over Trent, and then nothing until she woke up this morning."

"Not even the shower?" he asked, sounding worried. "She was standing and moving around. She was talkin' to you."

I knew what he was thinking—if she could take a shower and not remember it, what else could she have forgotten?

"I still believe she's innocent, Teddy."

He nodded and stared out into the fields. "I can't lose her again, Summer. I can't."

I grabbed his hand and squeezed. "You won't. *We* won't. You have me to help this time around, and remember that Baumgartner stubbornness? I won't stop until we know she's safe."

He swallowed, his Adam's apple bobbing as he nodded. "Yeah. You're right." A grin tipped up the corners of his mouth. "You were always the most stubborn out of all of us."

I grinned. "That's right. I won't stop until we prove she's innocent, but we've got a fight ahead of us, Teddy. I'm pretty sure Trent's trying to set her up, and he's got help on the police force to do it."

His eyes widened as I told him about my encounter with Elijah.

"Do you trust me?" I asked. "You and I worked different sides of the same case last time. Let's work together to free Dixie from her demons."

He hesitated, then nodded. "Okay."

I threw my arms around his neck and squeezed tight. "Thank you, Teddy."

"No." His voice was muffled in my ear. "Thank *you*, Summer."

I released him and said, "As much as I hate this next part, I have to get it on camera."

He nodded with a resigned look. "I know."

I motioned to Tony and Chuck to head over as I said to Teddy, "I'm going to tell you that I'm investigating Dixie, and you react however you want. If you want to fight me on it, go ahead. Just remember that this reaction is the one people are going to see. It might not ring true if you immediately agree."

"Okay."

Once the guys were ready, I repeated that I wanted to investigate what had happened to Dixie, although this time I didn't mention it was for the show. Following my lead, Teddy protested, arguing it would open old wounds, but he ultimately caved. I hugged him again, amazed that he played his role so convincingly, but then again, he'd been an informant for the sheriff's department. He'd already proved that he knew how to convince people to believe what he wanted.

"So I think we should work together," I said, reiterating what I'd said before.

He rubbed his chin and stared out into the fields. "Yeah. That's a good idea. My contacts are somewhat compromised since word got out that I was working for the sheriff, but I can still get information."

"What do you know about Elijah Sterling?" I asked. "Luke told me his application was pushed through by the mayor and city council, and now Luke's stuck with him."

Teddy gave me a disgusted look. "Cry me a river."

"He says Elijah and Trent were buddies."

Luke hesitated. "Yeah, I guess they were, but I'm not sure how close."

"Close enough for him to plant evidence at Trent's request?"

His eyes bugged out. "What?" He was playing his part well.

I repeated my encounter with the officer that morning. "It's suspicious," I finished.

"But not conclusive."

"So you think I'm overreacting?" I asked defensively.

"No, we just need harder evidence to prove he's crooked."

But all this talk about Officer Sterling reminded me about something else. "Oh, crap! Luke wanted me to file a report at the station, and I haven't done it yet. Maybe he's hoping to use it to fire him."

"More likely suspend him. If the mayor pushed him through the hiring process, he's not going to let Luke just fire him. He'll put up some kind of bureaucratic fight."

I frowned. Teddy was probably right.

His eyes hardened. "But I *do* know if he lays hands on you like that again, he'll be dealing with more than just a suspension."

"Teddy, don't do anything to get yourself in trouble. Save your outrage for Dixie."

"I have enough outrage to use on behalf of both Baumgartner girls, Summy."

"Well, venting your rage on a Sweet Briar police officer could land you in jail, so keep it under control."

He grinned but said nothing.

I narrowed my eyes. "Moving on . . ."

"Okay. What else?"

"What do you know about a guy named Rick Springfield? He lives off County Road 46 and has an alligator named Kitty in his backyard."

"Rick Springfield is trouble with a capital *T*. Stay away from that guy." He paused. "Does he have a connection to Dixie?"

"She said he was at Trent's party."

He gave me a suspicious look. "And how do you know about the other information?"

"He was part of a case we worked on this morning."

His voice hardened. "What case was that?"

"It's not important." I waved my hand in dismissal. "His alligator ate my client's chickens. What's important was that Big D was at the party, and I think his cousin was there too."

He looked confused. "His cousin?"

"Nash Jackson. He was at Rick's house when we asked him about his alligator."

Teddy was quiet for a moment. "I don't know him. The only cousin I know about is Herbert." His mouth twisted. "Why do you think his cousin was at the party? Did Dixie recognize him?"

"No. I think *he* recognized *her*, though. He did a double take when he saw her, like he was caught really off guard."

A grave look filled Teddy's eyes. "I'll ask around and let you know what I find out."

"Don't talk to him without me," I said.

"Without your cameras, you mean."

"Teddy . . ." I almost stopped him and restarted the question so we could cut it out, but I reconsidered. It seemed disingenuous not to acknowledge the cameras were part of this.

"Fine," he said, but he didn't look happy about it. "If I find out something big, I'll call you, and we'll look into it together, but I'm worried that both of us are too recognizable to be effective."

I hoped that wasn't the case. "What do you know about April Jean Thornberry?"

He looked uncomfortable. "Not much."

"She had a drawing of you hangin' on her livin' room wall that made me want to poke my eyes out."

"That thing's still up?" he asked in dismay.

"So you've seen it?"

"God, no. Not in person anyway. A friend of mine saw it and sent me a photo."

"A friend?"

"Never mind who." He held off a few seconds before he said, "April Jean's mother died a few years back, and her father left town when she was a baby. She has grandparents, but they practically disowned her when she started her career as an artist."

"She said Trent's stayed with her multiple times. She said they go way back."

His mouth twisted, and he partially shrugged.

"What's that mean?"

"It means she sleeps with multiple guys."

"So? It's the twenty-first century. Women can sleep with whoever they want."

He held up his hands in defense. "It means I don't know firsthand about her relationship status with Dunbar, but I *do* know that she's slept with a lot of guys, usually ones who have something she wants."

"What's that mean?"

"Just like it sounds. If there's something to the rumors that Trent Dunbar's selling drugs, she probably slept with him to get access. When she had a leaky kitchen sink, she slept with my friend Steve, who's a plumber. She dumped him the day after he installed a brand-new faucet and pipes in her kitchen."

"So it's possible that one of those guys could be pissed at being used by her."

"It's a fair assumption."

"Maybe it's also a possibility that one of those guys was pissed enough to burn her trailer down?"

"Yeah, I guess." He rubbed his chin. "We need to find out who responded to the call. It would be easy for you to find out if Luke handled it."

I shook my head. "The sheriff's department responded."

"Then we need to find out which of the Sweet Briar police officers was on call and why he didn't handle it," Teddy said.

"I doubt it was Luke," I said. "He spent the evening with me."

"They don't usually go on call until eleven, so that doesn't necessarily mean anything," Teddy said as he rubbed his chin. "They don't get many calls after midnight, so it's not like they're sitting around the station waiting for the phone to ring. The county 911 call center contacts the officer on call, and if they're tied up with something else, the dispatcher hands it off to a sheriff's deputy."

"So we need to find out why it got handed off."

Teddy nodded. "I'll check in with my buddy in the sheriff's department and see if I can get some info on their investigation . . . and why they got the case."

"Aren't they going to think it's weird that you're asking? We don't want to link this back to Dixie."

"Yeah, you're right. But I'll figure out a way to tie it in. I still work with them. Maybe I'll bring up the drug angle."

My stomach clenched at the thought of Teddy working with the Bixley County Sheriff's Department. He wasn't an official deputy, and when he'd worked for them a few months ago, he hadn't carried a gun. I was certain he'd pissed off more than a few people. It didn't sit well to think of him putting himself in more danger.

Another idea came to me. "What about your friend Garrett Newcomer? The volunteer firefighter. He might be able to tell us something useful, and then you won't have to bring in the sheriff's department."

His brow lifted. "Yeah. In fact, he might be able to provide a different angle than they would."

Garrett was cute, all the better for the camera, and he seemed like he might be open to discussing the cases. Plus, he'd worked Bruce Jepper's fire, which meant he might have more information than the sheriff's department. "Why don't you let me interview him?"

Teddy's eyes lit up. "Oh, yeah?"

I groaned. "Stop with the matchmaking. I'm with Luke."

He gave me his half shrug.

I'd win him to Luke's side. Eventually. "Garrett might also have some information about Trent. I remember him talking about a poker game they all played together."

He shrugged. "I'll text you his info. I'll bet he's willing to talk to you." He shifted his weight. "What else you got?"

I pulled out my phone, happy to see that Dixie had texted her list. "Dixie sent a list of the people she remembers being at the party. They must have seen what happened to her during the time she doesn't remember. We need to track them down and find out what they know."

"Who's on the list? I can help."

I started to protest, especially since she didn't want him to know, but he was right. He knew people. There were sixteen names altogether. When I took out Rick, Trent, and April Jean, that left thirteen people to interview. I read through the list, and he recognized most of the names.

"Some of them I know better than others," he said. "How about you start at the top of the list? I won't be able to start on it until tonight, but I'll work my way up from the bottom. If we get something useful, we'll share it with the other. And we won't stop until we save Dixie."

I had to believe that we would.

Chapter Fourteen

I left Teddy in the field and drove Tony and Chuck back to the farmhouse so we could move the gear into my car. They looked disappointed when they realized I didn't have a luxury sedan.

"I was forced into doing a reality show, and I just lost my house in foreclosure," I said as I unlocked my older Kia. "What did you expect?"

"Please tell me that the a/c works," Chuck said.

"It does." Mostly.

"So what do you want to do next?" Tony asked as he got into the passenger seat. Chuck climbed into the back seat.

"I need to call Garrett, the volunteer firefighter, and see if he'll tell me what he knows about the fires, particularly April Jean's, but first I have to go to the police station and file a complaint against Elijah Sterling."

"Are you sure you want to do that?" Chuck asked. "If he doesn't get fired, you could be creating a powerful enemy."

"It's too late to worry about that," I said. "He's already pissed off at me. Besides, if we're right about him wanting to plant evidence, he's dangerous with a badge."

"And after you file the report and talk to the firefighter?"

"I'm tryin' to decide if I should reach out to April Jean. She's open to being on the show, but she has to know I'm Dixie's cousin. Maybe we should hold off on talkin' to her and start goin' through the list of people at the party. We might find out something we can use when we meet with her."

"Good idea," Tony said.

"When we talk to the people who were at the party, I don't think *we* should mention that Dixie was likely drugged. I'm presuming Trent was the one who drugged her since he handed her the drink, but there's a chance someone else did it. If they suspect we're fishing for information, they're more likely to get defensive and lie. We need to come up with something else to make us seem less suspicious. Maybe say she lost something and we're trying to locate it."

"You really think that'll work?" Tony asked skeptically. "What are you going to say? That she lost her consciousness and now you're looking for it?"

I shot him a glare. "Hey, I'm open to ideas."

We discussed several possibilities on the way back into town— everything from saying we wanted to attend the next party to saying we were investigating a noise complaint from the neighbors. We didn't have a workable plan by the time I pulled into the Sweet Briar Municipal Complex, so we decided to table it until later.

Complex was a generous term. It was a one-story building with a small police station taking up the east side and city offices taking up the west side.

"Hey," I said when I saw a white Ford Explorer in the parking lot, "we might get that interview with April Jean quicker than I thought. That's her car."

Tony checked his camera. "I'm ready to get anything that comes our way."

Chuck leaned forward. "If the receptionist agrees to it, I can just use a boom mike, and that will capture any other people in the room."

"Sounds good."

Tony followed me to the entrance, his camera lowered, and Chuck trailed us with his boom mike and laptop. My strategy was to get Amber's permission to film at the station and then catch April Jean off guard, hopefully enough that she'd answer questions. I was certain both women would agree to be filmed, but Tony and Chuck were ready to capture any action that might spontaneously happen.

I opened the door and saw Amber sitting behind the receptionist desk. I knew bigger police departments had glass separating the waiting room from the reception clerks, but Sweet Briar was old-school, and Amber looked like she could be working for a dentist.

"Summer!" she said as I walked in, perking up when she saw Tony. She brushed her heavy auburn bangs out of her eyes, and I noticed she'd cut her long hair into a shoulder-length bob. "Are you filmin' in here?"

"If that's okay," I said. "We'll need you to sign a release to put you on TV, but I can have you fill it out later. I'm only here to fill out a form for Luke."

She waved her hand in excitement. "Sure, no problem."

"Great! Here's how this will work: I'll pretend like I just walked in, and you'll pretend like you just saw me, and then I'll tell you why I'm here."

She opened a drawer and pulled out her purse. "Can I touch up my makeup first?"

I really didn't want to wait, but I couldn't say I blamed her. "Sure. Your haircut's super cute, by the way."

She beamed.

I realized I hadn't checked my appearance since I'd gone to the bathroom after lunch, but I didn't really care. A glamorous look didn't really go with this job, despite Lauren's intentions last season.

A minute later, I walked through the front door. Tony followed me with the camera at first and then switched his position to capture a front view of my "entrance" from the lobby.

A necessary evil to make the show look good after editing.

Amber seemed fascinated by the process, and it took two takes before she realized when she was supposed to greet me, saying, "Hey, Summer. What can I do for you?"

I walked up to her counter. "Luke told me to come by and fill out a formal complaint for the way Officer Sterling treated me this morning."

Nodding, she grabbed a paper off her desk and set it on the ledge. "Luke's out on a call right now, but he left this for you to fill out. He said you could go into his office if you'd like."

I tried to hide my surprise. I suspected he hadn't planned on me bringing my film crew. "Thanks, but maybe I should stick to a more public area." Especially if I hoped to run into April Jean.

"Oh, okay." She pointed to several worn plastic waiting-room chairs. "You can sit over there." She bent down, grabbed a clipboard, and handed it to me. "Here. This will make it easier."

As I took the board, I said, "Hey, I saw April Jean's car in the parking lot. Is she here talking to somebody about the fire?"

Amber shook her head. "She's not here at the police station. She's over in the city offices."

"Oh." I hadn't considered that.

I sat down and started to fill out the dry-as-toast paperwork. The guys were still recording—which had to be like watching paint dry—so I was about to tell them they could take a break when Mayor Sterling walked into the station. Tall and good-looking for a man in his sixties, Mayor Garner Sterling was the epitome of a southern gentleman, from his combed and styled salt-and-pepper hair to his ever-present suit and tie. He'd given me a totally skeevy vibe the first time I'd met him in April, and this whole mess with his son had hardly endeared him to me.

He did a double take when he saw my film crew, straightening his tie before he said in a cheerful voice that belied the tension around his eyes, "Well, what a wonderful surprise to see you, Summer." He had a deep, genteel southern accent that didn't sound like anyone else's accent around here.

Tony backed up, widening his shot to include the mayor, but I knew he was already thinking ahead, planning to ask the mayor to re-create his entrance to capture the full effect for the show.

My lips formed a tight smile, the best I could manage, especially since the reason I was here was to file a report about the son he'd shoehorned into the police department. "Mayor Sterling, I didn't think you showed up at the city offices during the day. I thought your accounting business kept you too busy."

Sweet Briar—population 2,731—wasn't big enough to employ a full-time mayor, and I knew Mayor Sterling supplemented his income with his thriving accounting firm.

His smile looked strained. "And normally you'd be right, but there's a rash of fires I need to deal with. If you'll excuse me . . ."

He hurried toward the glass doors leading to the city offices, but they swung open before he could reach them. April Jean stood in the opening with her hand on her hip and her eyes full of anger. "What took you so long?" she demanded.

He shot a nervous glance at the cameras, then grabbed her upper arm and tugged her into the city office reception room. "Not here."

The doors closed, and I stared up at Tony, who looked just as confused as I felt. I leaned to the side, glancing around Chuck. "Hey, Amber, did you see what just happened?"

She chuckled. "Honey, there's not much I don't see."

This town was chock-full of busybodies and gossips. I was planning on using that to my advantage. "Do you have any idea what that was about?"

She waved her hand in dismissal. "Oh, yeah. She's probably thinkin' the mayor can help get justice against your cousin."

I stood and dropped the clipboard onto my seat. "What?"

Confusion wrinkled her eyes. "Surely you know that April Jean is blaming Dixie for the fire."

Suspecting it and seeing April Jean seek justice for it were two entirely different things. "Why's she goin' to the mayor? Why not Luke?"

"He said he's not working the case. Besides, Luke has a soft spot for Dixie, so I suspect April Jean wouldn't have trusted him to do anything anyway."

"Why isn't Willy workin' it? Why's the sheriff's handlin' it?"

"Willy was workin' an accident, so the dispatcher handed it off."

"What does she think the mayor can do?"

Amber shrugged, but the truth hit me like a two-by-four: his son was on the police force and had the power to do something. Wasn't I here to register a complaint because he'd been too free with his new authority?

I picked up the clipboard from the seat and waved it at Tony. The expression on his face told me that he'd figured it out too.

But what, if anything, should we do about it?

Tony lowered his camera and took a step toward me, keeping his voice low. "It looks like we're thinking the same thing."

"That April Jean wants the mayor to get his son to arrest Dixie. What if Mayor Sterling knew his son would plant the evidence in my truck?"

He gave me a grim look. "You can't turn in that paperwork. The mayor will know we're onto his son."

"There's no way Elijah Sterling doesn't know I'm suspicious of him."

"True, but you can pretend it was one of those in-the-heat-of-the-moment situations. You could even apologize," Tony said.

"Are you insane?" I hissed in a whisper. "Apologize for *what*?"

"For not cooperating."

There was no way *that* was going to happen. "I think I should call Luke . . . off camera."

Tony started to protest, then stopped. "Okay."

"I'm going to call him from his office. If April Jean comes out, try to keep her here so I can ask her some questions."

"Okay," he said, but he didn't sound very confident.

"I've decided to fill this out in Luke's office, after all," I said to Amber as I walked past her.

I suspected she knew I wasn't being entirely honest, but she didn't stop me.

Luke's office door was open, and my heart warmed when I saw his name painted on the frosted glass window. I was tempted to sit behind his big wooden desk to make the call, but it didn't feel right, so I sat on the leather sofa instead.

"Hey," he said when he answered the phone, his voice low and sultry. "I was just thinkin' about you."

I smiled to myself, parts of me heating up. "I'm sitting in your office right now."

"I *really* wish I were there," he said.

"I need some legal advice."

His tone instantly turned serious. "Are you in trouble?"

"No, not how you're thinkin'. I'm here at the station to fill out the complaint against Elijah Sterling, but his daddy just showed up, and he's meeting with April Jean at the city offices."

"Why's he meeting her there?"

"I'm not sure, but Amber thinks April Jean is wanting the mayor to do something about Dixie."

"Like what?" he asked, his voice cold, but I knew it wasn't directed at me. I also realized he and I had never discussed the possibility of a connection between Dixie and what happened to April Jean's trailer, but it had been on the *Sweet Happenings* page, which meant it was common knowledge.

"I don't know." I wasn't about to bring up my suspicion that Elijah had been hoping to plant evidence for his father. Not yet anyway. "What if Mayor Sterling has multiple reasons for wanting his son on the police force?"

Luke cursed under his breath. "You might be onto something, but you're not plannin' on confronting him, are you?"

"Well . . ."

"I'll take that as a yes."

"That wasn't my question," I said defensively.

"Okay," he said, but it sounded like he'd bit off the word to keep from saying something else. "Ask your question."

"I'm thinking that maybe I shouldn't fill out this complaint against Elijah Sterling."

"*Why?*"

"What if he thinks we're onto him?"

"Onto him doin' *what?*"

Dammit. Maybe I should tell him my suspicions, but then I told myself no. Luke was a bright man. He could put two and two together and get four. This was one of our don't-ask-don't-tell situations. If he thought I was going after his new officer to help Dixie, I suspected he'd put up a big fat stop sign. "Whatever it is that he's doin'," I finally said. "If he thinks he's getting away with it, we can try to catch them in the act."

"You have no proof that he's doin' anything other than being overexuberant at his job. And how do you propose to catch him in the act of something illegal, something which, I might remind you, you don't even know exists?"

"I don't know," I grumbled. "Why do *I* have to come up with all the ideas?"

"So you can say *Gotcha!* when you catch them in the act." There was the hint of a grin in his voice, but with his next words, it turned husky. "I wish I were there to kiss that scowl off your face."

"Who says I have a scowl?"

"I know how much you hate that line. Your scowl is a given." He turned serious. "Fill out the complaint, Summer. You won't be part of some elaborate scheme to catch the mayor and his son in some undercover sting."

"Why not?"

"Because you're working on your big case, and I suspect it has to be something to do with Dixie. You won't let the mayor get in the way of that."

I started to protest . . . until it occurred to me that he hadn't asked for any details. If I had to lie to him, much better to tell a lie of omission than a blatant untruth. As long as the mayor left Dixie alone, I'd let him go about this seedy business until next season.

Luke sighed. "Summer, fill out the paperwork, and help me get Elijah Sterling off the force. Trust me, he's much more dangerous running around with a badge than without, even if you're tryin' to tie him to something. We'll deal with him and Garner Sterling later."

"Promise?"

"Yeah."

"Thank you."

I could hear the relief in his voice when he asked, "How's tonight lookin' for you?"

"Too soon to tell," I said. "I've got a lot of people to interview, but I'll let you know as soon as I figure it out."

Right now I had to focus on getting Elijah Sterling off the force and protecting Dixie.

CHAPTER FIFTEEN

The form to file a complaint was more tedious than I'd expected, but I supposed it was serious business to accuse an officer of excessive force, and plenty of documentation was needed to back it up.

I was in the middle of writing my statement when I heard April Jean's voice in the waiting room. "My trailer's still burned down, Mayor Sterling!"

I moved to the opening of Luke's office. April Jean was standing in front of Amber's desk—directly in my line of sight—and she quickly turned her wrath on me. "Why were you really out at my trailer yesterday, Summer Baumgartner? Were you scopin' it out for your cousin?"

My mouth dropped open in shock. I advanced toward her, but the look on her face suggested she didn't want me too close, so I stopped several feet away. "No! It's just like we told you yesterday—I was with Luke when he got the call, and since he was off duty, I went with him. I would have been perfectly happy to hang out in the truck."

A sneer spread across her face. "You can't deny it's pretty convenient that you showed up at my trailer the day it went up in flames."

"April Jean," I said, softening my voice, "I don't know anything about what happened to your trailer, but I'd like to help you figure it out."

Disgust washed over her face. "More like help your cousin get away with it."

I pushed out a breath of frustration. "Dixie didn't do this, but I want to find out who *did*."

April Jean shook her head. "You just stay the hell away from me." Then she stomped out of the front door to her car.

"Ain't that a fine how-do-you-do?" Amber said from behind me. "I've never seen April Jean that snippy before."

"Well," I said, realizing belatedly that Tony was still filming, "she just lost her home, and she's under a lot of stress. Sometimes it brings out the worst in people."

"Like stress made you punch that guy in the pineapple shirt in public," she said with a nod, reminding me of the drunk guy who'd demanded I say *Gotcha!* In all fairness, I'd been on edge after just getting belittled by the reality TV producer for being too vanilla.

"Palm trees," I said with a grumble. Punching that guy had been the catalyst to get me here, so I couldn't regret it too much. Especially since he'd deserved it.

Amber glanced over the counter at the clipboard in my hand. "Did you finish your form?"

"Not yet." As hostile as April Jean had been, I was worried about Dixie. What if April Jean headed over to the office to confront her? I pulled out my phone and sent Dixie a text.

I just had a run-in with April Jean at the police station and wanted to warn you in case she shows up. xoxo.

I wanted to check on Dixie in person, so I finished the form as quickly as possible and handed it over to Amber.

"What now?" I asked. "Does Luke pull him off the force?"

"I don't know about that, but Luke wrote him up and made him take a paid leave. He'll be back to work in a few days."

Then what was the point? But I told myself Luke needed a paper trail, a solid foundation to back up his decisions regarding his renegade officer. At least I didn't need to worry about Officer Sterling harassing me in the near future. I could deal with Elijah Sterling, Sweet Briar resident. After this morning, I was even looking forward to it.

The guys packed up their equipment, and we headed out to my car. The clouds had cleared off, and the day was heating up. I turned on the a/c, but the vents were a touch loud, so I stepped out of the car to place my call to Garrett.

"Garrett Newcomer," he said when he answered.

"Hey, Garrett, this is Summer Butler, Teddy's cousin."

"Summer," he said, sounding surprised, "what can I do for you?"

"I know that you were working Bruce Jepper's fire, but I was wondering if you also responded to the fire at April Jean Thornberry's trailer out on Highway 10 last night."

"Yeah. I was there. I live out that way, and I was home for the night, so it was an easy drive. I keep all my gear in the trunk."

"I still can't believe you just volunteer your time to put out fires. If you lived in a big city, you'd get paid."

"Yeah," he said, "but I like livin' in Sweet Briar. Most people have hobbies. Mine just happens to be puttin' out fires."

Seemed like a dangerous hobby to me. "Say, do you think we could get together and talk about what you do as a volunteer firefighter?" When he didn't respond, I added, "Last season we focused on Teddy and what he did for the sheriff's department to help bring down Cale Malone. I'm sure the fires will play a part this season, so I'm thinking we could put you in the show—another hero, just a different branch." I wasn't sure that he'd be allowed to tell us many details, but it was worth a try.

He was silent for a moment, then said, "Sure. I'm guessin' you'll be bringin' your cameras."

"If we want to put you on the show," I teased. "And I *do* want to put you on the show."

"I have to work late, but I can be home by seven. Will that work?"

I hid my disappointment and frustration. I had hoped to have dinner with Luke, but figuring out who'd set April Jean's fire was more important than my love life. Maybe I could still head over to Luke's for a late dinner after shooting at Garrett's house. "That sounds great, Garrett. Thanks."

"I'll text you my address."

I hung up and looked back at the guys. If we couldn't see Garrett until seven, we needed to start interviewing the people who'd attended the party. Which included Rick Springfield's mysterious cousin. I still knew next to nothing about Nash Jackson, but it occurred to me that I might be close to a source who did. Hopefully, she'd give me the info I wanted without being too gabby about my asking.

I held up a finger to the guys, then went back inside the police station.

Amber's face lifted as the door opened. "Oh, you're back." She glanced around me. "You didn't bring your cameras this time."

"That's because I just have a quick question. This morning I ran into someone when I was working on a case, and since you said you see and hear all kinds of things, I thought you might know something about him."

She grinned from ear to ear. "Finally, someone takes me seriously." She rested her hands on the counter and leaned forward. "Shoot."

"Well," I said, resting my hip on the short counter wall, "this morning I was talking to Rick Springfield out on County Road—"

Her eyes flew wide open. "Rick Springfield? I have two questions. What were you talkin' to him about, and does Luke know?"

"The quick answers are his alligator and no."

166

"His alligator? He really has one? I thought that was an urban legend."

I grimaced. "I can assure you that Kitty very much exists."

"Kitty?"

"Yep. I got up close and personal with Kitty right before Rick's cousin tossed me up onto my truck. I want to know more about the cousin."

"Herbert? His beer gut's so big I'm surprised he could lift you up and over the bulge, let alone toss you."

I shook my head. "Not Herbert. This guy was in his late twenties or early thirties and had dark-brown hair. He was tall and pretty fit."

She winked. "No wonder you want to find him."

I laughed and rolled my eyes. "Not for that. I'm datin' Luke."

Amber looked like she was a five-year-old who'd just gotten a pony for Christmas. "You two are *datin'*?"

Oh crap. Luke hadn't told her . . . Then a new thought hit me.

Oh. Crap. He hadn't told people we were together. Did that mean he was waiting to see if we worked out?

As soon as the panic eased off, I reminded myself that he'd kissed me in public this morning after declaring himself my boyfriend on the show last night. I was being paranoid.

Waving off her question, I said, "He came over for dinner last night."

"With Teddy? He *hates* Luke."

Sounded like Amber knew her stuff, all right. "Back to Rick's cousin. His name is Nash Jackson, and he drives a really nice blue Dodge Ram pickup. What can you tell me about him?"

Her mouth twisted to the side. "He doesn't sound familiar."

"Really?"

She shrugged. "Sorry. It happens occasionally. I'll keep my ears open for anything about him."

"Can you keep it from Luke?"

Her eyes narrowed, and her back stiffened. "So you *are* interested in this Nash Jackson."

At least she was loyal to her boss.

"No," I groaned out. "I'm not. I just don't want Luke to know because I'm trying to keep my big case from him. The more he finds out about it, the more likely he is to guess what I'm doin'." I paused and leaned my arm on the counter. "You know, you could be a big help to the show, Amber. I need someone to feed me information without blasting everything on the *Sweet Happenings* page."

She chuckled. "Maybelline has a hard time sittin' on a scoop."

I knew she was capable of it. She'd kept quiet about something involving Otto this past April, but I got the impression it was a one- or two-time thing, something I'd be foolish to count on. "But this has to stay between you and me. You can't tell Luke when you're givin' me information."

She looked leery. "What kind of information?"

I stood upright and held up both hands. "Nothing confidential. Right now I'm more interested in what you know about people around town."

Her face brightened. "Okay."

"But—and this is the but that might make you change your mind—I don't want you to share the information with me on camera."

Excitement filled her eyes. "Oh! I'll be like your Deep Throat."

I grinned. "Exactly. You can be my mysterious, anonymous source, and everyone will go crazy trying to figure out who you are."

She clapped her hands together. "I love it."

For a spur-of-the-moment plan, this was going better than could be expected. I pulled out my phone. "If you've got a moment, we could start right now. There are a few people I'm hoping to question, and it might help if you could tell me what you know about them first."

She settled back in her seat, beaming. "Go for it."

"Gabby Casey."

Amber rolled her eyes. "*Total. Bitch.* She tries to pass off cheap knockoffs as designer. It works around here because no one knows the difference, which only makes the whole thing pathetic and sad since no one even cares."

Ouch.

I copied the whole list of party guests, pasted it in a note on my phone, and typed in what Amber had said. "Do you know if she's friends with Dixie or April Jean?"

"Nah, I know she and Dixie worked at the Dairy Queen together when Dixie came back from . . ." Amber cringed. "You know."

Juvie.

She shifted in her seat. "I don't think they were enemies or anything, but Dixie was interested in Trent, which made Gabby instantly dislike her. April Jean dislikes them both for the same reason."

"*How much* does April Jean dislike Dixie? Enough to set her up?"

Amber went still. "I don't know. She seemed genuinely upset when she came in lookin' for Luke and then the mayor. She lost all her drawings in the fire, and she was pretty proud of 'em."

"Did you see them?" I asked with a raised brow.

She leaned forward with a conspiratorial gleam in her eyes. "No. But I heard about 'em. Everyone in town has."

"I saw them in person yesterday. They were . . . something. It truly was a loss, but do we know if they really burned up? She could have taken them down, *then* set a fire."

Amber looked surprised. "You think April Jean burned down her own trailer and is blaming Dixie to throw off the sheriff?"

I rubbed my temple. "Honestly? I'm not sure." I needed to be more careful about brainstorming aloud. "Back to Gabby Casey," I said. "Do you happen to know where I might find her? I take it she doesn't work for the Dairy Queen anymore."

"Nope. She works for an insurance agent. Thelma Kuntz."

I perked up. "Hey, that's Bruce Jepper's insurance agent." Now I *really* needed to talk to Gabby. "Anything else about her?"

"I think she's still livin' with Mark Willis, but last I heard, they were fightin' big-time since Trent came back to town."

"He's jealous?" I asked. His name was also on the list of attendees. Was he the Mark who'd been at the poker game with Bruce, Trent, Wizard, and Garrett?

"Like I said, it's no secret she's always had a thing for Trent Dunbar." She shrugged. "Most girls did."

"And you?"

She rolled her eyes so far back in her head I saw mostly white. "Please. I'm not stupid."

But neither was Dixie. I reminded myself that loyalty had played a part—she'd stuck by him because he'd stuck by her while she was in juvie. "You're too young to have graduated with them. At least by a couple of years." I guessed her to be around twenty-one or twenty-two. "How do you know so much about them?"

"My sister graduated with Trent. And it wasn't a big graduating class. About fifty."

"Gotcha. And Mark Willis? Did he graduate with them too?"

"He graduated with Trent's brother, Troy."

"Ah . . . Troy." I felt bad for thinking ill of the dead, especially someone who'd died so young, but Troy had been as much of a scumbag as his brother.

"Did you know Troy?" she asked.

"Yeah. He was in Teddy's class." And Teddy had had plenty of run-ins with the kid. I cocked my head. "If Mark Willis was pissed about his girlfriend wanting Trent, then Trent probably isn't his favorite person."

"That's an understatement."

"Where does Mark work?"

"Dunbar Lumber. In the lumberyard."

Now, *that* had to sting. "Do you know if he has a grudge against April Jean or Dixie?"

She shrugged. "Not really, but I know for a fact he slept with April Jean before he started datin' Gabby. April Jean had a drawing of him up on her wall. When Gabby found out, she was *pissed*."

"And when did she find out?"

"A couple of weeks ago. She and Mark have only been together for a month or so. He slept with April Jean a month or two before that. Gabby and April Jean got into a huge girl fight over it, hair pulling included. Willy had to go break it up."

"Did he charge either of them?"

"Nah. He has a crush on Gabby, and April Jean scares him, so he let them off with a warning."

"How did Mark feel about being up on April Jean's wall?"

"He loved it . . . until Gabby found out. When he asked April Jean to pull it down, she told him no."

So Mark had a motive to burn down the trailer too. Interesting.

I was getting ready to ask her about the next name on the list—Amelia Bourdain—when my phone vibrated with a text. I slipped it out of my pocket, my heart catching when I saw it was from Dixie.

I have a situation at the office. Can you come ASAP?

I answered, I'm still at the police station. I'll be right there.

I slipped a business card out of my pocket and handed it to Amber. "Would you text me at this number so I can get ahold of you later? I have more names on my list, but I need to get back to the office."

Before she could do anything other than grab the card, her phone rang. Holding up a finger, she answered, "Sweet Briar Police Department, how can I direct your call?" Frowning, she shook her head. "Slow down, Hugo." She paused and listened for a moment. "Okay, I'll send Luke or Willy over. No!" she said emphatically. "Do *not* do anything. Willy or Luke will take care of it." She hung up, groaning, and shot me a sympathetic grimace. "There's a disturbance of some kind outside your office. I'm calling Willy to go check it out. I think he's closer."

"Thanks, Amber." I headed for the door, then stopped and turned around. "You've really helped me. If I can ever help you with anything, just let me know, okay?"

She looked surprised. "Okay. Thanks."

When I got in the car, Tony said, "What were you doing in there? Writing up the whole damn town?"

"I was getting information about the people on my list until Amber got a call about a disturbance outside our office." I pulled out of the parking space. "And seconds before that, I got a text from Dixie asking us to come back ASAP."

"Any idea what's going on?" Chuck asked.

"Not a clue, but I'm worried April Jean might have done something."

"Oh, shit," Tony said.

It was a short drive, but I used it to fill them in on everything I'd learned about Gabby and Mark, particularly the fact that both of them had some kind of motive. I'd just gotten to the part about giving Amber my business card so she could continue to be our secret source when I cut myself off midsentence. A crowd of about twenty people was on the sidewalk in front of our office. There was shouting, but I couldn't make out any words, and the crowd was too dense for any of us to see what was going on.

After I parallel-parked across from the office, I darted across Main Street, dodging a car in my haste to make sure Dixie was okay.

The crowd parted slightly, revealing a middle-aged couple standing about six feet from each other. The woman was wearing white capris and a loose denim shirt covered in paint splotches. The man was dressed business casual—khakis and a polo shirt—and had a serious comb-over. They were the type of normal middle-aged couple you normally wouldn't look at twice, only today they were shouting at each other in public while the woman held something above her head. The man held out his hands like he was prepared to catch it.

Dixie stood in the open doorway of our office, her mouth drawn as she watched. Bill, bless him, stood beside her, getting everything on camera, and Tony and Chuck were already capturing the action from a different angle.

"You think I'm cheating on you?" the woman shouted, waving the object in her hand. Now that I was closer, I could see it was a bright-red model car. "You're an idiot!" She chucked the car at his head.

He reached up to grab it, but her throw was to the left, and he missed. The car hit the head of the woman behind him before bouncing to the sidewalk.

The woman who'd taken the hit screamed and grabbed her head as if she'd been shot.

"That was my '69 Mustang!" the man shouted as he bent down to get it. "You dented the bumper!" he said in dismay as he stood.

"That's what you get!"

"This must be Dixie's cheating-wife case," Tony muttered under his breath.

I suspected he was right.

Dixie slid in next to me. "I'm sorry. I was conductin' his interview, and Margo showed up and started smashing his cars on the sidewalk."

"It's okay," I said. I kept my gaze on the couple, but I reached down, scooped her hand in mine, and squeezed. "You did great."

The woman reached into the oversize purse slung over her shoulder and pulled out a model of a bright-yellow sports car.

"Oh, my God, Margo," he cried out in horror. "*Not the Lamborghini!*"

She lifted it over her head and shook it. "This thing means more to you than I do!"

"That's not true," he said, but he didn't sound convincing. His eyes were fixed on the model as he clutched the red car to his chest like a newborn baby. Sweat beaded on his upper lip.

Margo's eyes filled with tears, and she darted to the middle of the street. "You have to choose, Harold! Me or the car!"

A pickup truck turned the corner and headed toward her.

"What?" Harold asked. "What are you talking about?"

She turned her back to the oncoming truck and shook the model at him. "You have to choose! Or you lose us both!"

The truck slowed to a crawl, and the man behind the wheel watched her in bewilderment.

"Hey, Margo," Willy called out in a good-natured tone from across the street. His thumbs were hooked in his waistband, and he looked like he was asking her about the weather. "Whatcha doin'?"

"I'm making him choose!" she shouted. "Me or his stupid car." She turned to face her husband, tears streaming down her face. "If you don't choose, that truck behind me will mow us both over!"

The truck was now driving so slowly that people on the sidewalk were walking past it in their haste to join the crowd.

"Why would you want to get run over, Margo?" Willy asked, standing next to the back bumper of my parked car.

"I want him to prove that I mean something to him," she said, her voice breaking off with a sob.

Harold edged toward her, moving slightly into the road, and I dared to hope he'd make the sort of loving gesture she clearly needed from him. Instead, he reached out his free hand and said, "Just hand over the car. No one has to get hurt."

Holding her Lab mix's leash with one hand, an elderly woman I recognized as Fredericka Mills marched forward and used her other hand to hit Harold over the head with a closed umbrella. "You stupid fool."

Clutching the red car to his chest, he reached for his head. "Ow! What'd you do that for?"

Fredericka turned her attention to Margo. "You're better off without him, honey."

Margo stared at her, slack-jawed.

"She's right!" another woman shouted. "He ain't worth the trouble!"

"Hey!" Harold protested, dropping his hand to his side.

A young woman with long dark hair started to approach the crowd, took one look at the situation, then turned around and strode purposely in the opposite direction.

"How'd you know I was here, anyway?" Harold asked his wife.

"It was on Maybelline's Facebook page, you fool!" she shouted. "You think I'm cheating on you? When would I have time? I'm too busy workin' at the bank and cookin' and cleanin' and starching your shirts!"

The truck honked, and Margo jumped, nearly dropping the model car.

Irritation covered Harold's face. "You found plenty of time to take your *art class*." He poured disdain into the last two words.

"So?" she asked, taking a step toward him. "You're busy playing with your toy cars."

"For the hundredth time, Margo, they aren't toy cars! They're CMCs, for God's sake! And you weren't makin' my dinner."

A chorus of groans erupted, and someone threw a half-eaten sandwich at him.

"Here's your dinner!" a woman shouted.

"This is gettin' out of hand," Dixie murmured, sounding worried.

Officer Willy Hawkins was so enthralled, all he needed was a bucket of popcorn. It was clear he didn't intend to do anything to stop this, so I heaved a sigh and walked out into the street. "Margo, you don't know me, but I want to help."

She gave me a look of contempt. "I know who you are, all right. You're Summer Butler, and you were takin' his side!"

The truck honked again, the driver's brow lifting in frustration.

"Margo, let's let the truck pass so that man can be on his way," I suggested.

"No! He can just mow me down!" She held her hands straight out to her sides—like she was being crucified—and closed her eyes. "Goodbye, Harold! Bury your smashed car in my casket!"

The truck driver's mouth dropped open, and then he shook his head as if trying to clear a hallucination.

"I'm not takin' anyone's side, Margo," I said. "Your husband contacted us, and Dixie was interviewin' him to see if we wanted to take the case. That's all."

Her arms lowered slightly, then she lifted them again and leaned her head back. "Well, the fool still doesn't appreciate me. I'm ready to meet my maker."

The truck let out a long horn blast, and I shot him a glare, waving my hand to the street corner behind him. "Back up!"

He lifted his hands with a look of *What the hell?* but he put the truck in reverse and headed toward the end of the street.

Margo's eyes flew open, and she spun around in dismay. "Where's he goin'?"

"Don't worry, honey," Fredericka said soothingly. "There'll be another car. There always is."

"But it's kind of late in the day," another woman said, "so it might be a minute or so."

"It was supposed to be a homogram," Fredericka said.

"I think you mean a metaphor," another woman said.

Fredericka's brow wrinkled. "Are you sure?"

"What difference does it make?" Harold shouted. "I want my Lamborghini back!"

A car engine revved somewhere in the distance.

I had a bad feeling about that . . .

"Margo," I said, prepared to try again, "why don't we go into our office and sort this out in there?"

"Out here's just fine," she said, her eyes narrowed on her husband. "What do you choose, Harold?"

"You made your choice when you started taking that damn art class!" he said.

"Your wife can't have a hobby?" a woman shouted, and a chorus of boos rang out.

The loud car engine was moving closer.

"But what about my dinner?" Harold asked.

More food flew through the air at him—part of a loaf of French bread, a cupcake, and someone's leftovers from Maybelline's—mashed potatoes and meat loaf, from the looks of it.

An old convertible skidded around the corner, tires squealing, and stopped two blocks down in the middle of the street. A woman rose up from behind the wheel, her long dark hair blowing around her, and I realized she was the woman I'd noticed earlier—the one who'd walked away from the crowd. She looked like she was in her midtwenties, and the flat expression on her face said she didn't tolerate bullshit.

"Make your damn choice, Uncle Harold," she called out to him, her voice clearly heard on the now über-quiet street.

Harold wiped cupcake from his cheek and licked his finger. "What the hell are you doin', Amelia?"

Amelia? Amelia Bourdain from Dixie's list? I cast a quick glance to my cousin, who was focused on the latest addition to the madness.

"I'm helpin' Aunt Margo," Amelia shouted. "Either you tell her you love her and you're sorry, or I'm goin' to put her out of her misery." She paused. "Your choice."

Well, crap. Amelia looked crazy enough to run her aunt over, and the look of terror on Dixie's face confirmed it.

"Amelia," I shouted, "let's just talk this over."

She revved the engine, and a sarcastic look covered her face as she cupped her hand to her ear, pretending she couldn't hear me. Obviously there wouldn't be any reasoning with her. I needed to get Margo out of the way.

"Margo," I pleaded, "let's just—"

My words were cut off as the car shot forward with a squeal of tires on the asphalt. I grabbed Margo's arm and tried to pull her, but she flung her arms wide again, bending her knees to lower her center of gravity.

"Margo!" I shouted as the car zoomed closer. I was stuck with a split-second decision: leave Margo to her chosen fate and leap out of the way, or die trying to drag her to safety.

With the car twenty feet away and still speeding toward us, I switched sides and grabbed Margo's arm, pulling her toward my car with all my strength. But my change in direction caught her off guard, and she stumbled.

I was bracing for impact when someone plowed into both of us, sending us flying toward my car. As the convertible zoomed past— not even braking—my back smashed into the trunk of my car. I fell to my bare knees as Margo landed on her butt on the street between the back of my car and the car behind it.

Amelia's convertible skidded to a screeching halt at the next intersection.

I glanced up at the man who'd tackled us, expecting to see Teddy or maybe even a newly inspired Willy, but my mouth dropped open when I realized who it was.

Nash Jackson.

"Are you fucking crazy?" Fire lit his eyes as he got to his feet. "Do you have a damned death wish? That's twice in one day!"

If he expected me to thank him now, he had another think coming. "I was tryin' to save her!"

"And doin' a piss-poor job of it," he said with contempt. He turned to Margo, who was sitting on her butt, staring up at him like he was an angel. Reaching a hand toward her, he grabbed hold of her arm and hauled her to her feet. "Are you okay?" he asked in a gentler voice than he'd used with me.

What the hell?

"I had it covered!" I said as I got to my feet too, my knees stinging from their scrapes.

He shot me a glare and turned back to Margo.

She glanced down at her empty hands and said, "Harold's car . . ."

The yellow Lamborghini sat in the middle of the street, amazingly enough, still intact.

Still stopped at the corner, Amelia lifted her butt off the seat and glanced over her shoulder, her gaze landing on the model. A smile spread across her face as she revved the engine.

"Don't you even think about it, Amelia!" Harold shouted, much more concerned now than he'd been for his wife.

Her grin spread.

Harold took a tentative step out into the street.

Amelia stretched her arm across the bench seat as she stared over her shoulder with a look of determination. She jerked in reverse—tires squealing—and Harold barely had time to skitter back onto the sidewalk before her back tires ran over the model with a satisfying crunch. Then she shot forward, running over it again, and tore through the stop sign, turning the corner at the bank and heading out of town.

Willy stared after her in awe.

"Willy!" I called out to him. "Aren't you gonna do something?"

"Like what?"

"Arrest her? She nearly ran us over!"

"But she didn't," he said, still staring after her with moony eyes.

Go figure.

I was hopping mad, but when I turned to give Nash Jackson a piece of my mind, he was gone.

Again.

Chapter Sixteen

"Start again," Luke said in exasperation. "From the top."

I was sitting on top of my desk while Dixie perched on her chair. She had the first-aid kit open on her lap.

"I want to know what you plan to do about—Ow!" I shouted as Dixie sprayed disinfectant on the scrape on my knee.

"Stop bein' a baby," she said as she blew on it.

I gritted my teeth as the stinging faded. "Willy just stood there watchin' like he was at a theater-in-the-park production of *Thelma and Louise*."

"And which one were you?" Luke asked with a hint of a grin.

"Neither! I was nearly run over, Luke!"

"Amelia Bourdain's crazy, but not that crazy," Luke said.

"She looked pretty damn crazy to me," Bill called out from the editing room.

"Bill's right," Dixie said with a frown. "Sure, she's a loose cannon most of the time, but she was really gonna run Summer and Margo down. If that guy hadn't tackled them, they'd both be roadkill."

Luke perked up. "You're sure she would have run them over? She wasn't bluffin'?"

"We've got the footage in here if you want to see it," Tony called out. "There was no way she could have stopped in time."

"It's great footage too!" Chuck called out in excitement. "This is going to make our season!"

"Happy to entertain," I grumbled. But I had to admit that this would make great TV—probably better than anything Connor could cobble together today.

A scowl lowered Luke's brow as he leaped out of his chair and headed to the back.

I glanced down at Dixie. "Are you okay?" I said in an undertone.

"*Me?* You're the one who nearly got run over."

I lifted my shoulder into a half shrug.

"Was that the guy from Rick Springfield's place who tackled you out of the way?"

"Yeah," I said, but I couldn't bring myself to sound overly appreciative after the way he'd talked to me. "Tell me what you know about Amelia."

The corners of her mouth drew back into a grimace. "She was a grade ahead of me in school. She's had a rough life."

"How so?"

"Deadbeat parents. She practically raised herself. She drove herself to school in that Cadillac when she was fifteen."

"How'd she get away with *that*?"

"Most of the men in this town are either scared of her or infatuated with her, so she does pretty much whatever she wants."

"And which side does Luke fall into?" I was surprised at the sudden pulse of jealousy coursing through my blood.

Her mouth parted in surprise, and then, as if to punish me for questioning Luke's good sense, she placed an alcohol wipe on my other knee.

"Ow!"

Luke emerged from the back, his jaw clenched tight. "I'm gonna need both of your statements, but right now I have to go find Amelia." He was out the door before either of us could say another word.

Dixie watched him walk out, then turned and blew on my knee.

"So," I said, "I take it you were interviewing Harold when Margo showed up."

"Yep." She grabbed a bandage and antibiotic ointment from the box. "I couldn't get ahold of Bruce to set up an interview with him. His phone went straight to voice mail."

I glanced down at my scrapes, and although one of them looked kind of gross, I didn't plan on walking around looking like a preschooler with two bandaged knees. I help up my hand. "Not necessary."

"But—"

"Nope." I slid off the desk and tried not to wince. "At least they took the argument outside. This could have been worse."

"Margo showed up and stood outside shouting at him. He tried to ignore her until she smashed his '68 Camaro on the sidewalk. He was so pissed, I worried he was gonna hit her, but then the crowd gathered, and I texted you. I probably should have called Amber."

I shook my head. "Someone else called her just as you sent the text." I pushed out a sigh. "It never occurred to me that Maybelline might post our clients on her Facebook page."

"I should have thought of it, but I just haven't been myself today," she said dejectedly.

I dragged one of the client chairs in front of her and took her hand. "How are you doin'? *Really?*"

Tears flooded her eyes. "I'm scared."

"Have you remembered anything else?"

She glanced down and shook her head. "No."

Dixie was a people person, and while she'd had Bill with her, it wasn't the same as being with all of us. Still, I wasn't convinced about the wisdom of bringing her with us. I needed to find her another project to keep her busy and distracted. "I haven't found out anything yet. I had to go to the police station to fill out that report about

Elijah. But you need to know that April Jean was there trying to get the mayor to help her."

Her eyes widened. "What does she expect the mayor to do?"

"I don't know, but Elijah has been suspended for a few days."

She pursed her lips and nodded.

"What do you have planned for the rest of the afternoon?" I asked as an idea came to me.

"Harold was the only person available to come by for an interview on such short notice, so nothing."

"How do you feel about being a spy?"

She gave me a hesitant look. "That's a loaded question."

"I'm super curious to know what Connor's up to." I paused, giving her a chance to stop me, but her eyes glittered with interest.

"Go on."

I sat up. "I want you to find him and his team, tell them you blame me for what happened this afternoon, and say you want to switch sides. You can even tell them I can't find any cases and you want to earn your keep. It will make Connor cocky and Lauren gloat. But we'll be onto what they're doin."

The devious glint in her eyes shouldn't have made me so happy, but it was good to see Dixie acting like Dixie. Not feeling defeated. "I'll tell them you decided to cut me out," she said. "They'll be more likely to trust me that way."

"You might need to do a couch interview about what happened and why you want to work with Connor."

She made a face and waved a hand in dismissal. "Not a problem." She grinned. "I'm gonna love this."

I gave her a hesitant look. "Remind me to never get on your bad side."

She laughed, then grabbed her purse out of her desk drawer. "I'll see you later."

I stood, my stomach flip-flopping. "Are you sure you want to do this? The idea *just* came to me. Maybe we should discuss it more."

"What's there to discuss?" she asked with her hand already on the doorknob. "It's brilliant. I'll know what they're up to, and you can find out if I burned down April Jean's trailer."

My heart squeezed tight. "Dixie . . ."

She lifted her chin with a defiant look. "Stop. Either I did or I didn't, but I'm countin' on you to find out the truth."

"Don't talk to anyone about this, okay?" I asked. "Just let Teddy and me sort it all out. We don't want anyone accusing you of anything."

"April Jean's already accusin' me. I don't know who you think you're foolin'. When you start askin' questions, people are gonna know what you're up to."

"You let me worry about that part," I said, but I was already thinking about how much faster my work would go with two cameramen.

Her eyes softened. "Summer . . . thank you. You doin' this means a lot."

"I failed you before, Dix. I won't fail you again."

Tears glistened in her eyes. She looked like she was about to say something, but then she gave me a sharp nod and walked out the door.

A few seconds later, Bill emerged from the back room. "You let her go to Connor?"

"You think it was a bad idea?"

"No, I think it was brilliant, but I know how much you hate the guy. You know he's gonna gloat and hold this over your head."

I shrugged, refusing to admit how hard it would be to deal with his attitude. "She's a spy. And she'll be distracted and feel useful. It's a win-win. I can live with his gloating in the short term, especially since I'll get the last laugh."

"I agree," Bill said as he stared out the window. "She wasn't herself this afternoon. She needs something to keep her mind off all this." His glance shifted to me. "So what do you want to do now?"

"I want to talk to Gabby, but she's at work."

"At the insurance office," Tony said, rounding the corner.

I could see he had a plan. "Yeah . . . ?"

"I think we should go see Thelma Kuntz, the insurance agent, and talk to her about Bruce's fire."

"But that's Connor's case. We're already pushing it if we interview Bruce."

Tony grinned. "Your real interview is her assistant, Gabby Casey." He turned to Bill, who hadn't been at the police station with us. "Gabby was at Trent's party last night, and she and April Jean don't get along. They got into a fight at the Piggly Wiggly last week."

"Because Gabby's jealous over her boyfriend sleepin' with April Jean. The fact that Gabby's got a thing for Trent Dunbar, and April Jean and Dixie do too, doesn't help," Bill said, sounding defeated. My eyebrows shot up, and he shrugged. "She told me everything."

I tilted my head. "Define *everything*."

"I know Dixie's been seeing Trent Dunbar since he came back to town."

I sucked in a breath and slowly released it. "I'm sorry."

The side of his mouth scrunched in self-disgust. "I'm not surprised. I know I'm not the handsomest guy around. Girls like Dixie go for guys like Trent Dunbar."

I started to argue, but he wasn't entirely wrong. Bill wasn't unattractive, but he was average-looking. If he were standing next to Trent in a Mr. Hot Stuff contest, it wouldn't even be close. But the only thing Trent had going for him was a pretty face, and I sure hoped Dixie was smarter than to base her choice on that. Whatever her reasons for taking up with Trent again, she'd hurt Bill in the process. "I'm sorry," I repeated. "Maybe you'd rather not work on this case."

"And what would I work on?" he asked bitterly. "Because unlike Dixie, I'm not switching sides, and I'm not quitting either. This case is our key to a successful Season Two."

My guilt was overwhelming. "Bill . . ."

"Stop," he said. "I'm a professional. I can deal with this."

"If you can't deal with it, let me know."

"And have you fire me? I assure you, I can separate my professional life from the personal. We need to go to the insurance office and meet with Gabby Casey."

"I'm still not sure I get the point of interviewing Thelma first," I said.

"That's because you're still thinking logically," Tony said. "You need to think like a reality show. What's more entertaining? Interviewing Gabby at her house, or going to her work and talking to her boss, and *boom*, all of a sudden Gabby's giving us unexpected information."

I crossed my arms over my chest. "It feels wrong."

"Nevertheless," Tony said, "it's what you signed up for. Sure, we've got a real case, and this afternoon will make for some good entertainment, but we need more drama or people are going to fall asleep in their La-Z-Boys watching." When I didn't respond, he shifted his weight and lowered his voice. "Look, what you, Bill, and Dixie did last season was really good, but it could have been better."

I gasped and started to protest, but Tony held up his hand as Chuck walked around the corner and joined him.

"He's right," Chuck said. "This *is* a reality TV show, not a documentary or an investigative-reporting show. You need the personal crap and drama to flesh it out."

"We can still make this real," Tony said, "but we need it to be entertaining."

I dropped my arms to my side. "I see your point, but I don't like it."

Tony nodded. "Duly noted. Now set up the interview at the insurance office."

I nodded my head. "Fine, I'll set up the interview, but I don't think she's gonna talk on camera at her office."

Bill gave me a smile that suggested I was an idiot. "Don't you remember the guy from April who talked about using drugs and where he got them? All while on camera. If you let the cameras roll long enough, they forget they're there. Some of the things you and Dixie have said . . . I know you've forgotten too."

He had a point. "I still think it would be better to catch her somewhere else."

"If nothing else, you'll piss off Connor. That has to be a plus."

I gave him a long look, then pulled my cell phone out of my pocket. "I'll call Thelma and see if we can talk to her before she leaves the office, but we should also arrange to talk to someone who was at the party and is sympathetic to Dixie. Did she happen to mention if anyone fits the bill?"

"Yeah," he said, his voice losing the sharp edge he'd had before. "Clementine Roland. Dixie said they were friends."

"Did she happen to mention anything about Clementine?"

"Nope."

I would need to track down Clementine, and I didn't want to ask Dixie. While I considered asking Amber, I wanted to save her goodwill for when I really needed it. Then I realized I could probably find her on the *Sweet Happenings* Facebook page.

Sitting down at my desk, I booted up the computer and searched for the Sweet Briar page. I wasn't surprised to see that the showdown in the street with Amelia was the top post, but the number of photographs caught me off guard. If TMZ was watching the page—and they would if they were smart (not that I planned to tip them off)—I suspected this would be national news by this evening.

How would Connor feel about that? He was here to get his next fifteen minutes of fame and promote his book. I scrolled down the page to see if there was any mention of him. Other than a visitor post comparing him to a Jehovah's Witness—he'd stolen her coffee and replaced it with green tea, then tried to convert her to the Connor Life all while on camera—there was nothing. If Connor knew about the page, he'd be pissed by the lack of coverage.

But I was getting off track, so I clicked to see who had liked the page and began to scroll. I was thankful that word about the page hadn't gotten out because Sweet Briar had fewer than three thousand residents, and the page only had 1,273 likes. When it became public knowledge, that number would skyrocket. As it was, it took me seconds to find Clementine Roland. Thankfully she hadn't made her profile very private, and I could see she worked at Precious Darlings Daycare.

I rolled my eyes. No doubt that was a play on my old nickname.

She had lots of photos of her with her mother, several girls—including Dixie—and some of the kids at daycare, which I wasn't sure was legal, but it *was* Sweet Briar.

I jotted the information on a notepad, then looked up the daycare and decided to take a chance and call. Sweet Briar was a small town, and sometimes folks were a little freer with information—just like Clementine clearly was with her photos.

Bill started filming as I made the call on speakerphone.

A cheerful woman answered. "Precious Darlin's Daycare."

"Hi, may I speak to Clementine?"

"This is her."

I took a moment to regroup. I hadn't planned on having such easy access to her. "Hey, Clementine, this is Summer Butler. Dixie Baumgartner's cous—"

"Oh, I know who you are. Dixie's so excited that you're back."

My chest warmed, and I felt a little emotional when I said, "I'm glad to be back. But Dixie's the reason I'm calling."

"Oh?"

"She was at Trent Dunbar's party last night, and she said you were there too."

Clementine was silent for a moment, then lowered her voice. "I was."

"Do you think I could ask you a few questions about the party? What time do you get off?"

"I was just leavin' now. But I can't talk to you here."

I sat up straighter, and Bill perked up. "Tell me when and where."

"I haven't eaten all day. Meet me at Maybelline's in ten minutes." Her voice hardened. "I know you're goin' around town with your cameras, and I'll tell you what I know, but not on camera. My boss can't know."

"Okay. Done. See you in ten minutes." I hung up and lifted my gaze to the guys, who looked like they'd just been rejected at a school dance. "Sorry, guys. She works at a daycare. If she was part of something seedy, she's not gonna want her boss—and the parents—findin' out."

"We can hide a camera," Tony said.

"She'll never sign a release."

"We could at least leave your mike hot," Chuck said. "Then we can take her voice and layer it over some shots of the diner or something."

My jaw tightened. "No."

Tony started to say something, but I held up my hand. "Yeah, Tony, I know this is a reality TV show, but it's also Dixie's life. I know she didn't start that fire. I know someone drugged her. I plan to prove it, camera or no, with or without you." I took a breath. "If Clementine has something good, maybe we can convince her to an on-camera interview if we can hide her identity. Smudge her face and distort her voice. But I agreed to no cameras for this first interview. I'm not goin' back on that."

"This is bad TV," Tony said.

"But it makes me a decent human being." I frowned, worried that Tony's attitude leaned more closely toward Lauren's than my own, but pleased to know that at least *I* had some boundaries. "Why don't y'all take a break, and we'll meet back here at six forty-five before we head to Garrett's house."

"What about the insurance agent and her assistant?" Bill asked.

"It's almost four. I'm sure they close at five, but I can call and set something up for tomorrow." But Gabby Casey would be at work tomorrow, and I still doubted she'd do much on-camera talking in front of her boss. Besides, I didn't want to wait that long. "How about I call Thelma and ask for an interview tomorrow. You guys can head over there to get some B-roll while I'm at Maybelline's. It'll be close to closing, so Thelma probably won't want to talk, but you can try to find out what Gabby's doin' tonight. Maybe we can interview her after we talk to Garrett."

"If I ask her, you do realize I'm gonna look like an old fart hitting on her, right?" Tony said.

My mouth twisted to the side as I studied him. He was right. Tony was in his late thirties or early forties and had a dad-bod thing going on. "Then have Bill find out."

Bill started to protest, and I held up my hand. "We're getting ahead of ourselves. Let me see if you can go over first."

I called the insurance agency and asked to speak to Thelma. When we were connected, I introduced myself and asked her if I could set up an interview with her.

"I already spoke with that old costar of yours . . . strange fellow . . . talking some nonsense about the Connor Life."

Connor would end up without any cases because he was pissing off half the town. If he kept it up, no one would talk to him. "While he's workin' Bruce Jepper's case, I'm interviewing professionals who have come into contact with people affected by devastating fires. In fact, I'm speaking with Garrett Newcomer, a volunteer firefighter, tonight."

"Well . . . ," she drawled out, "I'd rather help you than that lame-brain, but I'll tell you up front what I told him—I can't speak about any specific cases."

"Like I said, I'm not goin' that angle, so that won't be a problem."

"When would you like to come over?"

"I have a quick interview in a few minutes, but it's off camera, so if it's okay with you, I want to send my camera crew over to get some B-roll—the background shots we use between interviews. I promise they'll be out of your hair by five so y'all won't have to stay late. Then you and I can talk tomorrow."

"We're open until six on Tuesdays," Thelma said. "So no worry there. Send your crew on over, and you can interview me when you're done with your other one."

I brightened, and the guys perked up. "Thanks, Miss Thelma. I'll send them over and see you in a little bit."

I hung up and relayed the information, and the guys started to pack up.

I checked the time and stuffed my notepad in my purse. I couldn't record my meeting with Clementine, but I *could* take notes so long as she didn't object. "I'm heading to Maybelline's. I'll meet you over at the insurance office. You guys take my car. It's only two blocks from the restaurant, so I'll walk."

I handed Tony the keys as I headed out the door, but I found myself lingering on the sidewalk outside the office, staring at Dixie's empty desk through the office window. I had a feeling something bad was coming, and I had no idea how to stop it.

Chapter Seventeen

Four o'clock was the perfect time for a semiprivate conversation at Maybelline's Diner. It was well past the lunch hour and still too early for most folks to want dinner, with the exception of a few senior citizens, and they were usually hard of hearing.

A young woman wearing jeans and a T-shirt covered in teddy bears was sitting in a booth facing the door. Her light-brown hair was pulled back in a ponytail. Her mouth was drawn, and the moment she laid eyes on me, she looked close to bolting.

I gave her a soft smile and approached her table slowly. "Clementine?"

She leaned forward to look around me. "Where's Dixie?"

Oh, crap. It had never occurred to me that she'd expect Dixie to be with me, but then of course she would. Dixie and I had been like eggs and bacon back in April.

I stopped at the edge of the table. "She's workin' on another case. We both agreed she shouldn't be workin' on something related to her."

She gave a quick nod, reached into her purse, and pulled out a cigarette. Then, as though realizing where she was, she stuffed it back in her purse.

"Would you be more comfortable talking somewhere else?" I asked. "Somewhere you can smoke?"

She shook her head and folded her hands on the table. "No. I'm hungry."

I tilted my head toward the seat across from her. "Is it okay if I sit?"

She nodded, then her eyes darted toward the door.

Why was she so nervous? That, and the fact that she hadn't asked me why I wanted to talk to her, told me that she definitely knew something.

I slid into the booth seat and grimaced when my knee hit the pole under the table.

"I heard about Amelia nearly runnin' you down this afternoon," she said.

I gave a half shrug, seeing no reason to comment any further. The whole town had no doubt heard about it, and soon it would probably become wider news. I settled onto the seat and tried to figure out how to proceed. Clementine was so spooked, I worried she'd take off running—whether she'd eaten or not. I needed to seem harmless.

Maybelline sauntered over with a glass of tea in one hand and water in the other. Her usual carrot-orange hair had a redder tint than usual, and her blue waitress dress was stained with something brown. She set the tea in front of me and the water in front of Clementine, then put a hand on her hip. "What can I get you girls?"

"Nothing for me," I said, "but Clementine's hungry, and I'm paying."

Clementine's eyes narrowed slightly, but she ordered a club sandwich and fries along with a Coke.

Maybelline turned to go back to the kitchen, but I called out, "Bring me a nonsweet tea, please."

She stopped and glanced over her shoulder. "There's only one kind of tea, Summer Baumgartner, and that's the kind you have in front of ya. Don't you dare suggest something they serve out in

Cal-eh-forn-I-ay." She butchered the pronunciation of *California* with a lot of attitude before stomping back into the kitchen with a huff.

I cringed, but a genuine smile spread across Clementine's face. "That's sure to make the Facebook page," she said.

Her comment sobered me. "And so is me meetin' you here. Are you okay with that?"

She shrugged. "They don't know what we're talkin' about."

"But some people might figure it out."

Her eyebrows rose. "Like Trent? I don't care. I just don't want my boss to figure out I was at that party on a weeknight. Or that I showed up to work this mornin' still stoned. I like my job. I don't want to lose it."

I wasn't sure I'd want a stoned employee watching my kids, but I sure wasn't going to heap any judgment on her. I wanted answers. "I won't tell anyone what we discuss here."

"Even your camerapeople?"

I hesitated. "Not specifically, but I'm not gonna lie to you. I'm looking for leads, and I plan to follow up on anything you tell me that might be helpful. I'll keep your name out of it as much as I can, and I won't use your name on camera unless you give me express permission. Are you okay with all that?"

She swiped at the condensation on her glass, staring at it for a moment or two before she nodded. "Yeah. Okay."

"How long have you known Dixie?"

She looked up and smiled. "Since kindergarten. Dixie has always been bigger than life, ya know?"

I smiled back. "Yeah. I do."

"Back then she wasn't scared of nothin', and she refused to take crap from bullies. She'd stand up to anyone." She dropped her hand from the glass. "I think that's why Troy couldn't get a handle on her."

"You mean Trent," I said.

"No. Troy. Trent's brother."

A cold shiver went down my back. "*Troy?* What are you talking about?"

"Troy couldn't stand Dixie, although no one knew. He hid it well."

"Before or after the fire?" I asked, my fingers numb.

"Oh . . . before. Troy was *long gone* by the time Dixie came home from her time at juvie."

"So you could tell he didn't like Dixie, but everyone else thought he did?"

"I'm not sure anyone gave it much thought, to be honest. Troy and his friends were three years older than us, so they didn't hang out with us much. But sometimes when Troy and Trent's parents were gone, they'd throw joint parties. It was at one of those parties that she fell onto his radar."

"What happened?"

She shrugged again, starting to look uncomfortable. "Maybe you should talk to Dixie about this."

I swallowed, my stomach in knots. "She gave me permission to talk to people about her. We want to get to the bottom of things, one way or the other."

Her dark-brown eyes searched my face, as if trying to gauge my seriousness, then she nodded. "Everybody was drunk and high, and things got a little crazy."

"Back when you were in high school? At a party at the Dunbar ranch?"

A wry grin twisted her lips. "I've always found it funny that they insist on callin' it a ranch. Like we were in the Wild West."

"So what happened at the ranch?"

"Troy was hittin' on some girl, only she was so drunk, she didn't say no."

"He raped her?" I said, my mouth going dry.

"No. It didn't get that far. Dixie realized what was happening and put a stop to it. Troy didn't like it one bit, and he got physical with her, saying she could take her place instead. Then he started to haul her to his room."

"Oh, my God . . ."

Clementine's eyes flew wide, and she covered my hand on the table with her own. "Oh, no. He didn't do it. Dixie stopped him before he even reached the hall. Teddy had taught her a bunch of self-defense moves, and she brought Troy to his knees—literally—and made him beg for mercy before she let him go. When she did, I thought Troy was gonna backhand her, but Trent stopped him. And that's when Trent and Dixie became a thing."

"And she was fifteen?"

"Yeah. It was only a month or so before the fire."

"Troy graduated with Teddy. Wasn't Troy in college at the time?"

She made a face. "Troy was an on-and-off-again student. Plus, he didn't go to college right away. He stayed home to 'find himself'"—she used air quotes—"but it was more like 'get himself in trouble.' He went to college the next year, and everyone was sure that his daddy made him leave so he wouldn't get arrested anymore."

My mind was spinning with wild ideas. "What do you know about the barn fire?"

Clementine squirmed. "Only what Dixie's told me." But the way she said it made me believe she was fudging the truth.

"Which is?"

"That she and Trent were partying, and she blacked out. When she came to, she reeked of gasoline, and the barn was on fire."

"And where was Trent?"

She gave me a questioning look. "I don't know. Dixie never said."

"Did you believe Dixie started the fire?"

"Everyone said she did . . ."

I heard the hesitation in her voice. "But?"

"But it just didn't seem like her. She loved her parents and grandfather. She never would have intentionally hurt them, even if she was high. Even if she wasn't thinking it would *kill* them. The drugs changed her, but never like that."

"You said the drugs changed her. How so?"

"You know. Typical user stuff. Sneaky. Secretive. She got a bit of an attitude, but that was Trent's influence. Still, I never would have suspected she was capable of arson, especially at the farm."

"And you never questioned the official story?"

"Luke was so sure she did it," she said with an innocent earnestness. "And Dixie believed it too."

I felt sick to my stomach. "Where was Troy the night of the fire?" I asked. "If he hated Dixie, he could have set her up. He was the one who gave Trent the drugs that night."

"I don't know, probably around."

He must have had an alibi if Luke had let him off, but I kept my thoughts to myself. I had learned my lesson about blurting out suspicions.

But Clementine must have figured out where my head was going, because her mouth dropped open. "You think Troy started it?"

"Was he ever a suspect?"

"Not as far as I know, but I was a kid, you know? I wasn't payin' much attention to anyone but Dixie."

"He'd sure have a motive," I said, then a thought hit me. "Wait. You said no one suspected he didn't like Dixie. How could that be after she humiliated him like that?"

"That one's easy," she said. "Once she started hangin' around with Trent, Troy publicly forgave her and said she was a perfect fit for the Dunbar family. Everyone believed him."

"But not you?"

"Nah. Troy was known for his grudges."

Which made him suspect number one for the barn fire. But I still had no idea who'd drugged Dixie the night before. I could rule out Troy since he was dead. "Did you know that Trent visited Dixie at juvie?" I asked.

"No," she said with a look of surprise. "But she never wanted to talk about those two years."

"Do you think Trent loved Dixie?"

She chuckled, but it sounded bitter. "Trent Dunbar loves one person—Trent Dunbar. He's incapable of loving anyone else."

So then why was he so loyal to Dixie? But the answer hit me as soon as I asked myself the question. Guilt—not because he'd supplied the drugs, but because his brother had started the fire and set Dixie up to take the fall for hurting her own family.

Now I had to prove it.

Maybelline emerged from the kitchen with two plates and slid them onto the table—a sandwich and fries for Clementine and an order of fries for me.

"I didn't order these," I said.

Maybelline rolled her eyes. "Girl, you need more meat on those bones. Eat the fries."

"We've already been over this, Maybelline. I have to watch my weight for my job."

"You've already got a job," she said, crossing her arms over her ample breasts. "You've got two of them—that show and your PI office—and neither one of them say you have to look like a damn toothpick. *Now eat.*"

I jumped, picked up a fry, and stuffed it into my mouth while she watched with narrowed eyes. As soon as the fry was in my mouth, she gave me a curt nod and dropped her arms. "That's a good start. Now keep goin'."

I ate another fry as she headed into the back, then turned to see Clementine watching me with fear in her eyes.

"She scares me."

I grinned. "She scares me too."

I let Clementine devour half her sandwich before I resumed asking questions. "Can you tell me what you remember about last night at Trent's party?"

Her gaze dropped to her plate. "Like what?"

"Like when you got there and what happened. What you remember about Dixie."

"It started pretty late—not weekend late—but late for a work night. A lot of us were sayin' we needed to head home, but no one did."

"What time did the party start?"

"About nine."

"And why didn't all y'all leave?" I asked.

"Because Trent can hold a grudge too, and he said we were all a bunch of pussies. We knew if we left, he'd likely never invite us again."

"So what were y'all doin'?" I asked.

She shrugged. "You know, partyin'."

"Was there a bonfire?"

She made a face that suggested my question was ridiculous. "While it wasn't that warm last night, it was far too hot for a fire."

"So there wasn't a fire of any kind?" I asked.

Her gaze narrowed. "Why do you keep askin' about a fire? Is it because April Jean's trailer caught fire?"

I wasn't about to tell her Dixie had smelled like smoke. "Just curious. So y'all showed up around nine?"

"Yeah."

"And you sat around and partied."

"Basically."

"On Trent's property."

"At the pond behind his house."

"His parents didn't mind?"

She gave me a wry grin. "Typical Dunbar party—his parents weren't home. Business trip."

200

"Who was there?"

She gave me a leery glance.

"Dixie already gave me a list," I said, pulling out my phone. "How about I read it to you and you can tell me if I'm missing someone."

"Okay . . ." But I could tell she wasn't happy about it.

I leaned forward and lowered my voice. "No one will know I got any names from you. I'll say I got them all from Dixie, and for all we know, I already have the entire guest list."

She gave me a hesitant nod.

"Gabby Casey and Mark Willis."

She nodded again. "They were fightin' like cats and dogs. Mark's jealous as shit over Trent, and Gabby's jealous of April Jean."

"Who was also there."

"Oh, yeah. She was hangin' on Trent like a sock out of the dryer."

"And how did Dixie react to that?"

She fiddled with a fry on her plate, then looked up at me. "Do you think Dixie started April Jean's fire?"

Her question caught me off guard. "Do *you*?"

"No . . . but she started the barn fire, and she was acting so weird last night."

"How so?"

"She was ticked at April Jean for hangin' on Trent, and irritated at Trent for lettin' her, but she really got mad when he started givin' out drugs."

"Has he done that before?"

"Never when she was around. He's been weird about drugs around her. He'll drink like a fish but no drugs. Until last night."

"So what made last night different?"

"I don't know. He said something weird like he didn't owe her shit anymore. She got upset, and he told her to chill. She wanted to go home, but he refused to take her."

I wanted to beat the crap out of him.

"And no one offered to take her instead?" I asked, irritation bleeding into my words.

A guilty look washed over her face. "Like I said, no one wanted to tick him off."

"Why? What's so damn special about Trent Dunbar?"

Her face reddened. "He's gonna take over Dunbar Lumber someday."

Money.

The guilt in her eyes increased. "We're the inner circle. We were his friends back in high school, and he hasn't forgotten us."

And here I'd somewhat respected her for being Dixie's friend. "So back to last night . . . Dixie got upset, and Trent gave her a Coke, told her to chill, and proceeded to ignore her. Then she got into a disagreement with April Jean."

Clementine frowned. "Yes and no."

"What's the no part?"

"After she had her fight with Trent, she went inside to go to the bathroom. She was gone for about ten minutes, so I thought maybe she'd left. When she came back out, she had red eyes like she'd been crying, but she seemed different."

"How so?" I asked.

"When she went inside, she seemed defeated, but when she came out, she had her fire back, you know? Like she wasn't takin' crap from anyone. That's why she got into it with April Jean. April Jean was giving Dixie shit about Trent, and Dixie said she could have him."

That fell in line with what Dixie had told me, other than the going-inside part. "Did she take her drink with her inside?"

"Yeah, I guess so."

I leaned forward again. "No guessing. I need to know who had access to Dixie's drink."

"I was kind of out of it, you know?"

She was stoned, but it wouldn't do me any good to point that out. I needed every piece of information I could get. "This is really important. Trent handed Dixie the Coke, and then what? She sat down?"

"Yeah, and she was holding it against her chest until she went inside."

"That's helpful," I said, trying to soften my words. "She had the drink when she came back out?"

"Yeah. She sat down again and took a few sips before setting it on the ground next to her chair."

"Could someone have picked it up?"

"I'm not sure. Maybe. About ten minutes later, she got into it with April Jean. Then she sat down and fell asleep in her chair. She was still there when I left."

"And when was that?"

"I don't know . . . around midnight. I told Trent I had to be at work, and then he finally agreed to let me and some of the others go."

Agreed to let her go. Really? "You didn't think to take Dixie home?" I asked, trying to hide my outrage.

Her shoulders stiffened. "I was goin' to, but Trent said he'd do it."

I really needed to have another talk with Trent. "How many other people were at the party? Who were they?"

"About twelve or so." She took a breath as if gathering her courage. "Monica and Blane Hyde. Rebecca Smelt. Matt Greenwood. And Amelia. Oh, and Rick Springfield." She paused. "That's it."

That lined up with the list Dixie had given me. Neither of them had mentioned Nash Jackson. "What about Rick's cousin?"

Her eyes narrowed in disbelief. "Why would Rick's cousin show up at Trent's party?"

Her tone indicated she was talking about the bald one Amber had mentioned. "Not Herbert. Nash."

"Who's Nash?"

Why had no one heard of this guy? I shook my head. "Rick's cousin, Nash Jackson, has been hanging around, and no one seems to know who he is. Could he have been there?"

She shrugged. "Maybe . . . ? Rick didn't stay long. He showed up early but left while Dixie was in the bathroom."

"Rick was in the house while Dixie was there?"

"He may not have gone in the house. Most of us use the gate at the side of the house. The Dunbars added one of those fancy iron fences a few years back."

"But he could have gone inside." And if Dixie had left her drink on a counter or table, he would have had access to drug her. But why drug her if he was leaving? So far I had more questions than answers. "Who was still there when you left?"

"Amelia. And Gabby and Mark. Wait . . . ," she said, her eyes widening. "Bruce showed up around the time I was leavin'."

"Bruce Jepper?" He wasn't on Dixie's list, but then he wouldn't have been if he'd arrived after she lost consciousness.

"Yeah. He looked pissed and drunk, but his house had just burned down, so who could blame him? We met him in the driveway, and he wanted to know where he could find Trent. He was talking about a poker game."

"How did Bruce feel about Dixie?"

"They dated for a bit. It didn't end well." She grimaced. "That happens a lot with Dixie."

"How so?"

She shrugged. "A lot of guys really like Dixie, but she can't seem to commit. I used to wonder if she was waitin' for Trent to grow up and marry her, but now I wonder if she just needed to let go of him, you know?"

"Yeah." It only brought home how much I didn't know about my cousin's life. But that was one of the reasons I'd come home—to get to know my cousins better. But first I needed to find out who'd drugged

Dixie . . . and why. "Do you know if anyone else was in the house when she went to the bathroom?"

"I don't remember," she said. "Maybe. People were comin' and goin', gettin' more drinks. Trent had beer on tap in his dad's bar inside."

My phone vibrated in my pocket, and I pulled it out to see a text from Bill.

> We've gotten as much B-roll as we need. Are you going to make it over, or should we leave?

I glanced up at Clementine. I doubted she had much else to tell me.

> I'm wrapping up and I'm about to walk over. We REALLY need to talk to Gabby and Mark. Especially if they were part of the small group who'd stayed at the party late into the night.

After I stuffed my phone back into my pocket, I pulled out a business card and slid it across the table to Clementine. "If you think of anything else that you think might be helpful, could you let me know?"

She picked up the card and scanned it before lifting her eyes to mine. "What exactly are you lookin' for?"

I hadn't told her about Dixie being drugged, and although I was sure she could figure it out from my line of questioning, I wasn't ready to just announce it yet. I reached into my purse, pulled out a twenty-dollar bill, and set it on the table. "I think someone wants to hurt Dixie, and I'm trying to figure out who it is."

"Then April Jean is your number one suspect, because she *hates* that girl."

I stood and gave her a grim smile. "Thanks. I'll keep that in mind."

I headed back in the direction of the office, then turned right. The insurance office was two blocks to the east, a few buildings down from the theater.

After I'd walked one block, I caught the faint hint of smoke. I crossed the street, and something caught my eye halfway down the block. Someone wearing a gray hoodie darted out of an abandoned thrift store—a guy, based on his height and his broader upper body. He took off running toward the end of the street, sticking close to the buildings and staying in the shadows.

Why would someone wear a hoodie in this heat, and why was he sneaking off? This guy was obviously up to something.

"Hey!" I called out, heading toward him, but he raced across the street and around the corner, over to Main Street.

I stopped, realizing it was pointless to pursue him. Just as I was about to turn around and continue toward the insurance office, the burning smell became stronger, and wisps of smoke floated up from the thrift store.

Oh, crap. I'd just seen the arsonist in action, and I knew for a fact it hadn't been Dixie.

Chapter Eighteen

I dug out my phone as I ran down the street, dialing 911. The building was quickly becoming engulfed in flames. The dispatcher answered within two rings.

"I just saw someone set a fire," I said, trying to stay calm as the smoke grew thicker. The building was sandwiched between another vacant building and a bakery that had closed at two. I glanced at the address painted above the doorway, which was difficult to see through the smoke escaping out of the broken window in the door. "It's at 501 Pine Street. The old thrift shop. Send someone quick. It's spreading fast."

"We'll have someone there right away."

I hung up and called Bill. "Get over to Pine Street. I just saw someone set the abandoned thrift store on fire!"

"*What?*"

I heard sirens in the distance. "Hurry."

Just as I was hanging up, I saw a car turn the corner. It barely came to a halt before Connor's crew jumped out and started unpacking their gear, but there was no sign of Connor himself. Nearly a minute later, Connor rounded the corner, his chest heaving with exertion. Lauren said something to him, and he jogged toward the front of the burning building. She shot me a glare when she saw me.

Connor took one look at me, and anger filled his eyes. "Back off, Summer!"

He pulled his cell phone out of his pocket to check his appearance in the screen, but something else fell out of his pocket and hit the ground.

A lighter.

"And we're rolling," Lauren shouted as she shot me a dirty look. She held up three fingers and began to count down. "Three, two . . ."

Connor's face lit up with his fake smile, and he started talking to the cameras. "The arsonist has struck again in the once-sleepy town of Sweet Briar."

"How do you know it's an arsonist?" I called out to him.

"Go away, Summer!" he shouted.

I moved closer to him, surprised to see his face covered in sweat. It was hot outside, but not hot enough for him to be *that* sweaty. How long had he been out in the heat? "How do you know the fire was started by an arsonist?"

"Because there's an arsonist running around town!"

That was true, but why did he seem so manic about it? Was he that desperate for a good case? "But a lot of fires are accidental. You can't know for certain that it was arson."

"Get out of here, Summer! Go get your own story!"

My crew pulled into a parking space toward the end of the street, so I left Connor to his guessing game and headed down toward them. Bill got out, cursing under his breath. "Lauren beat us here."

"Connor's certain it was the arsonist, and of course he's right, but he's just guessing. He doesn't know anything."

Connor continued with a stream of word vomit, clearly uncertain about what he was supposed to be saying. "*We* arrived first to the scene to look for clues." He glanced behind him toward the burning building. "Yes, the building is on fire, our first clue that this heinous act was perpetrated by an arsonist."

"I'm surprised Connor knows such a big word," Tony said.

"And he seems to think he's a news reporter," Chuck said with a grin.

Lauren stood behind the cameras, reached into the bag hanging from her shoulder, and pulled out a flask. She took a long drag, then stuffed it back into her purse and started barking orders.

I took satisfaction in the confirmation that working with Connor was a nightmare. Maybe it would help her appreciate me more.

"I wonder if he started it," Tony said.

I turned to him in surprise. "What makes you say that?"

He shrugged. "I know someone on the camera crew working with Connor. She texted earlier to ask about you nearly getting run over in the street." He held up a hand when I started to protest. "I didn't tell her anything. I'm loyal to you, especially since it sounds like her day was a snooze. She texted that Connor said not to worry, he had his own excitement planned."

"You think Connor Blake started this fire?" Bill asked with a deadpan expression.

Oh, my God. What if Tony was right?

"I saw someone," I said. "A man, I think, in a gray hoodie. I saw him run out of the building, and then he took off, sticking to the shadows."

"Really?" Bill asked with excitement in his voice.

"Yeah. Connor's team showed up as soon as I called the fire in, but he didn't show up until nearly a minute later, running and out of breath. He was all hot and sweaty. And . . ." I paused, wondering if I should share this next part, but why not? We were just speculating, and this was too good not to mention. "He pulled his cell phone out of his pocket, and a lighter fell out."

"So the lighter was on top of the cell phone," Tony said. "Because he'd just set the fire."

"Maybe," I said. "But we can't jump to that conclusion."

"We know he's not a smoker," Chuck said. "Thanks to the Connor Life."

Tony chuckled. "My friend Dee said he threw a fit this morning when they stopped at a convenience store so Karen could go to the bathroom. He complained about being too close to the gas fumes."

"Did you see how tall the guy was?" Bill asked. "Was he Connor's height?"

I grimaced. "It all happened so fast, and then he darted into the shadows."

"What kind of pants did he have on?" Bill asked.

"Jeans."

Connor was a sweaty mess, his perfect hair now damp and plastered to his forehead. He kept shooting nervous glances at the fire like it was going to jump out and cause him to burst into flames.

Tony eyed my ex-costar suspiciously. "Connor has on jeans."

"And so do half of the other people in this town," Chuck said.

"But those people don't look as suspicious as he does."

"That doesn't make any sense," I said. "Connor just got into town a day or two ago. The first fire was last Friday."

"Connor got into town last Friday," Tony said. "Dee said Karen was complaining about trying to keep him under wraps so Lauren could surprise you with him on Monday."

"That's a stretch, don't you think?" I asked. "He's probably nervous because he's terrible at this. Look." I gestured toward him.

Connor had started rambling about items that could have caught on fire inside the building. ". . . a desk, possibly an office chair . . . although the metal wouldn't catch on fire . . ." He swiped his forehead with the back of his hand. "There could be *pencils* in there. Made of *wood*. I'm sure those are *very* flammable."

Bill stared at him in disbelief. "He's not known for thinking things through. The tabloids have been full of stories of Connor Blake going off the deep end. Maybe he decided to create his own stories."

"Before the show even started?" I asked. "Lauren gave him all the good stories. Why would he bother?"

"Maybe he didn't know that," Tony said. "Dee said he's obsessed with having better segments than you. And you're coming up with your own. He can't let you best him with that too."

I sucked in a breath and instantly regretted it when I got a lungful of smoky air. I coughed.

"And there's something else," Tony added. "You said he was at the fire yesterday. He was working the scene before you got there."

"And," Bill said, "he was insistent that *he* get the fire cases."

"True." Still, we couldn't just accuse him of arson. "Maybe Dixie knows something," I said, scanning the growing crowd. "I don't see her anywhere." Had Lauren turned her away? Surely Dixie would have told me before now. I sent her a quick text.

Where are you? There's a fire downtown on Pine Street, and I saw the arsonist.

A fire truck pulled up in front of the fire from the opposite side of the street, and we watched the firefighters jump out and start suiting up. More cars pulled into the nearby parking spots as people stopped to check out the latest excitement.

"I'm telling you," Tony said, gesturing to Connor. "He looks guilty as shit."

He had a point. Connor's shirt was soaked through, although to be fair, he was standing close to a now-raging fire. Still, there was no denying that the look on his face read pure guilt. We might be onto something.

"I saw the person who started the fire," I said, "but I never saw his face, so we should be careful about accusing Connor without more proof. He's liable to sue us for slander." Lord knew I had enough potential lawsuits on my hands.

"You saw who started the fire?" a male voice asked behind me. I turned around to see Garrett Newcomer opening the trunk of the car next to us.

"Oh, hey . . . yeah."

He pulled out a pair of pants attached to boots from the trunk and dropped them to the ground. "What did you see?"

As he kicked off his shoes and stepped into the pants, I told him what I'd told my crew.

His mouth pinched with concern as he pulled his suspenders over his shoulders. "This is the fourth fire in less than a week. This guy is dangerous. Where's Luke?" He looked around the crowd as he grabbed his fireman's jacket out of his open trunk. "You need to tell *him*."

"I plan to."

"But *you* saw the arsonist," Tony said, obviously gloating. "You need to let us interview you on camera with the fire in the background." A huge grin spread across his face. "Connor can't report seeing himself."

I shot him a dark look.

"Hey, it's true."

Garrett slipped his arms through the straps of his oxygen tank. "I would think the fact that you personally saw the arsonist would be great for your show. You should definitely play it up. The publicity might help us catch him."

He was right, but the suggestion caught me by surprise. I was sure Luke would have asked me to keep quiet.

As though sensing my hesitation, Garrett said, "If this guy is worried about you identifying him, it might make you a target."

"What?"

"Hear me out." He moved closer and held my gaze. "But if you take this to the public, the whole world will be watching. I suspect the guy will be less likely to go after you."

I made a face. "Not the whole world. Only about thirty percent of the eighteen-to-twenty-five demographic."

Bill chuckled.

Garrett tugged his helmet onto his head. "You and I should definitely talk later, cameras or no cameras." He started to walk off, then stopped. "But in the meantime, promise me you'll tell Luke."

I couldn't figure out why he thought I wouldn't, but he took my confusion as hesitation.

He looked me in the eye. "As soon as I finish here, I'm texting Teddy to let him know what's going on. I know he'll make sure you're safe." Then, before I could protest, he ran over and grabbed a hose to help several other guys who were already spraying down the fire.

I grumbled under my breath about being able to take care of myself.

"Are you going to tell Luke?" Bill asked.

"Of course I will," I said, regretting that I sounded so indignant. "I'm not sure why Garrett thinks I'd try keepin' it to myself."

"Because it's a scoop, and that's exactly what Connor would do," Tony said.

"Well, I'm not Connor," I said in disgust while I scanned their group. "*Where's Dixie?* I can't believe she hasn't shown up for this." I glanced down at my phone, getting worried when I didn't see a reply from her.

"Maybe Lauren turned her down, and she left," Bill said, voicing my own thought.

I sent her another text.

Dixie, I need you to answer me. This is important.

When another minute passed without her responding, I started getting really worried.

Connor was making exaggerated gestures toward the building, and I was about to walk over and ask Lauren if she knew where Dixie was when Luke's patrol car turned down the street. As soon as he parked next to Garrett's car, he got out and headed straight for me. "You were the one who called this in?"

"Yeah."

He shook his head. "Are you actually *looking* for trouble everywhere you go, or do you just stumble into it?"

I saw no reason to answer, but I didn't appreciate his attitude. I put my hand on my hip and gave him a deadly glare. "Would you prefer for me to ignore it next time?"

He scrubbed a hand over his face, then dropped it. "No. And sorry. You've been part of two emergency calls in as many hours. I can't help worrying about you."

He had a point.

"I was walking over to the insurance office and smelled smoke. Then I saw someone run out of the building that's now on fire."

His eyes went round. "You saw the arsonist?"

"Yeah, but not enough to identify anyone. Sorry."

"What did you see?"

I told him about the person in the hoodie and how he'd slunk through the shadows.

"How tall was he?"

"I'm not sure. Tallish." Some detective I turned out to be. "I'm sorry. I wish I'd paid better attention."

Luke wrapped an arm around my shoulders and snugged my side next to his. Leaning over, he placed a kiss on top of my head. "You've given us more than anyone else so far. Besides, the important thing is that you're safe."

"But I could have helped find the arsonist."

He turned me to face him and gave me a sympathetic look. "Summer. It's okay. Really."

But it wasn't enough, and we both knew it. "I don't suppose anyone has any security cameras on this street."

He pursed his lips as he watched the firefighters spray down the building. "Not likely. There aren't many break-ins, so these businesses can't justify the expense. Most are barely making it as it is." His gaze landed on the vacant business next to the fire, which was now engulfed in flames too. "Or didn't make it at all. But we'll ask around and see if we get lucky."

"Tell him the rest," Bill said.

Luke gave me a pointed look. "There's *more*?"

I frowned. "Speculation."

"Observations," Tony said.

Luke studied my crew. "Did you guys see this too?"

"No," Tony said. "We were at the insurance office waiting for Summer."

Luke turned back to me. "Why weren't you with them?"

"I had another interview."

"Not on camera?" When I didn't answer, I could tell he wanted to ask more questions about my interview, but he shook it off and asked, "What else did you see?"

I told him about Connor showing up late and out of breath and dropping the lighter. "I hate to accuse him of anything."

"But he's shown up early at two fires now," Bill said. "He was at this one before the fire trucks showed up. It feels suspicious."

Luke squinted at Connor. He was gesturing widely while a firefighter tried to push him out of the way. "Do you know if he showed up at April Jean's fire?" he asked.

"I don't know."

It was obvious from the look on his face that he didn't believe me.

"I swear. I've been working on other things." Okay, it was the same thing, just a different angle than he probably thought . . .

Luke frowned, then put his hands on my shoulders. "I'm going over to talk to the firefighters. Promise me you'll stay here and wait until I'm done."

I nodded. "I will."

The crowd had started moving closer to the fire, so Luke began to push everyone back. Once he made sure we were all a safe distance away, he walked over and started talking to several of the firefighters.

They had the fire contained within fifteen minutes, and once the flames were extinguished, two firefighters headed for the front door of the thrift store. A few minutes later, they came out of the building and headed straight for the fire chief. They told him something, and his head jerked up. "Montgomery," he shouted toward Luke.

Luke perked up, gave me a grim look, then headed for the small group.

Connor was with his crew about twenty feet away from the building, and he got a wild look in his eyes as he talked to the camera.

"What's he sayin'?" I asked a nearby bystander. Her eyes were glued on Connor.

"I can't make it out," she mumbled. "It sounded like he's sayin' they found something shoddy."

Something shoddy? Connor had totally lost it.

"They think someone's inside," Bill said in a quiet voice behind me. I spun around to face him. "What?"

"Those two firemen went in before they cleared the entire building. When they came out, they went straight for the fire chief—and they called over the chief of police too."

I started to protest, but then I realized Connor hadn't been saying *shoddy*. He'd been saying *body*. "But how? The store was abandoned."

Tony shrugged. "Maybe it was a homeless person."

As far as I knew, Sweet Briar didn't have a homeless problem, but then, maybe the town did a really good job of hiding it. That meant I hadn't just seen an arsonist, I'd potentially seen a murderer.

My head went numb.

Where was Dixie?

I pulled up her number and called her, even more worried when the phone went straight to voice mail.

Anxiety gnawed at the lining of my stomach. Something was really, really wrong. I just didn't know what yet.

"Summer," Bill whispered in my ear, "what's wrong?"

"I can't get ahold of Dixie."

Bill frowned. "Maybe she's in the middle of something."

"Her phone went straight to voice mail. That means it's either turned off or the phone is dead, but I know for a fact she charged it after lunch—I saw her plug it in—and she never turns it off."

Luke had been listening to the firefighters for several seconds. One of them reached out and put a hand on his shoulder. Luke stiffened and took several seconds to process whatever he'd been told before he broke loose and headed toward the fire engine, the firefighters following him.

"Something bad's happening," I said, feeling like I was about to throw up.

Luke made a call on his cell phone and talked to whoever was on the other line for nearly a minute while one of the firefighters pulled a pair of fireman overalls off the fire truck and dropped them to the ground. I watched in disbelief as Luke kicked off his shoes and stepped into the overalls and attached boots.

"Oh, God," I said in horror. I took an involuntary step forward. "Why's he goin' inside that still-smoldering house?"

"I don't know," Bill said, but his camera was lifted to his shoulder. He was recording this, and so was Tony. I suspected Tony had been filming ever since Luke had told me to stay put.

I called Teddy on my cell, and he answered with a warm hello.

"Have you talked to Dixie?" I asked, trying to hide my rising hysteria. There was no basis for my fear. I was sure there was a logical explanation for Dixie not responding. But I didn't like it.

He paused. "Not since this morning. Why?"

I tried to swallow the lump in my throat, but my words still sounded strangled. "I can't get ahold of her."

"She's not with you? Why'd you let her out of your sight?" he asked, his voice rising.

He was right. What had I been thinking? My job had been to watch her and keep her safe, and now she was missing. That was on me. "I'm sorry," I pushed out in a tight voice. "There's been another fire, Teddy."

"What? Where?"

"On Pine Street. In the old thrift shop." I paused. "I think they just found a body."

"Stay put, Summer," he said, sounding panicked. "Just stay put and wait for me. I'm on my way."

Willy had shown up, along with a couple of deputy sheriffs. They were stringing crime scene tape from one side of the street to the other to keep the crowd back. Luke was now wearing the firefighter pants, and he started to put on the jacket.

"What's he doin'?" I asked, trying not to sound hysterical.

"Summer," Bill said, grabbing my shoulder with one hand and turning me to face him. He tilted the camera so it pointed to the street. "Why are you so freaked out?"

"Luke's goin' into that burning building."

"It's not burning anymore," Tony said. "It's just smoking now. It's bound to be mostly safe or they wouldn't let him go in. Besides, it's a small town. I suspect he's helped put out a fire or two."

"Why's he going inside in the first place?"

Tony leaned into my ear. "To look at the body."

I gasped, feeling light-headed. Bill lowered the camera to his side and put his hand on my back, lightly rubbing back and forth. When Luke put on his helmet, the only way I could distinguish him from the other guys was a streak of blue on his pants.

The two firemen led Luke and the fire chief into the building while Willy and one of the sheriff's deputies got the crowd moved back and the crime scene tape firmly in place. Two more sheriff's deputies arrived at the opposite end of the street and headed straight for Connor and his crew, who had a direct shot inside the shop. One of the deputies moved Connor and the rest to the opposite end of the street, and the other worked on setting up crime scene tape on his end.

I understood their need to keep us back, but I couldn't see inside, which meant I had no idea what Luke was up to. Without thinking, I lifted the crime scene tape and ducked underneath, intent on getting a better look.

Willy saw me and hurried over. "You need to get behind the crime scene tape, Summer," he said in a gentle tone, one that set off alarm bells in my head.

I jerked my arm away from him. "Why are you bein' so nice?"

His eyes widened like he was a paparazzo caught in a house's floodlights at 3:00 a.m. "What are you talkin' about? I'm always nice to you."

"Except when you tried to arrest me for being a Peeping Tom in April."

He gave me a sheepish grin, then glanced over his shoulder with a worried look.

"What's goin' on, Willy?"

A deputy walked over, and before he even reached us, I steeled my back.

"Causing trouble, Ms. Butler?" Deputy Ryan Dixon asked with a hint of contempt.

The contempt was mutual. This idiot had accused me of moving Otto Olson's body to the lake so I could pretend to find him in order to boost ratings for my show. He'd actually believed I'd given myself a concussion for authenticity.

I lifted my chin and gave him my best haughty stare. "*I* was the one who called this fire in." As soon as the words were out of my mouth, I regretted it. The interest that sparked in his eyes confirmed it had been a mistake. For all I knew, he'd accuse me of setting the fire for the show.

Just like we'd speculated about Connor.

"Ms. Butler, you need to get back. This is a crime scene, and you don't have permission to be on this side of the tape." Then he gave me a glare. "Whether you called it in or not."

I moved back to the other side but stood at the very edge of the tape, trying to figure out why I was so panicky. Bill was right—this was likely not the first time Luke had gone into a building damaged by fire. But my inability to reach Dixie was worrying me.

Firefighters started to emerge from the building, and I held my breath until I saw a figure with a blue streak on the leg of his pants.

Relief swept through me as I placed a hand over my racing heart. Luke, at least, was okay.

But he seemed like a man with a purpose as he ripped off his air mask and headed for the fire truck. I watched in horror as he jerked off his helmet, squatted next to the engine's back wheel, and promptly threw up.

"He saw something," Bill said.

"Or some*one*," Chuck said.

What could have upset him like that? Someone who'd been caught in a fire would be in terrible shape, and Luke took the safety of his citizens seriously, but he'd seen bodies before . . . When he glanced over, his gaze held mine for a couple of seconds, the world fell away, and an awful certainty filled me.

"Dixie."

"What about her?" Bill asked, but the tightness at the end of his sentence hinted that he knew exactly what I meant.

Luke stood and wiped his mouth with the back of his hand, then stripped off the oxygen tank and jacket in record time. As he kicked off his pants, Garrett approached him. He put a hand on Luke's shoulder and leaned into his ear. Luke hung his head and nodded.

What had Luke found inside that building?

I couldn't wait any longer.

Lifting the crime scene tape again, I ducked underneath it. I heard Bill shouting my name, but it sounded far away. The only thing I could concentrate on was getting to Luke.

Luke's gaze jerked up to mine, and the devastation on his face confirmed my worst fears.

"No . . ."

I felt a hand grab my arm and tug backward, but my body was deadweight.

"Get behind the line!" I heard Deputy Dixon shout, but the words were muffled, like I was underwater, and he was above the surface shouting down to me.

Luke was crossing the distance in bounding steps, the pain on his face morphing to anger as he reached us. He placed his palms on the deputy's chest and shoved hard.

Deputy Dixon stumbled backward, then a dark look crossed his face before he lunged at Luke.

That brought me to my senses. I moved between them, putting a hand on Luke's chest. "No. Stop. He's not worth it."

The deputy looked ready to hit someone, but one of his fellow deputies grabbed his arm and tugged. "This is personal to him, Dixon. Let it go."

The fury in Deputy Dixon's eyes suggested he wasn't even close to letting it go—that he wasn't the type of person who knew how—but he took several steps back and finally spun away.

Luke's chest muscles were tight under my hand, but he wrapped an arm around my back and steered me back toward the crowd.

"It's her, isn't it?" I asked, surprised I sounded so calm, like I'd just asked Maybelline to hold the cheese on my burger.

"Not here, Summer," Luke said, his voice rough.

We reached the crime scene tape where Bill and Tony still stood waiting for me. Bill had given up all pretense of filming, but Tony had his camera trained on both of us.

Luke lifted the tape so I could duck underneath, and he quickly followed. He turned to my crew and said, "We're going to the police station. You will *not* be coming."

"What's going on?" Chuck asked, holding the boom mike over our heads. When had he gotten that out? But then why was I surprised? That was his job, and my crew were professionals. I couldn't begrudge them for trying to do their jobs.

Luke ignored them, moving me through the crowd at a dizzying speed and then settling me in the front seat of his patrol car.

"Am I in trouble?" I asked when he got behind the wheel.

"What? No." He ran a hand over his face, then reached over and grabbed my hand and squeezed, his eyes filling with tears. "Let's get to the station."

I wanted him to voice my worst fear, but as long as I didn't ask him, it wouldn't be true. Dixie wouldn't be dead.

No. Dixie wasn't dead.

What was Teddy going to say?

Oh, crap. Teddy. He'd told me to stay put.

I sent him a quick text telling him to meet me at the police station. Lord only knew what he'd think of that, but there was no gentle way to share my fears with him, and I didn't want him going to the crime scene.

We reached the police station within minutes, and I was out of the car before Luke could walk around to get me. The air had grown thin inside the vehicle, and I could barely breathe.

"It was her, wasn't it?" I asked, my skin crawling with panic.

"No." Luke's eyes were glassy with unshed tears. "Let's just go inside, Summer. We'll talk in there."

If it wasn't her, then why was he so upset? Was he lying to keep me from freaking out?

Oh, my God.

No. *No.* This couldn't be happening. I rested my hands on my legs and curled over as I took several deep breaths, fighting the panic.

I heard tires squealing behind me, and a vehicle screeched to a halt.

"Summer!" Teddy shouted behind me, and I stood upright. He reached me within seconds, grabbing my shoulders. "Where is she?"

I started to cry. "I don't know."

His eyes were wild with panic. "They said there's a body. Was she in that fire?"

"I don't know." My body was racked with sobs, and I felt Luke pull me from Teddy's grasp and haul me to his chest.

"It wasn't her," Luke said. "Let's go inside."

There it was again—the tightness in his voice. He was hiding something big.

"Where the fuck is my sister, Luke?"

"We really should discuss this inside, Teddy." Luke's voice broke.

"No, we'll discuss this *now*. Was Dixie caught in this?"

Luke cupped my cheek and tilted my face up to his. "You can handle this, and I'll help you. I swear it. Do you trust me?"

Fresh tears filled my eyes. "It was her. She's dead, isn't she?"

"Summer." His voice was harsh, and his eyes hardened. "Do you trust me?"

Why was he asking me that question? But there was no hesitation with my answer. "Yes."

Luke shook his head, holding my gaze, then looked up at Teddy. "It wasn't Dixie. We're pretty damn sure it was April Jean's body, but Dixie is the prime suspect."

Chapter Nineteen

I was caught between relief and horror.

"What the hell are you talkin' about, Montgomery?" Teddy asked in a deadly quiet tone as he took a step toward us. His hands were fisted at his sides.

Luke angled his body so I was partially behind him. "We should take this inside, Teddy."

"Why? So you can get us in there and trick us into helping you build your case *against* her?"

"No," Luke said in a firm tone. "So I can prove she didn't do it."

Teddy shook his head. "I fell for that bullshit once. I'm not doin' it again." He reached a hand out for me. "Summer, let's go."

I took a step away from Luke and stood between them. "Wait," I said, focusing on Luke. "How can you possibly name Dixie as a suspect when you *just* found April Jean's body? She was in a fire." But images of April Jean filled my head—her trailer, her drawings, the encounter between her and the mayor at the police station. I'd seen her just over an hour ago. "How can you be sure it was April Jean?"

"She was only partially burned. One of the firefighters identified a tattoo on her ankle. They'll check dental records—and fingerprints if they can get them. They won't release her name until it's been confirmed and her grandparents have been notified, but we're sure it's her."

"What makes Dixie the number-one suspect?" Teddy demanded in a snotty tone. "The fact that April Jean died in a *fire*?"

"I saw the arsonist run out of the building, and he was nearly a foot taller than Dixie," I protested.

"I'll tell you what I know, but I need to go inside and tell Amber I'm leaving for the day," Luke said. "They'll lock everything down tight before the media starts circling like vultures."

"Why do you keep saying *they*?" I asked.

Luke swallowed, then held my gaze. "The fire chief made me call in the sheriff's department and give them the case. With you here, and Dixie bein' in the middle of this, the media's gonna be all over it. I can't be impartial, and everyone knows it."

"So you tossed her to Deputy Dixon?" I asked in disbelief.

"The sheriff's department loves Teddy," Luke said. "They'll handle this with kid gloves because of him, and they'll be even more careful than usual since the media will be watching their every move. They won't make a hasty arrest, but when they *do* arrest her, it will make big news. Sheriff Bromley's up for reelection, and he'll play this case like a fiddle to aid his campaign." He turned to Teddy. "You know I'm right."

"You arrested her for a crime she didn't commit nine years ago," Teddy said in a gravelly voice. "How come you're so sure Dixie didn't do it this time?"

"Because April Jean was shot in the head, and Dixie's not a stone-cold killer," Luke said.

I gasped. "Someone shot her?"

Luke ignored my question as he turned to me. "I'm goin' inside to talk to Amber, but I want you both to know I'm devoting my full attention to this until we clear her."

"Can't you get in trouble for interfering with the sheriff's investigation?" I asked. "Last time this happened, they told you in no uncertain terms to back off."

"You're right, but you can work it," he said. "Teddy can officially hire you to investigate."

We'd dealt with the same issue back in April. The sheriff's department had been in charge of the investigation of Otto Olson's death, and Luke had gotten called on the carpet for conducting his own inquiries. But private investigators could work active investigations, and Luke had encouraged me to pursue it . . . until my crew and I stumbled upon another body. Not that I'd let Ed Reynolds's death or Luke Montgomery's orders stop me. He had to know I'd be even more persistent to save Dixie.

"I'll take leave if I have to, but I'd rather keep this aboveboard." He paused. "But there's no sense in you two working separately from me. We'll save time if we work together."

"Don't trust him, Summer," Teddy said. "He hurt her before. He'll do it again. Besides, you can do things he can't. Working with him could slow us down."

"Wait. Teddy's right," I said. "What will they focus on in their investigation? The fact that Dixie was convicted of arson before?"

Luke swallowed, and his face lost color. "April Jean was clutching a necklace. It was dangling from her hand. The clasp was broken, like she'd grabbed it during a struggle."

"So?" Teddy asked, but he didn't sound as defiant.

"It was Dixie's, Teddy," Luke said, his hand tightening on my shoulder. "It was the one you gave her for her eighteenth birthday. With three charms—a yellow tulip, a *D*, and an infinity sign." He pushed out a breath. "It was hers."

Rage filled Teddy's face. "How do you know about that necklace?"

"Because I've seen her wear it before. She was so happy when you gave it to her. She'd just come back from serving her time, and you welcomed her home with open arms. Your belief in her made her believe she could get past the things she'd done."

"And you were there for her too," Teddy said. "Why? Waitin' for her to screw up so you could arrest her again?"

Anger darkened Luke's eyes. "No, and you damn well know it. She's a good kid, and I could tell she'd gotten caught up in something out of her control. I hated arresting her. I hated that losing her was one more blow to *you*, Teddy. You'd already lost your parents. And I hate that she lost two years of her life for a stupid mistake. When she got out, she needed all the support she could get, and I knew you were the only one who was goin' to give it to her. Your grandmother's grudges run deep. Dixie killed her only son and her husband, whether she intended to or not. She wasn't gonna forgive that overnight."

I moved away from Luke. My own guilt was smothering. While Dixie and Teddy had been going through hell, I'd been going through my own pity party in Hollywood.

"So you befriended her because you're just that selfless of a guy," Teddy goaded.

Luke groaned. "I know you don't trust me, Teddy, and I know I've given you plenty of reasons not to. But I swear to you, I genuinely care about Dixie, and I want to help her."

Teddy turned at the waist and glanced at the smoke rising into the air behind the police station.

"I didn't have to tell you about her necklace," Luke said. "In fact, I could get fired for it."

"You want me to fall to my knees with gratitude?" Teddy sneered.

"Teddy," I barked. "Stop it. Luke's right. He could have kept this to himself." I turned to Luke. "So why did you tell us?"

Luke's eyes pleaded with mine. "I know she didn't do it, and I know you'll be working day and night to prove as much. Let's work together."

Luke was right about the press. This would be big news, and Dixie would be the easy, big-name arrest. Partly because of me. And her necklace was the perfect plant to prove she'd done it. Just like drenching her with gasoline had been the perfect piece of evidence to prove she'd set the barn fire.

"Fine, you can help," I said.

"Summer!" Teddy shouted.

I held Luke's gaze. "On one condition."

"What is it?"

"I'm not only interested in proving her innocence for this murder. I aim to prove she didn't start that fire nine years ago. You have to agree to help with that too."

Luke's face went blank. "What are you talking about?"

"Dixie didn't start the barn fire, Luke. And I'm going to prove it."

"Do you have any leads?" Teddy asked, sounding hopeful.

I lifted my gaze to his. "As a matter of fact, I do. And I'm pretty sure I know who started it."

Luke's brow lowered with suspicion. "Who?"

I shook my head. "I'm not telling you anything until you agree to my terms. There's more."

"What?"

"If you start to think she may be guilty, you have to bow out of our investigation."

His eyes hardened. "What does that mean?"

"If you find compelling evidence against her, you have to tell me, and we'll part ways on our investigation."

"Summer . . ."

I shook my head. "Teddy, let's go." I started to walk toward his truck.

"Summer!" Luke called after me. "Wait."

I stopped and turned around to face him.

His eyes met mine. "If we prove she didn't start the barn fire, then that means I put an innocent girl in juvie for two years."

The anguish in his eyes proved that the thought alone was killing him.

I walked toward him. "I mean to prove it with or without you." I stopped in front of him and lowered my voice, putting my hand on his shoulder. "Dixie herself believes she did it, and the evidence all pointed to her. I understand why you didn't dig deeper."

Luke's voice broke. "I'll help you. With all of it. What do you have?"

"You agree to my terms? Because I realize your job is to find the truth and arrest the arsonist, but my job is to protect Dixie. At the first sign that our goals are going in different directions, I need you to remove yourself from our investigation."

He nodded, but he wouldn't meet my eyes. "Yeah. I agree."

I turned to Teddy. "You in?"

"You're standing there asking me if I want to save my sister?" The contempt in his voice hurt, but I knew it wasn't really aimed toward me. He turned to Luke and pointed a finger in his face. "If you try to hurt Dixie, I swear to God, I will do whatever it takes to bury you."

Luke's eyes hardened. "Literal or figurative?"

"I'll let you figure that one out." He motioned to the building. "Now get your ass in there and do whatever you need to do. If you're not out in five minutes, we're goin' without you."

I rubbed my forehead. "Teddy's right. We need to find Dixie, and I know where to start."

Luke's face went blank. "What do you mean we need to find Dixie? Where is she?"

"If we knew, we wouldn't have to find her, now would we?" Teddy asked in disgust, then turned to me. "Why do you want to work with this guy?"

"Because he really does care about Dixie, and he's been doin' this a hell of a lot longer than I have. We need all the help we can get."

Teddy flicked a finger toward Luke. "You have four minutes and thirty-nine seconds. Go."

The two of them working together was going to be a disaster, but I didn't see any other option.

Chapter Twenty

Teddy's eyes were glued to the screen on his phone, and I realized he'd set a timer.

"You're seriously timing him?"

"You bet your ass I am." He glanced up at me, his eyes full of pain and fear.

"Oh, Teddy." I threw my arms around his neck and clung to him. "I'm sorry. We'll find her. We'll prove she didn't do this. I promise."

His arms tightened around my back, and he buried his face in my neck. "I can't lose her again. I can't . . ."

I leaned back and stared up into his face. "You won't."

He dropped his arms and took a step backward. "Why do you want to work with him, Summy?" He motioned to the building. "He may have experience, but you know what you're doin'. Your investigation flushed out Cale Malone. What happened to our agreement? Dixie before everything else?"

I groaned in frustration. "Luke's the one who told us she's a suspect. He could have kept that to himself. We're getting a head start because of him. He's going to investigate whether he's with us or not, even if he's not supposed to."

"You're dating him, Summer. Can you really cut him loose if he starts to believe she's guilty?"

My voice hardened. "Dixie comes first."

"You're willing to give up Luke to save her?" he asked.

"I hope it doesn't come to that, but Dixie comes first. I refuse to let her down again."

He studied me for several seconds before he said, "Okay."

I pushed out a breath, ready for the next fight. "Luke doesn't know about Dixie bein' drugged. As far as I know, he doesn't know anything about the party last night. But if we want his help, we have to tell him."

Teddy frowned, and I took it as a good sign that he didn't say no. His gaze shifted to the police station, and irritation filled his eyes. I turned to see what had caught his attention.

Luke was walking out of the building wearing jeans and a dark-gray T-shirt that clung to the muscles of his arms and chest. I couldn't help staring at him as he headed toward us.

"Priorities, Summer," Teddy muttered in disgust.

He was right. There would be plenty of time for ogling later.

"You changed clothes," I said as Luke reached us.

He opened the door to his truck and tossed his folded uniform inside the cab. "I figure I'll blend in more this way. You said you know where to go first?"

I glanced up at Teddy, then back at Luke. "I figure we should try to find out who saw her last." After looking around to make sure no one was listening in, I motioned for Teddy to move closer so we were in a huddle. "Which means we need to talk to Lauren. I say we go to the train station and see if they're there."

Luke's eyebrows rose, but Teddy looked pissed.

"Why would she be with that witch?" Teddy asked.

I leaned closer and whispered, "Because I sent Dixie to work with them." I paused, guilt stealing my breath away.

Teddy looked furious, but Luke spoke before he could, keeping his voice low. "Why would you send Dixie to work with Lauren and Connor? Did you two have a fight? Because punishment is the only reason I can come up with for you to send your cousin to those scumbags."

"She couldn't be with us while we were investigating," I said. "We shouldn't talk about this next part outside."

"Let's go into my office."

Teddy and I followed him inside, and once he shut his office door, I told him about Dixie calling me in the middle of the night and how out of it she was when I picked her up at the lake. I left out the part about her smelling like smoke.

"Why didn't you call me?" Luke asked, sounding hurt. He shot an angry glance at Teddy before turning back to me. "I understand him not calling me, but *you*?"

"I'm sorry."

Teddy glared at him. "Take your damn feelings out of it."

"Dixie was drugged," Luke said in a no-nonsense tone, his voice beginning to rise with his anger. "You *have* to know that. She could have been raped. She should have been drug tested. Given a rape kit. What you two did was completely irresponsible."

"She refused to go!" I argued. "But we convinced her to pee in a mason jar, and Teddy took it to the county lab."

Luke shot Teddy a dark look.

Teddy glared back. "I have friends."

"Have you gotten the results yet?"

"No."

"Do you think she was raped?" Luke asked, his words tight.

"She didn't think so, but we all know that doesn't mean anything. The last thing she remembers is . . ." I took a moment to regroup. How much did I want to tell him?

"You still don't trust me," he said, and there was no denying the pain in his voice this time.

I pushed out a breath of frustration. "You're a cop, Luke. You've always wanted to be a cop. I'm not sure you're capable of separating

Luke my boyfriend from Luke the cop." I gave him a tearful smile. "I need Luke my boyfriend right now, because I'm scared. I'm scared something really bad happened to her."

His face went blank. "Why do you think something happened to her?"

"She never turns off her phone, but she won't pick up. And I saw a man running out of that burning building, Luke, not Dixie. That guy set her up, and she's either hiding somewhere, or he's kidnapped her."

Luke shook his head. "Summer, that's a stretch. I'm sure there's a logical explanation. We'll find her and figure out how April Jean got ahold of her necklace."

"They had an argument last night at the party."

"Who? April Jean and Dixie?" When I nodded, he rested his hands on his hips, but I could tell he was frustrated. I hadn't told him everything, and we all knew it. "What did they fight about?"

"April Jean was jealous over Dixie and Trent. I think it might have gotten a little physical. April Jean didn't tell you when she came to you about her trailer being burned down?"

"No. I stopped her as soon as she showed up and told her to talk to the sheriff because he was in charge of the investigation."

"The last thing Dixie remembers from last night is her disagreement with April Jean, but I talked to someone who was at that party, and she said Dixie fell asleep in her chair after the fight."

"Who told you this?"

"I promised not to say." Although in hindsight, it would be easy for him to figure out. We ate at Maybelline's, so he only had to ask around . . . or even check Maybelline's Facebook page.

I had so much to learn about subterfuge.

"That was your interview before you saw the arsonist," Luke said, putting things together. No wonder he was a cop. "You didn't bring the cameras with you."

"We're wastin' time we could be usin' lookin' for my sister," Teddy said. "Let's go. I'm drivin' my own truck." He stomped out of the office, leaving me feeling torn between following him and staying.

Luke put his hand on my shoulder. "It's okay. Go with him. He needs you right now."

I reached up on my tiptoes and gave him a kiss. "Thank you."

"We'll prove she didn't do this, Summer. I promise."

At the moment, I was more worried about finding her.

Teddy had started his truck by the time I reached it, and I'd barely gotten the door closed before he backed out of his parking spot.

I studied him as he took off. His Adam's apple bobbed as he swallowed.

"None of this means anything unless we find her," he said.

I grabbed his hand and clung to him. "We will."

"I have a really, really bad feeling about this, Summer."

"I do too," I admitted.

He pulled up to a stop sign and turned to catch my gaze. "Luke agreed to your rules, but I never agreed to shit. I will do whatever it takes to find her and prove she didn't do this." He leaned closer, and his voice deepened. "Do you understand what I'm sayin'?"

The blood rushed from my head. "Gettin' her back doesn't mean squat if you're in prison for doin' something you'll regret, Teddy."

He turned back to face the road and drove through the intersection. We didn't say anything as we continued to the train station. I tried to come up with a plan for confronting Lauren, but all I could think about was Teddy's threat. How far would he be willing to go? Based on the extreme measures he'd taken to get her drug-dealer ex out of the picture, I was thinking he'd go pretty far.

Teddy parked in a space a half block down from the train station, and Luke pulled in next to him on my side. I hopped out and met Luke as he started to open his door.

"Luke, you need to stay out here. Teddy, you can come in with me."

"*What?*" Luke said.

I shook my head. "We can't all go inside, and you're a whole lot more intimidating than Teddy. We'll tell you what we find out."

He gave me a skeptical look, not that I blamed him. I'd pretty much admitted I didn't fully trust him, so he had no guarantee I'd be honest about what I found out.

"You have to trust me, Luke. Just like you're asking me to trust you."

I knew he could push the issue. He was the police chief, but he searched my face, then nodded. "Okay. I'll wait out here."

Teddy didn't waste any time heading for Connor's office. Based on the cars parked in front of it, there were at least a few people inside, but I only needed one person: someone who'd seen her and could tell me where to find her.

I slipped my phone out of my pocket, giving it one last look to make sure Dixie hadn't gotten back to me, then stopped a few feet from the front door and glanced up at Teddy. "Let me do the talkin'."

Teddy didn't say a word, instead reaching for the front door and holding it open for me to enter.

I strode through the door and stopped in the middle of the room. Connor was sitting at his desk. His hair was damp and freshly washed, and he'd changed shirts. He was watching a video of himself on his computer while Lauren and Karen stood behind the film editors. Their screens were full of videos of the fire on Pine Street.

"There!" Lauren said, pointing to a screen. "Freeze that screen. Is that a body?"

"Seriously?" I asked before I could stop myself.

Lauren stood upright and turned to face me. A smug look covered her face. "Ready to throw in the towel?"

"Not a chance," I said in a dry tone.

Teddy stood behind me, and Lauren's gaze lifted to take him in. "Hey, Teddy. What brings you into town again? Two days in a row. I thought you liked to stay out on that farm of yours."

"I'm lookin' for Dixie," he said. "Summer seems to have misplaced her, so I thought I'd check here."

So much for letting me do the talking, but he had a good approach. And Lauren was far more likely to spill to him instead of me.

Karen rolled her office chair away from her desk. "We haven't seen her since this morning."

My stomach dropped. I'd hoped that Lauren had put her to work and had maybe confiscated her phone. But no. She'd never even made it to the office.

"You sure about that?" Teddy asked.

"Yeah. We know Summer left her at their office to deal with that psycho couple. Then we noticed she wasn't at the fire this afternoon. We figured Summer had left her behind again."

Teddy shot me a glance as though asking if I believed her.

I turned to Connor. "Congrats on getting to the scene of the fire so quickly. Y'all are gonna have great coverage for the show."

"Thanks." But he seemed off and refused to look me in the eye.

"If you see Dixie, will you let me know?" I asked.

"Yeah, sure," he said, confusion covering his face. I was sure it was because he wasn't used to me being nice to him.

We went outside and stood on the sidewalk in front of Luke's truck. He was where I'd left him, but now his phone was pressed to his ear. The irritation on his face suggested the conversation wasn't going well.

"Do you believe them?" Teddy asked.

"Yeah. I do."

"When did Dixie leave your office?"

"I don't know, three thirty. Three forty-five at the latest."

"It's five thirty now," he said as he scanned the street. "Two hours."

"Yeah." A lot could have happened in two hours.

"You rode in together this morning, so she didn't have a car. She planned to walk from your office?"

"Yeah. And I saw her headin' in this direction," I said.

"So something happened to her between your office and here." Teddy glanced up the street. "We need to find out if anyone saw her."

"It's after five thirty. Everything's closed."

"Not Maybelline's." Then he headed across the street.

Luke was still on the phone, so I sent him a one-word text—Maybelline's—then hurried to catch up to Teddy, not an easy feat since his legs were nearly twice as long as mine.

"We should start calling her friends to see if they know where she is," I said.

"That list is pretty small, and I suspect it's the same people who were at that party last night."

"While we're at Maybelline's, let's place a to-go order and take it back to my office. I can fill you and Luke in on what else I know, and we can place some calls. We need to work out a game plan."

He stopped walking and stared down at me like I'd lost my mind. "Dixie's missing and you want to *eat*?"

"Teddy . . ."

He closed his eyes for a couple of seconds, then opened them. "You're right. It's a good plan. It'll seem less suspicious if we ask Maybelline questions after we make an order."

We continued walking, but I pulled up the Sweet Briar page to see if news had broken out about Dixie.

Teddy glanced over my shoulder. "Anything?"

I scrolled down the page until I got to the post about Amelia nearly running Margo and me down. "There's a post about the fire and the speculation about a body. There's a mention that I caught a glimpse of the arsonist, but nothing about who died or Dixie being a suspect."

His mouth pursed. "That won't last long. Not in this town."

"Push comes to shove, we can ask Maybelline to post on the page and find out if anyone's seen her."

Teddy shook his head. "She's already a suspect. If the sheriff's department finds out that she's missin', they'll presume she's run off because she's guilty."

"But she's innocent, so at least they might find her."

"Yeah, then slap handcuffs on her and toss her in a jail cell. You didn't see her before, Summer. Being arrested nearly destroyed her. That's not happening again."

I nodded. "Okay. Besides, we have a better shot at findin' her than they do. People will be more willin' to talk to us."

"Even more so if Dudley Do-Right isn't with us."

I started to protest, but he had a point. "We'll deal with him on a case-by-case basis. He didn't force his way into Connor's office."

He pressed his lips together and didn't comment. When we reached Maybelline's, he held the door open for me and then followed me inside. The place had gotten a lot busier than when I'd been there earlier, and all eyes were glued on me as Teddy and I headed toward the counter.

Maybelline darted right for us. "There's my girl."

I gave Teddy a grimace, and he rested a hand on my shoulder in support.

"And look at you, Theodore Baumgartner! You finally came off that farm and deigned to walk into my café."

He grunted. "It's not like that, Maybelline."

"When was the last time you came in here?" she asked.

"Maybelline . . ."

She waved him off and glanced around. "Where's Dixie? She and Summer are like two peas in a pod, and this is twice today I've seen Summer without her."

"That's why we're here," Teddy said, leaning closer. "Summer sent Dixie on an assignment, and now Dix's phone's died. I was wondering when you last saw her."

"Well . . . ," she said, her mouth twisting as she thought, "I guess it would have been during the ruckus Margo and Harold made outside the Darling Investigations office."

My heart sank. "You didn't see her after that?"

Her eyes narrowed on me. "You don't know where she is?"

"Like I said," Teddy said good-naturedly, "Dixie's phone died, and see . . ." He lowered his voice. "She and Summer had a little bit of a disagreement, and I'm tryin' to make these two stubborn girls make up. You sure you haven't seen her? She left the office around three thirty to three forty-five and was headed down to Connor's office."

Once again, Teddy's quick thinking impressed me. He'd taken exactly the right tack.

Maybelline chuckled. "She must've been mighty pissed if she ran off to Connor Blake's team. What did ya do, girl?"

I made a face. "I was stupid, and now I'm trying to find her so I can apologize. You sure you haven't seen her?"

"Sorry, darlin'. But if I do, I'll tell her you're lookin' for her."

"We want to order some food to go," I said. "Do you mind if we ask around while we wait for it?"

"Help yourself," she said. "How about I make up a couple of Tuesday specials?"

The door opened, and Luke filled the opening, drawing the eye of every female in the place, Maybelline included, although to be fair, they'd shifted their attention to Teddy before Luke showed up.

"Make it three," I said, then turned to meet Luke in the middle of the room.

He leaned into my ear. "I'm supposing Lauren was a bust."

"Yeah. No one saw her." My chest tightened at the admission. "And Maybelline doesn't know anything."

"Hey," he whispered, tilting my chin up to look at him, "we'll find her." Then he leaned over and gave me a soft kiss.

A man catcalled, and Teddy shot him a glare so dark the guy looked like he wanted to run out the back door.

I pulled Luke's head down to whisper in his ear. "We're tellin' people that Dixie and I had a fight, and I'm tryin' to find her to apologize."

He straightened and gave me a look of pride. "Good thinkin'."

"It was Teddy's idea."

He grinned, but it looked strained. "No one ever accused the Baumgartners of being stupid. Stubborn as the day is long, but never stupid."

That was debatable, as far as I was concerned.

"What do you know about the fire, Luke?" a younger guy called out from a booth.

Luke held up his hand. "The sheriff's department is handling the case. I'll let them make a statement."

"Why aren't you handling it?" a woman called out.

"Because," Luke said, wrapping an arm around my back, "this is the fourth fire, and the sheriff has handled two of the other cases. They have better resources to handle it, so I deferred to them. Of course, I'm willing to give them any assistance they need."

"That's good to hear," a man said from the door, and I turned to see Officer Dixon standing in the doorway wearing a smart-ass grin. "The first thing you can do is help me find Dixie Baumgartner."

We'd just lost our advantage.

Chapter Twenty-One

Teddy plastered a grin on his face and turned to the deputy. "I'd love to help you with that, but I'd rather tell you outside. It's a little sensitive."

The deputy tilted his head and focused on Luke. "I'd rather hear it from the police chief."

"That won't do you much good," Luke said, "since I don't know where she is. Seems like her brother's a better source. Besides, as you can see, I'm off for the night and about to have dinner with my girlfriend."

Deputy Dixon's attention shifted to me. "When was the last time you saw your cousin?"

I had no idea what Teddy planned to tell him, but I decided to stick with the truth . . . or at least part of it. Answer the question and volunteer nothing more. "This afternoon after the ruckus outside our office." I cocked my head. "What makes you ask?"

He ignored my question. "Do you know where she went?"

"No." She had never arrived at Connor's office, so it was technically true.

Teddy gestured toward the door. "You ready, Deputy?"

Deputy Dixon scowled but turned around and walked out onto the sidewalk. Teddy followed, never giving me a second glance.

"What's Teddy going to tell him?" Luke whispered in my ear.

"I have no earthly idea." But I was worried. Wouldn't it be a crime if Teddy lied to him? But then, he'd worked with the sheriff's department. Surely, he knew the rules.

"We'll need to keep a low profile," Luke said.

"We were plannin' on goin' to my office after we get our dinner. I have more info I haven't told you all yet, and we need to make a plan. I'll pull the blinds, and no one will know what we're up to." I paused. "Who were you talkin' to on the phone?"

He frowned. "It was about another case. Bruce Jepper's fire."

"Oh?" I perked up.

He gave me a long look. "It's official business, Summer, and nothing to do with this."

"Are you certain of that? They're both fires."

"Only Bruce's didn't contain a body and—" He cut himself off. He had more information, and he wasn't sharing it with me. But I was doing the same thing, so how could I complain?

"Here's your food, Summer," Maybelline called out behind me.

I reached into my purse and handed her cash as Luke went for his wallet. "Thanks, Maybelline."

She leaned close and lowered her voice. "Why's Deputy Butthead lookin' for Dixie?"

"Deputy Butthead?"

"He tried to pin Otto's murder on you when any fool could see you were innocent. He's a butthead."

I chuckled. "I've missed you, Maybelline."

"Damn right you have." She motioned for the door. "Now get goin.'"

By the time Luke and I got out to the sidewalk, Deputy Dixon was gone.

"What did you tell him?" I asked.

Teddy shook his head. "You don't need to know. Now let's head to your office."

It was a short walk, but I had my keys out of my pocket and ready to unlock the door, only to find it was already unlocked—Bill, Tony, and Chuck were sitting at Dixie's desk and in client chairs eating sub sandwiches. For some reason, it hadn't occurred to me that my crew would be there too.

"What's going on, Summer?" Tony asked. "Why did you run off?"

Bill gave me a wide-eyed stare. "Was Dixie in that fire?"

I glanced back at Luke, unsure of what I should and shouldn't say, but Bill had stuck with me throughout Season One. He'd risked his life to get the footage of Cale. And despite everything, he clearly cared about Dixie. He had a right to know, and I should have told them sooner.

Luke mouthed *No*, but I turned back to Bill and said, "No. But she's the prime suspect."

"Summer," Luke said in a stern tone. "A word."

"No," I said, shaking my head. "He's one of us."

"That was confidential information, Summer." His words sounded stiff.

"Bill kept all kinds of secrets with the Otto Olson case. He won't tell anyone."

He flung a hand in the direction of Tony and Chuck. *"And the other two?"*

"Hey," Tony said as he got to his feet, "we all signed NDAs. We want to help . . . whatever it is you three are up to."

"You don't even know what she's accused of doing," Luke said.

"Starting the fire, right?" Tony asked.

"And murder," Bill said quietly. "Who was in that building?"

"April Jean," I said.

He lowered his head. "Shit."

"Yeah."

"So what do we do?" Chuck asked.

"*You* all are goin' home," Luke said. "We'll take it from here."

"You're not in charge," Tony said. "Summer's our boss."

"I'm helping," Bill said in a tone that said he wouldn't be dissuaded. "I'll work this on my own if I have to."

"No," Teddy said, "you can work with me."

I held up my hands. "All y'all stop *right now*. We're *all* workin' together."

"Summer," Luke said. *"A word."*

With a huff, I stomped back to the editing room, then spun around to face him as he shut the door.

"I'm not investigatin' this on your show. Is that your intention?"

I crossed my arms and pushed out a breath. "I don't know."

He flung his hand toward the door. "You have to know that if they're working with you, it's goin' on the damn show."

Dammit. He was right.

"You're seriously willing to exploit Dixie's disappearance and impending arrest for your *TV-show ratings*?"

I gasped at his crassness. He was missing the point—deliberately. Once word got out that Dixie was a suspect, everyone would presume she was guilty. If it went to trial, a jury of her peers would be tainted. But if we got footage of people's preconceived notions of her guilt, we might have a chance to prove she'd been arrested based on her poor reputation alone. God knew people got up in arms about true-crime shows that did a good job of proving bias.

Or was I just telling myself that to feel better about the whole thing?

What would Dixie want? I suspected she'd tell me to make it part of the show, but would she really mean it, or would she say it just for my benefit?

Luke was waiting for an answer, and I didn't have a decision yet. I dropped my arms to my sides. "I don't know."

Disgust washed over his face. "Then maybe you're not the person I thought you were."

Tears filled my eyes. He hadn't even let me explain. "You really mean that?"

"If you're gonna use your cousin's misfortune for your personal gain, then, yeah, maybe I do."

We stood facing each other for several seconds, then he flung the door open hard enough to hit the wall. Moments later, I heard the ding of the bell on the front door.

It was all too much. I was terrified that something awful had happened to Dixie, and I had no idea how to find her. Deputy Dixon was looking for her—probably to arrest her—and now I was pretty sure I'd just lost Luke.

Tears welled in my eyes, and I struggled to swallow the lump in my throat.

Teddy appeared in the doorway with a somewhat aggravating mixture of sympathy and satisfaction on his face. "So he's not working with us anymore?"

Given the way Luke had walked out, I didn't expect him to come back, but now wasn't the time to give in to self-pity. "I guess not. How much did you hear?"

"Pretty much all of it."

Great. I wiped the tears from my cheeks. "Do you think less of me now too?"

He leaned his shoulder into the door frame. "The way I see it, your cameras might get us access we might not get otherwise."

"What are you talking about?"

"People in this town are eager to be on your show. Your cameraman just told me that people tend to spill things because they forget the cameras are there. Your cameras could be the key to helping us find Dixie and ID'ing April Jean's murderer."

I nodded, more tears flowing down my cheeks. I'd been so focused on protecting Dixie, I hadn't even considered that the person who killed April Jean was still out there, possibly preparing to hurt someone else. Maybe he or she had Dixie.

Teddy closed the distance between us and pulled me into a hug. "Summy, I'm sorry it didn't work out with Luke."

I laughed despite my tears. "No, you're not, but thanks for not sayin' *I told you so.*"

He lifted my chin and grinned. "I'm waiting until we find Dixie so I can tell the both of you together."

My chin trembled. "What if we don't—"

He grabbed my upper arms in a tight grip. "We're gonna find her." He released his hold and took a step backward. "Now let's get out of here and figure out a plan."

I wiped my face again and followed him into the office area. All three guys looked solemn.

"Sorry about that," I said, then took a breath to steady myself. "As you've probably figured out, Luke has decided not to work with us."

"Thanks for stickin' up for us," Bill said. "And you should know that these walls are pretty thin. We heard most of what he said."

I nodded. I'd figured that out, thanks to Teddy. "You were part of this before. I know I can trust you."

"There are ways to work around the cameras, Summer," Tony said. "If you think someone won't talk on camera, we can put a hidden camera on you before you interview them, then figure out a way to coerce them into signing the release after the fact."

"Do we have any of those cameras?"

"Yeah. Lauren's got them at Connor's office. But we can easily grab one."

"Okay. We have two goals. One, find Dixie, and two, figure out who set the fires and murdered April Jean."

"We need to figure out where April Jean stayed last night," Teddy said. "Mobile homes can be a death trap in a fire. Maybe the killer tried to kill her last night too."

I sucked in a breath. He was right, but it was hard to think about someone being so evil.

I'd seen the whiteboard in the editing room, so I rolled it out and put it in front of my desk, then grabbed some tissues and started wiping off Lauren's lists. "We need a crime board. Like you see on TV." I turned around to face them. "Does anyone know how to do that?"

"Don't they usually have the murdered person in the middle of the board?" Chuck said. "Then the suspects are like spokes sticking out."

That sounded like a plan. "Okay."

I wrote *April Jean* in the middle, then wrote in the four corners: *Civil War marker fire*, *Bruce Jepper's fire*, *April Jean's trailer fire*, and *thrift store fire*. "Now what?"

"I think we're supposed to find a commonality between all of them," Chuck said.

Wasn't that the million-dollar question?

I groaned. "We're wasting time." I turned to Teddy. "Gut instinct— what happened to Dixie?"

He swallowed, and when he spoke, his voice was tight. "She had no reason to run away, and we know she didn't do this. If she was hiding somewhere, she would have called one of us by now, even if she doesn't have her phone. That leaves one conclusion. Someone took her."

I nodded. "Yeah. I agree. So now, gut instinct—who took her?"

"Trent Dunbar."

I nodded again. "And I haven't even told you about my interview with one of Dixie's friends who was at the party." I told the group everything Clementine had told me: Dixie going to the bathroom at right about the time Rick Springfield left; Dixie and April Jean fighting; Clementine leaving around midnight while Gabby, Mark, and Amelia stayed behind; and Bruce Jepper just showing up. "Bottom line, there was only a handful of people still there after my source left—and when she offered to take the very passed-out Dixie home, Trent said he would do it. We need to talk to Trent ASAP. Before someone else gets to him."

Teddy sat back in his chair and shook his head. "He's never gonna talk to me. We hate each other."

"I think he'll talk to me," I said, "but it's one of those no-cameras situations."

Tony tugged his phone out of his pocket. "On it. I can have the hidden camera in a half hour, tops."

Chuck cleared his throat. "You're forgetting something."

"What?" I asked.

"Your interview with the fireman."

"Crap."

"Garrett?" Teddy asked.

"Yeah."

Teddy pursed his lips. "See if you can meet Dunbar. Then we'll head to Garrett's after."

"You think meeting with Garrett is worth the time?" I asked. "Luke took a call at Maybelline's that was about Bruce's fire. He insisted the fire at the thrift store was different because there hadn't been a body in Bruce's house, and he was about to say something else when he cut himself off."

"Then we definitely need to talk to Garrett. He responded to all four fires," Teddy said. "That's how we start with finding our commonality. He'll talk."

"Okay. I need Trent's phone number." I grabbed my phone and texted Amber.

Do you have Trent Dunbar's cell number?

She answered in less than half a minute with the number, then sent another text immediately afterward.

What did you do to piss off Luke? He's madder than I've ever seen him.

At least we knew where he'd gone off to.

We had a difference of opinion. Is he still there?

Yeah, he's in his office making some phone calls. LOUD calls.

At least he wasn't yelling at me. But who was he talking to? The sheriff's department? I considered asking Amber but decided not to press my luck. Thanks. And good luck.

I glanced up at the guys. Tony had just left, presumably to get the equipment, and Bill had picked up his camera. "You're calling the douchebag next, right?"

"Yeah."

"Put him on speaker, and let me record it."

Chuck went into the back and returned with his boom microphone, which he held over my head. I glanced over at Teddy, who wore a grim expression. I suspected he already knew how this conversation was going to go down—and he clearly wasn't pleased with the notion of my playing Trent. Still, we all knew this was the best way to get information.

"Ready," Bill said.

I sat on top of Dixie's desk and then counted down with my fingers. "Three, two . . ."

I placed the call, still mulling over the best approach. Trent was used to women hanging on him, and any other time I'd play hard to get—it had driven him crazy at the lumber-mill office—but I didn't have time for a long-term plan. I needed to see him like five minutes ago.

"Hey," he said when he answered.

"Hey, yourself," I said in a sultry voice.

"Who is this?" He sounded intrigued.

"I'm hurt you've forgotten me already. Yesterday you seemed eager to spend time with me. There was mention of a threesome."

A dark look crossed Teddy's face.

"Summer?" he asked in surprise, then turned cocky. "You led me to believe you weren't interested."

"Well . . . I was with Luke, and I couldn't let him see I had a thing for you, now could I? I'm bored. This Podunk town's got nothin' goin' on, and rumor has it you're the source of all the local entertainment. Is that true?"

"What kind of excitement are you lookin' for?" he asked.

Teddy looked like he was about ready to snatch the phone out of my hand.

I ignored him, focusing on sounding breathy. "What's your specialty?"

"My parents are out of town. Why don't you come over and let me show you?" Trent sounded beside himself with excitement, but he was still trying to play it cool.

I rolled my eyes at the mention of his parents. "When?"

"Baby, I'm ready for you now."

"I'll be over soon."

I hung up and looked at the camera. "Let's hope this guy's horny enough to tell me what I want to know."

"Exactly how far are you willing to go to get it?" Teddy asked.

I pinned him with my gaze. "Exactly how far are *you* willing to go?"

He got up and walked out the door, but unlike Luke, he stuck around, pacing the sidewalk in front of the office.

"He has a valid point, Summer," Bill said. "This jackass is expecting to get laid, and I suspect he's not much into foreplay."

"Look," I said in disgust, "I have plenty of experience with guys who want to sleep with Isabelle Holmes of *Gotcha!* It's quite the trophy. They don't want me. They want a character I played over a decade ago. I suspect Trent Dunbar is the same way. I know how to handle him, and I'm leaving with information." My expression softened. "But Teddy shouldn't go with us. He's always been overprotective of both Dixie and me, and he won't be able to handle the situation without storming inside. We need to find something else for him to do."

"Maybe he can go prep Garrett," Chuck said.

"Yeah, maybe." But it didn't seem like enough. "How about we send Tony with Teddy to talk to Gabby and Mark? He can get them to tell him what happened after Clementine left."

"You can't be serious," Bill said. "He's not even on the show."

"He was on the show last season, and women loved him. It's perfect, but he'll need to set it up."

"What makes you think they'll talk to him on camera?" Bill asked. "There's only one hidden camera, and you'll be using it."

"Trust me, Gabby would *kill* to be on TV." Anyone so obsessed with designer purses and shoes would sell a kidney for her chance to be a Real Housewife . . . "Oh!" I ran to the door and called out, "Teddy, I have an idea."

He came inside, looking only slightly less peeved.

"I want you to go interview Gabby Casey and her boyfriend, Mark. I think you know him."

His expression didn't change. "We went to school together."

"One of the reasons the guys were at the insurance office was to set up an interview with Gabby about the party. I want you to ask her and Mark what they remember about Dixie from that night—"

"What makes you think they'll talk to me?"

It was risky to send Teddy, and I could only hope my plan worked. "Gabby will kill to be on TV, so she'll agree to the interview, but the second part involves some lying."

Denise Grover Swank

His eyes darkened. "I'm good with that."

I blinked. "Okay . . . first let them believe you're just looking for information about the party. Act like you're good and ticked at Dixie so you don't give the impression that you'll beat Mark's ass for anything they tell you."

"That's gonna be difficult, but if I can pretend to be a drug dealer, I can handle this."

"We still haven't gotten to the big lie."

His head jutted back. "Okay . . ."

"Tell Gabby that the network is so happy with the show and the town that they're lookin' into doin' a *Real Housewives of Sweet Briar*, and your interview is also an audition for the show. She'll spill her guts."

He looked skeptical. "How can you be so sure?"

"Because I've met more Gabby Caseys than I can count, and for a while they thought if they were BFFs with me, I'd be their golden ticket to fame and fortune."

His expression softened. "I'm sorry, Summy."

I shrugged even though the memories still stung a bit. "It's in the past, but we can use my hard-earned lessons to our advantage. I hate playin' her like that, but—"

"I'm not Luke Montgomery," Teddy said. "You don't need to convince me. I'm totally on board." He paused. "But I take it this is your plan to get me out of the way when you go see Trent."

I gave him a twisted grin.

He pushed out a breath and rubbed the back of his neck. "I guess we each have our own row to hoe."

"Yeah," I said with a lump in my throat.

He slid his phone out of his pocket and made a call. "Hey, Mark," he said, sounding light and breezy, and I realized I wasn't the only one in the family who'd gotten the acting gene. "It's Teddy Baumgartner." He paused, then said, "Say, my cousin Summer's given me a job on

254

her show, and I wanted to talk to you and Gabby about it . . . Gabby in particular. We've got her in mind for a special project comin' down the pike. I was wonderin' if I could drop over . . . like within the next half hour." He listened for a few seconds, grinning at me. "Sounds great. Text me the address, and I'll see you in a bit."

His approach was brilliant.

He hung up and gave me a half shrug. "I figured it would be easier to get in the door if I lead with the opportunity. I can ask about the party as part of her audition."

My shook my head in amazement. "You're a natural."

"Pawpaw always said Baumgartners are natural-born bullshitters."

His statement tickled a few memories. "Yeah. I guess he was right. You sure you want to do this?"

He reached for the forgotten takeout bag of food and pulled out a Styrofoam container and some plasticware as he sat down in a client chair. "I'll have a hard time waitin' thirty minutes to go over, but I suspect Gabby's gonna want time to pick up her house first."

I grinned. "That's pretty astute of you."

He shrugged as he shoved a forkful of mashed potatoes into his mouth. "I've had a girlfriend or two," he said with a mouthful of potatoes.

"Eww . . . I take it back," I teased.

"You need to eat too," he said, pulling out another container and shoving it toward me. "It was your idea."

I slid off the desk and took the container, then sat in the chair next to him. "I'm not sure I should eat before going to see that scumbag. I might lose it later."

He stopped with the fork halfway to his mouth. "You don't have to go see him. There's another way to get information out of him."

I lifted an eyebrow. "Does it involve you goin' over and beatin' the crap out of him until he talks?"

"I plead the Fifth, but it's probably better if no cameras are involved."

I opened the container, and my stomach started growling as soon as I got a whiff of Maybelline's pork tenderloin. "That's not gonna work, and you know it. Even if he talks under pressure, we can't be sure he's telling us the truth, and if we're gonna use this, we don't want to make the viewers hate you. That meme of you shirtless in the cotton field from last season is makin' the rounds on social media. We're likely to get even more viewers, thanks to you and your abs." I bumped my shoulder into his arm.

He grinned, but it slid off just as quickly. "If beatin' the crap out of Trent Dunbar is what it takes to find Dixie, I'll gladly do it, many times over."

"I think my way is a much more effective approach with Trent Dunbar," I said. "But if it doesn't work, we'll explore other options . . . including your fists, should it come to it."

I only hoped Trent knew something useful.

CHAPTER TWENTY-TWO

I'd never been to the Dunbar property, but everyone knew where to find it. The Dunbars owned countless acres off County Road 172, and the huge log-and-stone house was clearly visible from the road even though it was set back several hundred feet. It was easy to see why they called it a ranch. When the wrought-iron fence lining the road came into view, I slowed down and glanced over my shoulder at Bill, who was sitting in the back seat.

"This is it."

He scrunched down so that he was lying sideways in the seat, trying to stay out of view. "Turn your camera on so I can make sure it works before you pull in," he said. "You'll only have two hours of battery, but let's hope you get what you need long before then."

My hidden camera was a completely nondescript pendant hanging from a necklace. I reached behind it and flipped the switch as I turned through the open gate onto the long stone driveway. "Looks like he's prepared for me," I said. "From what I hear, the gate's usually closed."

"Or he forgot to close it after his party."

"Possible . . ."

"Are you nervous?"

"Of him? Nah. I can handle Trent Dunbar. I'm nervous that I'll handle this all wrong and walk away with nothing."

"He could be a murderer, Summer. Don't underestimate him."

Bill was right, but I couldn't let myself consider that. I was just here to find out everything I could about the party last night. Still, I found myself saying, "What if Trent killed April Jean and hid Dixie away to protect her?"

"Or make her a suspect," Bill said in a dry tone.

Or worse . . . but my mind couldn't go there.

Trent was the obvious culprit, but something just didn't feel right. "Trent spent all those years being nice to her. He visited her at juvie. I find it hard to believe he'd just turn on her."

"Didn't Clementine tell you that he snapped at Dixie last night? Told her he didn't owe her anything anymore?"

My stomach cramped. "True, but it doesn't matter, Bill. I need to know what Trent knows. Whoever took Dixie from the party probably started the fire at April Jean's. If he can tell me who she left with, at least we'll have something."

"You can get that easy, Summer. Don't underestimate yourself."

I glanced over at him. "Thanks."

I parked in the circular drive, leaving my car facing the front of the house to help Bill stay hidden. My stomach churned, and my palms were sweaty. I took a deep breath and slowly pushed it out.

"We need a code word in case you get into trouble and need help getting out," Bill said.

I turned off the engine and wiped my hands on the skirt of my dress. "Pickles, although I'm not sure what you can do to help. Just call 911."

"I'll have your back if things go badly." He said it with the utmost sincerity.

I took another deep breath and pushed it out. "Wish me luck." But I was already out and had the door closed before he could answer. No turning back now.

I walked up to the double front doors and shook my head a little when I saw the door knockers—each in the shape of a bear's head. I was reaching for the one on the right when the door opened.

Trent filled the doorway, wearing a pair of tight jeans and nothing else. A devilish smile lit up his eyes. "You came."

I resisted the urge to make a that's-what-she-said crack. Instead, I gave him plenty of sass. "I *was* the one who called *you*." Best if I sent a message right away about who, exactly, was in control.

He backed out of the way and gestured for me to walk in. I smelled beer on his breath as I walked through the two-story round entryway leading into an equally tall living room with a stone fireplace. A wall of windows faced a swimming pool, and beyond that, I could see the infamous pond.

"What's your poison?" he asked as he made his way to a wet bar.

For a brief moment, I took his words literally. *Get it together, Summer.* I turned at the waist to face him. "What are *you* havin'?" Even though it was obvious from his breath.

"A beer. My dad has a great import on tap."

"Sounds good."

He pulled two glasses, then walked over and handed me one.

"You have a beautiful view," I said as I took the glass.

He held on to it so that our fingers touched, and stared into my face. "Yes, I do." Then he gave me a grin that I was sure worked on most of the women in this town, but I'd swum with enough sharks to recognize one sidling up to me.

I gave the glass a tug, pulled it from his grasp, and moved a few feet away. I couldn't make this *too* easy for him. "I bet you say that to all the girls."

His grin spread. "But I don't mean it with *them*, sugar."

"So you're admitting that you're a liar?" I asked in a playful tone.

He laughed. "When you put it like that . . ." Then he took a long pull of his drink.

I took a sip and walked the perimeter of the room, openly taking in the artwork and knickknacks. "No other friends tonight?"

"You heard about my party?"

I picked up a ceramic bird from a bookshelf and pretended to study it. "How could I not? I was a little hurt you didn't invite me."

"No offense, Summer," he said sarcastically, "but your TV show busted Cale Malone for distributing drugs. Not exactly the guest a host with certain . . . *refreshments* wants at his party."

"Touché." I set the bird down and turned to face him. "Of course, we can have *other* fun." I paused. "I know I told you Sweet Briar bores me, and it does, but I'm also sick and tired of the noise. Of everyone always wanting something. Aren't you?"

A strange look crossed his face. "Yeah."

I sat down on a chair. "That's part of the reason I came back. Back in Hollywood, the people I met always had an agenda." I drummed my fingertips on the chair arm. "They still do here, but they don't want quite *as much*."

He sat down on the ottoman in front of me, all traces of his previous ass-hattery gone. "Yeah. I get that. I'm sure you face it more, but my dad runs the second-largest lumber company in the country. When people realize he's worth millions, I'm never sure if they want to be my friend for me or his money."

"Is that why you came back?" I asked, cocking my head to study him.

"Yeah. Among other things." Then anguish filled his eyes, and he got up and moved to the windows.

He was giving me major mixed signals, and I wasn't sure I was playing this right. Did Trent Dunbar actually have some depth? I decided to try a more down-to-earth approach. "I know you and Dixie used to have a thing. I understand if you don't want to start something with me."

Keeping his gaze on the pool, he took a sip of his beer and didn't answer, but he looked heartbroken. Had Dixie broken up with *him*? She hadn't shared any details, but then, she really hadn't told me much about him.

I got up and moved closer. "Sometimes first loves aren't meant to work out. Even if you give them some time apart. The time and distance only shines a spotlight on how different you are. Sometimes you need to grow up to see it."

He turned to me. "Dixie told you?"

Shit. How did I answer? I decided to tell the truth. Mostly. "No. I was talking about me and Luke. There's still major chemistry there, but he's lived this nice, quiet life, and I've lived *bigger*, you know? He can't relate to that." I shrugged. "And now I'm back, and we're a decade older and a lot more grown up, and I'm just not sure it's meant to be anymore."

His eyes widened before settling back into melancholy. "Yeah . . . I get that."

"I know you stuck with Dixie when everyone else abandoned her . . . including me. Thank you for that. She's very loyal to you because of it."

A mocking grin twisted his lips. "And that's the problem. Dixie is very loyal. To a fault."

"What does that mean?"

He downed his beer and walked over to the wet bar. "Need a refill?" I shook my head and watched as he refilled his glass and downed a third of it. "You need to keep up, Summer. I've already gotten a head start."

"I like to pace myself."

"Can't let me get shit-faced on my own. Then I'll look like a douche."

Ordinarily, I would have wholeheartedly agreed with him—even if I kept it to myself—but right now, I found myself feeling sorry for him. "What happened with Dixie, Trent?"

Tears filled his eyes, and he shook his head and chuckled. "I may be drunk, but I'm not drunk enough to go *there*." The way he ended his sentence had an ominous tone.

Was he talking about their relationship or something he'd done to her? He was giving off a strange vibe, and honestly, I thought it could go either way. I needed him to keep talking.

He drained another third of his beer, then topped it off again. "Let's go sit in the hot tub."

I laughed, hoping my nerves didn't show. "I didn't bring a suit."

He winked, and asshole Trent was back. "Why would you need a suit?" Then he opened the back door and left it wide-open as he unfastened the button of his jeans and walked toward the Jacuzzi.

My phone rang, and I wasn't surprised to see it was Bill. I answered, and the first thing he said was, "Do not get in that hot tub with him."

"Well, hello to you too."

"I'm serious, Summer."

"Will the camera still work if I get in but keep it out of the water?"

"Yeah, but that's not the point."

I hung up and walked out to the patio.

Trent was shucking his jeans, revealing a skin-tight pair of BVD navy-blue boxer briefs, and he was angling his body so that I had a good view of his bulge. I was just thankful he wasn't going commando. "Come on, Summer, live a little."

"Maybe I've lived too much, and that's why I'm back here in Sweet Briar." Only that was *his* story, not mine. I hadn't lived much at all back in Hollywood. It was like I'd been hanging out, waiting for my life to start . . . or restart. Had I secretly hoped Luke and I would find our way back to each other? I'd never had another relationship that lived up to what the two of us had shared, but we'd been kids. Head over heels in love and too young to fully know ourselves. Now I worried I'd lost my chance with him forever.

Trent held out his glass and shook his head. "Nope. I see the look on your face. No thinking about the assholes who have hurt us. Only onward and upward."

I moved my glass a few inches from his. "I've spilled my stupid guts about what happened with Luke. Why are you leavin' Dixie behind?"

"Because that's what she wants, okay?" he blurted out. "I've loved Dixie since we were kids, but after the fire, Daddy said I couldn't be with her or he'd disinherit me. So away I went"—he scissored his index and middle finger to mimic walking—"because stayin' here . . ." His voice trailed off, then he slammed his glass into mine, and a satisfied grin lit up his face. "That's all you get until I see more skin."

He walked down the steps into the sunken tub, holding his glass out of the water. "Come on, Summer Butler," he coaxed as he sat down. "You know you want to."

"It's too damn hot to get in a hot tub," I said as I kicked off my sandals, "but I'll sit on the edge."

"Suit yourself." A sleazy grin lifted his lips. "Or, in our case, no suit yourself."

I shook my head as I sat on the edge, tucking my legs to the side. "You're drunk."

"And you're not. You need to catch up."

I took a sip of my beer, trying to figure out how to naturally move the conversation to Dixie and the party.

"You have gorgeous legs," he said, stretching his arm along the edge of the pool as his gaze drifted to my legs. "Why're you coverin' them up?"

"Because I'm not sitting cross-legged in a dress, and it's too hot to soak my legs in the tub."

He crossed the distance between us faster than I'd expect a drunk guy to move, but then I suspected Trent Dunbar spent most of his life drunk. He grabbed my legs and swung them around so they were in

263

front of me, then pulled my feet and calves into the water. I winced from the heat, but a satisfied gleam filled his eyes. "That's better."

"That's called manhandling, Trent, and maybe you've been with women who like that kind of Neanderthal behavior, but I'm not one of them."

He stayed sunk down in the water, holding his beer with one hand while the other caressed my right calf. "For a woman who claims she's interested in other things, you don't seem very interested."

"Ever heard of foreplay?" I asked before I could stop myself. *Dammit. Dammit. Dammit.*

His eyes hooded as his hand slid up to the edge of my dress.

"I didn't mean that literally, Trent," I said, trying to stay calm. I was worried that he'd be too distracted by his efforts to sleep with me to answer my questions. "I want to talk."

"Talk?" The word came out in a whine.

"You know, something grown-ups do. Something that can lead to sex."

"You have an obsession with grown-ups," he said, his hand sliding several inches under my dress. "Grown-ups can also have sex without all the talking."

His hand slid farther up my leg, and I was a half second from kicking him in the groin when my phone began to ring.

He stilled and gave me an exasperated look.

I knew it was Bill—the timing was a dead giveaway. "I'm not going to answer it, but I'm also not going to have sex with you five minutes after showing up at your front door. Show a little more class, Trent."

He dropped his hands and slunk back to the other side of the tub. "So you want to *talk* . . ."

I kept my feet in the water. "Yeah, you know, have a conversation."

A cocky grin spread across his face. "All the other girls just drop their panties, sweetheart."

"All the other girls except Dixie," I said, taking a chance. "She's different."

His upper lip curled. "Yeah, she's different, but she's not available. I told you I left to stay away from her, but my self-righteous dad made me come back home. Doesn't matter, though, because she's still not an option. Let it go."

"He made you come back because you got in trouble one time too many," I said, then added off the top of my head, "because you were trying to forget her."

He pushed out a frustrated breath. "What's your obsession with your cousin?"

"Look," I said, affecting a high-and-mighty tone, "I'm Summer Butler. I'm not gonna be sloppy seconds to anyone, let alone my cousin."

He stared at me in disbelief, then started to laugh.

"And why is that so funny?"

"You. *You* called *me*, Summer. What are you doin' here?"

I was screwing this up big-time, but I wasn't about to give up. I couldn't afford to walk out of here with nothing. He was going to talk whether he liked it or not. "Do you love Dixie?"

"For the love of God, I just—"

"Stop," I said softly. "Just answer the damn question. Do you love her?"

He didn't verbally acknowledge it, but the look in his eyes was enough.

"Dixie's in trouble. Do you know anything about that?"

He froze. "What kind of trouble?"

"How did she get home last night?"

Fear filled his eyes. "I never saw her leave. I figured she woke up and left with someone else. She was pissed and wanted to go home earlier, but I knew if she had enough time to cool off, she'd change her mind."

"Change her mind about what?"

"About never seeing me again." He ran a hand over his head. "Who took her home?"

"You really don't know?"

"No! I just told you I didn't!"

"Did you drug her?" I asked. "To make sure she stayed until she cooled down and changed her mind?"

"What?" He stood, looking outraged. "Dixie hates drugs after what happened. She never even drinks. If I did something like that, I'd *never* have any chance of getting her back!"

"Why are you wasting her time? If your daddy won't let you have a relationship with her, then why won't you just let her go?"

"Because I planned to leave!" he shouted, moving closer to me. "And I asked her to go with me, but she said no."

"What?" I took a breath. "I had no idea . . . Dixie never told me."

"Yeah, I guessed that about five seconds after you called me," he said in disgust.

"What about April Jean?" I asked.

"What about her?"

"You must not love Dixie very much if you got drunk off your ass and went home with her two nights ago."

"I don't even remember goin' home with her," he said, then added, "And a man has needs."

To think I'd started feeling sorry for the asshole. "Well, there you go . . . ," I said in a flippant tone.

Derision filled his eyes. "You think Luke Montgomery hasn't had his fair share of women?"

"We broke up years ago, so of course he's slept with other women, just like I've slept with other men. And Dixie had relationships while you were gone, but she hasn't been with anyone since she broke up with Ryker months ago. You tried to sleep with April Jean *days* ago, Trent."

His jaw clenched. "*Tried* to sleep with her? What did she tell you?" When I didn't answer, he slapped his hand on top of the water. "Did she tell you I couldn't get it up?"

I gave him a haughty look. "Maybe she did."

"What the fuck?" He threw his glass against the concrete, and pieces of shattered glass scattered across the pool deck and into the pool. "How many people did she tell?"

"Looks like she pissed you off."

"You're damn straight she did! This isn't the first time she's pulled that shit. It's not even the third."

"That's why you killed her, isn't it?"

His face fell. "What?"

Shit. I shouldn't have told him that. Luke was going to *kill* me.

His complexion paled, and tears filled his eyes. "April Jean's dead?"

"Yeah."

He stumbled backward and fell onto one of the hot-tub benches on his butt. "How?"

I was surprised by how hard he was taking this. "I'm sorry. I shouldn't have told you like that."

He shot me a glare. "You mean by accusing me of murder?"

I grimaced.

"How'd she die?"

"I can't tell you that. You're not supposed to even know, but knowing Maybelline, it'll be public knowledge tomorrow."

"I can't believe it . . ."

"Trent, there's more."

Wide eyes lifted to mine.

"Dixie's missing. We can't find her anywhere."

If he'd looked shocked before, he now looked like he was close to passing out. "Oh, God. Someone kidnapped her from my house."

"No. She came home, although she called me from a remote place at three in the morning. Here's what I know: you refused to take her home and gave her a Coke. Soon after, she went to the bathroom for about ten minutes, then came back and got into a fight with April Jean. She fell asleep in a chair, and when some people left at midnight, she was still there. When was the last time you saw her?"

He squinted at me, and his mouth dropped open. "*Shit.* You're not here to sleep with me. You're here finding out what I know about Dixie!"

So much for my undercover skills. "We weren't sure about your involvement."

Disgust washed over his face. "And when you say *we*, you mean you and Luke . . . and Teddy."

The answer was so obvious, I didn't respond.

"Teddy hates me, and I told Dixie he would never forgive me for what happened. Not in a million years."

"Can you blame him?" I asked, not unkindly. "You were the one who gave her the drugs that got her high enough to burn down the barn. You and those drugs destroyed his whole world."

Trent climbed out of the hot tub, water dripping onto the concrete.

"But it wasn't you, was it?" I asked. "It was your brother, Troy."

He turned around to face me, his jaw dropping.

"Troy started that fire, didn't he?"

Shock filled his eyes. But there was acknowledgment too.

"He did it to get back at Dixie after she kept him from raping that girl." When he didn't contradict me, I asked, "Did you help him start the fire?"

"What?" He took a step back, bumping into a pool deck chair. "No!"

I stood and took a step toward him. "Did you know he had something planned?"

No response.

"You knew your brother was going to hurt Dixie, and you just let him?" I asked in disgust.

"No!" His eyes squinted shut, and he shook his head. "Yes. I mean I knew he was gonna retaliate, but I had no idea when or how."

"Bullshit."

His eyes flew open. "He was a mean son of a bitch, Summer. Once he decided to hurt her, there was no stopping him."

"Teddy would have beat the ever-lovin' crap out of him." I took a breath. "But Dunbars stick together, don't they? Your daddy got you both out of plenty of trouble, didn't he?"

Anguish covered his face.

I needed to get him to admit that Troy had started the fire. "When did you figure out what Troy was doing?"

"After I got to Dixie's. I was waiting in the surveyor's house, but she was stuck in the barn cleaning up horse shit. Troy showed up and said he wanted to party with us. I might have believed him, except he didn't have a girl with him."

No witnesses. "Did Dixie know he was there?"

"No! Because he left . . . or I thought he did. But he left a bottle of vodka."

"Along with some Xanax."

He nodded.

"Dixie blacked out, but you never did, did you?"

"I tried to stop him! He started goofing around with matches."

"And gasoline," I added.

Trent winced. "He never meant to kill anyone. He said he only wanted to teach Dixie a lesson."

"And you let her believe she killed her parents." Because there was no way in hell he'd turn in his brother.

Tears filled his eyes.

"Why did she smell like gasoline? Troy doused her with it, huh?"

He looked down. "Yeah."

"He could have killed her, Trent!"

"I was out of it. I wasn't thinking straight."

"Dixie figured it out, didn't she?"

"Not for a while. And she never knew for certain, but at first she couldn't figure out why I kept coming to see her while she was incarcerated."

"Because you couldn't handle your guilt." Then it hit me. "She *just* found out. That's why she ended it with you."

"I told her the truth." He bit his lip, then released a chuckle. "You know what's funny? I didn't give a shit about her before the fire. I thought I was cool for screwing Teddy Baumgartner's little sister."

"He would beat the shit out of you if he heard you say that."

A grin lit up his face, but his eyes were dead. He wiggled his fingers at me. "Tell him to come at me."

The sick part was he probably *wanted* Teddy to beat the shit out of him.

Then a new thought hit me. "Who else knows about Troy starting the fire? Who else would try to protect your secret?"

Trent opened his mouth, about to speak, when I heard Elijah Sterling behind me. "Don't you dare answer that question, Dunbar."

I pivoted to see Elijah walking toward us, his face screwed up with determination and loathing. "Well, well, well," he said. "Summer Butler's paying Trent a call. Lookin' for your slut of a cousin?"

My shock that he knew Dixie was missing quickly morphed into anger.

"That's right." He laughed, then stopped in front of me. "You may have gotten me suspended, but I still know what's goin' on in this town. And when I get back on the force, you better watch your back, little Summer." He lifted his hand to my face, stroking a finger down my cheek.

I slapped his hand away, and his face turned red.

"Back off, Elijah," Trent said, sounding pissed.

"That's right, Elijah," I said. "Back off." I gave Elijah's chest a hard shove, and he stumbled backward.

Elijah wasn't even close to backing off. He closed the distance between us and lifted a hand to slap me.

I dropped to a crouch, then brought up my fist into his crotch.

He doubled over as I fell back onto my butt and scrambled backward. I was sure I didn't look very badass, but it got the job done. Not too bad after only a few self-defense lessons.

I stood and brushed off my dress, then walked over to him. "Next time I say back off, maybe you'll listen."

"I'm gonna make you pay, Summer," he wheezed out, still doubled over.

"Talk is cheap, Elijah. I'm not scared of you." I turned around and walked over to my sandals, scooping them up by the back straps. When I rose, I faced a still-stunned Trent. "If you see Dixie, will you *please* call me?"

"Don't answer her," Elijah said, still hunched over.

"Shut up, Elijah," Trent sighed out.

I started to head toward the house, but as I passed the still-hunched-over Elijah, I kicked him hard in the side, toppling him over into the pool. "Yeah, shut up, Elijah."

I was gonna pay for that later, but for now, I was gonna gloat in taking Elijah Sterling down.

Chapter Twenty-Three

I was already talking to Bill before I walked out the front door. "Bill, I need you to make a clip of Trent's confession about his brother all the way through Elijah showing up."

An old, restored pickup truck was perpendicularly parked behind my car, blocking it in against the house and landscaping. The positioning made his intentions clear.

That son of a bitch had known I was here, and he'd purposefully blocked me from leaving.

Panic hit hard. *"Bill!"*

"Over here." Bill popped up to my left from behind some bushes. He balanced the laptop on his left palm and closed the lid. "I saw that guy turn in from the street and realized he'd see me in the back seat, so I snuck out and hid."

"Good thinking. Especially since *that guy* is Elijah Sterling . . . the police officer I got suspended."

"Oh, shit!" he gushed. "Are you okay?"

"I am, but Elijah's not so great, which is why we need to get out of here ASAP before he comes out to kill me." I put my hands on my hips. "But we're blocked in." I walked around to the driver's side of Elijah's truck, surprised to find it unlocked. I glanced over the hood at Bill. "You drive my car. Be ready to take off."

Bill gave me a leery glance. "What are you going to do?"

"Commit a felony." I climbed into Elijah's truck, realizing I didn't have much time. "At least I think it's a felony."

It was too much to hope he'd left the keys in the ignition, but I put it in neutral and then hopped out and hurried to the front of the truck.

Bill stood next to the open driver's door of my car—sans computer—and he quickly realized what I planned to do. We both put our hands on the still-warm grille and gave a hard shove. The truck started rolling, and it was soon pushed back far enough for my car to get out.

"Okay," Bill said. "Let's go."

"Not yet." I ran for the driver's door again and got inside, turning the wheel to point the truck toward the pond. Then I jumped out, leaving the door open, and ran to the tailgate.

"Summer . . ."

I ignored him and pushed with all my might. The truck barely moved. Seconds later, Bill was next to me, leaning his shoulder against the tailgate.

"Maybe it's a misdemeanor," he said with a wink.

The truck began to roll.

We grinned at each other and continued pushing. The truck picked up momentum as it started down a slight incline, heading toward the pond. When it reached the edge, we gave it one last push, shoving it over the stone edge . . . then watched as it took a nosedive into the water.

"Oh, shit," Bill said. "I didn't think it was so deep."

I moved to the side and gasped. I'd expected it to be a shallow splash pool. This had to be more than three feet deep. "Oh. Crap. Neither did I."

The water was higher than the open driver's door, and it was filling the cab up fast.

"Crap," I said, taking a few steps backward. "I think it's *definitely* a felony."

"Time to go!" Bill said, running for my car. He jumped into the driver's seat, and I ran after him, climbing into the back seat as the front door of the house burst open.

Elijah stood in the opening, his soaked clothes dripping water, his face covered with rage.

Trent was behind him, grabbing his arm and taking in the scene with a panicked expression of his own. "Elijah! No!"

"Summer, you fucking bitch!" Elijah shouted. *"I'm gonna kill you!"*

I suspected he wasn't speaking figuratively. "Go!" I shouted to Bill.

Bill backed up, tires squealing, then drove forward, taking the turn in front of the house.

Moving right toward Elijah.

"What are you doing?" I shouted. "Why didn't you back up?"

"I don't know!" Bill shrieked, his eyes wide. "I don't think well under pressure!"

Elijah body-checked the rear passenger door, reaching for the handle.

"Lock the doors!" I screamed, grabbing my purse off the floor and reaching blindly inside.

"I don't know where the lock button is!!" Bill screamed back.

Bill was nearly all the way around the circle, but Elijah got the back door open.

"Bill!"

Wearing the face of a madman, Elijah reached for me. I knew if he grabbed ahold of me, I would be facing serious pain.

My hand landed on a cylindrical metal tube, and I whipped it out just as Elijah's fingers sank into the flesh of my thigh. He struggled to keep up with the car and started dragging me across the seat to the open door, probably intending to pull me out.

"*Let go!*" Holding up the tube of pepper spray, I gave his chest a shove and sprayed his face, trying to keep the can by the open door.

Surprise filled Elijah's eyes; then he started grunting and stumbled.

Bill reached the straight part of the driveway and punched the gas pedal. Elijah tripped, and the back door whacked him in the head as he fell.

"Oh, my God," Bill shouted, looking in his rearview mirror. "Did I kill him?"

Traces of the pepper spray lingered in the car, burning my nose and eyes, and I frantically reached for the window button.

"Summer?" Bill screeched, realizing something was wrong. "What happened?"

I pressed the button and stuck my head out, trying to get a glance back at Elijah, but my eyes were too teary. I doubted we'd be lucky enough to incapacitate Elijah Sterling long enough to keep him from doing us bodily harm.

"Summer!"

"Pepper spray," I choked out, but I'd only gotten traces of it. It surely could have been much worse. Elijah had gotten a face full of it.

"Oh, my God, oh, my God, oh, my God," Bill chanted, his hands shaking. "What do we do?"

"Go back into town," I shouted, my head still out the window. Thankfully the pepper spray was wearing off.

"Trent admitted his brother killed Dixie's family."

I slid back into the car and rolled up the window, then leaned my head back on the seat. "Yeah. And Elijah Sterling seemed to know all about his friend's dirty little secret." My family would finally have closure, but we were no closer to finding Dixie. If I was a betting woman, I'd put all my money on Trent having nothing to do with her disappearance. "Trent says he didn't see who Dixie left with last night. I should have asked him who was still there when he noticed her missing." I sighed. "I still have so much to learn."

"Are you kidding me?" Bill asked as he stopped at the country road and then took the turn toward town. "You got a hell of a lot further than anyone else has gotten."

"Sure, we cleared her of the past, but we still don't know where she is."

"Between you and Teddy, we'll find her."

I hoped he was right. "So you could hear his confession okay?"

"Yeah. It helped that there wasn't any wind when you went outside."

"And the video footage?"

"Not the best, but usable. Especially the confession. We need to wait a few days and interview him about something trivial enough to convince him to sign a release. He might agree if you promise to leave the past out of it. He doesn't know you were recording, and we'll make sure the release is retroactive." He glanced back at me. "What do you want to do with the clip you asked for? Give it to Luke?"

"That was my plan . . . but maybe I can just hold on to it and give it to him when he comes to arrest me for vandalizing Elijah's truck."

"Hey, you've got something on Elijah, and he's got something on you. You can use it to your advantage. He threatened you on tape. He won't want that to leak out."

I hadn't considered that, but Bill was right. "But right now it's my word against his. He has no idea I captured it all on video."

"When we get to the office, I'll make a short clip of him threatening you, and you can text or e-mail it to him, warning that if he turns you in for damaging his truck, you'll turn your video in to Luke and the sheriff."

That would clue Trent in on the camera situation, but saving my hide from Elijah seemed like the more immediate concern.

"I don't have his number . . ." But I knew who did. I sent Amber a text asking for Elijah's cell number. I expected to have to coerce her into it, but she was taking her job as my secret informant seriously. She sent it within seconds. "Amber gave me his number, and I take the fact that she didn't mention my vandalism to mean he hasn't turned me in yet."

"He might bypass Luke and go right to the sheriff," Bill said.

Crap. He was right. "I'm gonna send him a text letting him know I have video, and I'll hold on to it for now. No mention of his truck."

"Oh! That's good. Then it's not blackmail."

Agreed. No reason to add to my list of charges. I took a deep breath and composed a text to Elijah, figuring out a way to keep Trent from knowing about the hidden camera footage.

I have proof of you attacking me, but for now I'm keeping it to myself.

He didn't answer, but then again, he might be getting a milk bath to clear out his eyes.

"What do you want to do about the confession?" Bill asked.

"Good question . . . Let me tell Teddy. Maybe it will give him some clue about what's goin' on now. I can't help but think they're connected."

I sent Teddy a text. I'm headed back into town and got lots of information. You?

He responded a half minute later. Your plan worked like a charm. Don't head to the office. We're meeting Garrett at the Jackhammer.

I relayed the information to Bill, who released a groan. "It'll be next to impossible for us to film anything usable in there. The bar will be too noisy."

"We were supposed to meet Garrett at his house. I wonder what changed." I checked my phone again. Still nothing from Elijah. I wasn't sure if that was a good thing or not.

We rode in silence and were almost to the bar off Highway 10, a few miles outside of the city limits, when my phone rang. I jumped at the sound but pressed my hand to my chest in relief when I saw the name on the screen.

"Hey, Teddy," I said when I answered. "You on your way to the bar?"

"I'm already here. How far out are you?"

"Less than five minutes. Why are we meeting Garrett at the Jackhammer?"

"I called to tell him we were gonna be late, and he said he was running late at work since he had to take time off for the fire. He asked if we could meet at the bar instead. I figured, why not."

"We won't be able to film what he says," I said. "Too noisy."

"I hadn't thought of that."

"That's okay. We need that information right now. If he tells us anything good, we'll just reschedule and pretend to hear it for the first time."

"Spoken like a true reality TV star," he said, but his tone was teasing and not judgmental.

I grinned, grateful he was helping. "What did Gabby tell you?"

"I'll tell you when you get here. I'm waiting in the parking lot. Garrett won't be here for another fifteen to twenty minutes. You got something from Trent?"

"You'll be stunned at what I got from Trent." I hung up as we pulled into the parking lot. Teddy was already sitting on the tailgate of his truck, and Bill was parked next to him.

I opened the back door to get out, but as soon as I stepped onto the gravel, I realized I'd dropped my sandals somewhere in the process of pushing Elijah's truck into the pond.

Well, crap.

Teddy had hopped off the truck and, of course, noticed right away. "Where are your shoes?"

"We were in a hurry to leave. I must have dropped them along the way."

His eyes darkened. "Why were you in a hurry to leave?"

"I'm fine, Teddy. I took care of it."

"Boy, did she ever," Bill said in awe as he pushed open the driver's door. "I've got video evidence to prove what a badass she was."

I shot him a glare and shook my head, drawing my finger across my neck.

He cringed, realizing his mistake.

"What happened?" Teddy growled.

"Calm down," I said. "I'm perfectly unscathed."

"The other guy, not so much," Bill said. Chuckling, he got out of my car and moved to the trunk.

"Not helping," I said through gritted teeth. I took a breath and shot a fake smile up at my cousin. "What did you find out from Gabby?"

"Do you have a spare pair of shoes?" Teddy asked as his gaze drifted to my feet. "How are you gonna get inside?"

"I don't know . . ."

He opened his truck door, and I wondered if he was about to leave and get me a pair, but he leaned behind the seat and rummaged around before pulling out a pair of brown cowboy boots with tassels. "Here. See if these fit."

"You don't strike me as a guy who wears tasseled cowboy boots," I teased.

"Shut up. They belong to an old girlfriend."

"And you kept her boots?" I asked.

He tossed them at me. "I bought them as a gift, and we broke up before I could give them to Dix, but she hated Lorraine and would refuse to wear them on principle alone. If they fit you, they're yours."

I sat down on the back seat and stuffed my foot into one of the boots. "Hey. They do fit."

"Good, put the other one on, and I'll fill you in on what happened at Gabby and Mark's."

I had the boot on in no time, and Teddy and I sat on the tailgate to talk.

"Teddy, are you wearing a mike?" Bill asked. He had his camera in his arms.

"Yeah, and it's still on."

"Hey," I said, "where are Tony and Chuck?"

"I dropped them off at the office to get a new battery for Tony's camera and their car. They'll be here shortly." He turned to face me. "You were dead right about Gabby. She jumped at the chance to audition for the *Housewives* show and spilled everything. She and Mark were fighting, just like Clementine said, and she admitted to staying at the party after Clementine and some others left. But she said she and Mark stayed another half hour or so, or at least until Amelia left."

"So who was left?"

"April Jean and Bruce."

"Bruce was still there?"

"Yeah. And they both said he was acting weird. He kept trying to get April Jean to let him go home with her."

"Are you serious? Did she take him?"

"They left before there was a resolution. But they also said they thought they saw Rick slinkin' around in Trent's house."

My brow lowered. "Clementine said Rick left around the time Dixie went in to use the bathroom. What if he drugged her and then came back to get her later? Trent said he was planning to take her home eventually, but she left, and he had no idea who she went with."

"I estimate that puts us at twelve thirty to one a.m. at the latest," Teddy said. "And you got the call around three?"

"Yeah . . ." My brain was trying to put it all together. "We need to find out who was still at the party when Trent noticed Dixie was gone."

"Are you sure Trent wasn't lyin'?" Teddy asked. "He's probably got her locked in his room. Did you hear anything? Did you snoop around?"

"He doesn't have her, Teddy. He loves her."

"Bullshit."

"Yeah, I thought so too, but he was pretty convincin'. Or at least he loves her as much as he's capable of love. I believe him."

He started to protest, but I held up a hand. "I could explain it all to you, but I think you should just watch the video." I hopped down, and Bill backed up and motioned for Teddy to head over to the front passenger seat. Sure enough, the laptop was out. I grabbed it and sat down next to Teddy. Bill walked over and entered the password, then stepped back and resumed filming.

Thankfully the software was similar to basic video software. To my surprise, I realized the minicamera was still recording. I turned it off, then moved the cursor to the beginning and let it play.

Teddy watched the video, stone-faced. His jaw twitched when Trent dropped his pants, and he about leaped off the tailgate as he watched Trent try, again and again, to pull me into the hot tub.

I put my hand on his forearm and leaned my head into his shoulder. This was going to be equally hard and justifying for him. "Just wait."

We finally got to the part where Trent admitted to what his brother had done, and Teddy immediately went rigid. I was pretty sure there was a passing chance he might head down to the cemetery to beat the shit out of Troy Dunbar's body.

We got to the part when I asked Trent who else knew about what his brother had done, and when Elijah started talking, I pressed "Stop."

Teddy shot me a dark glance. "Who was that, and why did you turn it off?"

"Because the next part is liable to piss you off, and I'm scared of what you'll do."

His eyes became narrow slits. "Let me watch it, and then you'll find out for yourself."

"Teddy . . ."

He glanced up. "Bill. You just press 'Play'?"

"Yeah."

I almost fought him on it. I wasn't sure it was a good idea for him to see this in the Jackhammer parking lot, especially when Garrett was about to show up at any minute, but I also wanted his advice on how to handle the situation.

Teddy pressed "Play," and I was sure my cousin was going to have a stroke. When I ducked and punched Elijah in the crotch, Teddy wrapped an arm around my back and leaned his head on top of mine. "That's my hotheaded Summy."

He laughed when I pushed Elijah into the pool. "Remind me never to piss you off."

"Keep watching," Bill said. "There's more."

He grinned from ear to ear when we pushed the truck into the pond, but his face clouded over again when Elijah raced after the car and tried to snatch me. I played it all the way to our escape before stopping the footage.

He was silent for a few moments, then said, "You can definitely take care of yourself."

The pride in his voice made my eyes sting. "Thanks."

"Elijah is a dangerous loose cannon. We have to take this up with the sheriff's department."

"We can't," I said. "Sure, he threatened me, but my temper got the better of me, and I ruined his truck. I could get arrested for that."

"I have friends in the department, Summer. I'll call them."

"No. Deputy Dixon has a bee in his bonnet for me, and I don't want to press my luck."

"You plan to let this go?" he asked, his voice rising. "Someone like Elijah Sterling doesn't let things go, Summer."

"Just like Troy Dunbar."

Realization filled Teddy's eyes.

"They were best friends until Troy died," I added, "and Elijah certainly made it sound like they knew each other's secrets." What if Trent's daddy had convinced Mayor Sterling to hire Elijah to help protect the Dunbars' secrets?

And just like that, Elijah Sterling became my suspect number one.

CHAPTER TWENTY-FOUR

I opened my mouth to tell Teddy what I was thinking, but Garrett's car pulled into the spot on the other side of mine. Our time to talk privately had ended.

Teddy leaned into my ear as he shut the laptop. "We'll continue the discussion about Elijah later."

I nodded as Garrett got out of his car and headed toward us.

"Thanks for meetin' me here," he said, looking slightly flustered. "I had a devil of a time getting off. My boss is getting ticked about me bein' gone so much."

"Really?" I asked. "But you're performing a public service."

He frowned. "What are you gonna do? I love puttin' out fires and protecting the town." He paused and turned solemn. "Sorry about Dixie."

"She didn't do it," I said defensively, handing the computer off to Bill.

He gave a slight nod and a tight smile, but I knew he was just placating me. Still, he had information, and I had to be polite until I had what I needed.

"Do you mind goin' in?" he asked. "I'm starving, and it's wings night."

"Yeah . . . sure," I said, gesturing toward the building.

He grinned, his gaze scanning me up and down. "Ladies first." But then he glanced back at Bill, who was still recording. "But no cameras. This is off the record."

Bill's gaze caught mine, and his eyebrows lifted. He was waiting for orders from me.

"Take a break. Why don't you and the guys get some wings and a beer?" I held the pendant at my neck, flipping the switch on the back.

Bill grinned. "Thanks, Summer. Sounds good. I'll just wait out here for the other guys to show up."

Garrett and Teddy followed me inside, and I chose a table close to the stage. It was early enough that the live entertainment hadn't started yet. Teddy and I sat on one side, and Garrett sat across from us.

A waitress came over, and Garrett and Teddy put in their orders. I glanced up at the waitress. "Do you have bottled water?"

She laughed as her nose scrunched. "No. This ain't California, Isabella."

"My name's *Summer*, and bottled water isn't just a California thing. The Kum and Go has bottled water just down the street," I said with a sweeping gesture.

"Then feel free to head down the street to get one, because we don't have any here."

"Just get her a glass of water," Garrett said in a patronizing tone.

Oh, hell, no, he didn't. I turned and shot him a glare so dark Teddy looked like he was hurting himself trying not to laugh. "No." My tone was sharp. "Bring me a bottle of beer. Unopened."

She put a hand on her hip and looked down at me like I was a fool. "You plannin' on takin' it home? It don't work like that."

"Just bring it."

She walked off grumbling, and Garrett shot me a confused look. "What's the big deal?"

But I caught Teddy's gaze—I wouldn't need to tell *him* I was worried about being drugged. He gave me a tiny nod, then turned to his friend and said, "Thanks for meetin' us, Garrett. I know you're beat from workin' two fires in such a short period of time."

"Three, if you include Bruce's," I said, the only olive branch he was getting from me.

"Yeah, it's been crazy, but I know you've got two interests in this, and I want to help." He gave Teddy a sympathetic look. "I know Dixie means the world to you."

Teddy nodded once, his face blank. "Thanks."

"This can't be on your show," Garrett said again. "What I'm about to give you could get me in trouble."

"We know," I said. I wouldn't use the footage from the necklace camera on the show, but we could analyze it later.

"And again," Teddy said, "we appreciate you tellin' us."

The waitress showed up with our drinks and dropped a plastic container filled with buffalo wings and fries in front of Garrett. She handed me a still-closed bottle and gave me an annoyed look. "I suppose you want me to bring you a bottle opener?"

"Nope," Teddy said, reaching for the bottle. "I've got it covered, Olivia. Thanks." Then he opened it on the edge of the table and handed it to me.

"What's with the bottle thing?" Garrett asked.

As far as I knew, only a few people knew that Dixie had been drugged. I wasn't ready to let the information out into the wild. I was about to make up some story, but Teddy beat me to it.

"It's a California thing," Teddy said. "It keeps the beer colder a little longer."

Garrett gave him a look of disbelief. "For about thirty seconds longer."

I gave him a shrug, then lifted the bottle to my lips and took a drink. This was one situation where I was perfectly satisfied letting someone think I was a diva.

Garrett glanced at the door. "I'm not sure we should talk about this here."

Teddy leaned his forearms on the table. "You were the one who suggested we come here."

"That was before *he* showed up."

I glanced over my shoulder and saw Luke standing a few feet from the front door, scanning the room.

Great.

I knew it was too much to hope we wouldn't cross paths. He was still wearing his jeans and T-shirt, and something deep in my chest tightened at the sight of him. But I couldn't give in to my feelings. Dixie was counting on me, and time was running out.

He headed straight for our table, and the look on his face suggested his mood hadn't improved any since he'd stormed out of my office.

Stopping next to our table, he skipped the customary pleasantries and lifted his cell phone. "Summer, know anything about this?"

On his screen was a photo of Elijah's truck nose down in the three-foot pond.

How should I play this? Feigned innocence or outrage? Outrage was more likely to ring true. "And why would you think I'd know anything about that?" I asked with plenty of sass.

Garrett leaned closer, his mouth gaping. "Is that Elijah Sterling's truck?"

Teddy got a good look, then burst out laughing.

Luke's eyes narrowed. "Well?"

"Are you kiddin' me?" I asked in a huffy tone. "Someone drives their truck into a giant puddle, and you immediately think, 'Oh, this must be Summer's doin'?'"

"That and the fact Elijah Sterling texted this photo with the message, 'Ask Summer what she knows about my truck.'"

Well played, Elijah. Time to feign innocence. "And I just told you."

"No . . ." Luke sat in the seat next to Garrett, directly across from me, and grabbed my beer bottle off the table. "You didn't." He took a drink and glanced around the room. "What are y'all doing at the Jackhammer while Dixie's missin'?"

Teddy bristled. "I don't see that it's any of your damn business. And seein' how you're the only law enforcement at the table, what the hell are you doin' harassin' my cousin about a piece-of-shit truck when you should be out there lookin' for my sister?"

Regret washed over Luke's face, but he didn't apologize. Instead, he sat back in his chair. "It's funny you're both hangin' out with Garrett Newcomer."

"Not so strange," Teddy said, barely containing his rage, "considering Garrett and I are friends."

Luke's mouth twisted, and he gave a slight shrug, then took another sip of my beer.

Garrett eyed him cautiously.

"What do you want, Montgomery?" Teddy asked.

"I want to know what happened to Elijah's truck."

"Then what the hell are you doin' sittin' here for? You asked Summer, she gave you an answer. Now get the hell out."

"I saw Bill out front."

My breath caught. "He's waitin' for the rest of my crew so we can go to our next location."

"I showed him the photo of Elijah's truck too."

"You must be pretty damn proud of it since you seem to be showin' it to everyone," Teddy said. "Envious, Luke?"

Luke ignored him, keeping his gaze on me. "His reaction was interestin.'"

Do not take the bait, Summer. "Huh."

"His first reaction was fear, then he looked a little nervous."

I tilted my head. "Bill's been a little nervous over everything since getting shot. Besides, maybe he has a thing for old trucks. If you showed me a photo of a pair of Louboutins dropped into a big puddle like that, I'd likely have the same reaction."

A grin tugged at the corners of his lips, then he took a long drink of my beer.

My phone buzzed with a text, and I took a quick peek at the message from Elijah.

Two can play that game.

Luke tried to glance at my phone over the table, but I stuffed it back into my pocket and rolled my eyes.

"Seein' how you've drunk almost all my beer, I think I'll walk up to the bar and get a new one." Hopefully Luke would follow, and Garrett would loosen his lips. Teddy could fill me in later. We wouldn't get it on film, but we couldn't use the footage anyway.

I walked up to an open space at the bar and leaned both elbows on it. The bartender was at the opposite end, but I felt Luke walk up behind me. Lightly pressing his chest to my back, he rested his hand on my left hip and leaned into my ear. "Did you have another altercation with Elijah?" The worry in his voice was unmistakable, and I spun around to face him.

"I'm fine."

Anxiousness filled his eyes as his hand resettled on my hip. "That much is obvious, but if he's harassin' you, I need to know."

"I took care of it."

"By drivin' his truck into the Dunbars' pond?" When he saw the surprise in my eyes, he added. "I've been to the Dunbar ranch enough times to recognize the landscapin'."

Should I tell him about Trent's confession about his brother? Part of me wasn't ready to do that. I knew how profoundly it would affect Luke. Much better for me to break the news in private than in the middle of a bar.

"You went to see Trent." It wasn't a question.

"You know I'm investigatin'. Same as you. Just usin' different tactics."

"And he let Bill in with his camera?"

"Bill didn't go in."

His left eye twitched. "You were alone with Trent and Elijah?"

"I don't know why you and Teddy think I'm some delicate flower, but I've proven many times over that I can take care of myself."

His gaze was on my lips, and his hand tightened on my hip. "I know, but I still worry, Summer. Elijah Sterling is more of a hothead than when we were kids. He must have done something to you before you did this to his truck. Why won't you tell me what happened?"

Because I still wasn't sure if I could trust him, and while Trent's confession was illuminating, we weren't any closer to finding Dixie. The footage wasn't going anywhere.

"I'll show you later," I said.

"As much as I'd like that to be a dirty reference, I suspect you got some video even if Bill wasn't at your side."

"I got something very useful. Two somethings, and you wouldn't have either one without my cameras—the ones you claimed I was using to take advantage of Dixie's misfortunes."

Regret washed over his face. "You're right. I'm sorry."

I cocked an eyebrow. "Can you repeat that? I could have sworn you just apologized."

A sad smile lifted his mouth. "I'm so used to doin' things by the book . . . I refused to think outside the box. By the time I got to the police station, I knew I'd screwed up, but I wasn't sure what to do about it."

"So you tracked me down at the Jackhammer to ask me if I vandalized Elijah Sterling's truck?"

He made a face. "So I've got to work on my technique."

I gave him a wry grin. "I'll say."

"I was worried about you, Summer. Elijah was taunting me with that photo, and I'm pretty damn sure it was a threat to you. What happened?"

"I don't think I should tell you in here."

"My truck's out back. Why don't we go sit out there while Teddy quizzes Garrett about the fires?" My eyes widened, and he laughed. "You didn't think you were foolin' me, did you?"

"Well . . ." I sent Teddy a text saying I was going to wait outside with Luke, then left before he could send me a dirty look.

Luke wrapped an arm around my lower back and guided me toward his truck in the back of the lot. I reached up and flipped off the switch on my pendant. Bill and the guys didn't need to see what happened next.

After opening the passenger door, Luke grabbed my waist and lifted me up so I was sitting with my legs over the side of the seat. His gaze took me in before he said, "I thought I lost you with my idiocy." Then, before I could respond, he kissed me.

I wrapped my arms around his neck and pulled him close, savoring his gentle kiss.

"I was lookin' forward to spendin' time with you tonight," he said. "If you want, you can still come over after you finish for the night."

I leaned back. "I want to. You have to know that, but I don't want our first time to be with Dixie missin'. Not like this."

"I know," he said with a soft smile. "I understand."

"I'm scared we're not gonna work out," I said, deciding to at least be honest about my fears. "You got mad and just left, and I was pretty sure you were walkin' out on me for good."

He lifted a hand to my cheek. "I know, Summer, and I'm so sorry."

"If we're gonna try this, I need to know that you're committed to it. We might not work out in the end, but if I'm gonna put effort into us, I have to know that you're not just gonna bolt at the first sign of trouble."

"I swear to you that I'm all in, but you also know that when it comes to you, sometimes I'm quick to react and slow to come to my senses. I'll promise to do my best to keep a lid on it, and I also promise that if I get mad again—which, let's face it, we both know I will—that if I walk out, I'm not walking out on you, okay? I'm only leaving to keep myself from saying something I'll regret later. And if . . ." He took a deep breath, and sadness filled his eyes. "If we don't work out, we won't officially end things in a fit of anger, but in a calm discussion." His expression turned fierce. "But you need to know that I'm goin' into this plannin' on forever, Summer. You are the love of my life, and I only want you."

Tears stung my eyes. "I feel the same way." I tugged his mouth to mine, and he spread my legs apart, pressing his body into mine. His hands tangled in my hair as his lips became more demanding.

I heard his phone ringing, and at first I thought he was going to ignore it, but he pulled away with a groan of frustration and glanced at his screen. His face went blank, and he answered in a somber tone. "Montgomery."

He was silent for more than half a minute, his face giving nothing away, which was my clue that this was serious and probably not news I wanted to hear.

"I'll meet you there," he said, then hung up, lifting his gaze to mine.

My stomach churned, and I felt nauseated. This was about Dixie. I knew it in my gut. "What happened?"

"Deputy Dixon found Dixie."

Relief washed through me, but then I realized that Luke wasn't nearly as relieved as he should have been.

Horror washed through me, and I felt faint. "She's dead."

"What? No!" He shook his head and grabbed my upper arms. "Oh, God, Summer. No. I'm sorry."

"Then why do you look so upset?"

"He found her in her car in a picnic area."

"What? She didn't have her car with her today. And what do you mean *found her*?"

"It was definitely her car, but she was totally out of it. There's more."

I forced myself to settle down and concentrate. "Okay . . ."

"They found a needle and syringe on the passenger seat. And he found a handgun, an empty gasoline container, and a lighter in the trunk."

Dixie had been set up. Again.

Chapter Twenty-Five

I shook my head. "No. She didn't do it."

"I *know* she didn't do it. We'll find out what happened and clear her of it, but they took her to Sweet Briar Hospital, so we've got to get over there."

"*Teddy.*"

"I'll go in and tell him, and I'll tell Bill too. You just wait here and ride with me to the hospital."

It would be so easy to let Luke handle it all, but I couldn't be that woman. I needed to take care of my own shit. "I'll tell Teddy. You tell Bill. But I'll ride to the hospital with you."

Uncertainty wavered in his eyes, but he said, "Okay."

He grabbed my waist and slid me off the seat, then wrapped his arms around my back and pulled me close. "I'm here for you, Summer, no matter what you need, okay? Don't shut me out."

"Thanks."

He released me, and we headed for the front of the bar. I opened the door to go inside, but Teddy was on his way out with a wild look in his eyes. "Summer. They found Dixie."

"Luke just got a call. I was on my way in to tell you."

"We need to go to Sweet Briar Hospital."

Teddy looked so upset, I couldn't possibly let him go alone. I glanced back at Luke.

Luke gave me a reassuring nod. "Go with Teddy. I'll meet you there."

Teddy was holding his keys, so I took them from him and grabbed his hand, linking our fingers. "What else did you hear?"

"Everything." He sounded devastated.

I should have gathered that by his reaction.

"She didn't do it, Summer. She would never kill April Jean, let alone shoot herself up with heroin."

"I know that. You don't have to convince me of anything."

"But the sheriff's department is fallin' for it hook, line and sinker."

Luke was telling my crew about Dixie while Teddy got into the passenger door of his truck. I climbed up into the driver's side, and Luke glanced over at me, mouthing *It's gonna be okay.*

I bit my bottom lip and nodded. I sure hoped he was right.

I backed out of the parking space, then turned onto the highway. "The sheriff's department may have bought it, but we know it's not true. We'll prove she didn't do it. Now focus. What did Garrett tell you?"

"Uh . . ." He scrubbed his face with his hands. "The last fire was completely different from the ones at April Jean's and Bruce's."

"How so?"

"April Jean's and Bruce's fires had one point of ignition, while the fire at the thrift store looked like it had been doused with gasoline."

"Like the fire that killed your parents."

"Yeah."

"But Troy's dead," I said. "And we know Dixie didn't do it, so obviously someone was trying to mimic the barn fire."

"It could be anyone," Teddy said in frustration. "Everyone knows the barn was doused with gasoline."

"Did he say anything else?"

"That it looks like the arsonist today was trying to mimic the previous fires but didn't know anything about them."

"So we're lookin' at two different arsonists," I said. I turned and cast him a glance. "Which means there goes our theory that the murderer tried to kill April Jean by burnin' up her trailer."

Teddy groaned in frustration. "We're no closer than we were before."

"I know it feels like it, Teddy, but we're gettin' there, bit by bit."

He reached over and captured my hand in his. "I don't know what I'd do if you weren't here, Summer."

"Good thing you don't have to find out. I'm not goin' anywhere anytime soon."

We were silent for a minute before Teddy said, "I take it you and Luke kissed and made up."

I wasn't going to admit that it was true in a literal sense. "He admitted that he screwed up."

"Well, that's something, I guess."

I shrugged. "We can't help who we love."

"*Do* you love him, Summy?"

I realized what I'd just said. "Honestly? I don't know. I know I'm still hung up on him. We agreed we're gonna give this a real try . . . no runnin' when things get hard. So I guess we'll see."

He was silent for a moment. "He still loves you. He always has, but you're right. You're different people now. Just know it might end badly."

"I know." I couldn't see us ending things and staying on good terms.

"But if it does," he said, "ask yourself if you're gonna run away and leave me and Dixie behind. Because it's going to be awkward as hell with the two of you in the same town."

I hoped it never came to that.

I pulled into the hospital parking lot, and Teddy was out of the truck before I was finished parking. I chased after him, coming to a full stop in the ER waiting room. Two deputies had blocked Teddy's admittance through the door to the back.

"Is she under arrest?" Teddy demanded.

"No, but—"

"But nothin'," Teddy said. "She's my sister, and I want to see her."

"Sorry, Teddy," one of the deputies said in a sympathetic tone. "We have orders to keep you and your cousin out."

"You can't keep *me* out," Luke said from behind me.

The deputies straightened as Luke walked across the room. "Chief Montgomery," they said in unison.

Luke stopped next to Teddy. "Where's Deputy Dixon?"

"He had to step out for a bit."

"Then get out of the way, Keith. I'm goin' back to see one of my citizens."

"We're not supposed to let *anyone* back, Chief."

"This is my damned town," Luke said, his voice calm but direct. "And I'm goin' back there."

The deputy scowled, but he stepped to the side. Luke pushed the door open, then glanced back at my cousin. "Teddy, my department's short an officer since Sterling's on leave. Mind fillin' in for a day or two?"

Teddy perked up when he realized what Luke was up to. "Not a problem."

"Deputies," Luke said, "I'm going to need Special Officer Baumgartner to accompany me to the back."

"That's bullshit, and you know it," the other deputy said.

Luke moved closer and looked him in the eye. "In case y'all have forgotten, we are in Sweet Briar, and Dixie Baumgartner was found *within* city limits. I'm the damn chief of police in this town, so I'll go back and see the suspect if I damn well please, and I'll bring my staff with me."

"But, Chief . . ."

Luke ignored him, pushing the door open wider. "Teddy, let's go." Just when I was starting to think I'd have to stay behind, Luke shifted his gaze to me. "Summer, as special consultant, you need to come back too."

The deputy started to protest, but Luke silenced him with a dark look. I followed them back and down the hall. Luke studied the doors and opened the one at the end of the short hall, holding it open for me and Teddy to enter first.

Dixie was on a hospital bed wearing a hospital gown, and one wrist was handcuffed to the metal rail. She looked terrified.

"Dixie," Teddy said, rushing to her side.

I hung back against the wall at the foot of her bed. She looked so tiny and helpless, and I was overwhelmed by the thought that getting her out of this rested on my shoulders.

She scanned the room. "What happened?"

"They found you in your car," Luke said, moving to the end of her bed. "Dixie, you overdosed."

Her eyes flew wide, and she shook her head vigorously. "No. I didn't take anything." She looked up at Teddy and started to cry. "I didn't do it, Teddy. *I swear.*"

He ran a hand over the top of her head. "It's okay, Dix."

"But I didn't do it!"

"Dixie," Luke said, his voice gentle, "what's the last thing you remember before you woke up?"

She started crying. "I don't know."

"I need you to think about it, okay?" he asked, continuing to be sweet with her as he moved to the other side of her bed. "You were heading to Connor's office and never made it. Do you remember what happened next?" He pulled a chair up to her bed and sat down, then leaned closer.

"I was walking toward his office, and I heard someone call my name as I was crossing Willow Street. I walked toward the voice, and then . . . nothing." Her gaze found mine. "What happened after that?"

"Male voice or female?"

"Male."

"Dixie," Luke said, "do you remember seeing anyone as you headed toward the voice?"

She shook her head.

"Do you remember anyone hitting you over the head or covering your face?"

"No. Last I remember, I was walkin' past the dumpster."

"Until you woke up in your car hours later?" Luke asked.

"Yeah. Deputy Dixon was there shakin' me and yellin' at me."

"Did he ask you questions?"

"I think so, but I was so tired, I kept fallin' asleep." Her gaze landed on me. "What happened, Summer?"

"You've been missin' for hours. We've been lookin' for you."

"I don't understand what happened . . ."

Luke stood and moved closer to me. "I'm gonna go talk to the medical staff and let you two have a moment alone with her."

He headed out the door, and I followed him into the hall. Grabbing his arm, I whispered, "Why is she wearing handcuffs?"

He looked guarded. "They think she's a flight risk."

"They said she hasn't been arrested yet."

"But she's in custody," he said with a frown. "I suspect they're waiting for toxicology results to arrest her for drug possession and possibly driving under the influence. They'll want to keep her locked up until they can build the murder and arson case." He shook his head. "But it's already pretty damning. They're tryin' to make sure the charges stick."

My head swam. "She's not comin' home, is she?"

He paused, then said, "No, Summer. She's not. Not yet."

Part of me wanted to cry and admit defeat, but the rest of me was good and riled up. I was going to save my cousin and take down whatever no-good bastard had done this to her.

Luke tilted my head back and gave me a gentle kiss, then looked into my eyes. "We'll do whatever we need to do to get her out of this. Now go back inside and reassure her while I find a nurse and figure out what happened. Dixie needs you and Teddy right now."

I nodded and started to go back in, but Luke grabbed my arm.

Anger filled his eyes. "Summer, someone set her up, and we're gonna figure out who. But we both know that you can do things I can't." He paused and dropped his hand. "We need to keep workin' this separately, and you need to use every trick at your disposal to clear her name because I think you're the one who's gonna crack this." Then he turned around and walked down the hall.

Chapter Twenty-Six

By the time I'd gone back inside, Teddy had broken the news about April Jean and the fire. Part of me was upset with him. Dixie looked too fragile to handle the news, but she needed to know the truth, and better to hear it from her brother than Deputy Butthead.

Her gaze landed on me, her eyes wild with fear.

I rushed to the other side of the bed. "I'm gonna get you out of this, Dix. I swear it."

She nodded as tears rolled down her cheeks.

"I need you to be straight with me, okay? I need you to tell me more about what happened at Trent's party."

Her eyes shuttered.

"Don't you *dare* shut down on me."

She jolted at my harsh tone.

I continued, even though I could tell Teddy thought I was pushing too hard. "I talked to Trent tonight. I know you know the truth about Troy setting the barn fire."

Her eyes flew wide with surprise.

"What can I say?" I said flippantly. "We had a really great chat, but I need you to fill in some of the blank spaces. When did he tell you about Troy?"

She was quiet for a few seconds, and at first I didn't think she was going to answer. "Before everyone showed up at the party. We were in the kitchen."

"How did you take it?"

Anger flashed in her eyes. "How do you think I took it? I told him I was gonna tell Luke and that he was an accessory to murder and who knew what else, but he begged me to stay quiet. He offered me money to keep it to myself." She shook her head in disgust. "But first he asked me to run off with him, can you believe it? He let the whole world think I killed Momma, Daddy, and Pawpaw—even though he *knew* I was innocent—and then he had the nerve to expect I'd run off into the sunset with him." Her face fell. "Besides, I knew he didn't mean it. I think he thought that's what I wanted, and suggestin' it would keep me quiet."

"Why didn't you call me to come get you?" Teddy asked. "Why in God's name did you stay?"

"Because I was still upset over dinner. And people had already started arriving for the party. In fact, April Jean was standing at the back door after I told Trent what he could do with his offer to run off together."

"Wait," I said. "Do you think April Jean heard Trent's admission about his brother?"

Confusion washed over her face. "I don't know. Maybe."

I sat down on the chair Luke had used and grabbed her hand, careful not to disturb her IVs. "Think, Dixie. Did she say anything to make you think she did? I know you two got into that argument. Maybe she let something slip then?"

She thought it over for a moment before shaking her head. "I don't think so. Although I heard her say my name when she was talkin' to Rick Springfield in the house."

My eyes flew wide. "What? When was that?"

"When I went in to use the bathroom."

"Did you set your Coke down when you went to the bathroom?"

She hesitated. "Yeah . . ." Her body stiffened. "April Jean and Rick saw me put it down. They stopped their conversation to wait for me to walk down the hall."

My gaze lifted to Teddy. "We have to find Rick Springfield."

He gave me a sharp nod.

"You think the two of them drugged me?" Dixie asked.

"Rick was seen at the house while you were in the bathroom. He left the party at around that time, but when Gabby left with Mark, she thought she saw Rick in the house."

"What if Rick took her?" I asked Teddy.

"And then what?" He turned to Dixie. "Did he and April Jean look angry with one another? Were they arguin'?"

"No, they looked like they were cookin' up a plan."

"I think Rick took her," I said, getting excited. "His cousin recognized her when we did that shoot at Rick's house, and he looked nervous. I think he saw her with Rick."

"Only no one seems to know this mysterious cousin," Teddy said. "Where do we find him?"

"Why don't we ask Rick?"

Fresh tears filled Dixie's eyes. "Thank you for believin' me."

I gasped. "Why wouldn't I believe you?"

"Because everyone else is so eager to believe I did it. And it looks pretty bad."

The door opened, and Deputy Dixon said, "You have *no idea* how bad this looks." He stopped at the corner of the bed. "You two need to leave. Now."

Fear filled Dixie's eyes.

Teddy grabbed her hand. "It's gonna be okay, Dix."

The deputy stood at the end of her bed. "Dixie Baumgartner, you're under arrest for possession of a controlled substance."

Teddy jumped to his feet. "You can't arrest her for OD'ing. What about the Good Samaritan law?"

"That only applies if the suspect calls 911 seeking medical attention. Your sister did not. I found her unconscious behind the wheel of her car. Not only that," Deputy Dixon said, sounding a little too smug for my liking, "we found a stash of heroin in the glove box."

"It was planted," Teddy said, puffing out his chest.

"Face it," Deputy Dixon said. "Your sister has always been a user. All your parading around at the sheriff's department couldn't save her sorry ass."

Teddy launched toward him, but Luke appeared out of nowhere and jumped in front of him. "Don't do it, Teddy. He's goadin' you, and it's workin'."

Teddy still looked like he was about to rip Ryan Dixon limb from limb.

"Get him out of here," I said to Luke, sounding more in control than I felt.

"Dixie!" Teddy called out as Luke dragged him out of the room. "We'll get you out of this."

"I'm okay, Teddy!"

I turned to Dixie. "Don't you say a word to anyone, you hear me? I'll get you the best damn lawyer in the state, and we'll get you out of this, but keep your mouth shut. Got it?"

She nodded, her eyes brimming with tears.

I grabbed the back of her head and brought our foreheads together. "I'm here this time, Dixie," I whispered, "and I'm not goin' anywhere, got it?"

She nodded, tears tracking down her face. "Got it."

"You need to leave, Ms. Butler," the deputy said.

"I love you, Summer," Dixie said, starting to sob.

"I love you too." All I wanted to do was hold her close and tell her everything would be all right. But that wouldn't make it true. I had to go out and make it right myself.

I kissed her forehead and walked around the bed to leave. The satisfied gleam in Deputy Ryan's eyes made me sick. "There's a special place in hell for people like you, Deputy."

"What? For making the world a better place?"

"Is that what you think you're doin'?" I asked in contempt. "Once again, you've gotten it wrong. Maybe you should go to detective school and learn how to solve a case."

A derisive laugh bubbled in his chest. "Like you do on your TV show?"

I jutted my head back with a smirk. "My track record's beatin' yours, so maybe you shouldn't look so smug."

I headed for the door, where Luke was watching us with a dark look.

"You shouldn't have antagonized him like that," he said, falling into step with me as I marched down the hall. "You could make it worse for Dixie."

Dammit. He was right, but it was too late to do anything about that now.

"I found out that Dixie was unresponsive when Dixon found her, but the ambulance gave her Narcan, and she came around on the way to the hospital. They want to keep her overnight to keep an eye on her, so she'll stay here until her arraignment tomorrow morning at nine."

"Where's Teddy?"

"I don't know, but he took off, mutterin' something about Rick Springfield."

I came to a full stop. "What?"

"Is Teddy goin' to see him?" Luke asked, sounding concerned.

"I don't know. Maybe." Probably.

"You have to call him off, Summer. Rick Springfield is nearly as crazy as Elijah Sterling."

"This town is overrun with lunatics." I shook my head. "You're right, but nothing I say will call Teddy back." Even though I knew I'd stew until I heard from him. "Dammit."

I walked out to the parking lot as fast as I could, but sure enough, Teddy's truck was already gone. "He left me." But I was more worried about him facing Rick on his own than about finding a ride.

Bill must have driven my car to the hospital, because my crew was sitting on the hood, and they jumped to their feet when they saw me come out. "How's Dixie?" Bill asked.

"Luke wouldn't tell us anything," Chuck said.

"Dixie overdosed on heroin, but she's awake and scared." I scanned their shocked faces. "She didn't do this to herself. Someone did this to her, and if you believe otherwise, pack up your stuff and go work for Connor."

All three looked solemn, but Tony said, "We all know she was kidnapped. The important thing is that she's okay. We all want to find out who did this to her."

"Thanks," I said, taking a moment to get myself together. "They're arresting her for drug possession, but they found things in the trunk of her car that set her up for the murder and the fire. She doesn't remember anything, but she *did* fill us in on some more information about the party. Did Teddy say *anything* before he took off?"

"No," Tony said. "We asked about Dixie, but he didn't answer. Then we asked if he wanted a camera crew to come with him, and he said just said no and drove off."

"What do we do now?" Bill asked.

I took a good look at them and realized they looked as exhausted as I felt. This had to be the longest day ever. "We're done for the night.

Go back to your hotel and get some sleep, but be at the office by eight so we can get going early."

"Where do you plan to start?" Tony asked.

I shook my head, feeling overwhelmed. "I don't know."

Luke wrapped an arm around my shoulders. "I think Summer needs a good night's sleep too. Y'all can start fresh tomorrow."

Bill shot Luke a glare. He obviously still held a grudge over Luke walking out earlier.

"He's right," I said. "We're exhausted, and I can't think straight. Hopefully we'll have some ideas in the morning."

"Okay." Bill opened the car door and pulled out his laptop. "I didn't want to leave your car, so the guys and I drove over here separately. I'll get my things out of here and catch a ride with them."

I took the necklace and handed it to Tony. "Make sure this is charged. I have a feeling I'm gonna need it tomorrow."

He gave me a curt nod. "Consider it done."

I walked over to Luke's truck with him. "Thanks for gettin' us back to see Dixie."

He rested his hand on my shoulder. "She needed you. She needed to know she has your support."

I nodded, then lowered my voice. "She told us more about the party. Information that might help us figure out who really did it." I heaved out a sigh. "I'm going home. I'm tired, and even if I came into contact with the real killer right now, I'd be too exhausted to ask the right questions. I'll see you tomorrow."

He held on to my shoulder. "You're not ditchin' me yet. I'm comin' home with you."

"Why?" I asked, feeling edgy all over again.

"Because you're gonna need help tellin' your grandma."

Oh. Crap. How had I completely forgotten about breaking the news to Meemaw? She wasn't going to take it well. This could be the straw that destroyed our family.

Luke could read my emotional turmoil. "I'm gonna help you break it to her, so why don't you ride with me? We'll pick up your car tomorrow."

I started to say no, that I didn't want to be stuck without a car, but then I remembered that I'd left the truck out at the farm. "Okay. It's probably a good idea for me to ride with you. Then I can tell you everything I found out at Trent's. It might help us break the news to Meemaw." Although I knew how much it was bound to hurt Luke, he needed to know.

By the time Luke parked in front of the farmhouse, I'd told him everything—about Trent's confession (which put a pained grimace on his face), my encounter with Elijah, and what Dixie had told Teddy and me while he was checking with the hospital staff.

He turned off the engine and turned to me. I braced myself for a lecture about Elijah, but he just looked worried. "Are you really okay after your encounter with Elijah? Are you sure you didn't leave anything out?

"I told you everything."

His gentleness fell away. "I need you to file another report."

I shook my head. "No. Elijah and I are at a stalemate. We both hold the power to destroy each other . . . which he wouldn't have if I'd kept my temper."

"If you tell anyone I told you this, I'll deny it to my dying breath, but I'm glad you pushed his precious baby into that pond."

That got a grin out of me, but it quickly faded as I turned to face the house. My stomach flip-flopped at the prospect of repeating all this to Meemaw, but something told me it wasn't time just yet. Luke was still stewing over the big news about Dixie's past. I needed to give him a moment to work through it.

"What are you gonna do with Trent's confession?"

Anguish filled his eyes. "I sent her to jail, Summer."

"You didn't know."

"I should have investigated more. Asked more questions . . . but I was young and had only been doin' this for a year or so, and my boss agreed that it was clear-cut . . ."

"Luke."

He stopped but wouldn't look at me. "The thing is, if it happened to someone else now—the exact same way—I'm not so sure I would do anything different. All these years of experience, and I'd probably make the same mistake."

"It looked so obvious. I can see why you didn't search more. It's the whole don't-look-for-a-zebra-when-it's-likely-a-horse thing."

He picked at a flake of loose leather on his steering wheel. "Yeah." But he didn't sound convinced.

"Dixie won't blame you for what happened. And I don't either. You did the best you could."

He shook his head. "Teddy must hate me even more."

"You're human. You made a mistake."

"A mistake that ruined Dixie's life."

"Not ruined. She's okay." But we both knew it had affected her in more ways than either of us probably realized. "When this is all said and done, I want to make this public," I said. "I'm sick of hearing people make ugly comments to her."

He swallowed and then nodded. "Agreed. I'll figure out a way to make it happen."

"You don't have to think too hard," I teased. "You can just tell Maybelline and let her post it on her Facebook page."

"Dixie deserves better than that. And I suspect the Dunbars have done some behind-the-scenes work to make sure it stays buried . . . case in point, Elijah Sterling."

"I can't help but wonder if Roger Dunbar played some part in getting Elijah hired."

Luke made a face. "I'm pretty damn sure he did. I didn't mention it to you before, but rumor has it Elijah spent a shit ton of money on his new truck. The Sweet Briar Police Department salary is barely enough to live on, so where did the money come from? What if Roger Dunbar paid him extra to help protect this son?"

So we needed to prove Elijah had been paid off too. My to-do list just kept growing.

Luke shook his head in self-disgust. "What's done is done. I can't take back the time she lost, but I can try to make it right." He took a deep breath. "All right, it's time for me to go in there and convince your grandmother that I fucked up ten years ago and that Dixie's innocent now."

"If anyone can do it, you can. She loves you."

He opened his door. "We'll see if she still loves me when we're done."

Meemaw was watching TV when we walked in, and if she was surprised to see Luke, she didn't let on.

"Miss Viola," Luke said, "I need to talk to you."

"Is this about Dixie?" she asked, her gaze still on the TV screen.

Her disinterest hurt my heart. "So you heard?"

"Irma works in housekeepin' at the hospital and couldn't wait to tell me," she said in disgust.

Luke walked over to the TV and held his hand over the "Power" button. "May I?"

"Do whatever you gotta do, then turn it back on."

"How can you be like this?" I asked in dismay. "Dixie's in trouble. Don't you care?"

Her gaze lifted to mine. "I cared a decade ago, until that girl stole half my family from me."

"And then you chased me off too," I said, my anger rising. "You alienated me and Dixie and nearly ran Teddy off too, and all because of your stupid pride!"

Fire filled her eyes as she got to her feet. "Don't you be talkin' to me about runnin' off, Summer Lynn Baumgartner! You know a thing or two about that, don't ya?"

Tears filled my eyes, but I reminded myself this wasn't about me. It was about Dixie. "Well, you wrote her off for absolutely nothin'!" I shouted. "Because she didn't do it, and instead of bein' there for her when she needed you the most, you abandoned her!" I broke into a sob.

Her anger softened a bit, but she still looked irritated. "What are you talkin' about?"

"Summer." Luke's tone was gentle as he gripped my shoulders and bent at the knees to look me in the eye. "Why don't you go get a drink of water and let me tell her, okay?"

He was right. I was handling it all wrong. I nodded and headed to the kitchen, taking deep breaths in my attempt to calm down.

Why had I attacked Meemaw like that? It hadn't helped anything. Then the cold, hard truth hit me—I was angry with myself, and I was takin' it out on her. I'd abandoned Dixie too, but it was easier to put all the blame on my grandmother.

Oh, Dixie.

Five minutes later, Luke walked in looking like he'd been through an emotional wringer.

"You okay?" I asked.

"Yeah."

"And Meemaw?"

"She went to her room. She wants to be alone."

I nodded.

"Feel like takin' a walk?" he asked.

"Sure." After grabbing a flashlight on the kitchen table, I opened the back door and held it open.

He glanced down at my feet. "You sure you don't want to change shoes first?"

I realized I was still wearing my new boots. "Nah. I think this makes me more of a Baumgartner."

He followed me outside and captured my hand in his. "For what it's worth, there's no question that you're a Baumgartner, whether you're wearing cowboy boots or not."

I gave him a tight smile. "Thanks."

We walked in silence for nearly five minutes before the surveyor's house came into view.

"Mind if I check it out?" he asked.

I knew what he was doing. He was going over the events of that night, trying to see what he'd missed, even if any clues from the night would be long gone by now. I almost told him not to beat himself up over it, but then I realized how patronizing that would sound. I needed to let him work through his demons. He needed me to support him through it.

"No. Of course not." I handed him the flashlight.

We continued in silence until he reached the house. He walked around the outside, shining the flashlight beam at the base of the house, then checked the area all around it.

"Is it okay if I go inside?" he asked.

I looked up at him and kissed him on the lips. "Of course."

I wasn't surprised to find the front door unlocked. I flipped a light switch by the door, surprised that a lamp turned on, and equally surprised to find that the inside was in much better shape than the outside.

It was a tiny house, built in the late 1800s and intended to house a single man. The kitchen was archaic, but there was a dorm-size fridge next to the potbellied stove. Someone had moved an older sofa inside, and there was a bed in a small room off to the side.

"Someone's been stayin' out here," I said to myself.

"Dixie," Luke said, peering into the bedroom. "She mentioned that she's stayed out here from time to time after you left."

"When we were kids?"

"No. Back in May."

That caught me by surprise, but I kept it to myself. I could see how staying in the house with Meemaw might be unbearable at times. In fact, while I wanted to live in close proximity to my cousins, I wondered if I should consider moving out. We were grown adults practically living on top of each other.

"Maybe I should redo this place," I said, opening a cabinet door. One hinge was unscrewed, and the door went catawampus. "Dixie and I can move out here together."

"Can you afford it?"

"I have a little money left from last season, and I'll get paid for this one."

"Maybe you'd rather put the money toward your own land."

"*This* is my land." I stared out the window at the cotton fields, the white flowers filling me with a sense of contentment. "This is why I came back. This is what I was fighting for all those years." I turned back to face him. "Plus, as stupid as it sounds, I want to be close to Teddy and Dixie."

"It's not stupid, Summer. I get it. But what about your grandmother?"

I shook my head. I didn't want to think about her. It only added to my own guilt.

"For what it's worth, she's not taking this well."

"She turned her back on her own granddaughter. When Dixie needed her the most." I had too, but at least I was supporting her this time.

"I'm not sayin' what she did was right, but she lost her husband and her son. She was hurtin' too."

"Still . . ."

He pulled me into his arms. "You can't judge her for bein' the way she's always been, Summer," he said softly.

I sighed. "You're right. But I can hold a grudge for how much she's hurt Dixie."

"You Baumgartners are famous for your grudges."

I grinned and looked up at him. "But some of us are more forgiving than the others."

"Thank God for that."

He kissed me. His lips were soft and tender, but then he became bolder, and something stirred inside me, a deep craving for more. I wrapped my arms around his neck and pulled him closer, deepening the kiss.

He groaned, and his arm slipped around my back, pulling my body flush with his. His tongue parted my lips, coaxing mine into a passionate kiss.

I slipped my hands up his shirt, letting my hands explore his back. His free hand landed on my waist and then slid upward, cupping my breast over my dress.

I moaned and pressed myself into him, frustrated and needing more.

His head lifted. "I want you, Summer, but I know you want to wait—"

I cut him off with a kiss as I moved my hands down to his butt and pulled him even closer. "I don't want to wait. I need you."

He stilled and searched my eyes. "I'm in no hurry. We have the whole rest of our lives to sleep together."

I gave him a soft smile. "And sayin' things like that only makes me want to sleep with you more."

He glanced around the room. "Do you want to go home with me?"

I shook my head. "I've decided to move out here. Let's sleep here tonight. And if Dixie agrees to live out here too, I'll build her the best damn bedroom she's ever dreamed of."

He smiled and cupped my cheek. "I love that you're so certain you'll find a way to prove her innocence."

"I refuse to consider anything less."

A strange look filled his eyes. "Do me a favor."

My eyes narrowed. "What?"

"Put that same determination into us, because I suspect if you keep doin' this, today's fight will be far from our last. But as long as we're stubbornly determined to make us work, we will."

My heart melted. "I promise." I took his hand and pulled him into the bedroom. The room was barely large enough to hold a full-size bed, a bedside table with a lamp, and a dresser. The bed was made with an old-fashioned white chenille spread I'd seen on my grandmother's bed when I was a kid. I turned on the lamp.

"Are you sure, Summer?" he asked. "We can just sleep together, and I'll hold you. I know you're exhausted."

"No," I said, reaching for the hem of his shirt. "I want to consummate our agreement. To make it official. Besides, I'm tired of waiting. I want you. All of you." I slowly lifted his shirt until it reached his shoulders, and then he pulled it the rest of the way over his head.

Smiling, I placed my palms on his chest, reveling in the feel of him under my fingertips.

"I want to see you too," he said in a husky voice.

I took a step back and reached for the bottom of my dress. Luke brushed my hands out of the way and took over, lifting my dress until I was standing in front of him wearing only my panties and bra. His gaze wandered over my body, and my breath caught when I saw the lust in his eyes.

"I've wanted you for so long," he murmured, dropping his mouth to my neck, his lips brushing the sensitive skin.

A shiver rushed through me, and my knees went weak. Closing my eyes, I rested my hands on his shoulders. How many times had I dreamed of this? Dared to hope to have a second chance with him?

His hand cupped my butt, digging into my flesh. I reached between us and found the button of his jeans, then undid his zipper and began to tug.

He helped me push them over his hips, then kicked off his shoes and jeans so he was standing in front of me wearing just his tight boxer-briefs.

I lifted my gaze to his, and he grinned. "Do you know how sexy you are standing like that in your lingerie and boots?"

I gave him a saucy look. "I had no idea you had a thing for cowboy boots."

He grinned. "I never did until just now." He gently pushed me backward until I was sitting on the bed. He slid off his underwear but didn't give me much time to look at him before he knelt in front of me and tugged off my boots. Resting a hand on my shoulder, he pushed me flat on my back. His lust-filled eyes held mine as he placed a light kiss on my calf, then blazed a trail up to my inner thigh with his lips and tongue.

"Birth control?" he asked as he hooked his fingers on the sides of my panties. "I want this worked out before we get much further." His hooded eyes lifted to mine. "Because once I get these off, I don't want to think about anything else but your gorgeous body."

"An IUD."

"Do you want me to wear a condom too?" he asked. "Because I don't have one."

"I haven't had sex in two years, so no chance of getting anything from me." I paused, surprised at the jealousy I felt asking, "You?"

He shook his head. "It's been a while. And I used a condom."

"Then we're good," I said. "We've had *the talk*."

He grinned, but his gaze darkened as he pulled my panties over my hips and down my legs. He rose slightly and placed a kiss on my abdomen.

I sucked in a breath as his mouth skimmed down to my pubic bone. He moved between my legs, stretching his arms out on either side of me, and I rested my hands on his biceps, needing to touch him.

It didn't take long before I was dangerously close. "Luke . . ."

His face lifted, and he kissed his way up my stomach to the underside of my breast. He undid the front clasp of my bra and let it fall to the side.

I moaned as his tongue tortured one nipple and his hand fondled the other.

My core throbbed with need, and I grabbed his arms and pulled him up so his face was over mine. "I want you," I said in a husky voice I barely recognized.

"I want to look at you," he said, his gaze sweeping my face and then my naked body as he hovered over me.

He leaned down and kissed me while his hand slipped between my legs. Soon I was squirming, and I lifted a leg and hooked it around the small of his back.

Lifting his head, he watched my face as he probed my entrance and then slowly slid inside me.

I closed my eyes, relishing the feel of him and desperately needing more. I arched my back, taking him deeper, and he groaned.

"I'm trying to make this last," he said through gritted teeth, "but you're makin' that difficult."

I captured his face with both hands. "I don't want you to make it last. I don't want you to go slow. I want you to make me yours."

My words set something loose inside him. He grabbed my hip and plunged in deep.

I cried out, trying to take him even deeper as he continued to thrust into me. Something inside me coiled tighter and tighter until it finally snapped, and wave after wave of pleasure rocked through my body, stealing my breath as he gave one final thrust and groaned.

When I came to my senses, I was lying on my side in his arms, and he was staring at me in wonderment.

"I love you, Summer Baumgartner," he said softly. "I always have, and I always will."

"I love you too." As I said the words, I realized that it was true. But I couldn't let my love life make me forget my priorities. Dixie's freedom came first.

Chapter Twenty-Seven

I woke up with Luke's arm wrapped around me and faint sunlight filtering through the window. I had to go to the bathroom, so I slid out from under his arm and grabbed my phone to check the time, but he pulled me back.

"Where are you goin'? You said you weren't goin' into the office until eight."

"I have to go to the bathroom, but even so, I'll have to go up to the house at some point to get ready. It's already six."

"You can't get up until I kiss you good morning." He rolled me onto my back and gave me a soft kiss, but then it became more insistent, and his hand slid up my side to my breast.

I squirmed as parts of me heated up. "I still need to go to the bathroom."

He groaned. "I have to get up anyway. I need to go home to shower and change before I head to the station. Willy was on call last night, and I'm takin' the fact that I never heard from him as a good sign." He tucked my hair behind my ear. "You gonna see if Teddy's back?"

Teddy had called me around eleven to say he hadn't found Rick, but he planned to hang out at the Jackhammer to see if he turned up. I hadn't heard from him yet. "Yeah, but part of me hopes he didn't find him."

He gave me a look of surprise.

"Look," I said, getting out of bed and scooping up my underwear and bra off the floor, "we both know that Teddy was gonna go in like a bull in a china shop. A guy like Rick Springfield's gonna take more finesse."

Luke sat upright as I padded out of the room. "And I take it you're suggestin' you have the smoother technique?"

"I got all kinds of information out of Trent Dunbar. More than anyone else ever did," I called to him before I shut the bathroom door.

I quickly did my business, looking around the small room and thinking about how I could possibly remodel. When I opened the door, already dressed in my lingerie, I found Luke outside the door waiting for me, his shoulder leaning into the door frame and blocking my exit.

"When you suggest you had a special way of getting information out of Trent Dunbar, which you plan to use on Rick Springfield, what exactly are you talkin' about?"

I ducked under his arm and headed back to the bedroom. "A girl has to use her feminine wiles."

He was hot on my heels. "And what exactly are those?"

I picked up my dress off the floor and grinned. "Jealous?"

"Yes," he admitted with a dark look. "Very."

I walked over and gave him a kiss. "You don't have to worry. All it takes is a little flirting."

His brow lowered. "Someone like Rick doesn't stop at just flirting, Summer."

I tugged my dress over my head. "I know how to take care of myself. I took care of Elijah, didn't I?"

"Springfield's ten times meaner than Elijah Sterling."

I pushed out a breath. "I'll be careful. I promise."

He wrapped an arm around my back and pulled me flush against his naked body. "If you go to see Rick Springfield, I want you to let me know."

"Why? So you can babysit me?"

"No. So I can be your backup. If I don't hear from you in fifteen minutes, I'll come and check on you."

"Oh." That could come in handy.

"That's not something I want to make a habit of, but Lord knows we need all the help we can get to clear Dixie's name."

I nodded. I starting to feel guilty over the time I'd spent with Luke. Dixie was lying in a hospital bed awaiting her arraignment.

"Hey," he said, lifting my chin, "Dixie's gonna be thrilled we're really together. You know she's been wanting this since the moment you came back."

I gave him a weak smile. "Yeah. You're right."

"Let me get dressed, and we can walk up to the house together. If you'd like, I'll help you make a game plan for today."

I almost told him I could do it alone but decided to shelve my pride and accept his help. He'd done this a whole lot more than I had. "Thanks."

After Luke dressed and we started walking, we both agreed—although Luke was reluctant to admit it—that Rick was at the top of my list of interviewees.

"I want to interview Rick's cousin too. Not Herbert," I quickly added. "I want to talk to the cousin no one seems to know about. Nash Jackson."

"The one who pushed you out of Amelia's path?"

"Yeah." I turned to look at him. "What happened when you went to see her?"

"I never found her. I need to get on that today."

"You should make Willy handle it," I said. "He actually saw the whole thing."

"You're right, but he gets tongue-tied when he's around her. He couldn't arrest her if she was robbing the Dairy Queen at gunpoint right in front of him."

"No offense," I said, "and I don't mean to judge, but why on earth do you have him on the force?"

"Because until lately, it hasn't been a problem. We've never had this much crime. If this keeps up, I'm gonna have to petition city council for another officer."

"Surely they'll see that it's justified."

"They probably will, but like everything else in city government, it's a matter of money. The city of Sweet Briar is strapped."

"Oh."

He snagged my hand and laced our fingers. "You worry about Darling Investigations, and let me worry about the Sweet Briar Police Department, okay?" A sexy smile spread across his face.

When he looked at me like that, I'd do almost anything for him, but I wasn't stupid enough to admit that. "Okay."

"So how do you propose to find this mysterious Nash?" Luke asked.

"It looked like he was stayin' out at Rick's house," I said. "Maybe I'll just ask Rick when I see him."

"You think he's just gonna tell you?"

I shrugged. "Stranger things have happened." I was hopin' he'd just be there. That would certainly make things easier.

"Who else is on your list?"

"I want to talk to Bruce. He showed up as some of the partygoers were leavin' at midnight, which seems kind of fishy. I know he stayed until Gabby and Mark left, so maybe he saw who took Dixie. Plus," I added, "I asked him to give me an interview about his house fire. I still need to set that up."

"I thought Connor Blake was handling the arson cases."

"He is," I said. "I originally set this up just to tick off Connor. Now Bruce might have something I can actually use."

"Who else?"

"I'd like to talk to Amelia too."

"You're not gonna harass her about nearly runnin' you over, are you? Because it'll be safer to let me handle it."

"She's an interesting . . . character," I said. "So I think she might have a different insight into what happened at Trent's party. Hey," I said as a thought hit me, "I just realized that Elijah Sterling wasn't on the guest list."

"He worked Monday night until I took over on call. And you said Trent was handing out drugs. Maybe Elijah had the sense to not be part of that."

I wasn't so sure Elijah had enough sense to work his way out of a paper bag, but I suspected that was my bitterness showing. I shouldn't underestimate him.

Then a new thought threw me into a panic. "Oh, my goodness! I need to hire an attorney for Dixie. How could I forget?"

He cringed. "Summer, it's okay. I already called someone to handle the arraignment. You don't have to use her for Dixie's case, but she's good and fair. The judges respect her, which is gonna be important. You can interview her later to see if you want to officially hire her."

I pushed out a breath of relief. "Thank you."

He gave me a sad smile. "I knew you were overwhelmed, and I have experience with the attorneys. Her name's Lindy Baker. I'll text you her number so you can set up an interview."

The house and barn came into view.

Luke broke away and moved toward the barn, then turned and glanced back at the surveyor's house.

I put a hand on his arm and rubbed lightly.

"I'm so sorry." His voice broke.

"I know." I slid my arms around his waist and pressed myself against him, my cheek resting on his chest. He sank into me, his arms encircling my back. We stood like that for nearly a minute before he finally said, "I consider you a gift, Summer. A gift I won't take for granted this time. Thank you for just . . . bein' here."

I smiled up at him. "That's what girlfriends are for, right?" Then I kissed him and stepped away. "Now I need to get ready for work, and so do you."

We started walking toward the house, and relief washed through me when I saw Teddy's truck on the other side of the barn, but it occurred to me that we had no idea who had taken Dixie's car and when.

"Did you ask Meemaw if she saw anyone pick up Dixie's car?" I asked as we walked to the back door.

"No. She was so upset, and I didn't want to press her when it could wait until today." A sly grin lit up his eyes. "Besides, you know your grandmother. If she saw someone take Dixie's car, she would have led with that last night when we walked in the door."

I knew he was right, but a surge of disappointment rose up. If Meemaw had seen the car thief, that would have made things too easy, and I'd used up easy at Trent's last night. "Yeah, you're right. I'll ask her this morning before I leave." I climbed a step to put me more on eye level with Luke. "Will you go to the arraignment?"

"I'm gonna try my best to be there, but I suspect it'll be more low-key and unimpressive than you think. The attorney will enter her not-guilty plea, and the district attorney will make a suggestion for bail. If it's low enough and you can post it, Dixie could be out of jail by this afternoon. But given the notoriety of your show and Dixie's past . . . there's a chance he'll deny bail or make it so high that none of you will be able to afford it."

"On a simple drug charge?" Teddy asked in disbelief from inside the kitchen.

Luke glanced up at my cousin, who now stood behind the screen door. "It's Bixley County, which means it's a crapshoot, but we'll hope for the best, and Lindy will fight for her. I promise you that."

"Lindy?" Teddy asked.

"Her attorney," I said. I turned to Luke and gave him a quick kiss, then whispered, "Be safe today."

Luke seemed to realize I was talking low so Teddy wouldn't hear, but he had other ideas. He hooked his arm around my waist and hauled me to his chest. "I want to see you after you finish for the day, but I know both of our schedules are crazy. Maybe you can stay at my house tonight." He gave me a lingering kiss. "Bring a bag." Then he released me and walked to the front of the house.

I walked inside, ready for Teddy to pounce on me, but he didn't say a word, just sipped his coffee while leaning his butt against the counter.

"Have you seen Meemaw today?" I asked.

"No. She's still in her room."

"I need to ask her about Dixie's car."

"I heard."

"No lectures?" I asked.

"You're a grown woman, Summer. You don't need me to run your love life."

Something was off. "Teddy. What's wrong?"

He dumped his coffee down the sink and rinsed out the cup. "What's wrong is that my sister was arrested for something she didn't do. What's wrong is that I couldn't find Rick Springfield. And since I couldn't find Springfield and beat the shit out of him to make him admit to kidnapping and drugging my sister, she's about to be arraigned. *Again*." His voice boomed throughout the room. "*That's* what's wrong."

So obviously an unfortunate choice of words . . .

He set the empty cup in the sink and turned to me. "Once again, I have to stand back and let the legal system steal my sister from me."

"No. We'll find him, and we'll prove she didn't do this. But first I need to get ready, then talk to Meemaw about Dixie's car. What do you have planned for the day?"

"I have to spend the morning checking the fields." He headed for the door. "I'm gonna get an early start and then clean up and head in for the arraignment. I'll see you there." He went outside, and the door banged shut behind him.

"Teddy!" I shouted through the screen.

He stopped and turned to look at me.

I pushed the door open. "I'm sorry."

"What do you have to be sorry for?"

For sleeping with Luke while he was trying to find Rick? Because he was going through this hell again? I said the only thing I knew to say. "I love you."

His Adam's apple bobbed. "I love you too, Summy." Then he headed into the barn.

I poured a cup of coffee and grabbed some clean clothes from my room and headed upstairs, groaning when I realized I hadn't checked on the status of the plumber for the downstairs bathroom.

I took a long shower, letting myself break down in tears when I thought about how frightened Dixie had to be, all alone in that hospital room. I considered trying to stop by to see her, but I doubted the sheriff's deputies would let me in, and the truth was that I would better serve Dixie by looking for the killer.

I dressed in a skirt and button-up shirt and pulled my damp hair back into a French braid. I kept my makeup light since I had no idea how much I'd be outside in the heat. After I headed downstairs and grabbed a pair of flats, I searched for Meemaw and found her in the kitchen. She sat at the kitchen table, staring at her half-full coffee cup. She didn't look up when I walked into the room.

"Good morning, Meemaw." I kept my tone light even though I was still angry with her. I could only assume the feeling was mutual, but hopefully she wasn't too angry to talk.

She still didn't answer, so I got a fresh cup of coffee and sat down across from her. "I need to ask you a question about Dixie's car."

"What about it?" she asked in a gruff tone.

Whew. "Dixie rode into town with me yesterday. After lunch, I came out and swapped the truck for my car, but at *some point* someone came and got Dixie's car. I'm trying to figure out how and when. Did you hear or see anything? It would have been anywhere between three thirty and . . . eight or eight thirty." I shook my head, realizing the window was even wider. "Strike that. He or she could have come to get it anytime after I left with the car. Did you hear *me* when I came to get it?"

"All y'all were so loud even your pawpaw heard ya out in the cemetery."

Relief washed through me. I had a shot at getting an answer. "So whoever took Dixie's car would have gotten it after that. Did you see or hear anything?"

"No, but I ran into town to do some grocery shopping midafternoon, and when I came back, her car was gone."

I scooted forward on my seat. "Okay, that's good. When did you leave, and when did you come home?"

"I was gone between two thirty and four."

Dixie was taken at around three thirty, and I saw the arsonist run out of the building around four thirty. The killer must have kidnapped Dixie and hidden her somewhere, lured April Jean into the building, killed her and set the fire, stolen Dixie's car, and then put Dixie in her car at the park—oh, and overdosed her with heroin . . .

that was a lot of steps. Plenty of room for something to go wrong. But then something hit me, and I felt like a fool, wondering why I hadn't thought of this before. The person who came and took Dixie's car couldn't have come out here on their own, which meant they had help.

This was another confirmation I was looking at two suspects.

CHAPTER TWENTY-EIGHT

Bill was already at the office when I got there, so we got a good half-hour head start on the day, not that it did us much good.

We went out to Rick's house, but there'd been neither hide nor hair of him. Nor was there any sign of Nash Jackson.

"Maybe he's hiding," Bill said. "If he killed April Jean and kidnapped and drugged Dixie, he might be lying low."

"Granted," I said, "I don't know him very well other than the fact he sicced his alligator on me, but I think it's safe to presume he's not a lie-low kind of guy." But I had to admit his disappearance was suspicious.

"True."

I'd gotten Amelia's address, and we stopped by her place on the way back to town, but she wasn't home either.

Despite batting zero, I made it to the courthouse with only a few minutes to spare. I didn't see Luke, but Teddy was sitting in the row directly behind the defense attorney's table, and I slid onto the seat next to him. But what shocked me the most was that Meemaw was sitting on the other side of him, her back ramrod stiff.

I grabbed Teddy's hand and squeezed, leaning forward slightly to verify I wasn't hallucinating—our grandmother had shown up for the arraignment.

A woman in a suit hurried down the aisle and dumped her bag on the defense table before turning around to face us. "I'm Lindy Baker, Dixie's attorney. You must be Summer and Teddy Baumgartner." She held out her hand, and we both got to our feet and shook her hand as though on autopilot.

Then she turned to Meemaw. "And you must be Viola."

Our grandmother didn't stand, but she nodded.

Lindy's gaze returned to Teddy and me. "I assure you that I will do my utmost to help Dixie, but we're pushin' a boulder uphill. It's important y'all know that before the arraignment because I suspect the DA's office is gonna play hardball, especially in light of the Cale Malone drug ring and murders a few months ago. The DA's office feels like it's in the hot seat, and they're trying to prove they're serious about ridding the county of crime." She gave Teddy a sympathetic look. "And what better poster child than the sister of the guy who busted Malone?"

Teddy merely nodded, and my stomach flip-flopped with nerves.

"Now this will go fast," she said, raising her hands and holding the palms together. "So fast you'll wonder how you missed it, but you need to stay seated and stay silent. No shouting about the unfairness of the bail. No demanding justice." Her eyebrows rose, and I could see she was waiting for our acknowledgment.

"What makes you think we'd do such a thing?" I asked.

She glanced at the aisle, and a half grin lifted her lips. "I may have gotten a little advance warning from him."

I turned to see Luke striding down the aisle. He was dressed in his uniform, and my insides turned to mush at the sight of him.

He slid into the seat next to me. "Sorry I'm running late."

"I was just fillin' the family in on what to expect," the attorney said, and the way she looked at him made it obvious Lindy Baker was a Luke Montgomery fan, and I suspected it didn't just include his police work.

A surge of jealousy rose in me, catching me off guard and irritating the crap out of me. I didn't have time to waste on my stupid insecurities.

Luke wrapped an arm around my back. "I appreciate you helpin' out Dixie, Lindy."

She blinked, and if I hadn't been looking, I would have never noticed her reaction. Her smile didn't quite reach her eyes. She was still processing this new information.

"After the arraignment, we'll file out, and I'll talk to you in the hall, but until then, it's important you remain silent."

None of us said anything.

She continued, avoiding looking at Luke or me. "You also need to know that while you'll see Dixie, you won't get an opportunity to talk to her. I know that will be hard, but if you press it, the judge will likely kick you out."

My grandmother grunted.

"Any questions?" Lindy asked. When we didn't ask anything, she said, "Okay. Let's see if I can get a decent bail set."

The bailiff came in moments later and called the court to order, and the judge entered the room. The next thing I knew, Dixie was marched in through a side door wearing a gray jumpsuit, with chains connecting her handcuffs to the manacles on her ankles.

Luke's arm tightened around me, and he leaned into my ear. "It's standard procedure. Don't let it alarm you."

It may have been standard, but this was Dixie, and she looked so small and frail, it was a wonder she could carry it all. She caught our gaze as she shuffled behind the table, her eyes growing wide when she saw Meemaw.

Our grandmother leaned over the waist-high fence. "You're a Baumgartner, and Baumgartners stick together. It took me a little bit to remember that, but I'm here for you, girl."

Tears filled Dixie's eyes, but Lindy shot Meemaw a glare and turned Dixie to face the front.

Lindy and Luke had been right. The arraignment was over in the blink of an eye. After very little persuading by the assistant DA, the judge withheld bail despite Lindy's insistence that Dixie had been a model citizen up to her arrest and that her whole world centered around her family and farm—she had nothing else to run to.

The next thing I knew, Dixie was gone.

The judge called the next case, and we left the courtroom, forming a huddle about twenty feet from the doors.

"No bail?" Teddy asked, his anger rising.

"We knew that was a possibility," Lindy said in a calm voice. "We'll just wait for the other charges to be filed, and then we'll see what kind of plea bargain they'll offer."

Teddy's voice rose. "Plea bargain?"

The courtroom door opened, and out of the corner of my eye, I saw a man walk out. I did a double take when I realized who he was.

Nash Jackson had come to Dixie's arraignment. Why?

But Teddy was becoming irate. He turned to Luke. "This is your idea of a *good attorney*?"

I wanted to run after Nash, but I didn't dare leave this powder keg. "Teddy, let's discuss this somewhere more private."

"No." He kept his glare on the attorney. "Let's make something perfectly clear right now. Dixie is innocent, and there will be no plea bargain. We did that before, and she was just as innocent then as she is now."

Lindy gave him a patient look. I suspected Teddy's reaction wasn't uncommon. "We have to be practical. I'm not saying she should take it, but we'll compare it with the evidence and decide what's in her best interest. A trial will be expensive and could net a longer sentence than a plea."

Teddy shook his head. "What about justice? She didn't do it!"

She gave him a sympathetic look. "We should meet in my office to discuss this further, but since we know additional charges are pending, I suggest we wait until they're filed. Then we'll know what we're facing."

Teddy stormed off, but Meemaw pointed her finger at the attorney. "My granddaughter's innocent, and I'll be damned if her own attorney says differently. We'll fight this, and if you don't wanna fight, then you best get *the hell* out of the way."

Lindy's face paled.

Meemaw turned to Luke. "I thought you said you got a good lawyer."

He looked chagrined. "Miss Viola, Lindy is one of the best—"

My grandmother turned to me. "Summer Lynn, you got any of that TV money left?"

"Yes, ma'am. Some."

"Then find your cousin the best damn lawyer that money will buy. I'll mortgage the farm if I have to."

I held up my hands. "Whoa. No mortgaging the farm. I'll find the money, but hopefully it won't come to that." I glanced down the hall Nash had walked down. Was it too late to catch up with him? "But right now I've got to go."

I took off down the hall, ignoring Luke as he called after me.

The hallway led to some offices and an elevator. I doubted he'd slipped into an office, and I didn't want to wait for the elevator, so I took the stairwell. No matter how fast I raced down those steps, I knew it was probably a lost cause. He had a good head start on me.

I pushed open the door, finding myself in a more crowded hallway. When I reached the courthouse entrance, I ran out the front door and scanned the sidewalk. A blue Dodge Ram truck was pulling out of the parking lot.

"Dammit!" There was no way I could get to my truck in time to catch up to him, but I took note that he was headed east on Highway 10.

"Summer!" Luke hollered, and I turned to see his worried face. "What happened?"

"Nash Jackson was in the courtroom."

His jaw dropped. "You're kidding."

"I saw him walk out while we were outside the courtroom talkin' to Lindy."

"Why didn't you say anything?" he asked, sounding exasperated.

"Because Teddy was goin' off on your girlfriend!"

He blinked. "What are you *talkin' about*?"

I put a hand on my hip and gave him plenty of attitude. "Oh, I *saw* the way she was lookin' at you. Did you two used to date?"

"Are you *seriously* standin' there accusin' me of dating Dixie's attorney while we have much more important things to deal with?"

"Yes! I am!"

He grinned, and before I knew what was happening, he kissed me.

"What are you doing?" I demanded, frustrated with myself for getting weak-kneed and breathless.

"She's not my girlfriend, nor has she ever been. We went on a couple of dates, but we agreed it didn't work, and that was the end of it."

"Well, you may have agreed, but she clearly didn't."

He shook his head.

"Trust me on this, but you're right. We have more important things to deal with. I need to find Nash Jackson."

"Did you happen to get a plate number? Even a few numbers?"

I shook my head. "That's probably the first lesson on day one of police school," I grumbled. "Memorize the license-plate numbers."

"Hey, you're learning." He frowned. "I'm not thrilled you're learning as you go, but I admit that you seem to have a knack for this."

I put my hand over my heart and beamed. "That's probably the sweetest thing you've ever said to me."

His brow lifted before a grin lit up his eyes. "Then I obviously need to throw out all my preconceived ideas of romance with you."

I reached up on tiptoes and gave him a peck on the lips. "I'll talk to you later."

Meemaw was walking out of the courthouse. "Summer Lynn!"

Luke took a step backward. "Don't hate me, but I'm heading back to the station."

"Chicken."

"I never denied havin' a healthy respect for your grandmother." He caught my gaze and held it for a moment. "Be safe. *Please.*"

"I will. You too."

He passed my grandmother and said something I couldn't hear. She waved him off—her primary focus seemed to be reaching me. Was she about to chastise me for running off so rudely?

"Meemaw, I can explain."

"Explain what?" she demanded. "I was the fool, not you. Now what I want to know is what you plan to do about clearin' Dixie's name."

"I'm workin' on it. In fact, that's why I ran out. I saw a suspect in the courtroom, but when I chased him outside, he was already gone."

"Then what are you still doin' here chattin' with me?" she asked. "Go help Dixie."

I hugged her, and she bristled, but then she relaxed and hugged me back.

"I've got a lot of makin' up to do—to all of you."

I kissed her on the cheek and took a step back. Maybe there was hope for us yet.

Since the courthouse was a half block from my office, I set out for it, bracing myself before I faced my crew. I knew they'd be as frustrated as I was that the investigation had come to a screeching halt after our great night of discovery.

"Do you have enough money to post Dixie's bail?" Tony asked.

I shut the door behind me. "They didn't give her bail."

"For drug charges?" Bill asked in disbelief.

I didn't respond. We all knew it was ridiculous. I clapped my hands together. "We need to focus on what we do have control of and come up with a game plan. We can't find Rick Springfield or Amelia, but we can still talk to Bruce."

"And Nash Jackson," Chuck said.

I told them about seeing him in court.

"Why would he show up?" Bill asked.

"Guilt?" Tony suggested.

None of us could think of a better reason.

"And another thought occurred to me this morning," I said, sitting on my desk. "Whoever took Dixie's car from the farm must have had help. Someone had to drive the person out there."

"Hey," Tony said, "you're right."

"He or she might not have known what was goin' on, but they would have seen something."

The bell on the front door dinged, and Lauren stepped into the opening. The smug grin on her face indicated I wouldn't like whatever she was about to say.

"Can we help you, Lauren?" I asked with a bright smile.

"As a matter of fact, I need to interview you about Dixie's arrest."

"Can we schedule that for later? We're in the middle of something."

"Nope. We need it now. Schapiro's orders."

Alarm bells went off, but she knew I could easily check up on her, and I wouldn't be surprised if Schapiro backed her up on it. "Fine. Let's get this over with so I can get back to work." I grabbed my purse. "Let's go."

"Oh, no," she said, turning sideways and motioning to someone I couldn't see. "It'll look better if we do it here."

Connor and his camera crew started walking past the windows.

Great. "My crew is quite capable of recording this," I said. "Connor's team is redundant."

"Oh, don't be silly," Lauren said. "Connor and his team have a great rapport. I wouldn't dream of splitting them up."

Bill headed to the back with Tony and Chuck while Connor's crew walked in and set down their equipment where my guys had been sitting. Connor came in last, strutting like a damn peacock. Who exactly was he trying to impress?

I sent Bill a quick text. Call Bruce and see if we can set up an interview after he gets off work. Then I sent him Bruce's number.

One of Connor's camerapeople told me to sit in a client chair in front of the window while the others set up light filters. While the reality segments were all about capturing things in real life—even if it took six takes—the couch interviews gave the illusion of comfort and intimacy while the interviewee spilled secrets. Apparently, people looked more trustworthy when bathed in filtered light.

Within ten minutes, we were ready to go. Someone used the clapboard to start the scene. Almost immediately afterward, Connor walked around the camera and sat in the chair beside me. "I think this will go better if I'm sitting with her."

My eyebrows shot up, but I decided to save my protest for later.

Connor leaned back in his seat. "Summer, I just want to ask you a few warm-up questions before we get to the meat of the story."

I glanced over at Lauren. "Isn't a producer supposed to ask me questions? A.k.a. *you*?"

She gave me a sarcastically sweet smile. "I thought you might feel more comfortable with Connor. Especially since you found me asking questions so onerous last time."

We spent the next hour of take after take of Connor trying to sensationalize every bit of Dixie's arrest. Lauren continued to be frustrated when I didn't give her what she was looking for—anger, outrage, tears—but I refused to cave, even when she threatened to call Schapiro and get me fired.

I sat back in my chair and folded my hands on top of my crossed leg. "I'm not going to condemn my cousin, so if that's what you're lookin' for, you're wastin' all of our time."

"We need a sound bite, Summer. Something to give the morning news shows."

"Well, why in the hell didn't you say so?" I asked. "I'd be happy to give you a sound bite."

She gave me a skeptical look.

I turned to the camera, and an idea came to me. "My dear cousin Dixie, who is also my assistant on *Darling Investigations*, was arraigned this morning on charges of possession of a controlled substance. There is a lot more to this story than the public knows, but I'd like to remind people that sometimes investigative work involves going undercover. I'd also like to add that my cousin takes her work very seriously." I paused to let that sink in. "I assure you that when everything is resolved, Dixie will be cleared, and the people who were eager to condemn her will be eating crow." I refrained from saying, *And I will be gloating over every bite.* Instead, I stood. "And cut."

"I want another take," Lauren said, trying to regain the upper hand.

"Don't overthink it, Lauren." I leaned to the side. "Bill. You and the guys ready to go get some lunch?"

"Yeah," Tony said emerging from the back. "We're starving."

We walked out in silence, but instead of heading toward Maybelline's—the gossip hub of the county—I led the way to the hole-in-the-wall pizza joint a few doors down. After we ordered our food at the counter, we found a table in the back. I looked around to make sure Lauren's people hadn't followed us. "Did you get ahold of Bruce?" I asked in an undertone.

"I did," Bill said, "but he was reluctant."

"I don't get it. He seemed eager a couple of days ago. Did he finally agree?"

Bill gave me a hopeful look. "He didn't say no."

Tony grunted. "He said he wanted to think about it."

Had someone told him not to talk? I pushed out a sigh. "Dammit. Now we have *nothing*."

"No," Tony said. "Springfield is our best suspect. We need to find out who his friends are and who he hangs out with."

"Aren't those one and the same?" I asked.

"Look who you just spent the last hour with," Tony said.

"Touché."

"And how are we going to find that out?" Chuck said. "Go ask his alligator?"

My mouth twisted to the side. "We could go look through his house."

"Are you out of *your mind*?" Bill asked. "What if he came home and found you? If he's the one who killed April Jean and set up Dixie, you know he won't bat an eye at killing *you*."

Chuck swallowed, and his voice came out in a squeak. "And anyone with you."

"I can ask Teddy who his friends are."

"He's not going to tell you," Bill said. "You need to find someone else who knows something."

"I'll text Amber." But five minutes later, Amber proved to be no help. I read her text and broke the news to the guys. "She says that she knows the sheriff has been called out to the Jackhammer a few times when Rick was involved in disturbances, but that's it."

"What about going back to the crazy chicken lady?" Chuck said. "She might be able to help."

We all looked at him like he'd lost his mind.

"We don't need to ask anyone else for information," I said. "We just got our answer."

"Huh?" Tony asked.

"I told you!" Chuck said, pointing his finger at the guys.

"Not the chicken lady," I said. "The Jackhammer. Amber just said he's gotten into trouble out there multiple times. And Teddy was lookin' for him there last night. He must frequent it. And if he's lying low and not showing up at his usual hangouts, we can still ask around about him. And when we talk to them . . . maybe we could offer a reward for any information that helps free Dixie. They'll be more willing to talk."

The guys looked at one another for a few seconds before Tony said, "It's actually a good idea."

"Then it's set. We'll start with collecting names at the Jackhammer, then we'll figure out where to go from there."

"Summer Butler," Deputy Dixon said behind me.

I spun around in my seat to face him, hoping my fear over seeing him didn't show. I didn't want to give him the satisfaction. "Are you here to harass me, Deputy?"

"I'm here to give you a personal escort to the sheriff's department."

CHAPTER TWENTY-NINE

Bill stood and faced him. "Is she under arrest?"

The deputy lifted an eyebrow in an amused sneer. "Should she be?"

"What's this about?" I asked, my heart pounding against my chest as I got to my feet.

He reached for my arm. "Just come with me and you'll find out."

I backed into the table, just out of reach.

"Is she under arrest?" Bill asked with more force.

Deputy Dixon's eyes narrowed as he focused on Bill. "You wanting to join us?"

"She has a right to know if she's under arrest."

The deputy cocked his head and grinned, but it didn't reach his eyes. "Well, now, she didn't ask me, did she?"

I squared my shoulders. "Am I under arrest?"

He didn't answer, just grinned like the fool he was.

Another deputy walked through the door, scanning the small space until his gaze landed on us. He must have picked up on the tension, because he immediately said, "Is there a problem, Dixon?"

"This one's giving me sass," he said, motioning to me with his shoulder.

I wanted to rip this guy to shreds, but I remembered Luke's warning from the day before. Be polite. Cooperate. "Actually, sir, Deputy Dixon is rudely insistent that I go with him, yet he refuses to say if

I'm under arrest. Because if I am under arrest, I need to contact my attorney and ask her to meet me at the sheriff's department."

The other deputy shot Deputy Dixon a glare before turning back to me. "You're not under arrest. We just need a statement about what you saw before you reported the fire. We're here to ask you to come in today to assist with our investigation."

While part of me was glad they were interested in my statement, I couldn't help wondering if this was some kind of trap. What if they thought I'd made up my story to help Dixie get away with it? "I think maybe I'll call my attorney anyway. Do you have a card so she can make the appointment?"

He frowned and dug a card out of his shirt pocket. "I assure you that this is routine procedure, Ms. Butler."

I gave him a tight smile. "And while I would love to believe you, Deputy, your fellow officer has made that rather difficult."

Now the new deputy looked downright pissed at Deputy Dixon, and I had to admit I felt pretty satisfied.

I took the card and read the name. "Thank you, Deputy Vincent. I'll call my attorney when we finish here. You both have a good afternoon."

Deputy Dixon shot darts of hate at me, but the other deputy nodded. "We'll let you get back to your lunch."

The two men left, and Bill and I took our seats.

"What do you think they want?" Tony asked.

"I'm certain they want to know more about what I reported to Luke and Garrett. Are they really taking this as a possible lead, or are they trying to say I'm covering for Dixie? Or maybe they think there are two suspects like I do . . . only they think it's me and Dixie. Either way, I'd rather bring an attorney just to be on the safe side."

"So who are you gonna call?" Bill asked, sounding worried.

Dammit. I was gonna have to suck up my pride.

At six that evening, I left the sheriff's department with Lindy Baker by my side. I'd just spent several hours in an interrogation room. Deputies had come and gone, asking me a wide array of questions and bringing me various mug shots to look at, which was an obvious attempt to lull me into complacency. I'd fully admitted that I'd never seen the guy's face.

The hot evening air felt like a sauna after spending the day in air conditioning, and from the way Lindy dabbed her forehead with a tissue, she must have been feeling it too.

"Let's sit in my car and discuss this," she said in a brisk tone.

I followed her to a small Honda and sat in the passenger seat as she turned the a/c on full blast. The hot air hit my face.

"Don't sugarcoat it for me," I said. "Gut instinct—are they trying to make me an accomplice?"

She paused for a moment. "Possibly."

I pushed out a breath and groaned. Not only had I wasted the entire day, but now I was a suspect too. This day just kept cycling from bad to worse.

"I know you've been investigating Dixie's case, but from this moment on, you need to stay as far away from the investigation as possible," she said. "Otherwise you could be seen as tampering with witnesses. You could hurt her instead of help her."

"What?" My mouth dropped open. "But the investigation is part of my show." Then a new thought hit me. What if that had been the plan all along? Was Connor involved in this somehow?

"Right now they have nothing, so I don't think you're in imminent danger of arrest, but I think you should be careful. Stay away from Dixie's case."

Dammit. "Do you think they believed me about Dixie being drugged?"

"They might have been more receptive if y'all had reported it when it happened. Now it seems a little too convenient."

"But Teddy took her pee to the lab."

"And they said they would check into that, but for right now, she's still the prime suspect, and I wouldn't be surprised if they go after you for helping her cover it up."

Well, shit.

"Oh . . . ," she said. "There's something else." She lifted her phone and showed me her screen—a report from TMZ with the headline "More Trouble in Darlingland—Drugs, Arson, Murder, Oh, My!" She gave me a wry look. "That broke fast."

Lauren.

I reached for the door handle and started to get out, but she called after me. "Summer."

"Yeah," I said with a sigh. She hesitated long enough that I turned, anticipating something bad.

Her lips puckered like she'd taken a huge bite out of a lemon. "Luke's a good man. Don't let him get caught up in all this."

"What does that mean?"

She gave me a sympathetic look. "Look, Luke's a great guy—down-to-earth, thoughtful . . . very attractive, especially with his shirt off. I totally get why you're interested in him."

Jealousy rose up inside me like a thunderhead. When had she seen him with his shirt off?

"But Luke's not a complicated guy, and he likes the rules. Needs them. That should be obvious enough since he's the police chief." She paused. "I can already tell you like to skirt them. So if you really care about Luke, ask yourself if being with you is going to make his life better or worse, because from where I'm sitting, you're nothin' but drama."

I had to admit that she was right, and I hated her for it. I hated her even more when I realized she'd made the entire speech without a shred of gloating. "Thank you for helping me with the sheriff's department, and while you're right about everything, you're fired."

"*What?*"

"I hope to God you were really telling me that as Luke's friend and not his scorned lover, but the fact is that I can't trust you, Ms. Baker, and if I can't trust you, you're worthless to me. Send me a bill for today, for the work you've done for Dixie and me, and we'll find a new attorney." I climbed out of the car. "And I'll be telling Luke about this conversation, so I hope it was worth it."

I slammed the door and walked over to my truck. I sat behind the steering wheel for nearly a minute, embracing my self-pity. Then I realized Deputy Dixon was watching me from a window with a wide grin. He thought I was sitting here stewing over him. As if.

I lifted my hand and gave him a one-finger salute (sorry, Luke, good sense be damned) and backed out of the parking spot. Where the hell was I going to go? I couldn't face the guys right now, I didn't want to see Luke, and the last thing I wanted to do was admit to Teddy that things were even worse than they'd seemed this morning. What I really needed was a drink.

I was going to the Jackhammer.

I turned right and continued out of town, grabbing my phone out of my purse and turning it on. The messages and missed calls began to roll up my screen, half a dozen of them from Luke. I'd texted and told him about the appointment, but I hadn't told him where, or that it would take hours. First I needed to call the guys.

Bill answered right away. "Are you okay?" he asked, sounding worried. The echo of his voice let me know he'd put me on speakerphone.

"I'm okay for now." Then I proceeded to tell him everything that had happened with the exception of my firing Lindy and why. "So y'all take off for the night, and I'll see you in the morning."

"Are you really giving up Dixie's investigation?" Tony asked.

"No, but I can't risk hurting Dixie either," I said. "I need to figure out a way around this, but I also need a drink, so I'm going to the Jackhammer. Maybe a few shots of whiskey will help me think straighter."

"Said no one the next day ever," Bill said. "What if Rick Springfield's out there?"

"I seriously doubt I could get so lucky." Then I hung up.

I started to call Luke, but I couldn't handle talking to him. I kept hearing Lindy asking me if I was making Luke's life better or worse. I used my voice control to send him a text.

I'm fine. Sorry to worry you. I need some time alone.

The parking lot was fairly empty, but then it was only six thirty on a Wednesday night. I headed inside and took a seat on a bar stool as far from the door as possible.

"What can I get ya?" a woman asked, her shirt unbuttoned far enough that I got a very good view of her cleavage.

"Jameson. Two fingers. Neat."

She laughed and put her hand on her hip. "Bad day?"

"The worst."

She grabbed a glass, gave me a generous pour, and set it in front of me. "Want me to open a tab?"

"Might as well. I'm not goin' anywhere."

She tapped the counter and smiled. "I'm Brandy. Let me know if you need anything else."

I picked up the glass. "Don't go far, because this won't last long." The glass was empty in a couple of minutes, and I asked for another.

She grabbed the bottle and poured another generous amount into my glass. "You might want to pace yourself."

I lifted my glass and took a long sip.

She grinned. "Or not. I get it. Sometimes you just need to get shit-faced. You got anyone joinin' ya?"

I thought about Luke, and tears stung my eyes. "Not tonight."

"Bad breakup?"

"Not yet."

"Ah . . . ," she said, shaking her head. "Girlfriend, say no more."

I knew she had misunderstood, but I didn't correct her as I sipped my whiskey. Just this morning I'd vowed to Luke to stubbornly fight for us. Was I really going to be a liar? But there was no denying I had the power to destroy him with my imminent arrest. Would he stick through it with me out of love? Honor and obligation? If he did, would he eventually hate me for taking away everything he'd dreamed of? Because there was no doubt if I was arrested as an accomplice, it could and probably *would* destroy his career. At the very least, it would destroy his credibility.

I'd just finished my second drink when the door opened and Bill walked in. He scanned the room until his gaze landed on me.

I patted the stool next to me. "Have a seat, buddy." Then I patted it some more.

"Oh, my God. Are you drunk already?" he asked in dismay.

Brandy leaned her elbow on the counter, her eyes narrowing. "Is this the guy?"

I stared at her for a moment, then realized what she was asking. I laughed. "No . . . this is my . . ." I almost said *cameraman*, then caught myself. "Bill."

Brandy grinned. "Welcome, my Bill. Your friend's had two doubles already. You want to play catch-up?"

He gave me a dubious look.

"*Billllll*," I said, "don't let me drink alone."

He sighed, then sat on the stool. "Just give me a beer."

"And put it on my tab," I called after her.

She walked away, and Bill leaned closer. "Come on, Summer. What the hell are you doing?"

"Isn't obvious? I'm getting drunk."

"Summer . . ."

"Sometimes a person just needs to get shit-faced, right, Brandy?" I asked her as she slid Bill's beer across the counter.

She grinned. "That's right, girlfriend."

"Bring me another."

Brandy gave me a look, then headed to the other end of the bar.

"I think we can convince Bruce to talk to us."

I shook my head. "Stupid Lindy says I can't investigate or I might hurt Dixie. I need to think this through."

"But if you clear Dixie's name, you won't have to worry about any of this."

I looked into Bill's face. "I was soooo stupid." How could I believe that I could get my family back and Luke back and finally, *finally* be surrounded by love? My mother had taught me years ago—by words and deeds—that we came into this world alone, and no one stuck with us until the end. How could I forget that?

Sympathy filled his eyes. "When were you stupid?"

Tears stung my eyes again, and I shook my head. "Nope. I'm not gonna be that loser that gets drunk in a bar and cries."

He picked up his glass and took a sip, turning to look over the room. "Luke's worried about you. Why won't you take his calls?"

"He called you?"

"Like I said, he's worried."

"We'll put that blame on stupid Lindy too."

"Summer . . ."

"I don't want to talk about it."

"Okay." He checked his phone and put his glass on the bar. "I have to check in with the guys. I'll be right back."

"Okay . . ."

Brandy came back with a basket of fries and a burger and set it in front of me.

"I didn't order that."

"I know, but the rules are I can't serve you once you get too drunk, and I like havin' you around. If you eat that, I'll serve you more whiskey."

That seemed fair.

She set a glass of ice water next to it. "Drink this too."

I eyed it suspiciously. "Who's touched it?"

"Just me. And . . . smart girl." She winked. "I knew I liked you."

Bill returned a few minutes later, looking guilty as hell.

"What happened?" I asked.

"I told the guys I found you drunk and feeling sorry for yourself and told them to go home."

I scowled. "I already told all y'all to go home."

He picked up one of my fries. "Well, we'd hoped you'd come to your senses."

My phone buzzed in my purse, and I pulled it out. A pang shot through my chest when I saw Luke's name.

"You're really not being fair to him," Bill said.

I turned off the ringer. "He deserves better than me."

"You need to let him be the judge of that."

"Hmm . . ."

As soon as I finished half the food, I flagged Brandy down. "I'm ready for another drink."

She gave the basket the once-over and then nodded, taking my empty glass and getting me a new one.

Bill still sipped his beer while looking around the room. "We're already here. We could ask around about Springfield."

I took a generous gulp, then shook my head. "Lindy says it's witness tampering." Could I meet people on the sly? How was I going to get around this?

He leaned closer. "Think about how nonsensical that sounds, Summer. How are you tampering with witnesses if you and Dixie supposedly did it?"

I had to admit he had a point, but I wasn't sure if it really made sense, or if the alcohol in my bloodstream just thought so. "I don't want to think about it tonight."

Bill finished his beer and set the glass down on the bar. "I bet Dixie doesn't want to think about it either . . . while she's sitting in the county jail."

Dammit. I was pretty sure he was right about that too.

"I brought something for you." He took the pendant out of his pocket and put it in my palm. "All charged up. If Springfield shows, call me." He moved his face closer to mine. "I mean it. Call. Me. *Do not* try to engage him while you're still drunk, and definitely don't do it alone. But if he shows up, it wouldn't hurt to film who he's hanging out with. We can follow up tomorrow."

"I don't deserve you either, Bill."

He sighed, then shook his head. "Now you're *really* drunk, and I think you should go home. Let me take you. Or I'll call Teddy."

"No. No Teddy. I can't go home and face him right now."

"Then Luke."

I shook my head.

"He's crazy about you, Summer. Don't give him up because some jealous lawyer with lots of bad advice thinks you should." He grinned. "Come on. You're made of stronger stuff than that."

"Not tonight I'm not."

He gave me a sad smile. "Yeah, you are. You're just overwhelmed and scared, but remember that you're not facing this alone. You've got a lot of people to help."

I blinked to clear my eyes. "Thanks, Bill."

"Hey, that's what friends are for. I'll call and check on you later." He paused. "Don't screen my calls."

I grinned. "Okay."

He left, and I stared at the pendant in my hand. I knew he'd given it to me to make me remember my purpose. I unclasped the chain and hung it around my neck.

"Your friend left," Brandy said, picking up his empty bottle. She motioned to my drink. "Want another?"

"I'll take another water. Do you really not have bottled water?"

"Sure don't."

"Well, you should," I said, still feeling drunk. I needed to get myself together in case Rick Springfield showed up. "How many women do you think have been roofied in here?"

"Women have been roofied here?" I heard a man ask in alarm from the other end of the bar.

He made his way toward me, and I gasped. "It's you."

Nash Jackson was standing right in front of me.

"What were you saying about women getting roofied?"

"I was saying this bar needs to have bottled water so women can try to sober up and not worry about getting drugged."

His mouth pursed, and he looked like he was considering it. "You have a valid point."

I licked my finger, then stuck it in the air and brought it down like I was marking my point, but I misjudged the distance and slid my slobbery finger down his forehead.

"Oops," I said. "I didn't mean to do that."

His jaw clenched, and it was obvious he didn't appreciate the spit bath. He grabbed a cocktail napkin and swiped at his forehead.

"You big baby," I mocked.

"Back to the bottled water. Do you know someone who was roofied?" The expression on his face was weird, like he was missing a puzzle piece and thought I had it.

"What are you doin' here?" I asked.

"Summer, do you know someone who was drugged?" He sounded more insistent.

"Hey, you know my name."

He rolled his eyes. "Everyone knows your name."

"Not everyone," I said, lifting my chin. "Brandy doesn't know my name."

"Brandy *definitely* knows your name, and she's hopin' you'll leave her a big tip."

A lump formed in my throat. I was used to everyone in LA trying to use me, but I'd thought Sweet Briar would be different. Turned out what I'd said to Trent was more accurate than I wanted to admit. As stupid as it was, for some weird reason I'd thought Brandy actually liked me. My stupid tears were back. Dammit. Why did I always forget that I wasn't a giggly drunk? I was the emotional, I-love-everybody kind of drunk, as already evidenced here tonight. But my chin trembled anyway.

"What did you say to her?" Brandy demanded, shoving Nash out of the way. "What did he say to you, girlfriend?"

"He said you know who I am."

"Well, of course I know who you are," she said. "Everyone does, but you were here intent on getting hammered. You didn't need me gushing over your résumé. You need someone to take care of you."

"Nash said you were only doin' it because you wanted a big tip."

"He *what*?" She shot a glare at him before turning back to me. "Don't pay any attention to him. He's our new owner, and he doesn't know jack shit about anyone. He's from Atlanta, which apparently means he's suspicious of everyone and everything."

Nash shook his head in disgust.

"The new owner? What happened to Rudy?"

Nash gave me a dry look. "He got tired of dealing with emotional drunk women." His gaze drifted to the door, and his scowl deepened. "Brandy, sober her up, then we'll send her on her way. Call her a cab if necessary." He moved purposely around the bar and into the main room.

I stared at Brandy in disbelief. "He's kickin' me out?"

"I can't believe he thinks we have *cabs* here." She shook her head back and forth. "I have yet to figure that man out, but it's only been a few days, so I hope he gets his shit together or I might be lookin' for a new job."

I glanced over my shoulder and saw that Nash had intercepted a customer who'd just walked in through the front door. He was leading him to a table close to the bar.

I couldn't believe my luck—both good and bad.

Rick Springfield had just shown up, but I was too drunk to do anything about it.

CHAPTER THIRTY

I reached up and ran my thumb along the back of the pendant, flipping the switch to start recording. Should I call Bill back? I suspected Rick had murdered April Jean. If and when I dealt with him, I needed to be on top of my game. Which meant I had no business talking to him now. Maybe I'd just keep an eye on him.

Rick didn't seem to like the table Nash had picked out for him, but he finally sat down, and Nash sat with him.

Was Nash suspect number two? Had he been interested in my statement about women getting roofied because he was part of it?

I needed to sit here and play it cool because I was definitely too drunk to drive, which meant I was stuck. The thought of no avenue of escape made me nervous. I picked up my phone and called Luke.

"Summer. Goddammit," he snapped when he answered. *"Where are you?"*

To my dismay, I started to cry. Why couldn't I be a fun drunk?

His voice softened immediately. "Summer, what's wrong? Where are you?"

I sniffed. "The Jackhammer."

"What are you doin' there? Is Bill with you?"

"I'm gettin' drunk. And I sent him home."

"You're there alone?"

"No," I said, wiping a stray tear. "Brandy's here."

"Brandy who?" Then, as though putting it together, he said, "Brandy the bartender? Tell her I want to talk to Rudy."

"He's not here," I said as more tears flowed. "Nash said he retired." Why was I crying? I'd met the guy once.

"Nash? Nash Jackson is there?"

"He bought the place."

He released a few curse words. "Do you know *anyone* there besides Brandy?"

"No," I said, starting to cry. "I don't have any friends."

"Summer, what happened?" he asked. "Why are you upset?" Probably to help move the conversation along, he added, "Besides the no-friends situation?"

"The sheriff's gonna arrest me as an accomplice."

"*What*? No. I know your imagination is running wild, but I can—"

"Even stupid Lindy thinks so."

"Wait. *What*? When did she say that, and why?"

"Probably because we spent the afternoon at the sheriff's department, and Deputy Dickhead looked at me like I was the next contestant in a dogfight."

"Your appointment was at the sheriff's department? Did they arrest you?"

"No. They asked me to come to the station."

"Why didn't you call me, Summer?" The disappointment in his voice made my heart hurt.

But it was a very good question. Why *hadn't* I called him? Maybe because I was so used to doing everything on my own. Maybe I was too scared to rely on him. Everyone I'd loved had left me at some point. "I don't know," I said, breaking down.

"It's okay," he said, his voice soft and understanding. "We'll talk about that part later."

"Maybe we shouldn't," I said, sniffling. "Maybe we should just . . ." Break up? My tears started flowing even more.

"Darlin', I'm on my way to get you. Just sit tight."

"Maybe you should just leave me here," I said. "Stupid Lindy thinks I should break up with you." Where the hell was my filter? Oh, yeah. Whiskey.

"She said that?" he asked in shock.

"She says you're too good for me. That I'm gonna ruin you." I grabbed the half-empty whiskey glass and took a generous drink. "She's probably right. You should run away from me as fast as you can."

"I'm not havin' this conversation on the phone while you're drunk," he said, his voice rough. "Just stay there."

My phone beeped, and I pulled it away from my ear to show my battery was at 3 percent, but I also saw a group text from Garrett to me and Teddy.

"Luke, I've got to go. My phone's about to die, but I just got a text saying April Jean's drawings weren't in her trailer when it burned down. Do you think the person who set it on fire took them?"

"That helps narrow the suspects . . . and rules out Dixie. Why would she want the drawings? But forget about the case, and worry about protecting yourself. What's Nash up to?"

"He's sitting at a table with Rick Springfield."

"What the hell, Summer?" he shouted in my ear. "*Rick Springfield's there*? Maybe lead with that next time."

"You're mad at me again."

I heard him take a deep breath. "Summer, I'm worried about you. He's dangerous, and you're sitting at the bar alone and drunk. Dammit." He paused. "I'd call the sheriff's department, but if you're on their radar, I don't want to call any more attention to you. If you're in imminent danger, though, I'll take the chance."

"I'm fine. Perfectly fine. Now just break up with me and be done with it. Then you won't have to worry anymore."

"Summer," he said, his voice calmer, "I'm sorry. Just listen to me, okay? Does he know you're there?"

"Who? Nash and I had a conversation about roofies."

"You accused Nash of drugging Dixie?"

"No. I told him if he's the owner now that he needs to have bottled water so women can't get dosed while they're trying to sober up."

"What about Springfield?"

"I didn't accuse him of anything either," I said, getting huffy.

"No," Luke said, getting exasperated. "Does he know you're there?"

"Oh . . . I don't think so. Nash saw him walk in and headed him off before he got to the bar."

"You need to get out of there. Now."

"But I can't drive."

"Just go sit in your truck. I'll find you there and take you home."

"Fine."

"Summer? Just remember—" he said. And then there was nothing.

I held out my phone and looked at the screen. Dead as a doorstop.

I took another drink of my water, then waved Brandy over. "I need to close out my tab."

She glanced around. "Why? You got someone pickin' you up?"

I was alert enough to figure out that telling her I was going to wait in my truck would look weird enough to draw attention. "Yeah, my boyfriend, so I want to be ready."

She walked over to the register, pulled up a receipt, and handed it to me. "Since the cat's out of the bag that I know who you are, I just want you to know how sorry I am about Dixie."

A lump formed in my throat. Why'd I have to throw a pity party and get shit-faced? I could be finding useful information to save

Dixie, Lindy's warning or not. Instead, I was feeling sorry for myself. Again.

"Thanks," I said as I pulled some cash out of my purse and handed it to her.

She shook her head. "It's such a shame. I thought she'd got her crap together, so color me surprised when I saw her car goin' ninety to nothin' yesterday afternoon while I was on my way to work."

I blinked. Trying to get a clear head. "You saw Dixie's car?"

"Yep."

"When did you come to work?"

Putting her hand on her hip, she sucked in a deep breath. "I had to come in early yesterday, so it was probably about three."

I sat up straighter. "You're sure it was Dixie's car?"

"Yeah, she's got that beat-up clunker, and I saw her long blonde hair, although she was goin' too fast for me to see her face. I noticed because she doesn't usually drive like that. She's been so careful since she came back . . ." Then she flashed me a sad grin. "Except with men. She's run around with plenty of them."

Her timeline made no sense. Dixie had been at the office with Bill and then me until I sent her to Connor's at three thirty. "You're sure about seeing Dixie? It couldn't have been after three thirty?"

"Yeah, because I was a few minutes late to work at three. I suppose it might not have been Dixie, but what other blonde woman would be drivin' her car?"

Who indeed? The only other blonde I could think of at the moment was April Jean, and that made absolutely no sense. Why would she be driving Dixie's car to set up her own murder?

What if she hadn't known her partner was about to murder her?

But one thing was clear—Dixie had about twenty people to support her alibi. She'd been watching Margo pitch her fit around three.

Brandy handed me my change. "Thanks." I stood and leaned closer as I left a generous tip. "Would you be willing to tell that to the sheriff?"

"Yeah, but I don't want to get her into any more trouble. She's a good kid. Maybe she got so high she thought April Jean was a monster or something, because I can't see her hurtin' anyone purposefully, you know?"

"You won't get her in more trouble," I said, trying to hide my excitement. "That would help her more than you know." I centered myself to keep from wobbling, then took a practice step.

"Where do you think you're goin'?" she asked.

"I'm gonna wait for Luke outside." I took several more steps, pretty proud of myself for not wobbling more.

"Don't you dare drive!" she called after me, loud enough to catch people's attention. Including Rick Springfield's. His gaze landed on me, and something dark flashed in his eyes.

Oh, shit.

I hurried outside and tried to remember where I'd parked my truck since the lot was fuller now. It was close to the street, and if he ran out after me, he'd catch me in a heartbeat. Instead, I ran around to the other side of the building, nearly falling on my face when I rounded the corner. Maybe if he didn't see me, he'd go back inside.

"Summer Butler!" I heard him shout. "Where the fuck are you? We have some things to discuss!"

My heart hammered in my chest. How far away was Luke? Could I hide until he got here?

"Summer," I heard someone whisper behind me.

Startled, I shrieked and then immediately clamped a hand over my mouth to keep from giving myself away any more than I already had. I was relieved to see Bruce Jepper.

"Are you okay?" he asked with wide eyes.

"No. Rick Springfield is after me."

"Rick Springfield? What did you do to piss *him* off?"

"I know about his involvement in April Jean's murder. I suspect he got April Jean to drive Dixie's car from our farm."

He stared at me for several long seconds as though he was thinking about something. "Did he tell you what he did?"

"No," I whispered. "I've been collecting facts, but I'm too drunk to confront him with it. I'm waiting for Luke to come get me. I just need to hide from Rick until he gets here."

"I'll help you hide. We can go get in my car, and I'll call Teddy so he doesn't worry about you."

"Thanks, Bruce."

He took my arm and led me along the side of the building and then around the back. I saw an older Cadillac in the corner by the dumpster.

"Summer Butler!" Rick shouted, sounding closer.

"Leave her alone," Nash said. "You're makin' a scene."

"That bitch knows too much. She's gonna ruin everything."

"*Leave her alone.*"

Bruce was practically running toward the car, dragging me with him. He opened the back door. "Here. Get inside, and I'll get rid of him."

I fell into the car, none too gracefully, and he shoved my feet inside before shutting the door.

"Jepper!" Rick said. "You're late. You got it?"

"Shut up," Bruce said, then there was silence.

I popped up in the back seat enough to look out the tinted back window. Bruce was standing in front of Rick, but I didn't see Nash anywhere.

Why was Bruce talking to Rick? Was he actually trying to get rid of him?

Rick grabbed the front of Bruce's shirt and hauled him closer. Bruce's face screwed up, but he pushed the bigger man's hand away.

As soon as he was freed up, he removed an envelope from his back pocket and handed it to Rick.

Why was Bruce giving Rick money?

Rick opened the envelope, peered inside, and stuffed it into his back pocket. He put his hand on Bruce's shirt to smooth out the wrinkles, then clapped his hand on Bruce's cheek. Whistling a tune I didn't recognize, Rick headed toward the front of the building.

Bruce watched him walk away, his chest heaving. Then he glanced down at the ground and stared at it for several long seconds.

I wasn't sure what was going on, but I was pretty sure I didn't want to find out . . . at least not in this state. Now seemed like a good time to leave. I grabbed the door handle, but the door didn't open. Frantically searching for the door locks, I realized they'd been removed. Who in their right mind removed door locks from the back of a car?

Oh, shit.

Chapter Thirty-One

I dove between the two front seats, aiming for the driver's door, just in time to see Bruce standing outside the window, watching me with a look of pity.

I tried to hit the "Lock" button to keep him out, but he opened the door before I could push it.

"Let me out of this car, Bruce Jepper!"

"I can't!" he said, sounding pissed. "You know too much."

"I don't know what he has on you, but we can go to the police together," I said. "We can bring him down."

He shook his head as he leaned over and pushed me hard into the back seat. Without a backward glance, he got inside the car and locked it.

"Why are you doing this?"

He remained silent.

"Oh, my God," I said as the truth hit me hard. "*You* killed April Jean."

"Shut up, Summer," he said, starting the engine.

"Luke is gonna find out you did this! If you turn yourself in, maybe you can get a plea bargain if you help them bring down Rick."

He shook his head as he gripped the steering wheel and reached for the key in the ignition. "No. I can't. I'll never get out of prison. Her murder was too cold-blooded."

He started to back up, and I knew if he got out of this parking lot, I was as good as dead.

"Stop! Wait! I can help you out of this."

The car came to a halt, but it was still in reverse, which meant I had some fancy talking to do. We could see the highway from here, but the back windows were tinted, which meant no one would be able to see in.

"Let's just look at the facts, okay? Maybe there's a way out, because I know you don't want to kill me." He was friends with Teddy. I needed to play that up. "Think about Teddy. Dixie's in jail and will probably be sentenced to life. If you kill me, Teddy will lose his shit. Don't you owe it to your friend to at least entertain another possibility?"

He shoved the gearshift into park. "You have a couple of minutes. This needs to be done before Luke gets here." He sounded exhausted.

Where to start? My brain was fuzzy. I decided to pitch my ideas and see if any stuck. "Rick drugged Dixie."

"Duh."

Not duh to me, but I was drunk, so I'd give it to him. I thought about April Jean and Rick commiserating in the house at Luke's party. Dixie said they'd acted like they were scheming. "April Jean was in on it."

"Yeah."

My mind was rolling now. "April Jean stuck around at the party until Rick came back, then she helped him get Dixie into his truck . . . But why? Did Rick rape her?"

"Hell if I know. I *do* know Dixie wouldn't give him the time of day, and it pissed him off. So . . ."

"So . . . ," I said, "if he had her in a position to do whatever he liked, he'd take advantage of that."

"Rick sees what he wants, and he takes it." I was horrified that he sounded envious.

I gasped as another thought hit me. "Did *you* rape her?"

"No."

I wasn't sure I believed him. But I had to figure out their plan. Why would they drug Dixie and dump her by the lake?

Then I realized I was an idiot.

Garrett had told Teddy and me in the group message that April Jean's precious drawings hadn't burned down with the trailer. "It was April Jean's plan. She got Rick to drug Dixie and then set fire to her trailer. They made sure she was close enough to the fire to smell like smoke before dumping her at the lake. April Jean was setting her up. She'd get the insurance money, and Dixie would end up in jail." And out of the way for her to go after Trent.

Bruce's jaw tightened.

"You didn't help?"

"I wasn't part of their plan." But the way he said it was cagey.

He'd been hitting on April Jean at the party, and she'd shot him down. If he'd seen her leave with Rick . . . "You saw them put Dixie into Rick's truck."

He didn't deny it.

"Did you follow them?"

"They didn't come straight to her trailer. So I was there waitin' on them when they showed up a half hour later."

"You were waiting to confront April Jean at her trailer?"

"At the party she told me she'd give me a shot, so I thought if I was there, she might let me in," he said, his anger rising. "Especially after she found out . . ."

"Found out what?"

He looked at me in the rearview mirror. "You know I can't let you go, right?" he asked. "In fact, you won't leave this parking lot. You know too much. I feel like it's only fair to tell you that."

My stomach roiled, and my heart jumped into my throat. *Keep him talking. Buy time.* If he shot me, hopefully my pendant was recording, and my death wouldn't be in vain. At least I'd save Dixie. I snuck a glance toward the highway, trying not to be obvious about it. If I shifted to the right, I could make it look like I was trying to see him, but I'd get a view of the highway. I could see when Luke pulled in.

"I know." I prayed Luke would get here before it came to that. But I still needed to come up with a plan to let him know I was back here. "April Jean found out something about you . . . the fires at your place and hers were the same," I said, thinking out loud. "Garrett said the last one was different."

"We were all drinkin', and I'd had too much. I knew she liked bad boys, so I thought if I told her . . ."

"That you started your own fire for the insurance money?"

"I wanted her to think I was dark enough for her." He paused before adding, "I've lost a lot of money since Trent came back to town. I figured if I could just get out from under it . . ."

"But she used it against you?"

"Rick made me start *her* fire."

"In her trailer?"

"Yeah."

"So what happened after you started the fire?"

"Rick said I was part of it, so he made me help him take Dixie to the lake. To make sure I was good and involved."

"And you'd keep their secret."

"Yeah."

"If they were setting Dixie up for starting the fire, why text me? Why not make an anonymous call to 911? The sheriff would find out about April Jean's fire, figure out she'd been arguing with Dixie, and then there'd be Dixie herself, drugged up and smelling like smoke. Nice and airtight. Why take the long way around?"

"That was my doin'. Teddy's my friend, and I felt bad hurtin' him like that, so I told them I'd take care of the call. Instead, I used Dixie's fingerprint to unlock her phone, and I texted you. I figured if anyone could keep her safe, you could."

Only I hadn't. "I bet April Jean was pissed the next day, huh? She expected Dixie to be in custody, and she figured you must have screwed her over."

"She was madder than a wet hornet and threatened to turn me in for settin' both fires, but I knew part of her plan had been to hurt Dixie, so I told her that we could still set Dixie up."

"So you both went out to our farm, and April Jean took Dixie's car. You planned to stash Dixie's car somewhere, shoot her up with heroin, and stow the arson kit in her trunk. Where'd you get the heroin? Rick?"

He didn't answer, but there wasn't any need. It was obvious enough.

I realized we were getting dangerously close to the end of his story. "You waited until you had the right opportunity, then kidnapped her. But why did you kill April Jean?"

"I didn't plan to . . . not in the beginnin'. But she kept humiliatin' me. She told me she'd never sleep with someone like me. That she was usin' me at the party as cover until Rick turned up to get Dixie, and I'd been too stupid to figure it out." He shrugged. "I snapped."

"How'd you get her in the thrift store?"

"That part wasn't hard. She was already dead. In fact, I shot her right where you're sitting." He reached into the glove compartment and got out a gun. I didn't know a lot about guns, but I was pretty sure the long, skinny thing attached to the barrel was a silencer.

My adrenaline spiked, and I felt like I was going to vomit. He sounded so cold. Absolutely remorseless. And now he was about to shoot me in the very seat where I was sitting.

Don't give in to panic, Summer. Figure a way out of this.

I considered the timeline. April Jean was seen in Dixie's car around three, and Dixie disappeared after three thirty. "But you kidnapped Dixie first."

"April Jean insisted on watching the whole thing so she could make sure it was done right. She sat in the back and played back-seat driver. Kept laughing at me for struggling to get Dixie in the car, and when I got inside, she told me that she bet I was like Trent and couldn't get it up. She said she'd never know for sure, so she'd just believe it. And in that moment, I knew what I had to do. Women are supposed to respect men, and she wasn't respecting me. So I got the gun, turned around, and shot her." He turned around to face me, his face completely blank. "That's how I'll shoot you. It won't hurt."

The way he was so casually talking about murdering me set my nerves on edge. "But it would have been loud. Didn't it hurt your eardrums?"

He pulled out a pair of padded headphones. "I wear these at the gun ranges. I figured the silencer would muffle most of the sound, but I decided to play it safe. So I put them on before I got the gun out. She made fun of me for that too. She wasn't laughing about five seconds later."

My breath was coming in rapid pants. Freaking out wouldn't help me, although at least I was feeling a lot more alert than before. I supposed imminent death would sober anyone up.

Keep him talking.

"So Rick found out that April Jean had been murdered." I thought about the envelope of money. "He figured out you did it and blackmailed you. But you had dirt on him too." I thought about my stalemate with Elijah Sterling. "If one of you caved, the other one fell too."

"But mine was a whole lot worse than his."

"Trust me, save your money. Rick's not gonna risk goin' to prison." No, I suspected Rick would kill Bruce first and feed him to his alligator.

I saw Luke's truck pull into the parking lot, and I fought hard to not show a reaction. "So you're just gonna keep payin' Rick money? He's the kind of guy who will bleed you dry."

He tapped his thumb on the steering wheel. "Yeah, I've considered that too. The thing about guys like Rick is that they're a lot like the April Jeans of the world—they don't think someone like me is capable of doing anything really bad."

Luke was already standing next to my truck, giving the empty interior a worried look.

How was I going to get his attention?

The real question was, How was I going to distract Bruce? Did I dare try to use my pepper spray in this enclosed car? But my biggest concern was to keep Bruce talking, because if he saw Luke, he'd shoot me immediately.

I slid to the side of the seat a bit to hide my purse, then leaned forward. "*I* never underestimated you," I said, riding a fine line of flirting and playing coy. I slipped my hand into my purse and started to rummage around, trying to keep my shoulder behind the headrest. "When I heard about your house fire, I took one look at you and thought to myself, 'Now that man looks like he could commit an arson.'"

A frown tugged at his lips. "You're just sayin' that to make me feel better."

My hand closed around the can of pepper spray. I transferred it to my left hand, the side with more access but a lower likelihood of success. "Nope. I may be with Luke, but when Teddy and I left your house, I asked him if you were single. And if you liked to play with fire."

Skepticism hardened his face. "And what did he say?"

"He said you were single, and he didn't know about the fires, but he warned me to stay away from you. He told me I couldn't date his friend."

He sat upright and turned to face me more, holding the gun out to his side and pointing it at the passenger window. "Teddy said that?" He sounded pissed.

The timing was never going to get better than this, especially since Luke was headed for the bar's entrance. This was far from fool-proof, but if it didn't work, I was getting shot anyway. Might as well go down fighting. Still, I'd never been more scared in my life. I had to play this role to the end.

"Yeah," I said in a husky voice, "but I've never been much of a rule follower, you know?" I leaned forward, parting my lips as though I was about to kiss him. I sure hoped the look in my eyes said *sultry* and not *so terrified I'm about to pee my pants.*

Bruce seemed surprised, but he twisted to get a better look at me.

Before he got too close, I lifted the can and sprayed, leaping past him to lay on the horn with my right hand.

He coughed and cursed. Although it hadn't been part of my initial plan, I'd managed to trap his gunslinging arm.

Bruce was still squirming and cussing me out. I could see Luke sprinting toward us as I kept the horn going, but Bruce was wriggling around with the gun, trying to angle it up toward me.

Pulling my left arm back, I smashed my elbow into his nose as hard as I could. He screamed in pain, and I reached for the "Unlock" button—the click of the doors unlocking the sweetest sound I'd ever heard.

I threw myself in the back seat and grabbed the door handle, getting the door open just before he clicked the locks again.

"Luke!" I screamed as I scrambled out. "He has a gun! Be careful."

The driver's door opened, and Bruce fell out, pointing his gun in front of him and pulling the trigger.

The gunshot echoed through the parking lot.

I was terrified for Luke. He was on the side of the building with absolutely no cover, but he ducked and lifted his own gun, aiming at Bruce.

I was on my hands and knees, trying to get to my feet as Bruce dove on top of me, tackling me to the ground. He pressed the gun to my temple and shouted, "I'll kill her, Luke. Back off."

"He's gonna kill me anyway," I said, trying not to cry. "He told me he won't let me go alive."

"Now hold on," Luke said, his voice friendly. "No one's gettin' killed today. I don't have the time for the paperwork. You havin' a bad day there, buddy?"

"Buddy?" Bruce shouted, pulling up to a kneeling position and tugging me with him. "Don't you know who I am, Luke?"

Luke squinted. *"Bruce?"*

I glanced over my shoulder and realized why Luke hadn't recognized him. Bruce's face was covered in blood and tears and snot.

"Yeah," Bruce said, "and you're right, I'm having a *really* bad day, thanks to your girlfriend."

Luke took a few steps closer, still pointing his gun toward us. "I know she has a way of gettin' into things," he said in light tone. "But she's pretty harmless."

"Look at *my face*!" Bruce shouted, and jerked me to my feet. He pointed the gun at my right temple while his left hand gripped my left bicep. "Does that look harmless?"

"She's clumsy when she's drunk," Luke said, taking two more steps closer.

"She did this on purpose! She humiliated me!" He jammed the gun into my temple, making me wince.

"Hey, now," Luke said, his voice rising, "we're havin' a civil conversation here. No need to be gettin' rough. And that's not Summer's way. She would never humiliate someone. I'm sure you just took it wrong."

"She made me think she was gonna kiss me, then sprayed me with pepper spray and broke my nose! I'd call that humiliatin'!"

Pride filled Luke's eyes, but then he grimaced, trying to affect camaraderie. "Well . . . maybe she felt threatened, Bruce."

"Women need to know their place! The good book says women are supposed to submit to men."

"No . . . ," Luke said, inching closer. "It says *wives* are supposed to submit to their *husbands*, and unless you two had some secret ceremony that I don't know about, that doesn't apply to you. And besides, Bruce," he said good-naturedly, "we both know women are the weaker sex. They need us to feel protected. If she lashed out, it meant she was afraid. Did you give her reason to be afraid?"

"I don't want to kill her."

"And you don't have to. Just let her go."

"She needs to be punished for hurting me!"

"You're right, and I'll make sure that happens. Just let her go." He was about six feet in front of us now, and I couldn't believe how confident and in control he looked. Like this was just another day at work.

"I tried to get him to work out a plea," I said, hoping I was giving him something he could use. "He has information on Rick Springfield."

"You have shit on Springfield?" Luke asked, sounding hopeful. "We can *definitely* work something out. But that's never gonna happen if you shoot Summer in front of me." His voice hardened, and he took a moment before he said, "The moment you kill someone else, there's absolutely no compromise, and the DA will throw the book at you and the kitchen sink too. So just put down the gun and let her go."

Bruce hesitated. His fingers wiggled on my arm. "You'll get time off my sentence if I tell you about Rick?"

"I *guarantee* it. The DA will be very happy to talk to you."

Bruce hesitated. His hold on my arm loosened, and he lowered the gun from my temple.

A loud gunshot cracked the air from overhead.

Bruce was falling to the ground. I hit the side of the car with a hard thud as Luke dove for me, then looked up to see where the shot had come from.

Sirens wailed in the distance. Luke shoved me under the back end of the car while he crouched next to me. "Suspect down," he said into his radio. "Active shooter, possibly from the bar roof."

"Copy," a voice crackled over his radio. "I have backup two minutes out."

"Summer," Luke said, his voice tight as he leaned over to look at me, "are you all right?"

"I think so."

"Are you sure?"

"Only a few bumps and bruises so far."

About a half minute later, muffled screams and a gunshot came from inside the bar. Luke tensed.

"The shooter's in there, isn't he?" I asked, my voice shaking. "You need to go in there."

"I'm not leaving you."

"You have to help those people, Luke. I could never live with myself if someone got hurt because you stayed with me."

A war waged in his eyes before he said, "I want you to *stay put*. You hear me?"

"Yes." I had no desire to get shot.

He ran over to Bruce and pressed two fingers to his neck, then ran for the back door of the bar.

I was surprised when the door opened. Luke slipped inside.

The night was quiet except for the sounds of the sirens coming closer and crickets in the woods behind me. After what felt like forever but was likely only thirty seconds, I heard a crack several feet away in the trees and felt a prickle between my shoulder blades like I was being watched. I couldn't help thinking about the fact that Bruce had been shot the moment he agreed to tell Luke about Rick. And the person who'd shot Bruce knew that I had the same information.

Rick was in the woods behind me, and I had no doubt he planned to kill me.

Staying put was no longer an option. "Sorry, Luke," I mumbled to myself as I scrambled out from underneath the car and dove for Bruce's gun on the pavement. I'd just grabbed it and rolled over to my butt, lifting the barrel, when Rick walked around the trunk of the car, his gun aimed at my chest.

"Summer Butler," he said with a grin. "You are a tenacious thing . . ."

"I'm gonna take that as a compliment." My hand was shaking—so much for looking badass—but the gun was aimed at his chest. If I pulled the trigger, he'd suffer serious damage. But then again, so would I. But I planned to get him to confess for the pendant camera. "Why'd you shoot Bruce?"

"Oh, come on now, Summer, don't play stupid. You seem like a smart girl. You know why."

"Why are you gonna shoot me?"

"Same reason."

"So why haven't you done it yet?" I asked, surprised I wasn't terrified. I was *pissed*.

An evil smile lit up his eyes. "Because unlike Kitty, I like to play with my kill first."

The blood in my veins turned to sludge.

"Don't be stupid, Rick," I heard Nash say from my side.

I didn't dare steal a glance at him. Was he here to help Rick?

"I told you to stay out of it, Nash," Rick sneered.

Nash took several steps closer to me. "I got dragged into it the moment I saw that girl in your truck the other night. I knew she was drugged and not sleeping. Summer confirmed it."

"Well, she's not gonna stick around to confirm anything." His eyebrows rose in a menacing look.

"She isn't worth it," Nash said. "Your best bet is to get the fuck out of here and run. The cops are gonna be here any second, and if they see you, you're a dead man. Go."

Rick's confidence lagged. "She's gonna squeal."

"I know how to take care of her. Get out of here." He dug into his pocket, then tossed a set of keys to his cousin. "Take my truck. Yours is too recognizable."

"Thanks, cuz. You're all right."

Nash's upper lip curled as though he took it as an insult. "Yeah. Go."

Rick ran along the back of the building, heading to the other side.

I stared up at Nash in disbelief. "He just shot a man and you're *lettin' him go*?"

"Are you all right?" It sounded like it pained him to ask.

"I'm more concerned with your cousin getting aw—"

"Put your hands up," someone shouted on the other side of the building. Seconds later, multiple gunshots went off.

"Luke!" I jumped to my feet, and Nash grabbed my arm in a firm grip.

I shot him a dark glare. "You're about two seconds away from losing the ability to father children, so I suggest you let me go."

He dropped my arm like it was on fire. "I was trying to keep you from running into gunfire."

"I realize you think I'm stupid, but I do have some sense in my head!" I spat out.

"My mistake."

Luke ran around from the front of the building, then held his gun on Nash.

"Put it down." I patted the air as I dropped the gun to the ground. "He just saved me."

"Happy to hear you're so grateful," Nash said in snarl.

"Yeah, well . . ."

Luke lowered his gun but still cast a wary eye on Nash. "What are you doin' back here?"

"Saving your girlfriend from my cousin. He was about to shoot her to shut her up. I convinced him to make a run for it instead."

Luke eyed him suspiciously. "You knowingly sent your cousin into a trap?"

Nash didn't answer for several seconds. "Well . . . he wasn't a nice man, so maybe I did the world a favor." His jaw twitched, and I could tell it hadn't been easy for him.

"Thank you," I said, feeling like a real bitch now.

"I didn't do it for just you. I think I'll go find someone to give my statement to so I can get it over with." Then he walked to the front with slow, heavy steps.

I felt another rush of guilt for feeling grateful that he was gone.

Luke grabbed my arms and looked me up and down. "Are you sure you're okay?"

"I'm fine."

He wrapped his arms around me and crushed me to his chest. "Jesus, Summer. You just scared the ever-lovin' shit out of me."

"You didn't look scared."

"I was terrified."

"I wasn't tryin' to interview anyone. I swear. I was on my way out to the truck, and I ran into Bruce—literally—while trying to hide from Rick. Bruce confessed, to everything, and he dished on Rick and April Jean too."

"Let me find a deputy to take your statement."

"Ask and you shall receive," Deputy Dixon said as he walked toward us.

Luke's body tensed. "Thanks, but we'll find someone else."

The deputy laughed. "What are you trying to hide now, Summer? And am I going to catch you lying to cover for her, Montgomery?

She's a joke. A humiliating joke, and she's gonna make you lose all credibility."

He was voicing my worst fears, and after our semicoherent phone conversation earlier, Luke had to know that. He put his arm around my shoulders. "A joke?" he laughed. "You've gotta be kiddin' me, Dixon. For the second time, she's solved a case for you, and this time she did it while drunk. So who's the joke now?"

Deputy Dixon's smile fell. "What the hell are you talking about?"

"Summer not only figured out who the arsonist was, but she also uncovered April Jean's murder. Maybe she should be workin' for the sheriff's department. At the very least, she should be gettin' some kind of consultant fee for doin' your job for you."

"What the hell are you talking about?" he repeated with more fury.

"Here's the CliffsNotes version," I said. "April Jean and Rick Springfield drugged Dixie and framed her for the arson of April Jean's trailer. Bruce Jepper figured out what they were doin', and instead of turning them in, he got wrapped up in it. He was the one who texted me the other night, hoping to help her for Teddy's sake. But then April Jean got pissed off, and she made him kidnap Dixie and set her up. Only April Jean pissed Bruce off. He shot her and then started the fire to make Dixie take the fall for that too."

Halfway through my speech, the deputy hooked his thumbs on his belt and gave me a smug grin. When I stopped, he lowered his hands and gave me a condescending look. "You realize there's one problem with your little story, don't you?"

Luke stiffened. "It's her word against three dead people."

"Wrong," Bill said, walking toward us with an open laptop. "Summer was recording the whole thing, and while some of the video is shit, the audio is perfect." He beamed at me. "Good job, Summer. Providing us with job security once again, and I'm thankful that I was nowhere near gunfire this time."

I pulled him into a hug, and he scrambled to keep hold of the laptop. "You're the best!"

Luke gave the deputy a dark grin. "As I said, my girlfriend solved two cases for you. She's two for oh, Dixon."

"Yeah," Bill said. "Suck on that!"

Deputy Dixon shot me a dark, dangerous look, and I knew I'd made an enemy for life. Somehow I couldn't bring myself to care.

CHAPTER THIRTY-TWO

Luke called the DA and got Dixie's charges dropped that night. By ten, Teddy, Luke, and I were in the waiting room of the county jail. We'd been waiting ten minutes, and Teddy and I were pacing while Luke sat in a chair with his arms crossed over his chest.

"You two are makin' me anxious," Luke said. "And Summer already reached her quota for making me anxious for the next three months."

"I can't help it," I said, wringing my hands.

A buzzer sounded, and the door to the back finally opened. Dixie appeared, wearing a pair of mismatched sweats that were too big for her and carrying a plastic bag.

A female guard stood behind her and watched as she entered the waiting room. Then she shut the door.

Teddy reached her first, engulfing her in his arms. She broke down sobbing as he cradled her, cupping her head and whispering in her ear.

I felt like an interloper, watching something I had no business being a part of. Luke stood next to me. I buried my face in his chest, and he held me close.

"You okay?" he asked in a hushed voice.

I nodded, unable to explain the strange mix of relief and worry, sorrow and elation. Dixie was free, and her name would be cleared, but she'd lived through hell the last few days. How was she going to handle it?

"You did this," he said, tilting my face up to look at him. Pride filled his eyes. "*You* proved her innocence both now and in the past. So don't you dare let men like Dixon belittle you. Got it?"

Tears filled my eyes, and I nodded. "Yeah. But I overturned your case." I paused. "Does it bother you that I . . ."

"Challenged me?" he finished.

"Well . . . yeah . . ."

"Summer, that's one of the many things I love about you. You're not afraid to challenge anything that you think is wrong. Including me."

"But some men are threatened by strong women."

"You mean like Bruce? Don't you for one second think I believe that malarkey I was spewin' to Bruce when he was holdin' you at gunpoint. I would have told the man I was a leprechaun who peed gold to keep you safe."

I grinned.

"I love you, Summer. I love you more than when we first fell in love, because we've lived now and we've kissed a few frogs and recognize that we have something that's worth fightin' for, so no more listenin' to fools like Lindy Baker. I'm so damn proud of you I could bust. Don't ever think I could be ashamed of you."

Luke dropped his arms, and I realized Dixie was standing next to me.

One look at the dark circles under her eyes, and I started to cry. "Dixie, you have no idea how sorry I am for sending you to Connor's office. If I hadn't sent you—"

"Summer," she said with a shaky voice, "stop." Tears flowed down her face, and she took my hands in hers. "You . . ."

She took several breaths. Teddy moved next to her and wrapped an arm around her back. "You can do this later, Dix. You need to go home and rest."

Stubbornness settled on her face, and she shook her head. "No. I want to do this now."

Teddy leaned over and kissed her head, and for the first time, I was envious of them. Sure, I was a Baumgartner, but I would never have the bond that they shared. My own mother didn't want me. It hurt a lot more than I would have liked.

Dixie squeezed my hands. "Summer." She smiled through her tears. "You and Teddy . . . You believed in me even when I didn't believe in myself. You were both so sure—even years later—that I hadn't started that fire."

"We know your heart," I said. "We believed in that."

"But other people can believe it too since you recorded Trent's confession about his brother. What you did . . . I have no idea how I will ever thank you."

I shook my head, unable to speak, and reached for her and held her close as she cried on my shoulder. "You're not supposed to thank me, Dixie. You're just supposed to let me be one of you."

"Summer, how can you say that? You already are."

Teddy joined us, wrapping his arms around us both while we cried, and I knew I'd made the right decision to move back. This was where I belonged. This was my home.

Dixie took a step back and wiped her face, her eyes swollen and puffy. She turned to Luke, who, to my surprise, looked close to tears himself.

"Dixie." His voice broke. "Sayin' *I'm sorry* seems so inadequate. If you hate me for what I did, I understand. I hate myself."

Her eyes widened. "Luke! I could never hate you! I'll never forget how kind you were to me back then. I was devastated and so scared, and you held my hand every step of the way—sometimes literally."

"But that's just it, Dix," he said. "I was the person responsible for putting you in that hell. I stole your life. I stole Teddy's. If only I'd—"

She shook her head slowly and reached up to wipe a tear rolling down his cheek. "Luke, I could never hate you. You thought I was guilty. *I* thought I was guilty. But even though you thought I did it, besides Teddy, you were the only other person who stuck with me, and I will never forget you for it. Please don't hate yourself for this, because I don't."

She wrapped her arms around his waist and clung to him until he held her too. But I could see from the devastation on his face that her arrest and conviction would haunt him for a long, long time.

With a soft laugh, Dixie said, "I've had enough of jails to last the rest of my life. Let's go home."

I liked the sound of that.

◆ ◆ ◆

The next morning was packed full of remote morning-news-show interviews filmed in my office—half of which were live—about what happened in the parking lot of the Jackhammer. Thankfully, Lauren had hired a makeup person to help hide the dark circles under my eyes from lack of sleep. (From staying up so late with Dixie, not from another sleepover with Luke—I'd sent him home so I could give my cousin my full attention.)

Lauren, Karen, and my crew were present when I arrived, and Lauren was surprisingly quiet. I half expected Connor to sneak in at the last minute with his copy of *The Connor Life* in hand, but when I mentioned it to Chuck as he miked me up and put me in a chair, he gave me a devilish grin.

What was that about?

There were twelve interviews scheduled over the course of two hours, with only about five minutes between some of them.

The first two interviewers asked why Dixie wasn't with me. After I told them she was still recovering from her trauma, they tried to bring up the fire that had killed Pawpaw and my aunt and uncle, but I quickly changed the topic. Luke had convinced us to try to get Trent to give an official statement before we made the truth public. I couldn't help hoping we'd get him to sign a waiver so I could use the footage too.

The second interviewer was a perky blonde who looked like she'd drunk way too much coffee. "How much crime can one small town have?"

I gave her a cheesy grin. "I don't really know, but it has a little bit less than it did yesterday."

When we signed off, Lauren stormed over. "You're not promoting the show enough. That's the whole point of doing these things."

"It feels pretty arrogant to say, 'I'd tell you what happened, but you'll need to wait four months to see it for yourself.'"

"Then I'll do it," she grumbled, and had the makeup person fix her up too.

Lauren slid into the chair next to mine with seconds to spare before the third interview began—a live one this time.

The interview started off pretty much the same as the others, with Lauren dropping obnoxious hints that viewers should tune in if they wanted the real scoop, but it took a turn when the new interviewer, a younger man named Brad, said, "I'm surprised Connor's not with you to address the latest news."

I turned to Lauren and gave her an acquiescent smile.

She shifted in her seat. "Connor wasn't involved with this case."

"I'm not talking about the case," the man said. "I'm talking about the photos just posted to TMZ."

Lauren's eyes widened so much she looked like she had googly eyes. "Uh . . ."

I crossed my legs and rested my hands on my knees, giving the camera an inquisitive stare. "And what might those be, Brad?

"So this is the first you're hearing of it?" Brad asked.

Lauren looked panicked, and Tony and Chuck were shaking as they tried to control their laughter. Obviously they knew about whatever Brad was talking about, and I was beginning to suspect they were behind it.

Go, Team Summer.

I tilted my head and said in the same voice a mother would use for her naughty child, "And what has Connor done now?"

"We have the photos here." The screen switched from a view of the host to a slide show of Connor in various places in Sweet Briar. Connor eating a huge burger behind the train station. Connor smoking next to a dumpster behind Maybelline's. A video of Connor chewing out a little old woman who had hired him to look for her missing cat. But the most damning of all were a few stills of Connor handing money to Rick Springfield, then taking a small pouch in exchange.

"Summer," Brad said, "isn't this one of the suspects you helped apprehend?"

"Yes," I said. "That's Rick Springfield. He died last night in a gunfire battle with the Bixley sheriff's deputies."

"Was Connor working undercover there? It looks like he's making a drug deal."

"Uh . . ." How should I handle this? "Connor Blake has had a well-documented on again/off again struggle with drug use, so I see no reason to comment on that, but as to whether that is a photo of an actual drug deal? Well, I really can't comment on that either, Brad." I gave Lauren a wink. "You'll have to watch *Darling Investigations* in October."

I'd just figured out what my crew had been up to while I was being interviewed at the sheriff's office.

When we finished the interviews a couple of hours later, Lauren started to storm off, but stopped in the doorway and turned to glare at me.

"You think you got one over on me, Summer Butler, but revenge is a dish best served cold."

"Lauren," I said, sounding as exhausted as I felt, "can't we just let this go? Aren't you tired of all the animosity?"

She shook her head. "No one one-ups me and gets away with it."

"She's gotten away with it twice," Bill said.

I shot him a glare that read *not helping*.

Lauren's eyes narrowed to slits, then she stormed out the door.

As soon as she shut the door, I gave my full attention to my crew. "How on earth did you manage to get all those clips and photos of Connor?"

Tony laughed. "It was surprisingly easy."

"I guess the lighter was from his cigarette habit," I said. "What about the drug deal with Rick Springfield? We never found him that day."

"We didn't get that one," Chuck said. "That was Connor's crew the day before. Dee smuggled it to me."

I hoped my guys never turned on me like that.

"We'll have even more work now," Tony said, and when he saw my confused look, he added, "While you were doing your interviews, Connor caught wind of the photos and stormed out."

"He quit?" I asked in shock.

"Looks like it, and some people think they'll pull the book."

I wasn't surprised. Looked like even Connor couldn't live up to the Connor Life.

"Well, I know we've got a heavier workload now, but I say we take the rest of the day off. Get a fresh start tomorrow. Maybe Dixie will feel like comin' in too."

The guys all agreed, and soon I was alone in my office. I glanced up at the map on the wall, starting to believe I could make investigating a real profession, not just for the cameras. And maybe Luke could teach me a thing or two.

The bell on the door jingled, and I glanced up and saw Luke walking through the door in his uniform.

"Hey," I said as I stood, my face flushing at the sight of him. "What are you doin' here?"

"I saw your interview on *Good Morning America*, but after last night I needed to see you in person." He walked toward me and gave me a long, soulful kiss. "I still haven't recovered from your close call at the Jackhammer."

"Thanks for showing up to save me," I said.

"Let's not make a habit of it."

I didn't plan on it, but then again, I hadn't planned on it before either.

"I'm also here to see if you can get me a clip of that tape of Trent's admission."

"Yeah," I said, walking over to my desk and opening the drawer. "Bill already sliced it and made a file." I pulled out a flash drive and handed it to him. "I thought this wasn't admissible in court."

"It's not, but I can still use it to coerce him into giving me a statement."

"You're gonna go after him?"

He gave me a dark smile. "You bet your sweet little ass I am. But I'm also here to try to convince you to file charges against Elijah for attacking you at the Dunbar ranch."

I shook my head. "No way. He'll file charges against me. You know I can't risk it."

"But that means the city is stuck with him."

"Just gather more evidence against him," I said. "It won't be hard."

"But how many innocent people will be abused by him before we get it?" Luke asked, then shook his head. "I understand, Summer, I do, but I'm still frustrated."

"I'm sorry."

"No, darlin', don't be sorry. But until he's gone, you need to watch your back, okay? And call me at the first sign of trouble with him. Got it?"

I smiled. "Got it."

His phone began to ring, and he answered it, saying, "Hey, Amber." He paused, and his eyes became as wide as silver dollars. "Two o'clock is good. I'll alert the DA." He hung up, beaming.

"What was that about?"

"Trent Dunbar's attorney called. They want to come in and give a statement about Troy's involvement in the fire ten years ago, but he also wants to talk to the DA about workin' out a deal for other information."

"Other information?"

"About all his father's underhanded dealings, including bribery to clear his sons' names. The DA's been looking to bring Roger Dunbar down, and Trent might be his ticket."

Oh, crap. This was big.

"But before you think Trent's being all altruistic, consider this: If Roger Dunbar's in prison, guess who's running his multimillion-dollar lumber empire?"

My heart sank. "Trent." He was going to be rewarded for keeping his awful secret.

Luke sighed. "I was gonna invite you to lunch, but I've got to call the DA. Dinner tonight?"

Butterflies filled my stomach. "Yeah. I'm lookin' forward to it."

◆ ◆ ◆

I drove out to the farm and had lunch with Dixie and Meemaw, but I was worried about my cousin. She wasn't herself, but then, what had I expected? She'd been through hell.

We were lying on the sofa after lunch, watching a marathon of *Gilmore Girls*, when I heard a knock at the door.

She gave me a worried glance, so I hopped up and opened the front door, shocked to see Bill holding a large bouquet of flowers. He was even wearing a dress shirt and tie.

"Hey, Bill," I said in surprise.

"Is Dixie up for company?"

I glanced around the short entry wall and stared at my cousin, who was now sitting up.

She grimaced, then nodded.

"Yeah, come on in."

I stepped back and let Bill in, still in shock as I watched him make a beeline for Dixie. He sat down beside her, the bouquet still clutched in his hand, looking more nervous than I'd ever seen him. (He'd stared down the barrel of a gun and gotten shot, so that was saying something.)

"How you feeling, Dixie?"

"Better," she said. "Tired."

He nodded, then swallowed, his hand tightening around the flower stems. "Dixie, I know I'm not the most attractive man in the world—"

"Bill . . . ," she said softly, sounding embarrassed.

"No, hear me out."

She nodded, and her cheeks turned pink as she gnawed on her bottom lip.

"But I'm loyal. And thoughtful. And I cook without burning things." He laughed, and she laughed too. "I can be a great boyfriend, and I know you just went through something horrible, so maybe you don't want to even think about this now, but I want to be here for you, Dix. I want to be here holding your hand while you go through it."

She looked up at him with unshed tears in her eyes. "Oh, Bill. I was so awful to you. Why would you want me?"

He shook his head. "Because you're a beautiful person, Dixie Baumgartner, inside and out. You just need someone besides your family to help you believe it too."

A tear slid down her cheek.

"So will you give me a chance?" he asked.

She nodded. "I'd love nothin' more than to have you here holdin' my hand."

He grinned, and I walked over and took the flowers. "Let me put these in water for you and give you two a little privacy."

I took the bouquet into the kitchen and found Meemaw snapping beans.

"Meemaw," I said, "you never said why you called for a family dinner the other night. Do we need to schedule another one?"

She gave me a long look before shaking her head. "And have another disaster? It'll keep."

I put the flowers in water and then headed out to the surveyor's house. If I was going to remodel it to make it more livable, I needed to start a list of what needed to be done. Halfway down the dirt lane, my phone rang, and I was excited to see it was Marina.

"Marina," I said. "How's the world tour goin'? Where are you now?"

"It's a disaster. I'm in Cambodia," she said, sounding disgusted. "It's hot, and they have mosquitoes the size of airplanes." She paused and lowered her voice. "So tell me about sleepy little Sweet Briar, Alabama. I bet you're bored to tears. Are you sorry for moving there yet?"

I'd escaped an alligator, was almost run down by a car, and was nearly shot by April Jean's killer. All within a couple of days.

But happiness filled me when I took in the white and now-pink cotton fields that had bloomed for my family for nearly two centuries

Teddy, Dixie, and Meemaw gave me a sense of belonging I hadn't felt in years. And when I thought of Luke . . . I could see a glimpse of a future we could create together, and it gave me hope.

Did I regret coming back to Sweet Briar?

A grin spread across my face. "Not a chance."

I was here to stay.

ABOUT THE AUTHOR

Denise Grover Swank is the *New York Times*, *Wall Street Journal*, and *USA Today* bestselling author of the Rose Gardner Mysteries, the Magnolia Steele Mysteries, The Wedding Pact series, The Curse Keepers series, and others. She was born in Kansas City, Missouri, and lived in the area until she was nineteen. Then she became a nomad, living in five cities, four states, and ten houses over the course of ten years before moving back to her roots. Her hobbies include witty (in her own mind) Facebook comments and dancing in her kitchen with her children (quite badly, if you believe her offspring). Hidden talents include the gift of justification and the ability to drink massive amounts of caffeine and still fall asleep within two minutes. Her lack of the sense of smell allows her to perform many unspeakable tasks. She has six children and hasn't lost her sanity—or so she leads you to believe. For more information about Denise, please visit her at www.denisegroverswank.com.

ABOUT THE AUTHOR